I0661782

WHITE TIGER

ANDREW WARREN

B
Boldwood

First published in Great Britain in 2025 by Boldwood Books Ltd.

Copyright © Andrew Warren, 2025

Cover Design by Head Design Ltd.

Cover Images: iStock and [Paul Thomas Gooney] Figurestock

The moral right of Andrew Warren to be identified as the author of this work has been asserted in accordance with the Copyright, Designs and Patents Act 1988.

All rights reserved. No part of this book may be reproduced in any form or by any electronic or mechanical means, including information storage and retrieval systems, without written permission from the author, except for the use of brief quotations in a book review. This book is a work of fiction and, except in the case of historical fact, any resemblance to actual persons, living or dead, is purely coincidental.

Every effort has been made to obtain the necessary permissions with reference to copyright material, both illustrative and quoted. We apologise for any omissions in this respect and will be pleased to make the appropriate acknowledgements in any future edition.

A CIP catalogue record for this book is available from the British Library.

Paperback ISBN 978-1-83703-897-8

Large Print ISBN 978-1-83703-896-1

Hardback ISBN 978-1-83703-895-4

Trade Paperback ISBN 978-1-80656-050-9

Ebook ISBN 978-1-83703-899-2

Kindle ISBN 978-1-83703-899-2

Audio CD ISBN 978-1-83703-890-9

MP3 CD ISBN 978-1-83703-891-6

Digital audio download ISBN 978-1-83703-892-3

This book is printed on certified sustainable paper. Boldwood Books is dedicated to putting sustainability at the heart of our business. For more information please visit https://www.boldwoodbooks.com/about-us/sustainability/

Boldwood Books Ltd, 23 Bowerdean Street, London, SW6 3TN

www.boldwoodbooks.com

1

TOKYO, JAPAN

'Family,' the man in the blue kimono said. 'We yakuza are many things. Warriors. Criminals. Outlaws. But we are, above all other things, a family.'

Koichi Ogawa, *oyabun* of the Yoshizawa clan, contemplated the small stone bowl in his withered hands. The *chawan* was handcrafted, its depth and circumference calculated to ensure the steaming matcha tea within did not cool too rapidly in the cold winter air. The vessel was formed from a rough black ceramic. According to Tetsuo, his *wakagashira*, second-in-command, it was over 400 years old. Its history stretched back to the Edo period, when Japan was ruled by the Tokugawa shogunate.

At some point in its long, storied existence, the bowl had shattered. Whoever had patched it back together had filled in the cracks with thick gold lacquer. The shimmering lines of gold rippled through the stoneware like veins. The bowl's imperfections made it beautiful, unique. Like a fractured bone, long since healed, it was stronger along the break.

'When we quarrel, we must always remember that strife divides us,' Koichi continued. 'For the yakuza, for our family, times are not what they once were. Our numbers are dwindling. We are stronger when we join together.'

Koichi set the bowl back on the table. Tetsuo Mori, the younger man standing beside him, stiffened, and Koichi heard him suck in his breath. He realized he had committed a faux pas by not drinking the tea before setting down the bowl. He looked at the heavyset man sitting across the table from him.

Koichi's lips curled into a grin. 'What do I know about tea ceremonies, eh? I came into this life kicking over TUC shops behind pachinko parlors. I was a punk, fighting other punks in the street. Turf wars and gang feuds.'

He gestured to the scented smoke wafting from an incense stick at the far side of the low, flat table between them. 'Tetsuo tells me this incense is agarwood. It's supposed to be mild, so as not to interfere with our appreciation of the tea.' Koichi shrugged. 'I can barely smell it. The smells I associate with our life are beer, cigarettes. Cheap perfume and expensive whiskey. And, sad to say, blood. Spilled blood has a very particular scent. Once you've smelled it...'

His voice trailed off.

Across from him, Goro Watanabe shifted his weight and grunted. 'Ogawa-san,' he said, his voice deep and guttural. 'We come from the same place. The streets. The yakuza is our only home, the only place we belong. As you say, our family. Of late, our clans have been enemies. But it was not always so. This ceremony, this beautiful teahouse...' He gestured with one hand at the lacquered wood walls and paper screens surrounding them. 'This is a strange place for men such as us to meet. But it is beautiful all the same.'

The Nakajima-no-ochaya teahouse sat on a small island in the middle of the Hamarikyu Gardens, a green oasis in the center of Tokyo's urban labyrinth. The building's interior was made of wood, and soft tatami mats covered the floor. Behind Goro, ripples in a vast tidal pond lapped against the rocks. The pond's water flowed from Tokyo Bay, and sluice gates controlled the water level year round.

'Still, we are here for a purpose,' Goro continued. 'The men who raided your warehouse in Kyoto belonged to my organization. They acted on their own, out of greed and stupidity.'

Goro sighed and glanced up at Koichi. 'A new *oyabun* has seized power in the Koda Kai clan, up north.'

Koichi squinted at the man sitting across from him. 'I've heard rumors. A power struggle in Sapporo. More bloodshed. Who is this new *oyabun*?'

The heavyset man shook his head. 'I have not met him. No one has. He operates behind the scenes, using underlings to carry out his orders. But under his leadership, the Koda Kai have turned to human trafficking. They have seized ports, pressured contacts in the shipping industry. Their activity has cut into my smuggling operation. And as profits shrink, my men grow desperate.'

'I see,' Koichi said, his brow furrowing deeper. 'So that's why they tried to move on my territory?'

Goro nodded. 'I did not order them to do so. But they are my men, my responsibility. They will be dealt with. Of that, you have my word. Now, all that remains is *yubitsume*. The obligation I must fulfill, to prevent further bloodshed.'

He set his hand on the table. The pinkie finger of his left hand was missing, severed at the second joint. The wound had long since healed over, and only a fleshy nub remained.

Goro's second-in-command bowed and set a small fabric-wrapped bundle on the table. The heavyset man unwrapped the crimson square of cloth, revealing a tanto knife within its folds. The straight steel blade shimmered in the warm glow of the hanging rice paper lanterns. Goro picked up the knife and took a deep breath. He placed the blade over the first joint of his ring finger.

Koichi frowned. His bushy white eyebrows tilted towards each other, and a sea of wrinkles creased his forehead. He glanced down at his own left hand. It, too, was missing most of its pinkie finger.

He shook his head and raised his hand.

The heavyset man paused and stared back at him.

'Goro,' Koichi said. 'I think tonight I prefer the scent of agarwood to that of blood. Let us enjoy these beautiful surroundings. The cool night air. And this delicious tea. The point of the *yubitsume* is to prove that without our brothers, without our family, we are weaker. Strength lies in unity. But we are old enough to have learned this lesson many times over. I would like you to consider reuniting with our clan. Ending this fracture, and the strife that comes along with it. Promise me you will consider my proposal. That is all the obligation I ask.'

Goro Watanabe set the knife down, then leaned back. He pursed his lips and stared into Koichi's dark, sunken eyes. The *kobun*, the underlings surrounding them, tensed. The air was still, and for a moment the only sound was the water outside, slapping against the wood pilings of the teahouse's deck.

Goro nodded. 'I will give this my utmost consideration. You have my word.'

Goro bowed his head. Koichi bowed as well, but not as low as Goro. The Yoshizawa clan was larger, more powerful, than Goro's faction.

'All right then,' Koichi said with a smile. He glanced up at Tetsuo. 'Now, let's drink some tea.'

Tetsuo sighed and shook his head. Koichi laughed.

'Since when did young punks like these worry so much about following rules?' he asked.

Goro chuckled.

Koichi picked up the *chawan* of steaming tea once again. 'I'll do my best not to upset our sensitive younger brothers anymore. Let's see if I can remember how this goes.'

He held the bowl in both hands, then turned it until the front faced Goro. He brought the bowl to his lips and took a long sip. Then he set the bowl down.

Koichi gave a brief bow to Goro, then turned to the tea master, a matronly woman dressed in a simple white kimono. He bowed to her.

'*Kanpeki deshita*,' he said. 'That was perfect.' As the host of the ceremony, only he was allowed to comment on the tea.

The woman returned his bow, lowering her head even farther than Goro. She took the bowl and cleaned it. She refilled the bottom with matcha powder, then ladled in hot water. After frothing the tea with a bamboo whisk, she placed the bowl before Goro, bowed to both men, then stepped away from the table.

Goro lifted the bowl in both hands and inhaled the scent of the tea.

As he wafted the steam to his nose with one hand, Koichi frowned. A cold breeze blew through the ancient teahouse, carrying with it a sound... The buzzing whine of a distant motor.

Peering over Goro's shoulder, he saw the tidal pond's waters beyond the railing of the outer deck. Dark and deep, the black pool extended into the shadows. In the distance, he could just barely make out the garden's trees, their snow-laden branches bending down to kiss the water's surface.

As Goro sipped his tea, the noise grew louder. A silvery wake rippled across the pond's surface. A boat of some kind skimmed over the water, moving towards the teahouse's deck.

Koichi gestured to Tetsuo. The younger man leaned in closer.

'Is that the water taxi?' Koichi grunted. 'I thought they closed down after dark?'

Goro narrowed his eyes and stopped drinking. He set the *chawan* down and turned. The boat sped closer. A second watercraft darted behind it, moving parallel to the first.

The sounds of muffled shouts came from outside the front entrance.

Although the teahouse was normally open to visitors in the winter months, Tetsuo had booked out the entire venue for the sit-down between Koichi and Goro. And, at any rate, the hour was well past closing.

Tetsuo pulled a cell phone from his pocket and dialed a number. As he waited for an answer, he headed toward the front entrance of the teahouse.

Koichi narrowed his eyes. The boats moved closer, running parallel to the teahouse. With a loud sputter, their motors came to a stop, and they drifted sideways towards the outer deck. Three men in heavy black puffa jackets sat in each of the small watercraft. They stood up as the boats floated closer.

Each man carried a Howa Type 89 assault rifle in a two-handed grip. They raised their weapons, aiming them at the teahouse.

'Get down!' Koichi shouted. He reached out to Goro, but before he could grab the man, one of his *kobun* tackled him to the ground.

The flash of muzzle fire reflected across the black water, lighting up the fog-shrouded night. Gunfire screamed through the teahouse, accompanied by the tinkle of shattering glass. A stray bullet smashed through the teapot on the table. Koichi winced as boiling water splashed across his skin.

A woman's scream pierced the air. Koichi looked up and saw the tea master hit the floor a few feet away. A dark pool seeped beneath her body, turning the tatami mats beneath her crimson.

'Goro!' he shouted. 'Is he—'

Before Koichi could finish his sentence, he heard a strangled cry from across the table. Goro struck the ground with a loud thud. His men returned fire. The wood beams overhead splintered, and a shower of fine dust filled the air, like snow on a calm winter's eve.

One of Koichi's men flipped the table over, sending the remains of the teapot and the delicate *chawan* bowl crashing to the ground. From the corner of his eye, Koichi saw the ancient vessel shatter once more, and pieces of crockery skittered across the floor.

Koichi crawled across the tatami mats. Gunfire thundered above, and he heard shouts from the front entrance. Whoever had attacked them was flanking both his and Goro's men, attacking from the water and the land at the same time.

More glass shattered. Footsteps thudded across the outer deck. From his vantage point on the floor, Koichi couldn't see what was happening. But he could guess that the men from the boats had climbed up onto one of the wood bridges connecting the island to the garden and were now storming the teahouse. He grabbed a discarded pistol, then he fell across a bloody corpse lying on the floor. He froze, lying still.

The footsteps moved toward him. More gunfire echoed in the distance.

'*Are wa kare desu ka?*' a voice said. *Is that him?*

Koichi felt a boot prod his shoulder. The foot flipped him over. He sprawled across the tatami mats, eyes closed, chest stained with another man's blood.

Two of the men from the boats stood over him, cradling their weapons in their arms. '*Hai*,' one of the men said. 'He's dead. Let's finish here and—'

Koichi's eyes snapped open and his lips curled into a snarl. His pistol roared twice. A crimson hole exploded in the nearest thug's forehead. The man's muscles went limp and he collapsed to the floor. Koichi was already firing again, sending a double tap into the other man's chest.

The man tumbled beside his comrade, his breath a rasping wheeze. Koichi staggered to his feet and aimed his gun at the man's head.

'Fucking amateurs,' he muttered. He pulled the trigger. A fine red mist spattered his kimono.

From the corner of his eye, Koichi saw another of the armed men in the puffa jackets spin towards him, aiming his rifle. Koichi gave him a defiant stare. He did not bother raising his pistol. He knew he would not be able to fire in time. He spat on the ground and grinned.

Bang!

A crimson stain exploded across the man's coat. He fell to the ground, as one of Koichi's men raced across the teahouse.

It was Junko Fujioka, a new member of the gang. Koichi stared at the young man in shock as Junko traded gunfire with another assailant on the outer deck.

'*Oyabun*, we must leave!' Junko shouted. 'The teahouse is overrun!'

The young gangster grabbed Koichi's arm and dragged him towards the kitchen. As the old man staggered beside him, he looked into Junko's face. He knew the man was in his twenties, but to Koichi, he had the face of a teenager.

As Koichi limped through the teahouse's kitchen, Junko ejected the spent magazine from his pistol and reloaded. The slide snapped back with a loud click as they approached the metal doors leading out of the kitchen.

'Some of these *rokudenashi* infiltrated the garden grounds,' Junko said, breathing hard. 'They disguised themselves as the grounds staff.'

'Who are they?' Koichi demanded.

Junko kicked open the door and peered out into the darkness. 'I thought they were with Goro,' he whispered. 'This whole sit-down must have been a trap!'

'No,' Koichi said, shaking his head. 'They killed Goro and his men, too.'

The two of them staggered onto a walkway outside. Muted gunfire echoed from the rear of the teahouse, near the water. Koichi followed behind Junko as the young man led them around the side, towards one of the curved wooden bridges. Across the bridge, a black sedan was parked on the grass next to a dirt trail.

Two armed men took cover behind the vehicle, exchanging fire with a trio of gunmen on the bridge. Koichi watched as one of the attackers dropped his rifle and tumbled over the guardrail. His body struck the water with a loud splash.

'You ready, *oyabun*?' Junko asked.

Koichi gave the young man a sly grin. 'Don't wait for me, kid. I'll keep up.'

Junko stalked towards the bridge, pistol raised in a two-handed grip. He sent a double tap into the nearest attacker.

Koichi fired as well, taking down the remaining enemy. As they crossed the bridge, Koichi braced himself on the guardrail, panting to catch his breath. He heard a low gurgle from a body on the bridge. The man he had shot wasn't dead. Kneeling, he grabbed the wounded thug by the collar of his jacket and jerked him to a sitting position.

'Who sent you?' he demanded. He slammed his pistol butt into the dying man's face. 'Come on, you goddamned sewer rat! Talk, or you get another round in the belly!'

Junko spun around. More intruders were marching from the teahouse, heading for the bridge. '*Oyabun*,' he shouted. 'We have to go!'

'Guess this is your lucky day,' Koichi whispered to the dying man. He shoved the barrel of the pistol under the man's chin and pulled the trigger.

Koichi followed Junko to the car. But before they could finish crossing the curved wooden bridge to safety, one of the bodies ahead of them stirred. Junko lowered his pistol and fired. The prone man groaned and flung out his arm. A tiny black sphere fell from his hand and rolled toward them.

Junko's eyes opened wide and his face turned pale. He spun around, blocking Koichi's body with his own. 'Oyabun,' he shouted. 'Get down, it—'

A thundering explosion drowned out the younger man's words. Blinding light engulfed Koichi's vision, and a wave of hot air blasted across his skin. He felt Junko's body slam into his own, and the two of them tumbled over the railing of the bridge.

Koichi hit the water with a loud splash. His body went limp and he sank beneath the shimmering black surface. Burning slivers of wood rained across the water, hissing as they sank through the inky black void.

The old man closed his eyes. At first, he thought he smelled the soothing agarwood incense. But it was only a dream... stray neurons firing as his oxygen-deprived brain shut down. Cold darkness engulfed him, and he sank deeper and deeper into the shadows.

2

SEOUL, SOUTH KOREA

Gangnam District, 24 hours later

Thomas Caine couldn't say exactly why, but he was certain of one thing: the man sitting alone at the Octagon Club was a killer.

The man was Korean, handsome and well dressed. He drank whiskey, neat, from a highball glass. Sweeping spotlights lit his face with a neon glow, shifting from crimson to green, then blue.

Caine watched the man from the corner of his eye. The thumping beat of the club's music drowned out the surrounding chatter. They were both sitting in the VIP area above the main stage and the crowded dance floor. A row of padded white bench seats ran along either wall, and a railing gave them each a view of the VIP boxes on the level below them.

The foam-covered waters of a small swimming pool filled the floor between the VIP booths. The club's swirling lights shimmered off the pool's surface. Bikini-clad dancers splashed in the water, twirling their lithe bodies to the thumping beat of K-pop.

The man ignored the women in the pool and kept his attention on the VIP boxes surrounding it. As he drained the last drops of amber liquid from his glass, a cocktail waitress stopped by and set a fresh drink down on the table in front of his bench. The man smiled and chatted with her, but Caine could not hear what he said over the music. The waitress responded with a smile and laughter. She seemed at ease in his presence.

It was a cold February night, and the man wore clothes suited for the weather. His olive suede jacket covered a gray turtleneck sweater. Dark indigo jeans and black leather Chelsea boots completed the outfit. They looked expensive, as did the gold watch dangling from his left wrist.

Caine had spent years working in the field with assassins and cutthroats of all kinds. Soldiers, snipers, guns for hire. Women and men who seduced their targets, then slid a knife into their lovers' backs before their lips even parted.

He was no stranger to the ways of death. Blood stained his own hands as well.

But just what it was about the man at the bar that tipped him off, he couldn't say. He simply knew on an instinctual level that this man was, like him, a killer.

Caine had learned long ago to trust his instincts. The faint tingle on the back of his neck, a sixth sense for danger, honed over years in the field, surviving one deadly mission after another. He would not ignore them now.

His emerald-green eyes focused on the VIP box the man was watching on the level below... the same box Caine and his female partner were surveilling. Behind the glass walls, a group of men, all wearing business suits, sat at a long table. Chan Tae Young, a director at Korea's Ministry of Trade, Industry, and Energy, stood at the head of the table.

The other men laughed and shouted as a waitress cleared away empty glasses and plates. Another cocktail waitress deposited a fresh tray of green soju bottles on the table and began pouring drinks.

Most of the men appeared to be in their late twenties and early thirties. But Chan was older. Caine knew the man was in his fifties, though he seemed fit for his age. He wore glasses and had a mild-mannered look about him. He seemed a bit out of place in the chic, modern nightclub.

Chan straightened his tie, then raised his glass. '*Uahago areumdaun nareul wihayeo*,' he shouted. It was a common Korean toast, meaning 'to elegance and beauty'.

The other businessmen returned the toast, then downed their shots of clear, sweet soju. One of them grabbed the server's waist and cackled like a hyena. She swatted his hands away, an annoyed grimace on her face. Pulling free from his grasp, she left the table and sauntered to the bar at the far end of the room.

Shifting in his seat, Caine leaned closer to the attractive Korean woman sitting across from him. She wore a shimmering silver cocktail dress, and the dark roots of her hair showed through her blonde dye job. Her eyes scanned the lower level, watching the men, then moving across the rest of the crowd.

'Chan has a shadow,' Caine whispered into the woman's ear.

'*Al-ayo*,' she replied, her dark eyes sweeping over the crowd. 'Green jacket. On your six.'

'Have you seen him before?' he asked.

She gave a tiny shake of her head. Raising her hand, she caressed his hair, and her lips touched his neck.

'*Anibnida*,' she murmured. 'Negative. Let me get a closer look.'

Fishing around in her gaping Louis Vuitton purse, she removed a Samsung cell phone in a pink rhinestone case.

'*Ya, jiralhaji ma!*' she shouted. 'Don't be so lame... drink up!'

Sue Mi Bae was thirty-two years old, and based on her file, Caine knew she was a highly trained agent of South Korea's National Intelligence Service. But in her club attire and heavy makeup, she could easily pass for ten years younger. She swayed and giggled like any other drunk patron at one of Gangnam's exclusive clubs and bars, but Caine knew it was all an act.

Still, he couldn't help but be surprised when the attractive woman sashayed from her seat then deposited herself into his lap. Throwing his arm around her, he stopped her from hitting the table.

Laughing, she raised her phone and made a V symbol with her fingers.

'Selfie time!' she said, slurring her words. She planted a kiss on his cheek as she took several photos of them.

Caine smiled for the camera, then shot a glance at the booth behind them. The man in the green coat narrowed his eyes, watching them as Sue Mi threw her arms around Caine's neck. He returned the embrace, and her lips brushed against his.

'I think he made us,' Caine whispered.

Sue Mi shrugged. 'Maybe. Or maybe you're just too stiff to enjoy yourself.'

'I know how to work a cover,' he replied.

'Could have fooled me,' she said, peering into his eyes. 'You married? Trust me, you're not my type. But I've had worse assignments.'

Caine didn't reply. Deep down, he knew her words stung because she was right. He had worked undercover in similar situations many times before. But now, his feigned intimacy with the attractive young woman felt forced, awkward.

To sell your cover, you have to believe your cover, Caine thought. *Live the lie, until it becomes the truth.*

His on-again, off-again relationship with Rebecca Freeling, director of the CIA's National Clandestine Service, was finally back on track. And for Caine, his feelings for Rebecca made his performance with Sue Mi feel even more contrived by comparison.

The NIS operative climbed off his lap and raised her empty glass, flagging down a waitress. '*Yeogiyo*, hey!'

As the waitress hurried back, Sue Mi glanced over her shoulder. The man in the green jacket had returned his attention to the VIP booth below.

'I don't think he's paying attention to us,' she whispered to Caine. 'He's focused on Chan.'

Caine ordered another round of drinks from the waitress as Sue Mi flipped through the pictures she had taken. Once she found a clear angle on the man behind them, she texted the photo to a contact on her phone.

'I sent his picture to NIS,' she said after the waitress left. 'They'll run facial recognition on him.'

Caine returned his attention to the glass booth below. A woman climbed up from the pool, water dripping from her sleek, pale body. Caine shifted his gaze as she crossed his path, keeping his eyes on Chan in the VIP booth below.

He was standing, retrieving his credit card from one of the cocktail waitresses. The other men were still drinking, and he slapped one of them on the back.

'Looks like the party's over,' Sue Mi said, leaning her head on Caine's shoulder.

'Not for Chan,' Caine replied. 'His night's just beginning.'

Sue Mi's phone beeped. She frowned as she read a new text message. 'Subject unknown,' she said. 'No match to any known North Korean operatives on file. Other intelligence agencies are negative as well.'

Caine narrowed his eyes as Chan left the VIP box. The man in the green jacket threw some won notes on the table to cover his tab, then headed for the elevator leading down to the first floor.

Caine tapped the concealed earpiece microphone hidden within his right ear. 'All units, this is Blackbird One. Magpie is on the move. Be advised, potential hostile in field.'

'Copy that,' a voice crackled back. 'Do we abort?'

Caine thought for a moment, watching as Chan Tae Young took the stairs down to the dance floor. Chan's position at the ministry gave him access to high-level economic intel and access to South Korea's military intellectual property, as well as any trade secrets the US shared with their Korean allies. The man was respected and well liked by his peers. He had a family, a wife and two daughters, and a comfortable house.

Unfortunately, Chan Tae Young was a North Korean spy.

For nearly a decade, Chan – or whatever his real name was – had maintained his cover, worming deeper and deeper into the country's military industrial complex. On paper, he lived a quiet, unremarkable life. His North Korean handlers made sure he kept as low of a profile as possible, activating him only for matters of utmost importance.

But after one too many meetings with his foreign masters in Cambodia, usually coinciding with trade conferences of some sort, Chan fell into a CIA honey trap. An asset posing as a sex worker recorded Chan debriefing high-level members of North Korea's Reconnaissance General Bureau, the country's foreign intelligence service.

It was the latest in a string of setbacks for South Korea's beleaguered intelligence community. The CIA offered to expose the mole hiding within their government, in exchange for being allowed first crack at Chan and the secrets he could expose. Caine had been chosen to run the 'extraordinary rendition', essentially a government-sanctioned kidnapping.

The intel Chan could provide on North Korea, and their network of deep-cover assets, could be invaluable. And Caine was certain it was only a matter of time before Chan or his handlers realized he had been discovered.

Which might explain why an assassin was also shadowing Chan on this cold February night.

Caine watched as the man in the green jacket stepped into the elevator. The lights bathed his face in a kaleidoscopic array of colors once more. Then they swung away, leaving him a shadowy silhouette. The elevator doors closed.

Caine made his decision.

'Stand by,' he replied. 'Blackbird Two, stick with Magpie. I'm on the hostile. Operation Empty Nest is a go.'

3

After taking the stairs to the ground floor, Caine and Sue Mi shoved their way through a sea of dancing bodies. True to its name, the club was octagon-shaped, with a stage at the north side of the building. A DJ stood on the raised platform, mixing beats between popular K-pop songs as colorful spotlights swept across the crowd.

Caine squinted, struggling to see the edges of the club through the mass of dancing bodies. An older Caucasian male like himself fit in reasonably well up in the quieter VIP section. But down here, surrounded by young laughing faces, he knew he stuck out like a sore thumb.

Sue Mi, on the other hand, fit in perfectly. A young man in torn blue jeans and a leather jacket grabbed her and began grinding on her leg. The NIS agent shoved him aside and continued scanning the crowd.

'Chan's at the coat check,' she said, watching as an attendant handed the older man a black overcoat.

As the spotlights swung over the crowd again, Caine saw the elevator doors open at the far end of the club. The man in the green jacket exited the elevator. He shot a quick glance at the main doors, then turned and headed for the rear of the building.

'Stay on Chan,' Caine replied, never taking his eyes off his quarry. 'I'll contact you shortly.'

'Copy that,' Sue Mi replied. She broke away from Caine and danced through the crowd, her metallic dress shimmering in the lights as she made her way to the front of the club.

Caine shoved a swaying youth aside and headed for the edge of the dance floor. As he broke free from the crowd, he saw the man in the green jacket duck out a side door. Caine followed, pausing at the door for a few seconds before he opened it.

A frigid blast of wind slashed across his cheeks as he stepped into a wide alley. Traffic roared down Nonhyeon-ro, one of the major roads connecting Gangnam-gu to other residential areas nearby.

Caine spotted the man a few yards down the alley, heading west past the flashing purple lights of a twenty-four-hour bowling alley. A group of giggling girls wearing long puffa jackets over their cocktail dresses ran down the alley, heading towards the Octagon Club's entrance.

Caine flipped up the collar of his navy peacoat and stuck his hands in the front pockets. Hunching his shoulders to ward off the bitter chill, he followed the man down the alley, keeping his distance.

The ground beneath his feet was slick with ice, and scattered clumps of gray snow dotted the ground. It had been over a week since the last snowfall, but the freezing temperatures had prevented the filthy residue from melting away.

The man turned left on Bongeunsa-ro, a street named after the famous Bongeunsa temple. It was said that on a clear day, one could see the temple and its towering Buddha statue from the end of the street. But on this cold, windy night, Caine saw only clouds and the blinking lights of traffic in the darkness ahead.

Taxis wove through the traffic on the congested street. The man in the green jacket raised his arm, and an orange sedan with yellow stripes pulled over. Caine did likewise, keeping his eyes on his target as a similar sedan, this one white and green, darted to the curb.

Caine slid into the back seat just as the other taxi pulled away. He handed his driver a thick wad of Korean won notes.

'I need you to follow that orange cab,' he said in a low voice. 'Try to keep your distance. Stay three car lengths back.'

The driver adjusted his glasses and gave Caine a confused look.

'*Yeong-eo eobs-eum*,' he said. *No English.*

Caine pointed out the windshield and said, '*Geunyang gaseyo. Seodulleoyo!*'

Just go – hurry!

The driver slipped the folded bills into his vest pocket with a sigh and pulled away from the curb. As they merged with the local traffic, Caine leaned forward, keeping his eyes on the other vehicle. He tapped his earpiece.

'Magpie Two, status report,' he whispered. The driver's eyes glanced at him in the rearview mirror, but he continued maneuvering the cab through the traffic in silence.

'Magpie Two, copy,' Sue Mi replied, her voice crackling in his ear. 'Chan left the club. He texted Lee Seol Ah. Right on cue.'

Caine watched as the red taillights up ahead veered left, past a blinking LG billboard. Caine tapped the driver's shoulder.

'Left here,' he said, gesturing with his hands.

The driver muttered a curse in Korean, but Caine felt the sedan shudder as the engine roared louder. They sped through the intersection, beating the red light by a matter of seconds. Caine struggled to spot the other taxi in the sea of blinking taillights.

'Magpie Three,' he said, his eyes scanning the cars ahead of him. 'Are you in position?'

'*Junbi dwaesseo*,' a man's voice replied through his earpiece. *Good to go...*

Caine recognized the voice as Jae Yoon, the third member of his team. He clenched his fist as the taxi swerved around a delivery truck. The orange cab turned left again. Caine tapped the driver on the shoulder and pointed left. The car's brakes screeched as the driver spun the wheel.

So much for not attracting attention, Caine thought.

For a moment, he debated calling off the operation. The plan was simple – after discovering Chan's indiscretions in Cambodia, the NIS had kept him under tight surveillance, and soon discovered the man's sexual appetites at home were no less voracious.

Despite South Korea's recent crackdowns on prostitution, the country's billion-dollar sex industry continued to thrive, rivaling red-light districts in countries like Japan and the Netherlands. When the police raided a brothel or massage parlor in Hongdae, it simply closed shop and moved to Itaewon or some other area. And many sex workers had moved their operations to online systems, booking clients through anonymous web portals.

When the NIS discovered Chan's infatuation with an online escort named Lee Seol Ah, they brought her in for questioning. Once they offered to turn a blind eye to her illegal activities, it was a simple matter to recruit the woman as an asset.

Chan was a creature of habit, and he usually contacted Lee for a rendezvous on Thursday nights, after holding a business meeting with his department. Tonight was Thursday, and Chan's late-night meeting wrapped up at 10:30 p.m., just as it always did. Like clockwork, Chan had set up an appointment with Lee. They would rendezvous at a love hotel near the club. But tonight, Chan would get more than he bargained for...

Unless Caine called off the op.

He tapped his earpiece again as the driver swerved around a delivery van. The orange taxi was still several cars ahead of them.

'Magpie Three, stand by. Magpie Two, contact operations. Are your people running a B team here? Could this guy be working for you?'

'*Aniyo*,' she answered back. 'No, I already checked. And Chan's car just arrived onsite. He's getting out and approaching the hotel.'

Caine debated whether he believed her. It was always possible the NIS wasn't happy with the CIA's deal. Maybe they were trying to pull a double-cross and grab Chan before his team moved in.

Then why is this guy driving away from the operation site? The NIS know exactly where Chan is heading...

Caine paused. All his instincts told him that the man he was following was an enemy, a hostile operative. Which meant if they missed their chance to grab Chan tonight, they might not get another one.

'Do we abort?' Sue Mi asked, her voice a cool monotone.

'Negative,' Caine replied. 'Maintain radio silence until you have Chan in custody.'

Up ahead, the orange taxi pulled over on Gangnam-daero, a popular shopping street lined with stores and cafés. Neon signs hung over a crowd of pedestrians, advertising international brands like New Balance, Prada, Godiva chocolates, and more.

Caine tapped his driver on the shoulder. 'Pull over.'

The driver grunted in response, then turned the wheel. The cab slid up to the curb about twenty meters behind the other taxi. Caine waited a few moments, watching as the man in the green jacket paid his driver and exited the vehicle. He walked down the street, glancing at the flashing signs overhead.

Caine exited the taxi. The driver rolled down the window, waving Caine's change and calling out to him. Like many Asian countries, tipping was not a common custom in Korea. Some considered it rude, but Caine had no time for social niceties. Instead, he plunged into the crowd, following his quarry through the neon maze of shops.

The man in the green jacket shoved his way through a trio of young women drinking coffee from steaming Starbucks cups. One girl's drink spilled on the sidewalk. She shouted after him, her breath misting in the chilly night air.

'Ya, gaesaekki!' Hey, asshole...

The man ignored her and ducked into a large store underneath a glowing yellow sign. Caine peered through the towering glass windows. The store sold a variety of toys and accessories based on a series of online chat characters. Caine wasn't familiar with them, but they certainly seemed popular with the local crowd. The shimmering glass and steel edifice took up the first three floors of the sleek, modern office building. Clear plastic racks of merchandise filled each level of the store, and a mob of Koreans in their teens and twenties meandered through the shelves, grabbing plush dolls and clipping dangling charms to their cell phone cases.

Caine entered the store and walked past a plastic statue of a smiling blue cat. The sculpture was about Caine's height. He ducked behind it, then sauntered along the store's outer perimeter. Keeping an eye on his quarry, he grabbed a yellow stuffed animal from a display case and pretended to check the price tag. Cheerful music played through the store, barely audible beneath the chattering of the other shoppers.

An escalator led up to the store's second level, but the man in the green jacket remained on the ground floor. He walked past a rack of backpacks and tote bags, each one adorned with the smiling face of a different animal character.

'Dowadeurilkkayo?' a soft, lilting voice asked. Caine turned and saw a salesgirl approaching him. She wore a black T-shirt featuring the same blue cat from the entrance and held another yellow stuffed animal in her arms. 'May I help you? Are you shopping for... yourself?'

Caine smiled. 'No, I'm looking for my niece. But I'm not sure if she'll like this one. Is it a bear?'

The clerk waggled the toy she was holding in Caine's face and made a roaring sound. Caine ignored her, watching as the man in the green jacket moved closer to the rear of the store.

'No, silly,' she said, laughing. 'It's a lion.'

'Of course. It's perfect.' Caine handed her the doll. 'I'll take five. Can you gift-wrap them, please?'

The woman beamed at him as she gathered up three more dolls from the rack. 'Wow! You have a lot of nieces!'

'I'm going to keep looking around,' Caine said, heading toward the back of the store. He glanced left and right but saw no sign of the man he was following.

Damn, he thought. *I lost him...*

As he scanned the store, he glimpsed movement from the corner of his eye – a metal door next to the front counter hung open. A security guard shuffled out from behind the counter and moved towards the door.

As Caine passed the counter, the guard reached out, grabbing his arm.

'Excuse me,' he said, raising his hand. 'That area is off—'

A loud noise echoed through the store, cutting the man off. He turned and looked at the door. The other patrons in the store froze.

The sound was muffled, but Caine recognized it at once. It was a pistol shot.

Cheerful music played over the store's speakers, a surreal contrast to the panicked expression on the crowd's faces. A few of them set down their merchandise and headed for the front doors.

Caine twisted his arm free from the guard's feeble grip. Pivoting his body, he shoved the man away, causing him to stumble backwards. Then he reached up, grabbed the striped handle of a fire alarm next to the door, and yanked it down.

Panic surged through the crowd. They headed for the store's exit en masse. The alarm's high-pitched wail drowned out the music and the crowd's screams.

As the guard caught his balance, Caine nodded towards the checkout staff, who stood frozen in fear behind the front counter.

'Get these people out of here,' Caine said. 'Then call the police.'

Without waiting for a reply, he reached behind his back and drew a small pistol from a concealed holster. The NIS standard issue sidearm was the Beretta PX4 Storm, a weapon with which Caine was intimately familiar. Although they had balked at first, Rebecca had insisted that Caine be allowed to carry the firearm on the mission, despite the fact that he was a foreign agent.

Holding the weapon in a two-handed grip, Caine stalked through the door, then kicked it closed behind him.

He found himself in a large stockroom. The walls and floor were bare concrete, and towering metal shelves ran through the center of the cavernous chamber. Loose toys and boxes of merchandise filled the shelves. Fluorescent lights hung above, bathing the room in an industrial green glow.

Caine grabbed a chair and wedged it under the door handle, preventing anyone outside from gaining entrance.

Before Caine could take another step, two loud coughs echoed off the concrete walls. Caine ducked as bullets ricocheted off the door behind him.

As he crouched behind a table near the entrance, he heard a loud thunk, followed by a low hum. The lights went out, plunging the room into darkness.

4

Caine didn't wait for his eyes to adjust to the sudden change in lighting. He dropped to the ground and rolled behind one of the towering shelves.

Bullets tore into the storeroom's concrete walls. There was no muzzle flash; Caine couldn't see where the shots came from. But he knew his attacker was hiding somewhere among the shelves.

Must be using a suppressor, Caine thought. *Masked the muzzle flash.*

A split second later, the hum of a generator kicked in. Emergency lights glowed above, breaking up the shadows with pools of amber light. Caine stalked between the shelves, silent as a jungle cat. He paused as he reached the end of a rack, listening for his enemy's movements. He heard the patter of footsteps scuffling through the room. But between the droning fire alarm and the generator's hum, he couldn't pinpoint where the sound was coming from.

Caine swung out from behind the shelves and aimed his pistol down the gap between the rows. There was no sign of his opponent in the narrow circle of light. As he moved along the shelves, he spotted a dark mass crumpled on the floor, partially lit by the emergency lights overhead. Ducking into a low crouch, Caine peered down the row... All clear. He advanced toward the dark shape.

As he suspected, it was a body. A young Korean man in his early twenties lay on the ground, surrounded by a pool of sticky blood. In the dim orange light, Caine could just make out the cartoon characters adorning the man's black T-shirt.

Store employee, Caine thought. *Probably got in this guy's way, tried to stop him.*

Before Caine could check for a pulse, more gunshots erupted from the darkness. Despite the man's suppressor, the loud coughs echoed off the storeroom's concrete walls. Bullets tore through a cardboard box above Caine's head, showering him with bits of fabric and white stuffing.

Caine moved down the row, pausing next to a cargo dolly stacked with boxes and plastic bags. He reached up and shoved a stack of windup toys aside. As he cleared the shelf, he spotted a shadowy figure moving a few rows down.

Caine opened fire. Muzzle flash from his pistol lit up his face. Bullets sparked off the metal shelves in the distance.

Footsteps echoed in the shadows. Caine reversed course, moving away from the dolly and back toward the body on the floor. His enemy fired again, tearing holes in a large stuffed animal a few feet away.

Caine returned fire, aiming through the gaps in the shelves. Squinting as his gun flashed, he glimpsed the man's green coat, darting behind another row. Caine adjusted his aim and fired again.

He heard a low gasp and the footsteps stopped.

Got you, you son of a—

Before he could finish the thought, a metallic creak echoed through the room, followed by a loud crash. Plastic toys and cardboard boxes tumbled to the floor as the shelves ahead of him toppled like dominoes.

As the shelf above him teetered, Caine sprinted toward the cargo dolly. Leaping into the air, he crashed down onto the wheeled platform. His momentum sent the dolly rolling across the smooth concrete floor.

He sped into the center of the room just as the rack of shelves behind him struck the ground with a deafening crash. The man in the green jacket limped out from behind another collapsed shelf and opened fire. But he aimed high, and his bullets flew above Caine as he rolled across the floor.

As he sped behind another rack of shelves on the opposite side of the room, Caine tumbled off the dolly. It continued on its way, slamming into the wall with a loud crash and tipping over on its side.

Three more gunshots rang out. Bullets tore chunks of concrete from the wall above the crashed dolly. As footsteps stalked toward his position, Caine glanced left and right, unsure which way to run.

Then he looked up...

Jamming his pistol in his waistband, he climbed up the shelving rack. His ascent knocked stuffed animals and windup toys to the floor. The plastic animal characters spun and gyrated on the concrete beneath him.

The footsteps came closer. Caine gritted his teeth as he heaved himself onto the top shelf. The metal buckled beneath his weight, but it held. He could only hope the wailing alarm and generator noise would mask the creaking sound.

Caine crouched on the shelf, watching as the man rounded the corner. The killer approached the dolly, kicking toys and cardboard boxes out of his way. The emergency lights cast flickering shadows on the wall, and Caine could tell by the dark outline that his assumption was correct – the man's pistol had a long, thick noise suppressor attached to the barrel.

This guy is well equipped, and he's clearly been trained, Caine thought. *Why didn't he run an SRD, a search and detection routine, on his way here? Why did he make himself so easy to follow?*

The man swung his pistol left and right, searching the surrounding racks for any sign of movement. Caine inched toward the edge of the shelf. He held his breath, listening for any creak or groan from the thin metal that might give away his position.

The man shoved the dolly aside with a well-placed kick, aiming his pistol down the narrow space running between the wall and the shelves.

Caine slowly drew his pistol from his waistband. *Now or never...*

Caine pounced, leaping from the shelves and slamming into the man below. The impact drove the man forward, and he struck the concrete wall with a dull, fleshy thud. He struggled to spin around, but before he could get his bearings, Caine slammed the butt of his pistol into the man's skull. As he reeled from the blow, Caine drove his forearm into his opponent's neck, smashing his face back into the wall.

A muffled cry of pain escaped the man's lips. Caine grabbed the wrist of his gun arm and jabbed his thumb into the pressure point between his enemy's thumb and forefinger. A low grunt of pain echoed through the room as Caine increased the pressure, twisting the man's wrist until it snapped. The gun clattered to the floor as his fingers spasmed. Caine kicked the weapon behind him.

The man ducked, struggling to break free from the wrist hold. Caine jerked his opponent's arm behind his back. The man yelped as Caine pushed his bones to their breaking point.

Caine spun around, hurling the man away from the wall and into the shelves. He struck the rack with a metallic clang, sending boxes and toys spilling down around him.

The man blinked, then shook his head, recovering quickly from the impact. He raised his fists and lunged towards Caine. But before he could strike, he found himself staring down the barrel of Caine's Beretta. He froze in place.

'It's over,' Caine snarled. 'You want to live through this? Start talking.'

The man stared at Caine, relaxing his posture as he gasped for breath. His lips curled into a smile.

'Live?' He spoke perfect English, with no trace of an accent. 'You are a fool.' He spat blood on the floor between them. 'I'm already dead. Just like Chan. And just like your friends.'

Caine squinted as the emergency lights bathed them in a hellish glow. 'What are you—'

Before he could finish, the man screamed a war cry and charged at Caine, his hand held high.

Caine reacted on instinct. His gun roared twice as he sent a double tap into his enemy's chest. The man ceased his mad lunge, jerking to a stop like a marionette with its strings pulled. He touched his chest with his free hand. It came away slick with blood. The dark, dripping fluid looked black in the spinning orange lights.

Then he collapsed to the ground.

Caine rushed over to him and rolled the man onto his back. He examined the object clutched in the man's outstretched hand, expecting to find a weapon of some kind. But it was just a cell phone.

Bastard wanted me to shoot him, Caine thought.

Two gaping holes pierced his chest, near his heart. Blood ran down his shirt and soaked his clothes. The man's head lolled back, and his eyes fluttered closed.

Caine slapped him across the face. The man blinked, then glared up at Caine.

'I can get you medical attention,' Caine said. 'I can help you. Do you understand?'

The man did not respond. Caine grabbed a scrap a towel from the pile of toppled merchandise and the man gasped as Caine pressed the cloth against his wound, fighting to stop the blood loss.

'Who do you work for? Who sent you?' Caine demanded.

The man glanced up at him through half-lidded eyes. 'Defend unto death, our strong and prosperous nation,' he wheezed. 'And our... glorious leader...'

His eyes closed and his head sagged. Caine slapped him again, but there was no response.

He was dead.

Caine grabbed the man's cell phone. Glancing at the screen, he confirmed the model used a fingerprint sensor beneath the screen to unlock. Like all such sensors, it used a capacitive field to detect the faint electrical signals generated by a living body. The finger of a dead hand would not open it. He had mere seconds before the electrical charge dissipated from the man's corpse.

After tapping the unlock button, he grabbed the man's right thumb and pressed it against the sensor's glowing white circle.

Nothing happened. The screen remained black.

Muttering a curse, Caine tried the right forefinger, but again, the phone failed to unlock.

As the fire alarm wailed, Caine dropped the man's arm and grabbed his left hand. He pressed the thumb against the sensor.

The phone emitted a soft beep, and the screen glowed to life.

Caine stood and swiped his finger across the screen. The call log showed only a few calls from an unknown number. There were no texts or emails.

Caine opened the photo app. The gallery was nearly empty, save for pictures of Chan Tae Young and his mistress, Lee Seol Ah. As Caine continued swiping, he found pictures of Sue Mi, Jae, and even himself.

Checking the metadata, he saw the pictures were all sent weeks ago.

This op was blown from the start, he thought. *He wanted me to follow him. Split us up, divide and conquer.*

Caine grabbed the man's pistol from the floor, then tapped his earpiece. 'This is Magpie One. Empty Nest is Code Red!' he shouted. 'We're blown. Abort! I repeat, abort!'

Static crackled in his ear. There was no response.

The fire alarm ceased its wailing. Caine heard radio chatter from outside. Jogging over to the door, he removed the chair wedged in place then cracked it open and peered into the dimly lit store. The staff and customers had evacuated, and police cars gathered in the street. Their flashing red and blue lights reflected off the glass storefront.

Caine backed away from the door, then ran towards a glowing exit sign in the far corner of the storeroom. Outside, the frigid air blasted him once again as he raced down an alley, heading for the next street over. He had to find a vehicle, get back to his team before whoever was watching them struck.

But as his footsteps echoed down the frost-covered pavement, a cold, gnawing sensation grew in the pit of his stomach. He feared he was already too late.

5

The Hotel Strawberry sat on a quiet backstreet, away from the congestion and traffic of Nonhyeon-ro. A getaway for couples looking to escape the watchful eyes of their families, the hotel was designed with privacy in mind. A towering black glass slab, every window was tinted, preventing pedestrians on the street from looking in. Brick walls surrounded the parking lot, and private garages hid the hotel guests' vehicles from view, as well.

Caine's taxi pulled over across the street from the hotel. The driver gave Caine a knowing smile and a wink.

'Joh-eun bam bonaeseyo,' he said. *Have a good night.*

Everyone in Korea knew exactly what such hotels were for. And while there was no shame associated with visiting one, as a lone foreigner, Caine knew the driver mostly likely assumed he was paying for his evening's entertainment. Caine ignored the man's leer and handed him several won notes.

As the driver counted his change, Caine peered through the window at the building. Crimson neon letters hung along the side of the glossy black structure, facing toward the street. The word 'Hotel' was written in English, but the rest of the characters were Korean.

The landscaped sidewalks and walking paths surrounding the hotel were devoid of pedestrians. There was a pharmacy around the corner, and a few parked cars lined the street. Their interiors were dark, with no signs of passengers inside. Chan's car and driver were nowhere to be seen.

Chan probably sent the driver home, Caine thought. *He was planning to be here for a while...*

Caine took his change and exited the vehicle, keeping his fingers wrapped around the grip of the pistol in his coat pocket. The wind sent a shiver down his spine as he approached the eerily quiet hotel. All his instincts, all his years of experience, screamed in the back of his mind.

Death lurked in the hotel's penthouse suite. Either his own, or someone else's...

He entered the glass-enclosed lobby, his footsteps clicking across the marble tile floor. The front desk was unmanned, and he ignored the blinking automated check-in machine. He already had a key that could access any room in the hotel. As the elevator doors slid open, Caine glanced up and noticed his reflection in the dome of a security camera. Judging by the dust covering the smoked-plastic dome, and the loose wires hanging out the back of the tiny device, he doubted it still functioned.

He entered the elevator and swiped his card across the terminal. Then he pushed the button marked 'P'. Chan always booked the penthouse suite for his rendezvouses with Lee. Tonight was no exception.

The elevator car rumbled as it moved up the building. Caine ejected the magazine from his pistol and checked the load. The NIS had assigned him the small concealed-carry model of the weapon. Unlike the full-size model, its magazine only held ten shots, of which he had three remaining, including a round in the chamber. He slapped a fresh mag in the weapon and stuffed the old one in his coat pocket.

The elevator doors slid open with a chime. Caine stepped out, sweeping his gun left and right. He was alone in the tiny alcove. Soft pink carpet covered the floor, matted down by years of foot traffic. A row of white marble statues lined a shelf on the wall opposite the elevator. They resembled Greek gods, entwined in various lewd positions.

Caine moved into the corridor. There was only a single door at the end of the hall. It was carved from dark brown wood and marked with a gold plaque that read *Penthouse*.

The door was open just a crack, and the room beyond was dark and silent. Caine eased the door open with his foot. The hinges made a quiet creak. Caine winced at the sound, but he heard nothing else in the room.

He entered the dark space, staying close to the outer wall. As he swept his gun around the room, his eyes adjusted to the dim light. The twinkling lights of the Seoul skyline glimmered like stars through the room's panoramic windows. The Lotte World tower dwarfed the surrounding buildings. It rose over 500 meters, a spear of metal and glass outlined with purple lights, thrusting up into the ebony night sky.

Unlike the love hotels he had seen in Japan, the Hotel Strawberry's penthouse featured no extravagant or unusual decor. It had a modern, industrial design, with concrete walls, exposed air-conditioning ducts, and hardwood floors. The furniture was all mid-century style, in various shades of brown leather. A well-stocked bar, complete with counter and stools, filled the eastern wall. Glass bottles of high-end liquor sparkled in the shadows, reflecting the lights beyond the window like jade and amber gems.

Caine froze in place, clenching his pistol in a white-knuckled grip. As his eyes adjusted to the dim light, he spotted two bodies, a man and a woman, sprawled face down on a leather couch in the center of the room. The woman's long black hair flowed over her face, obscuring her features. Someone had slit her dress open down the back, revealing her pale skin. Zip ties secured her arms behind her.

Caine advanced toward the body, glancing in the shadows to make sure he was alone in the room. He kneeled on the floor and brushed the woman's hair aside with the barrel of his pistol.

It was Sue Mi.

Her cheeks had a pale, bluish tint, and her eyes gaped open, their pupils two tiny black pinpricks.

She was dead.

Dead because you got played, he thought.

The other corpse was Jae Yoon. His leather jacket draped across the floor, and his shirt was slit down the back as well. Caine narrowed his eyes as he examined the two bodies. The skin between their shoulders appeared marked or burned. Angry red blisters formed what looked like Korean *hangul* characters. The grisly markings were identical on both corpses.

Caine slid his cell phone from his pocket and took a picture of Sue Mi's back. He was careful not to touch her skin. North Korea's RGB had a penchant for using nerve toxins in their executions. The deadly substances could be spread by touch, and even a tiny amount could kill. They could also be sprayed into the air as an aerosol mist. But if that were the case, Caine knew he would have been dead already.

He turned and prepared to photograph Jae as well, but he froze as the muffled sound of breaking glass came from the bedroom.

Someone else was in the penthouse.

6

Caine grabbed a bottle from the bar then approached the bedroom. A faint glow shined beneath the door, barely visible in the dim light twinkling through the windows. Pausing, he heard the soft padding of footsteps moving in the other room.

The footsteps ceased.

Caine stood to one side of the door and rolled the bottle across the floor. As it crossed the light beneath the door, three gunshots rang out. Caine winced as the slugs tore through the wooden door and buried themselves in the opposite wall. A second later, more breaking glass sounded from behind the punctured door.

Taking a deep breath, Caine leaped in front of the door and kicked it open. The frame near the lock splintered with a loud crack, and the door swung in. Chan and his mistress lay naked on the raised circular bed. Their hands were bound, their bodies stiff and motionless above the rumpled satin sheets.

Next to the bed, a Korean woman sat on the windowsill. Glass shards sparkled on the floor beneath the shattered window.

Her hair was tied back, revealing a strong, almost masculine jawline and dark, pensive eyes staring back at him. Her clothes – a black sweater and olive-green pants – clung to her lithe, athletic figure. She wore no makeup, and her mouth was a thin, cruel slash, a bitter scowl cutting across her harsh features.

Whoever this woman was, Caine was certain she had killed Chan and then Lee, marking them just as she had marked the bodies outside.

The man in the green jacket, he thought. *She's working with him. But who the hell are they?*

Caine advanced into the room, holding his gun in a two-handed grip.

He fired, but the woman slipped through the broken window. She moved like an athlete, a gymnast. Caine's gunshots sparked off a fire escape railing. He heard the clank of metal striking the pavement below.

She dropped the ladder. She's getting away...

Caine leaned out the window. He heard footsteps pounding across the sidewalk below. Street lights cast the fleeing woman's shadow across the opposite buildings. He fired two quick shots, but he was too late. The woman turned, sprinting down an alley behind the hotel.

Caine crawled out onto the fire escape and slid down the ladder. He felt a shock wave run through his knees and ankles as he struck the pavement. Ignoring the pain, he raced after the woman.

He sucked in a lungful of cold air as his feet pounded across the ground. As he rounded the corner, he spotted the woman about fifty meters ahead of him. Pedestrians crowded the narrow brick street, forcing her to slow her pace. Red awnings jutted from the storefronts, and boxes of fresh produce lined either side of the alley.

As the woman raced around another corner, she grabbed a metal cart piled high with *hotteok* – deep-fried pastries stuffed with nuts or red bean paste. Hot oil sizzled across the pavement as the cart tipped over. Stacks of golden pancakes spilled onto the street.

Caine vaulted over the toppled cart. He continued to give chase as the cart's operator, a heavyset Korean man wearing a grease-stained apron, shouted after them, waving his fist in the air.

The alley grew even more narrow. A skeleton of metal beams and corrugated plastic sheets covered the street like a tunnel. Fluorescent lights beamed down from overhead, and a mélange of smells filled the air – fermented kimchi, fresh seafood, fragrant spices, and more.

A banner hung above the street. The writing was in Korean, but smaller English letters underneath identified the area as Yeongdong Market, one of the oldest open-air markets in South Korea.

Every kind of local produce and meat imaginable lay on display trays outside the market's tiny stores. Cafés and bars, their entrances covered with plastic sheets to keep out the cold, flanked both sides of the street. The crowd grew ever denser as shoppers inspected the wares. Groups of young people meandered in and out of the bars, laughing and swaying as their breath misted in the air.

Caine shoved past a pair of Korean men wearing leather jackets. He could barely see the woman up ahead. Her pace slowed to a jog as more people got in her way.

She glanced over her shoulder. Even from a distance, Caine could see her expression harden as she glared back at him. She stopped running, planted her feet in a shooter's stance, and drew a pistol from her waistband.

The last thing Caine wanted was a gunfight in the tight confines of the market. But it didn't look like she was going to give him a choice.

Drawing his pistol, he fired a shot into the air. 'Everyone get down!' he shouted.

The crowd screamed. Men and women surged past him as they struggled to make their way down the narrow side streets leading out of the market. Caine ducked behind a stack of barrels in front of a nearby store. Farther down the street, the woman aimed her pistol as the crowd rushed away from her. Drawing a bead on Caine, she opened fire. Her gun roared twice. Caine winced as the bullets struck the barrels with a dull thud.

As the crowd thinned out, he returned fire. The woman ducked behind a concrete pole, and his bullet ricocheted inches from her face. She fired again, then turned and ran. Caine heard her footsteps echo off the pavement.

He rose from behind the barrels and aimed his Beretta, but she was already turning down a side street. Taking a deep breath, Caine continued to give chase.

As he turned the corner, his feet slid across the slick, wet pavement. Struggling to maintain his balance, Caine glanced down. Soapy water covered the bricks beneath him. A mop and a yellow bucket filled with gray suds sat in the middle of the street, abandoned in the chaos.

The woman raced towards an abandoned booth in the middle of the street. Behind the booth's glass barrier, mung bean pancakes sizzled in vats of hot oil. Bins of rice cakes and skewered intestines were stacked on trays atop folding tables surrounding the cooking area.

A few stray pedestrians crouched behind carts and tables nearby, taking cover from the gunshots. On either side of the booth, Caine could see traffic lights filling the distant street. They were near the market's border. If he lost her now, she could escape into the city.

Caine raised his pistol and opened fire. Two shots ricocheted off the booth's metal counter, but the third grazed the woman's leg. She stumbled, crashing to the pavement.

Caine felt the pistol's trigger go dead as the slide locked back. The weapon was out of ammo. He reached into his pocket for the old mag... Only to find it was gone! Cursing, he realized it must have slipped from his pocket during the chase.

The woman picked herself up and rolled over the counter.

Caine sprinted toward her, running as fast as he could on the slick pavement.

As she landed on the other side, she spun around and opened fire. Caine gritted his teeth as the gunshots echoed through the enclosed market. Bullets ricocheted off a concrete pole to his right.

Caine dove to the ground, sliding towards the booth across the soapy bricks. The woman continued firing, her shots passing overhead as he slid under the counter.

Before she could adjust her aim, Caine grabbed her legs and stood up, hurling her backwards. She slammed down on a stack of produce boxes behind the counter. Melons and lotus roots crushed beneath her, and several yams rolled across the damp bricks.

Before she could get up, Caine tackled her, grabbing her gun hand and shoving it aside. The gun fired, and Caine winced as the sound battered his eardrums at close range. He heard a metallic twang, followed by the hiss of escaping gas. The stray bullet had pierced a propane tank under the cooking grill.

The woman struggled beneath him. Caine twisted his body to the side, narrowly avoiding a knee thrust to the groin. As she kicked her feet, she knocked the punctured propane tank loose from its mounting bracket. The metal cylinder rolled across the ground, coming to a stop in front of the darkened exterior of a dumpling shop.

Caine slammed her gun hand on the pavement. Once, twice...

Her pistol fired again. The dumpling shop's window shattered, and Caine heard a high-pitched scream from inside. Glancing over, he saw a young girl standing behind the shattered glass. She wore pink pajamas under a puffy blue jacket, and her black hair was tied in pigtails. She couldn't have been more than eight years old, and she stared wide-eyed at Caine and the struggling woman.

Caine slammed the woman's hand on the ground again. She lost her grip and the gun fell from her fingers. Releasing her hand, he swiped the weapon away, sending it skittering across the soaked bricks.

The woman curled her fingers into a fist and drove two quick punches into his kidney. Caine clenched his jaw and rolled off her. As she bounded to her feet, his fingers wrapped around the handle of a large meat cleaver, lying in a pile of cooking utensils on the ground.

A loud buzzing sound filled the air. Caine couldn't tell what it was, but as they both gasped for breath, flames leapt from the deep-fryer bin. The oil had been left unattended for too long and had reached its ignition point.

The woman grabbed the deep-fryer basket, crying out in pain as her fingers wrapped around the hot metal handle. She swung the basket at Caine, sending flaming oil splashing through the air.

The burning liquid spattered his shoulder as he dropped to the ground and rolled under the grill. More cooking oil flew overhead, igniting a stack of newspapers in front of the dumpling store. The little girl backed away from the fire as smoke wafted through the shattered window.

Still on his back, Caine kicked the grill over, sending the hot coals tumbling across the oil-soaked pavement near his opponent's feet.

An inferno engulfed the booth. The woman backed away as flames licked at her feet. Grabbing a towel, she swatted at the fire crawling up her pants leg. Then she turned, kicked a table out of her way, and hobbled towards the end of the market. As Caine rose to his feet, he saw a black unmarked van screech to a halt in the street. Heat from the fire rose, rippling the air like a mirage.

Caine hurled the cleaver at the fleeing assassin. The blade spun through the air with a high-pitched whistle. At the last second, the woman slipped left. The blade sailed past her head and buried itself in the door of a grocery store on the opposite side of the market.

The woman looked back at Caine, her eyes dark and lifeless as a shark. Then she staggered to the van. A cloud of smoke rose from the burning stand, obscuring Caine's view as the vehicle sped off down the street.

Caine heard coughing behind him. Spinning around, he saw the little girl, still standing in the dumpling store. Smoke from the fire now filled the tiny café. Tongues of orange flame rose as the slick of burning oil crept across the pavement. Caine followed the trail of fire with his eyes. Flames crawled up the storefront, and the door frame was charred and black. The fire was moving toward...

The propane tank!

Caine did not hesitate. Moving on pure instinct, he grabbed a plastic chair from the street and dove through the remains of the glass door. A jagged shard from the door frame cut his side, but the chair protected him from most of the glass fragments.

Grabbing the petrified girl in his arms, he picked her up and rolled over a metal counter, scattering plastic bins filled with napkins and chopsticks. The boxes tumbled over the counter, spilling their contents across the floor.

Kaboom!

An explosion tore through the store. The cabinet doors shook and rattled. Wood and glass flew overhead, crashing to the ground a few feet away. Caine held the little girl tight, coughing as a wave of smoke and dust washed over them.

A few seconds later, the echo of the thundering explosion faded away. Dust and debris fell to the ground, trickling from the ceiling above like sand in an hourglass. Smoke filled the tiny store, and a wall of flame engulfed the storefront.

Caine set the girl down. 'Are you okay?'

The girl nodded but remained silent. Her eyes were wide, and her pupils looked dilated.

Probably in shock, Caine thought. *Who could blame her?*

At the rear of the store, a set of rickety wooden stairs led up to a second level. Caine heard footsteps creaking above, and hushed voices, whispering. A Korean man and woman, both in their forties, hurried down the stairs. They wore T-shirts and sweatpants, and their hair was messy and unkempt. The woman gasped as she saw the flames roaring at the store's entrance.

The little girl ran over to them, and the woman scooped her up in a tight embrace. She peered at Caine with fearful eyes as she comforted the girl.

'*Nuguseyo?* Who are you?' the man shouted, glaring at Caine. 'You come to rob us?'

'No time,' Caine said. 'Fire! Go out the back, now!'

The man gave Caine one last angry look, then ushered the woman and child to the rear of the store. The crackling of the inferno grew louder. Orange tendrils of fire crawled across the ceiling and sweat dripped down Caine's brow.

He glanced around the smoky interior. In the flickering firelight, he saw an open cabinet door beneath the counter. A digital recording device sat on the shelf, nestled in a bundle of cables. One of the tangled wires led to a charred security camera mounted on the ceiling, pointing out the remains of the glass door.

Caine ejected a tiny memory card from the recorder. Slipping the card in his pocket, he made his way to the rear service door and exited into an alley running alongside the market.

More police lights blazed in the darkness. The family was nowhere to be seen, and cars blocked either end of the dark, narrow passage. Armed men advanced towards him. As they moved closer, Caine recognized the eagle emblem marking their uniforms.

The KNP, Korean National Police. Judging by their heavy body armor and the HK 416 rifles they carried, Caine was certain this was a Special Operations Unit team, formerly known as SWAT. A logical response, given the chaos he and the unidentified female assassin had unleashed on the market.

'*Mugileul beoliseyo!*' one of the SOU team members shouted. 'Drop your weapon! You are under arrest!'

Caine held up his hands, then dipped his thumb and forefinger into his waistband, gently removing his pistol. With slow, languid movements, he set the gun down on the pavement, then took two steps back. He placed his hands on his head and kneeled.

The SOU team rushed in, weapons raised. An officer confiscated his pistol. Someone clubbed him on the back with a rifle butt, knocking him down on the ground. He did not resist as the man snapped metal cuffs around his wrists. He said nothing as they dragged him to his feet and led him to one of the vans. A uniformed officer read him his rights, but he ignored them. He remained silent as they asked him further questions.

There was nothing he was permitted to say.

Chan Tae Young was dead. Whatever secrets he possessed regarding North Korea's deep-cover operations would go to the grave with him. Caine's team,

Jae and Sue Mi, were dead as well. Their passing would be marked by two nameless gold stars added to a black plaque displayed at the NIS exhibition hall – South Korea's equivalent of the Memorial Wall, back at CIA headquarters in Langley.

Their assassin had escaped. Operation Empty Nest was over.

He had failed.

7

After the SOU team escorted him from the market, Caine was taken to NIS headquarters, a sprawling white building in Naegok-dong district. A team of two NIS officers questioned him for approximately an hour, during which he said as little as possible.

They confiscated the memory stick taken from the market. They drove him to the US Embassy in the Yongsan district. After confirming his identity, Embassy officials sequestered him in a Sensitive Compartmentalized Information Facility room in the building's basement. There, he endured a lengthier debriefing via satellite connection with his handler at Langley, along with a CIA lawyer.

Rebecca was not on the video call.

Finally, he was assigned a new cover identity and given a reservation at a nearby hotel.

'Don't get too comfortable,' the lawyer on the screen said as the call was wrapping up. 'We got you some clothes and toiletries to replace the items at your previous hotel. But if I were you, I wouldn't bother unpacking. We're planning to get you out of the country as soon as possible.'

'Knock yourself out,' Caine replied. 'All I want to do is take a shower and go to sleep.'

Now, hours later, sleep refused to come. Caine paced back and forth in his spacious room at the Botanik hotel, in Myeongdong. The decor was modern and soothing: marble floors, wood furniture, white sheets and curtains. Outside, the lights of the Seoul skyline twinkled in the distance. The view was almost identical to the one from the love hotel's penthouse.

He stared out the window, watching as the Lotte tower changed color, shifting from purple to blue.

That tower was probably the last thing Sue Mi saw, Caine thought. He imagined her pupils dilating, her lungs spasming as the toxin cut off the flow of oxygen to her brain.

Caine wore gray sweatpants and brown leather slippers. He was shirtless, and he could see his reflection in the darkened windows. White bandages wrapped around his torso, covering the stitches in his side.

He picked up a half-finished bottle of Hite beer from the nightstand. Condensation dripped down the tapered amber glass. He drained the rest of the beer, then tossed the bottle into the trash can.

I got off easy, he thought. *Everyone else... Not so much.*

A soft electronic chime echoed from his nightstand. It was his cell phone, his personal one, retrieved from the embassy safe.

He glanced at the screen... He saw several missed calls and texts. They were all from Sean Tyler. He sighed as he stared at the screen.

Sean... Jack Tyler's son. Caine had never quite figured out when his former partner had found time to raise a family. Based on the few times he had spoken to Sean, Caine gathered Jack hadn't been around much when Sean was growing up.

And now, Jack was dead. Killed by the same people who had betrayed Caine, back in the deserts of Afghanistan. So much had happened since then, it seemed like a lifetime ago.

But every time Caine looked into Sean's eyes, it was like a one-way ticket back to that hole in the desert. A reminder of his promise to Jack, a promise to look after Sean.

A promise he had broken, like so many others.

It had been months since they last spoke. Sean kept reaching out, trying to form a connection. But something drove Caine to pull away, no matter how much he wanted to connect.

As he stared at the call log, a new number blinked on the screen. He didn't recognize it, but he knew who would be on the other line.

He tapped the screen. 'Hello?'

'Hey,' Rebecca's voice replied. 'Sorry to call you so late. Wanted to see how your meeting went with the Korean suppliers?'

Over the years, he and Rebecca had established a habit of using code phrases, known only to them. It was a way to ensure neither of them were speaking under duress, or in the presence of observers. But given the night's events, Caine was in no mood for games.

'Fine,' he replied. 'I was up watching some K-drama. Have you seen *The Innocent Man*?'

'That's a bit dark for my taste. I prefer a little romance mixed with my revenge. Like *The World of the Married*.'

Caine stared out the window and said nothing. Now that the exchange of meaningless phrases was complete, he found himself at a loss for words.

Rebecca broke the silence. 'Look, what happened tonight—'

'It was my fault.' Caine said, interrupting. 'I went off mission.'

'Really?' Rebecca replied. 'Based on the report the NIS sent me, it looks like your instincts were correct. This operation was blown from the start. The man you followed was working with the assassin.'

'Yeah,' Caine muttered. 'Tell that to Sue Mi and Jae. If I hadn't gone off on my own, if—'

'If what?' Rebecca snapped. 'If you had been there? These assassins, whoever they were, got to Chan's mistress before the NIS did. They were one step ahead of us the entire time. They wired the AC in the room with halothane gas canisters. Once everyone was unconscious, the assassin...' Rebecca's voice trailed off. 'Well, you saw what she did.'

'Some kind of nerve toxin, right?'

Rebecca was silent. Caine heard her shuffling papers in the background.

'Rebecca?' Caine prodded.

'Yes,' she replied. 'It was a unique compound, something we've never seen before. VX neurotoxin, combined with a stimulant and a corrosive acid.'

'So they were awake as they suffocated to death,' Caine said, spitting out the words as if they left a bitter taste in his mouth. 'And the acid... Those markings?'

'They were numbers,' Rebecca continued. 'Two nines. Nine is a significant number to the Kim regime in North Korea. Kim Il Sung declared September 9th to be the founding date of the DPRK. The family even owns a fast-food chain called Number 9 Farms. Internally, the NIS has designated Chan's group of deep-cover operatives as Unit 99.'

Caine glared back at his reflection in the window. 'So this wasn't just a counter-intel operation. They wanted to send a message. Keep their other people in line.'

Rebecca's voice softened. 'Tom, I know what it's like to lose people. But this isn't on you. We all knew the risks. The NIS has had one intelligence disaster after another. There was always a chance they were compromised from the inside.'

'Then why the hell did Paulis agree to this in the first place?' Caine snapped.

'He thought it was worth the risk. So did I, for that matter. If it had worked, we could have exposed this Unit 99, dismantled their network before—'

'Great,' Caine said, interrupting her. 'I'm sure those officers' families will sleep better knowing their loved ones died for nothing.'

Rebecca sucked in her breath.

Caine rubbed his temples. 'I'm sorry. It's been a long night.'

'Sue Mi and Jae were professionals. They knew the risks, same as you. It's disrespectful to assume otherwise.'

'You're right,' Caine replied. 'But you're not the one who got them killed.'

'Neither were you. Speaking of which, the NIS shared the files from the memory stick you retrieved.'

Caine ran his fingers through his hair. 'And?'

'No match on facial recognition. Whoever she is, neither the CIA nor the NIS has any record of her. Thanks to you, at least we know who we're looking for. She'll turn up sooner or later.'

Caine rubbed his eyes. 'Maybe.'

'You sound exhausted,' she said, a hint of softness creeping back into her voice. 'I expedited your pickup. Embassy security will send a car in the morning. They'll escort you to Seoul airport and put you on a diplomatic flight out. Try to get some sleep until then, okay?'

'Yeah,' Caine muttered. 'I will.'

'And maybe...' Her voice trailed off.

'What?' Caine asked.

'When's the last time you saw Sean?'

Caine blinked. 'Sean? I don't know. We had dinner once or twice. I've been busy—'

'You had dinner once, and that was months ago,' Rebecca replied.

'You keeping the kid under surveillance?'

'I don't have to,' she replied. 'He took a job with Human Rights Watch. They have an office in DC. I ran into him a couple of weeks ago. We talked. You know, like normal people do?'

Caine grunted. 'What we do is pretty damn far from normal.'

'You're the closest link Sean has to his father. Jack was your friend. And Sean, he—'

'I'm not cut out to be anyone's father figure, Rebecca.'

'No one's asking you to. Just be... there.'

Caine sighed. 'All right. I'll call him when I get back. But—'

Before he could finish his sentence, there was a knock at the door.

Caine froze. He listened for a few seconds but heard no other sound.

'Hello?' Rebecca's voice echoed from the phone.

'You said the embassy guys weren't coming until the morning?' he whispered.

'Right. Is something wrong?'

'Not sure. Stand by.' Caine dimmed the lights in the room and pulled the curtains closed. Cloaked in darkness, he approached the door and peeled back a strip of electrical tape covering the peephole.

The corridor outside was empty.

Caine opened the door. A small package sat on the carpet, in front of his room. It was wrapped in a silk cloth, a print with images of koi swimming up a waterfall.

Caine recognized the design instantly. It was the symbol of the Yoshizawa clan, a yakuza group based in Tokyo. He picked up the package and gave the corridor one last, wary glance. It was empty, and the lights were dim. At this hour, most of the guests were asleep. Only the soft hum of the elevators broke the hotel's slumbering silence.

'Tom?' Rebecca's voice crackled in his ear. 'Are you still there?'

'I'm here. Everything's fine. But I have to call you back.'

'All right,' she said in a suspicious voice. 'Keep me in the loop.'

'I will.'

He brought the strange package inside and closed the door. Then he turned on the lights and examined the carefully wrapped bundle. The intricately folded cloth was tied in a loose, floppy knot, almost like a bow on a present. The technique was known as *furoshiki* and traced its roots to the cloth wrappings used to bundle clothing when visiting Japan's public baths.

Caine set the package down on a table and gently tugged at the knot. The cloth fell away, revealing a small box carved from yew wood.

Caine thought for a moment. The box seemed too small to hold enough explosives to reliably kill anyone. Still, he knew it was not impossible. Mossad had targeted leaders of the Hezbollah terrorist group in Lebanon with explosive pagers, and those devices were even smaller. Given the intel possessed by these deep-cover North Korean operatives, it was not impossible for them to have located his whereabouts.

But it seemed far less likely that they could know about his history in Japan, working with the Yoshizawa clan. Or his relationship with the clan's current leader, Koichi Ogawa.

Caine shrugged, then flipped the box open. Inside, he found a Cathay Pacific airline ticket in the name of Mark Waters, along with a US passport matching his old cover identity. There was also an envelope marked with the same koi design as the silk cloth.

Caine opened the envelope and removed a card. Japanese calligraphy covered the tiny square of cream-colored paper.

'Apologies for the inconvenience. If it's not too much trouble, Ogawa-san asks if you wouldn't mind joining him for a drink? Please forgive the suddenness of this invitation, but time is of the essence. Also, Ogawa-san asks if Honda-san was able to assist you with your China problem?'

Caine set the card down and examined the airplane ticket. Then he checked the steel dive watch on his wrist. He had about two hours, and it was a ninety-minute cab ride to Incheon Airport.

Caine pulled the suitcase of clothes the embassy had provided from under the bed and got dressed. He would have to leave immediately to catch the flight. And despite the polite language of the note, Caine knew something terrible must have happened for Koichi to have asked him for help.

After Caine's mission in Japan, the old gangster had helped Caine several times, including providing a plane and pilot to smuggle Jia Zhou and her kidnapped daughter to safety.

But Caine knew he owed Koichi more than that.

Giri, he thought. *That's what Isato, Koichi's old boss, called it.*

A duty. An obligation. A debt...

Japan, the things that had happened to him there... They were the first steps on the road to rebuilding his life. The events they set in motion culminated in the death of Allan Bernatto and Walter Grissom, exposing them as Caine's betrayers, and allowing him to come in from the cold.

Allowing him to resume his relationship with Rebecca.

But *giri* was a double-edged sword. To be bound by such a debt was no small burden. And thus, to remind one of such an obligation, as Koichi's note had done, was considered rude and vulgar. Something only done as a last resort, when things were dire.

There was no time to explain things to Rebecca, no time to go through official channels. He would contact her later, tell her everything, just as he promised.

But first, he had to catch this flight to Japan.

8

OTARU, JAPAN

International waters

Frost clung to the chamber's metal walls. Chains creaked from the darkness above. Animal carcasses hung from the rafters, swaying back and forth.

'Gold General A4 to B3,' an electronic voice called out over a loudspeaker.

Akari Habu shivered as he slipped between a pair of slaughtered cattle. Their carcasses were skinned, and frost covered their butchered torsos. They swung back and forth, as if something was gently rocking the room.

The thirty-four-year-old Japanese man squinted, struggling to see in the dim light. His torso was bare, revealing the toned body of a casual athlete. His belly hung over his belt, forming a slight paunch. An elaborate black and red tattoo sleeve covered his right arm. The design featured a dragon surrounded by cherry blossoms. The beast's roaring maw stretched over his shoulders and snaked down across his chest.

His skin was pale. Bits of frost stuck in his hair. Bruises covered his face, and his right eye had swollen shut. He heard the jangle of chains again to his right. He spun around, raising his fists in a defensive posture.

The jangling sounded again, this time to Akari's right. Before he could react, another man charged toward him, planted his left foot on the floor, and swung his right leg into a roundhouse kick.

The blow connected with a bone-shattering crack. Akari fell to his knees and groaned in pain.

'Rook H8 to G7,' the other man said. His voice was a deep, gravely baritone, and it echoed off the chamber's metal walls like thunder.

He stood over Akari, his face hidden in shadow. Shafts of light beamed through a ventilation fan, revealing brief glimpses of the man's physique. He was tall, lean, and muscular. Unlike Akari, there was no softness in his stomach or abdomen. His smooth, tan chest looked as if it had been carved from oak, and thick cords of muscle rippled along his arms.

This man, too, was marked by an elaborate tattoo. Snow-covered mountains stretched along both arms, broken up by red tori gates and blue water streams.

'*Tachiagare, okubyoumono-me,*' he snarled. 'Get up, coward!'

He swung his arm out, driving the knife edge of his palm into Akari's left shoulder. The man cried out in pain as his arm went numb. He scrambled to his feet and swung his right arm out in a clumsy punch.

The other man slipped left, dodging the blow.

'Foot Soldier C3 to C4,' the voice called out over the speakers.

'Torazama-san, please!' Akari said, his voice trembling as shivers ran through his body. 'I swear, I thought—'

Torazama launched a quick jab with his left hand. Akari stepped back, then threw a left cross that slammed into his opponent's jaw. Torazama stepped back, then launched a front kick into Akari's torso. The man crumpled over, then collapsed to the floor. The savage blow knocked the wind from his lungs.

'Rook H8 to G7,' Torazama bellowed, rubbing his jaw. Although he was the superior fighter, Akari had landed a few solid blows. He grinned as he felt pain radiate through his muscles.

The thrill of the hunt was always proportional to the skill of the prey.

Akari groaned and rolled across the floor.

Torazama snarled as he launched another kick into the prone man's abdomen. Akari grunted in pain. He coughed a spatter of blood onto the frost-covered floor.

'Get up, you pathetic worm!' Torazama bellowed. 'Is this the best you can do? Again, you disappoint me. You failed to kill Ogawa-san in Tokyo. You let the girl slip through your fingers in Sapporo. And now, you cannot even present me with an amusing death!'

Akari staggered to his feet. 'Forgive me, *oyabun*,' he replied, spitting blood on the icy floor. 'It was not my fault!'

He launched a left hook at Torazama. The older man threw up his arm to block the strike. But the blow was just a feint. A split second later, Akari's right knee slammed into Torazama's side.

As Torazama grunted in pain, Akari pressed his attack. He threw a quick jab at Torazama, followed by a roundhouse kick that struck the older man's right thigh.

'Foot Soldier C3 to D3.' The strange, inhuman voice echoed through the metal room. Akari looked up, struggling to discern where the sound was coming from.

Torazama grinned, using the momentary distraction to step back, dodging another kick from Akari.

'Silver General I7 to H8,' he bellowed in response. As Akari swung his fist again, the older man slipped to the right. The blow struck a frozen beef carcass with a bone-shattering crack. Akari cried out in pain, cradling his swollen hand as he backed away from Torazama.

The older man stood half-hidden in shadow. His low, sinister laugh echoed off the metal walls as his breath misted the air.

'I should not be so hard on you, Akari,' he growled. 'Karate these days... It is not what it once was. All these rules. Forbidden strikes, gloves, padded helmets. How can I expect you to fight like a man, when you've been coddled like a child your whole life?'

He charged forward. Akari threw up his arms to block, but he was so tired and weak that Torazama's forward kick swept them aside like twigs. The blow connected with his chest, sending Akari reeling back into another swinging carcass. He bounced off the frozen meat with a loud thud, then fell to his hands and knees. Blood and saliva drooled from his mouth as he gasped for breath.

'Rook B2 is promoted. Rook B2 to G7. Opposing Rook is captured,' the electronic voice said.

'Silver General H8 to G7,' Torazama growled. 'Opposing Rook captured.'

He walked over to Akari and grabbed the man by his hair. He kneeled beside him and yanked the man's head up, forcing him to look into his eyes.

Akari's exhausted features contorted into a look of fear as he gazed upon Torazama's face. 'It... It's true, the stories...' he said, his teeth chattering from the cold. 'You... Your eyes...'

'I trained in Kyokushin Karate as a child,' Torazama said, his voice quiet and reflective. 'We practiced in the snow, in temperatures far colder than this. When we sparred, only full contact was allowed. I broke my arm three times, learning how to block a kick like that. I dislocated my shoulder twice and sprained my ankle more times than I could count. But I quickly learned that pain is the greatest teacher. To rise to greatness, there is no room for fear or doubt. One must strengthen both the body and the mind, in order to resist such weakness.'

He stood, dragging Akari to his feet.

'You, Akari-san, have not overcome pain. And that is why you fail me.'

Torazama's elbow swung out, striking Akari's skull with the force of a sledgehammer.

Akari's head whipped around. His legs wobbled like jelly, and he collapsed to the ground, striking the metal floor with a loud thud. He lay on his back, eyes twitching. Torazama raised his foot, then stamped down on the man's trachea.

A last gasp of pain escaped Akari's lips. Torazama turned away, and Akari gazed up at the tattoo covering the man's back... A white tiger perched upon the waves of a dark blue sea. The animal's fanged jaw hung open in a savage roar. A red sun rose behind its snarling face. Clouds filled the sky, and a lightning bolt streaked behind the ferocious-looking animal.

'Byakko-san,' Akari whispered, his voice a faint croak. 'To look into the white tiger's eyes...'

His voice trailed off and his eyes glazed over. Again, he heard the strange, computerized voice echoing through the meat locker.

'Silver General A3 to B2,' it said.

The next sound he heard was the icy whisper of his final breath escaping from his lungs. A quiet sigh, welcoming his release from pain. An acceptance of whatever fate lay beyond the pale white haze that filled his vision.

After that, he heard nothing more.

* * *

Torazama exited the freezing meat locker and emerged into a narrow corridor. A pair of men wearing dark suits flanked the door. One of them handed Torazama a white fur robe, which he slipped over his naked torso.

'Send some men to dispose of Akari,' he said. 'Perhaps the tiger sharks below will find him more entertaining than I.'

'*Hai, oyabun,*' one of the men grunted. They followed him down another corridor. He stopped at a door halfway down and placed his hand on the glowing surface of a security terminal. There was a soft beep, and the pad pulsed with light. The metal door slid open, and Torazama entered with his men in tow.

The room beyond was massive, with sloped metal walls curving up into the shadows. Rows of desks, each topped with a glowing computer monitor, filled the floor. The soft tapping of keyboards filled the air, as men and women wearing headsets entered lines of code, breached firewalls, and disseminated data throughout the world.

A pair of stairs near the back of the room led to a raised platform overlooking the workstations. A bank of massive screens hung from the ceiling, displaying news outlets from around the world. The news stories focused on events in the United States, South Korea, and Japan.

But the center screen displayed something different... A green grid, divided into thirty-six squares. Tiny white shields, their pointed ends facing opposite sides of the grid, moved along the board. A Japanese kanji character in black marked each shield, except for one, which was red.

It was a shogi board, the Japanese version of chess. The pieces on the board matched the grid coordinates called out by both Torazama and the electronic voice emanating from the speakers.

Torazama ascended the stairs and stood atop the platform, gazing out at the screens. He focused his attention on the news stories surrounding the game board. He did not need to see the board to play. He had memorized the position of both his and his opponent's pieces. He could play the game from memory alone, as he had during his fight with Akari.

'Gold General I6 to H7,' he said in an absent-minded voice, as he scanned a story concerning a viral outbreak in Los Angeles. There were no deaths reported so far, but the pathogen responsible was unknown, and case counts were on the rise. Similar stories flooded the South Korean and Japanese news outlets.

Torazama's lips curled into a grin.

One of the shield-like pieces moved a single square on the game board. Another piece, one in the opposing player's army, moved as well.

'Rook B2 to C3,' the voice responded.

Torazama nodded as he stroked his goatee, a satisfied gleam in his eye. His opponent had ignored his feint, instead defending against a possible future attack, thinking several moves ahead. They were learning, improving with each game. Soon, his opponent's skill would rival his own.

Torazama had taught them well.

A man sitting at a nearby computer glanced up. 'Torazama-san, I have—'

'Here, in this place, you will call me by my other name,' the older man said in an icy voice.

The man stood from his desk and gave a deep bow. 'Forgive me. Byakko-san. Miss Park is reporting. She has returned from Seoul, and is on her way—'

'Put her on the screen,' Torazama, the man known as Byakko, said.

The image of the game board vanished, replaced by the stern, emotionless face of a Korean woman. At the sight of her, Byakko's expression seemed to soften, like ice melting in the warm sun. His lips curled into a faint smile.

'You have returned to us. Is it done?' Byakko asked.

The woman nodded, her dark eyes betraying no hint of emotion. 'Chan has been silenced. He will no longer be a liability to us, or to our mission.'

Byakko's grin grew wider. '*Subarashii*. Excellent.'

The woman's face remained neutral, but her voice struck a concerned tone. 'There was a man, an American. I think he was CIA. He was working with NIS officers.'

Byakko nodded. 'It is of no matter. By the time they put the pieces together, it will be too late. The damage will be done.'

She tilted her head, peering into his eyes. Unlike Akari, she did not seem to find his gaze strange or unsettling. 'And Ogawa-san? The yakuza *oyabun* in Tokyo?'

Byakko's nostrils flared. The woman returned his steely gaze.

'Regrettably, my *wakagashira* failed in his task,' he said. 'I'll take care of it. I have applied pressure to a weak link in Ogawa-san's organization. He will be dead before the sun rises.'

'Another mistake, then,' the woman said. 'Like the girl. You grow careless.'

Byakko glared at the screen. 'In shogi, as in life, one must often sacrifice pawns to achieve victory.'

'We are playing a game we cannot afford to lose,' the woman replied, staring back at him. Her image blinked off the screen, replaced once more by the green shogi board.

Byakko gripped the platform's railing and took a deep breath. He exhaled with a low hiss, clearing his mind, calming his thoughts. It was his move. He would not allow anger or emotion to dictate his strategy. Not for Jiwoo Park, or anyone else.

'Send more men to the Sapporo address,' he said in a loud, firm voice. 'If Kanako Natsuki returns there, bring her to me. And if anyone else enters the apartment...'

He looked down at his men. '*Karera o korose*... Kill them.'

The men bowed. Byakko moved toward the exit door. But he paused and placed his hand on one of his men's shoulders. The man winced as the imposing gangster dug his fingers into his flesh.

'Do not fail me,' Byakko growled. 'Or you shall be my next sparring partner. *Wakarimasu ka?*'

'*Hai*, I understand,' the man gasped, bowing even deeper.

Byakko, the White Tiger, released the man. As he exited the room, he called out his next move.

'Silver General I3 to H3.'

The door slid closed behind him and the piece moved across the screen.

The game continued.

9

TOKYO, JAPAN

06:30 hours

Caine slept for most of the two-and-a-half-hour flight from Seoul to Tokyo. But the brief nap seemed to have little effect on his body as he lumbered down the jetway at Haneda Airport. His nerves were buzzing, jangling. His eyes felt red and bleary. He knew he was still suffering the effects of an adrenaline rush after the events in Seoul. The fight-or-flight instincts kicking in, the injuries he had suffered.

The raw, fresh scars of guilt after what had happened to his team.

He did not know why Koichi had reached out to him, but whatever the reason, a part of him was grateful for the distraction.

After passing through immigration, he slung his weekend bag over his shoulder and headed for the bathroom. He had traveled light, with just a carry-on and the clothes on his back. The embassy hadn't exactly splurged for a new wardrobe – he was still wearing the gray sweatpants from earlier, along with a white T-shirt and a navy-blue hoody. Black Asics sneakers completed the outfit. The bag contained a few more shirts, socks, and fresh underwear.

After splashing some hot water on his face and running a comb through his hair, he examined himself in the bathroom mirror. The traces of crow's feet surrounding his verdant green eyes were a bit more pronounced. Salt and pepper dusted his dark brown hair at the temples.

Caine shrugged. *Could be worse*, he thought.

His jaw was still firm, his face lean and tan. His eyes, though tired and red, still held a predatory gleam. Despite the years of pain and betrayal, and more injuries than he could count, he wasn't ready to be put out to pasture yet.

He washed his face again, knowing it might be some time until he could shower. Then he exited the bathroom and entered the sprawling international terminal.

Announcements blared through the speakers overhead, first in Japanese, then translated into English, Chinese, and Korean. Even at this early hour, hundreds of travelers surged through the modern glass and steel building. Above him, a glass barrier ran along an elevated balcony. Restaurants and cafés lined the upper level. Businesspeople sat in padded leather chairs, looking out over the terminal as they worked on laptops, or checked emails on their phones.

Caine followed the signs for ground transportation. He assumed if Koichi wanted to see him, he would send a car or arrange for a rental from the airport.

A small crowd of drivers, tour guides, and families waited beyond the security gates once Caine entered the landside of the airport. Scanning their faces, he spotted a young Japanese man in his twenties. He wore dark sunglasses and a burgundy sharkskin suit. His white dress shirt was open at the collar, and he wore no tie.

If the yakuza had an official uniform, this guy was wearing it, Caine thought.

The man held up a sign. The name 'Mark Waters' was written in English on the paper square.

Koichi didn't give his people my real name, Caine thought. *Interesting...*

As Caine approached, the man lowered the sign and pulled his cell phone from his pocket. Peering over the rim of his sunglasses, he checked the screen, then looked at Caine.

'I'm Mark Waters,' Caine said. He did not hold out his hand.

The man checked the phone screen one more time, then looked Caine in the eye. He gave a small bow. Caine nodded in return.

'*Hajimemashite*,' the man said. 'Pleased to meet you. I am Junko Fujioka. I am an associate of Ogawa-san. Please come with me.'

Caine looked the man up and down, noting the slight bulge beneath his jacket. 'You expecting trouble, Junko?'

The young man shifted on his feet and glanced around the airport. 'We should go,' he said. 'We may not have much time.'

Caine looked around as well. No one else in the crowd stood out to him. Bodies rushed past, eager to make their way to the taxis and shuttle buses pulling up beyond the glass doors.

Finally, he gave Junko a nod. 'After you.'

Relief filled the young man's eyes, and he relaxed his stiff posture. He turned and led Caine through the airport. 'I am parked nearby.'

Caine eyed a coffee stand in the middle of the airport, just before the glass doors that led to the parking area. 'Any chance we could stop for coffee? It's been a long night.'

Junko's shoulders tensed once more, and his mouth curled into a frown. '*Gomennasai*... I'm sorry, but—'

'Okay, okay, don't sweat it, kid,' Caine replied. 'I'm just tired.'

Junko nodded. 'There will be coffee at the hospital.'

Caine narrowed his eyes. 'Hospital? Wait, is Koichi... I mean, Ogawa-san... Is he okay?'

'I don't know. But the sooner we get there, the sooner we will find out.'

The second they stepped outside the airport, a blast of frigid air struck Caine's face, chilling him to the bone. It was still early morning, and the sky was dim, streaked with purple and orange haze. Caine paused for a moment... Lurking beneath the exhaust fumes and city smells, the air held a familiar scent. Trees, grass, damp earth – Japan.

The smells triggered a barrage of memories, carrying him back to the time he had spent working undercover in the country, posing as an international arms dealer to infiltrate the Yoshizawa crime family.

Familiar faces filled his thoughts. Isato Yoshizawa, the wily old crime boss. Koichi Ogawa, his tough-as-nails right-hand man. And Kenji, his son.

'This way, please.' Junko gestured to a walkway leading to the closest parking garage. Caine blinked, realizing he had been lost in thought. He shook his head, letting the cold wind blow the old memories away, like autumn leaves scattered on the snow-swept ground.

Junko led him to a sleek orange sports car near the edge of the parking structure. Caine gave a low whistle as he walked around the vehicle.

'Lexus LFA,' he said with an admiring glance. '4.8-liter V10 engine, zero to sixty in 3.6 seconds. They only made about 500 of these.'

Junko gave Caine a brief grin. He tapped his phone, and a series of beeps emitted from the low-slung vehicle. 'You know your cars.'

The vehicle's trunk popped open, and Caine slung his bag into the tiny cargo space. Junko opened the driver's side door and slid into the car. The engine roared to life. Caine felt the deep bass growl of the V10 rumble through his chest.

Again, his thoughts drifted back to Kenji, Isato's son. Without thinking, he rubbed the old scar just beneath his shoulder. The tiny white divot in his flesh, where he had taken a bullet to save the young boy's life.

Years later, when he'd returned to Tokyo, Caine had met Isato's son again, as a young man in his twenties. Kenji had driven a flashy, expensive sports car, similar to this one. And he'd betrayed both Caine and his own father.

The passenger window rolled down. 'You coming or what?' Junko asked.

Caine opened the door and got in. The car tore out of the garage, swiftly merging with the traffic on the expressway.

'You can sleep, if you want,' Junko said. 'Traffic is light. We'll be at the hospital soon.'

Caine nodded but said nothing. He did not sleep. Instead, he stared out the window, watching the other traffic speed by. Blooms of light pierced the shadowy clouds above, clusters of buildings lit brighter than the early morning sky.

His last trip to Japan had set him on a path. A path that had led him back to his old life, back to Rebecca. Back from the brink of death.

What, he wondered, would this trip bring?

* * *

After a twenty-minute ride, Junko pulled up outside the St. Luke's International Hospital, in Tokyo's Chuo ward. One of the most famous and well-respected medical centers in the world, the hospital comprised multiple beige buildings, spread out over a sprawling, landscaped campus. In the distance, a pair of towering spires, linked on the fourteenth floor by a glass-enclosed walkway, thrust up into the hazy morning sky. The Sumida River snaked past the twin towers, a ribbon of slate-gray water reflecting the fiery glow of the rising sun.

Caine followed Junko into the main building, and they took an elevator up to the twelfth floor.

'Ogawa-san has a floor to himself,' Junko explained as the car rose through the glass and metal tower. 'Security will be tight.' The young man gave Caine a questioning look. 'You will be searched.'

Caine shrugged. 'I'm not carrying.'

The elevator stopped, and the doors opened with a soft chime. A woman's voice played over the speakers.

'*Juunikai*,' the electronic voice said. 'Twelfth floor.'

The doors slid open with a soft chime. Caine followed Junko down a sterile white corridor to the nurse's station. The floor was silent, save for the distant beeps and humming of medical equipment.

A pair of women in white and lavender uniforms worked behind a desk, entering data into their computer terminals. In front of the desk, a group of men dressed in dark suits blocked the corridor. They mumbled to each other in low voices and gave Caine suspicious looks as Junko approached them. Caine spotted yakuza tattoos peeking out from under their shirt collars. A few of the men chewed on toothpicks or sucked on hard candies. The hospital didn't permit smoking on its grounds.

Junko put a hand on Caine's shoulder, and he stopped walking. One of the men stepped towards them with his hands shoved in his pockets. He rocked back and forth on his feet and looked Caine up and down. Then he ran his hand through his thinning gray hair.

'*Kore ga gaijin desu ka?*' he snarled. *This is the foreigner?*

Caine was fluent in Japanese, but he said nothing. He returned the man's steely stare with his own emerald gaze.

Junko whispered something in the gangster's ear. The man grunted, then shook his head. He looked at Caine and spread his arms out. Caine mimicked the gesture, and the glowering man searched him for weapons.

After a quick pat-down, the yakuza turned to the others. '*Kare wa buki mottenai*,' he said, raising his voice. *He's clean.*

The nurses behind the desk glanced up and gave the man a sharp look. He lowered his head, hunched his shoulders, and shuffled back to the group. The men parted, and another figure strode towards Caine and Junko. He was taller than the others, and he walked with a confident stride. The other men seemed to melt away, letting him pass. His youthful good looks resembled a Japanese TV star, and he wore his thick black hair slicked back with gel.

'Thank you for coming,' he said, giving Caine a slight bow. 'I am Tetsuo Mori.'

'Ogawa-san's *wakagashira*,' Junko said, bowing deeper to Tetsuo. 'His second-in-command.'

Caine held out his hand. Tetsuo gave him a firm shake.

'What exactly is going on here?' Caine asked. 'Is Koichi all right?'

The other men ceased their mumbling, and their eyes turned to Tetsuo. The handsome man sighed and again gave Caine a brief bow.

'Ogawa-san spoke highly of you. Coming here shows great respect. I know he would be pleased.'

'That doesn't answer my question,' Caine replied, his voice taking on a cold, hard edge.

'There was an attack... A rival clan struck, even as we worked to negotiate peace,' Tetsuo said, shuffling his feet. 'Ogawa-san was seriously injured and—'

'Spit it out,' Caine snarled.

'It pains me to say he is no longer with us,' Tetsuo said, bowing deeper. 'Koichi Ogawa died fifteen minutes ago.'

10

Caine glared at the young Japanese man as the words washed over him. The group of yakuza in the hall chattered amongst themselves even louder. The nurses behind the desk made a shushing sound, and the conversations lowered to a dim murmur.

'What do you mean?' Caine snapped. 'What the hell happened? Who attacked him?'

'Ogawa-san left some things for you,' Tetsuo continued. 'Papers, mementos of your time here. He asked that I give them to you immediately, in the event of... In light of what has occurred.'

Caine hesitated. Tetsuo gave him a solemn look and gestured down the corridor, back in the direction he had come.

'Please. It was his dying wish.'

Junko and Tetsuo led him back to the elevators. Caine clenched his fists and kept his eyes on the two men as the tiny car descended to the building's sixth floor.

Tetsuo's hiding something, he thought. *But what?*

As the elevators opened and they exited onto the sixth floor, Caine kept his distance from the two men, watching their movements for any sign of impending violence. His eyes darted left and right, noting the layout of the surrounding corridors. And marking the location of exit signs, in case he needed a quick escape route.

He could think of no reason why Tetsuo, a man he had never met until now, would wish him harm. But he knew better than to let his guard down. As he followed them, he noticed the walls in this part of the hospital were bright and colorful. Crayon and marker drawings decorated the doors of the rooms.

Children's ward, he thought.

That made even less sense. If this was a trap, why would they bring him here, away from the other men? But if not, what business could they possibly have on this floor?

The morning sun beamed in from a row of glass windows at the end of the hall. Junko opened a door and Tetsuo exited the hospital onto a rooftop garden. Caine followed, shoving his hands into his pockets as the cold winter air blasted his skin.

A concrete path meandered through the foliage. Ivory clumps of snow clung to the bows of evergreen trees, and white powder covered the grass and moss on the ground. The muted roar of traffic below drifted through the trees, occasionally broken by the loud, persistent calls of black crows circling overhead.

Caw, caw, caw... One of the birds landed on the gnarled branch of a cherry tree. It cocked its head, eying Caine with a dark, inquisitive gaze.

A sign blocked the concrete path, stating that the garden was closed for maintenance. Tetsuo and Junko ignored it and started down the path. Caine followed.

'Is Koichi's lawyer meeting us here?' he asked, glancing at another crow as it flapped its shadowy wings.

'Lawyer?' a rough, scratchy voice called out from the trees. 'That's the last thing I need! Only lawyers and painters can turn black to white.'

Caine turned the corner and was shocked to see Koichi Ogawa sitting in a wheelchair on a small concrete patio, hidden from view by a grove of trees.

'You tough old bastard!' Caine exclaimed.

Tetsuo seemed unperturbed by the old man's appearance, but Junko's eyes were wide with shock. He took a step forward and gave a deep bow.

'*Oyabun!*' he exclaimed. 'But I thought—'

'You thought what he wanted you to think,' Caine said with a grin.

Koichi smiled and nodded his head toward Caine. 'Pay attention, kid. You could learn a thing or two from this guy,' he said. 'He's pretty sharp for an old barbarian.'

Caine chuckled. 'Look who's talking.'

Koichi rolled up to a small metal table, flanked by a pair of garden chairs. A nurse hurried over and set down a tray. A teapot and two small cups rested on the black lacquered wood. She filled each cup with steaming tea and set the pot down. She smiled at Caine and gestured to the empty chair.

Koichi looked up at his men. 'Give us old-timers a few minutes to talk stories, eh?'

'Not too long,' the nurse said, draping a blanket over the old man's shoulders. '*Kaze o hiite shimaimasu yo*... You'll catch cold!'

Koichi shook his head and chuckled. 'Sure, sure. Bullets and grenades didn't do the trick, but a little wind will be the death of me.'

The nurse rolled her eyes and walked away, her heels clicking down the concrete path. Tetsuo and Junko gave one last bow, then turned and followed. Caine sat down at the table.

'Grenades?' He peered into Koichi's dark, secretive eyes. 'What the hell happened?'

He took a sip of tea, cradling the cup in his hands. He pursed his lips as he swallowed and stared at the trees in the distance, lost in thought.

'Koichi,' Caine prodded.

'*Sumimasen*. Sorry,' the old man said, putting the cup down. Steam wafted in the air between them. 'Truth is, I'm not exactly sure where to start. It seems I've made a new enemy. Not so unusual, in my line of work.' His eyes darted up, squinting at Caine. 'Or yours.'

'I haven't kept up with local events,' Caine replied, keeping his voice neutral. 'But I thought the Yoshizawa clan was building alliances, not fighting turf wars. At least, not under your leadership.'

Caine took a sip of tea, watching the old man's reaction.

Koichi gave a slow, weary nod. '*Hai*, that is true. But it seems I can't stop fighting just yet.'

'Who took a shot at you?' Caine asked.

'I wish I knew. In my day, things were different. Men like Isato... He had the guts to look his enemies in the eye when he pulled the trigger.'

Caine doubted that was true. The wily old gangster had his own code of honor. But when it came to killing, in Caine's experience, honor usually gave way to more practical concerns. He kept his thoughts to himself and sipped his tea in silence.

More birds circled overhead. Their persistent cries pierced the gloomy clouds overhead.

'Koichi, look. We both know I owe you, big time. But if this is some kind of yakuza beef, I can't—'

'Oh, look who's developed a conscience all of a sudden,' the old man countered, raising his bushy white eyebrows. 'Well, I wouldn't want to upset your delicate sensibilities.'

'Koichi, I'm sorry, but—'

Koichi slammed his fist on the table, rattling the teapot and cups. 'You think I wanted to bring you here? You think I want to be out here in the fucking cold with you? Instead of lying in my bed and getting a sponge bath from a pretty nurse?'

He leaned forward in his chair. 'You saw all those men when you came in here, didn't you? I don't need another monkey to pull a trigger. I don't need muscle... I need brains! Someone I can trust!'

'*Gomennasai*,' Caine said, giving Koichi a brief bow. 'I meant no offense. It's been a long couple of days. In Korea, things... didn't go my way.'

Koichi nodded. 'So I heard. Seems we were both betrayed by an inside man.'

'That's why you're playing dead?' Caine asked. 'You think someone in your organization set you up?'

Koichi wrinkled his eyes and pursed his lips, as if tasting something sour. 'I can't rule out the possibility, much as I hate to admit it.'

He looked up, meeting Caine's gaze head on. 'You know, it's funny. After all we went through together the last time you were here, I don't know all that much about you. Do you have family, Caine-san?'

Caine glanced up at the crows circling overhead. They dove towards the gardens, settling on the snow-draped branches of a mayten evergreen tree.

'Why do you ask?' he replied.

Koichi fished a cell phone from the folds of his robe. He tapped the screen and flicked through pictures in the gallery. 'Huh. My folks died when I was young. Not that my father was around much, anyway. And my mother... Well, after my father left her, she married the bottle. Sometimes, I wonder. If things had been different, would my life have turned out the same?'

He slid the phone across the table to Caine. 'Bah, listen to me. The older I get, the more I complain. *Fukusui bon ni kaerazu.*'

'Spilt water will not return to the tray,' Caine translated, picking up the phone.

He examined the picture on the screen. It was a photo taken at a bar or nightclub. Most of the faces were blurry and indistinct, and a smoky haze filled the air. The subject of the photo, a young Japanese woman in her twenties, stood out. A halo of light from the bar circled her head, giving her red hair a fiery glow.

Obviously a dye job, Caine thought. *But it suits her.*

Her high cheekbones, pert nose, and slim, dark eyes were classically beautiful by Japanese standards. Yet it was her mouth that stood out most to Caine. Her lips were large and full, accentuated in the photo by carefully applied burgundy lipstick. They parted in a sly, seductive smile, her eyes glancing to the left of the frame.

She wore a black evening gown and appeared to be pouring alcohol of some kind into a crystal glass.

Based on the camera angle, and her position in the frame, Caine had the impression she did not realize her picture was being taken.

'She's beautiful,' he said, setting the phone back on the table. 'Who is she?'

'Her name is Kanako Natsuki. She's a hostess in Sapporo.' The old man took another sip of tea. 'She is also my daughter.'

Caine squinted at Koichi in disbelief, then grabbed the phone again, checking the picture. 'Daughter? But, I mean... How old were you when—'

The old man shrugged. 'I'm a gangster, not a saint. I met her mother in my fifties, long before you stumbled across my path. She was a hostess too, at one of Isato's clubs.'

Caine shook his head. 'Are you close? I mean, does she know?'

Koichi shook his head. His eyes turned to the dead, shriveled branches of a cherry tree. 'Things didn't end well with us. My fault. I was a *baka*... a fool.' He glanced up at Caine and gave a thin smile. 'Some things never change, eh?'

'I'm sure this life isn't easy on relationships,' Caine replied.

The old man narrowed his eyes. 'She wanted me to leave the yakuza. To abandon Isato. When I refused, she left me. Took our child with her. I tried to honor her wishes, stay away. But she – the mother – died a few years ago. Cancer. Not long after, Kanako got herself in trouble with another yakuza clan up north. Drugs, money, the usual things.'

'What did you do?' Caine asked.

Koichi took another sip of tea and shrugged. 'I did my best to straighten things out from afar. I applied pressure where I could. Got the sharks she owed to back off. And she got off the drugs. Cleaned up on her own, nothing to do with me. She's a tough kid.'

Caine sipped his tea but said nothing. He waited for Koichi to continue.

'When I took over for Isato, I sent a couple of men to Sapporo to keep an eye on her. Just to make sure she was okay. No direct involvement. As I said, I honored the mother's wishes. I stayed out of Kanako's life.'

The old man coughed into his fist, then drank more tea.

'A few days ago, the men I sent to Sapporo failed to report in. I sent another man to check on them. He, too, disappeared without a trace. Then, I sat down for a peace meeting with Goro Watanabe. We've clashed a few times over the years, Goro and I. Stupid pissing contests over scraps of territory and bruised egos.'

'I've seen men kill for less,' Caine replied.

Koichi nodded. 'Perhaps. Before we could finish our meeting, someone attacked us. Tetsuo blames Goro's people, but...' Koichi's voice trailed off, and he shook his head.

'You don't buy it?'

The old man shrugged. 'Goro was killed in the fight. Before he died, I looked in the man's eyes, Caine-san. I saw something in him. The same thing I see in myself when I look in the mirror. He was tired. Tired of the killing, tired of spilling blood. He wanted something more than...'

Koichi gestured with his hands, waving at nothing in particular. 'More than just this.'

'All right,' Caine said, narrowing his eyes. 'And Kanako? Where does she fit into all this?'

'After the attack, I had Tetsuo call her, pretending to be a recruiter for a local hostess club. He was unable to reach her. And I can't help thinking that the attack on me, and now this... Perhaps it's all a coincidence, but—'

Caine shook his head. 'I don't believe in coincidence. Not when blood's been spilled.'

Koichi frowned. 'Me neither. There must be a connection. Only a few people knew the location of my sit-down with Goro. And even fewer know about Kanako.'

'So you got the hospital to fake your death,' Caine said. 'Nice trick.'

'After donating millions to this place, it's the least they can do. But I can't hide here forever. Word will get out that I'm alive. And when that happens...'

'Whoever attacked you will come back to finish the job.'

Koichi shook his head. 'I don't care what happens to me. But Kanako... I failed her, Caine-san. As a man, and as a father. I made my peace with death a long time ago. But I have to make sure my daughter is safe. I can't let my mistakes drown her in all this bloodshed as well.'

Caine nodded. 'I'll look into it, make sure she's okay. You have my word.'

As if on cue, footsteps clicked down the winding path. A pair of nurses appeared behind Koichi.

'*Tottemo samui desu!*' one of them exclaimed, as she draped another blanket over his shoulders. 'It is so cold! You must come inside. Your friend can continue his visit there.'

Caine stood. 'Actually, it appears I have some work to do.'

Koichi followed him with his eyes. 'Junko will take you to the airport. I've already booked your flight to Sapporo. Please, call me if you find anything.'

Caine nodded. 'I will. But let me ask you something. How did you know I would come?'

Wrinkles rippled across the old gangster's leathery face as he grinned and winked at Caine. 'You may be a *gaijin*, a barbarian. But even barbarians have honor.'

One of the nurses gave Caine a faint smile as she cleared the table. The other wheeled Koichi around and pushed him down the path. Caine walked in the opposite direction, back toward the children's ward. As he exited the garden, the flock of crows burst from the trees, screeching as they took to the air.

Caine watched them circle for a moment, then pulled out his phone. He dialed a number from memory.

A woman's voice answered. '*Moshi moshi*... Hello?'

'Hey,' Caine answered. 'It's me.'

There was a pause, then a faint chuckle came through the phone's speaker. 'Been a long time. Where are you?'

'I'm here in Tokyo,' he replied. 'But I can't stay long.'

'Knowing you, that means trouble,' the woman replied.

Caine grinned. 'You could say that. I need a favor. And you're not going to like it.'

11

GEORGETOWN, WASHINGTON DC, USA

The whoosh of steaming milk and the mechanical clatter of coffee bean grinders drowned out the customers' chatter in Café Georgetown. The quaint little coffee shop had gained a devoted local following and was about twenty minutes from popular tourist destinations such as the Washington Monument and the Jefferson Memorial. It was significantly closer, however, to the infamous Watergate Hotel. Officially, the CIA denied involvement in the 1972 break-in, and resulting scandal, although six of the seven men who stood trial were former CIA associates.

Rebecca Freeling, director of the CIA's National Clandestine Service, always found this amusing when she stopped at the café for her morning coffee, or a quick bite on her lunch break.

Normally, she preferred to sit outside, but February in Washington DC was far too cold for that. Frost clung to the windows next to her tiny square table, and a carpet of fresh snow blanketed the sidewalk outside. But the sun streaking in from the skylights above kept the café warm, and linen sheets draped through the rafters gave the light a soft, diffused glow.

Rebecca sipped the foam from her cappuccino as she watched pedestrians in colorful winter coats walk by outside. She glanced down at her phone, reading the text on the screen one more time.

Have to stop in Tokyo. I'll explain later.

It was from Tom, of course.

There was only the one short message. No details, no information, no hint as to why he had deviated from standard procedure. Still, as frustrating as it was, she knew that even this simple text was an acknowledgment of the trust they had managed to rebuild together. At least now she knew where he was. And that he was safe.

It wasn't enough... Far from it. But it was something. And after years of betrayal, living off the grid, surviving on his own, she knew trust didn't come easy for a man like Thomas Caine.

He had his own wounds to recover from, just as she had hers.

She was debating how to respond when the café's front door jingled open. Turning her head, she saw a tall, striking woman wearing a black wool Burberry overcoat step inside. The woman stamped her boots on the mat by the door, knocking off the loose snow and ice. Then she surveyed the crowd, her eyes blinking behind slim designer glasses.

Rebecca waved.

The woman nodded, then approached the counter and placed her order. Rebecca stood as the woman approached her table, balancing her weight on her cane.

'Rebecca!' Alejandra Zavala said, her eyes twinkling behind her glasses. Her lips curled into a smile. '*Que bueno verte!* So good to see you!'

She set down her coffee and embraced Rebecca, planting a light kiss on both her cheeks.

'It's been too long,' Rebecca replied, returning the woman's hug. 'It's nice to see you too, AJ. Especially when nobody's shooting at us.'

Alejandra 'AJ' Zavala chuckled as she sat and sipped her coffee. Both women had survived a brutal gunfight in the Georgetown area. Coming through that ordeal had forged a friendship between them, despite their initial mistrust of each other.

'So, how's life at the FBI?' Rebecca asked, taking a bite of her matcha scone. 'I hear the new director is quite a character.'

AJ sighed and rolled her eyes. '*No me lo recuerdes!* Don't remind me. Have you read his book?'

Rebecca laughed and shook her head. 'No, I did not. Director Paulis gave me his review. I believe he called it "somewhat less believable than a Holly-wood action movie, and far less entertaining". Or words to that effect.'

'To be honest, I haven't dealt with him much. I—' The Argentinian FBI Special Agent paused and glanced out the window. A flurry of thick white snowflakes descended from the gray sky. 'I put in for a transfer, actually. That's why I wanted to meet.'

Rebecca blinked. 'Oh. That's big news. Where to?'

'Los Angeles,' AJ said, peering at Rebecca over the rim of her glasses. 'I'll be working cold cases with ViCAP, the Violent Criminal Apprehension Program.'

'Other side of the country. Wow.' Rebecca nodded. She broke off another piece of her scone but did not eat it. 'Well, I'm sure you won't miss the winters here. When do you leave?'

'If they approve my request... maybe two weeks?'

AJ watched the snow again, then shook her head. 'It's hard to believe. Here we are, in this warm little café, enjoying coffee and pastries. But not too long ago, we were dodging bullets in the street, just a few minutes away from here. Grissom and Blackwing turned Georgetown into a war zone. You almost died, Rebecca. We both did.'

Rebecca reached out, put her hand over AJ's. 'But we didn't. We're still here.'

The other woman nodded, her eyes pensive behind her glasses. 'The Senate Intelligence Committee was on the brink of cutting a deal with Grissom. After all the violence, all the secrets, all that death. And what happened to Clayton...'

Her voice trailed off.

'AJ, you've been through a lot. I know, believe me,' Rebecca said, gripping her hand tight. 'But are you sure this is what you want?'

AJ gave her a sad smile. 'Am I sure? No, not really. But after all that's happened... Rebecca, you know I have a ton of respect for what you do. But I didn't join the FBI to work counter-intel or fight terrorists. I wanted to help people. Maybe a change of scenery will help me focus on that.'

'Have you told Clayton?' Rebecca asked, lowering her voice.

AJ sighed. 'Things with Clayton... They're not good.'

Rebecca sighed and looked down at her coffee. 'Yeah. I heard he was having a tough time after his injuries. I mean, I've been there...'

AJ nodded. 'Rebecca, you're one of the toughest women I've ever met. What you came back from... Most people would have given up.'

Rebecca shook her head. 'Don't say that, AJ. Seriously, I almost gave up more times than I can count. I was lucky. My injury wasn't as severe as it seemed. And even then, I'm still a long way from where I want to be.'

'*Gracias a Dios*, thank God, I know. But Clayton is a *soldado*, a field guy. When he realized that wasn't in the cards for him anymore, he changed. He's not the same person, Rebecca. He's so frustrated, angry. At himself, mostly. Which I totally get.'

AJ shrugged and sipped her coffee, staring at the falling snow outside as it blanketed the curb. 'Bottom line is, he doesn't want me in his life right now. And eventually, I got tired of fighting. He needs to take care of himself. And so do I.'

'Of course you do.' Rebecca gave her hand a squeeze, then slid the plate of scones between them. 'Here... It's no Dean & DeLuca, but the scones here are literally the next best thing to sex.'

AJ laughed. 'Really,' she replied, arching a single eyebrow. 'Well, that I have to try.'

She grabbed a pastry from the plate and took a bite. Her eyes opened wide. 'Wow, that *is* good!' She paused as she ate. 'Anyway, enough about my problems. How are things with you?'

Rebecca laughed. 'You know how it is. Every time a new administration comes in, it feels like one step forward, two steps back. Still, I guess I'm lucky to have a job.'

AJ shook her head. 'You and Paulis dismantled the single largest domestic threat the country has ever faced. They'd be crazy to let you go.'

'Yeah, well, the fallout from that implicated half the senators on the intelligence committee, so the other half don't think too...'

Rebecca cocked her head, watching as a young man in his twenties approached the counter. AJ turned, following her gaze. The scruffy-looking guy wore jeans and a North Face jacket. His eyes were a bright piercing blue, and his curly brown hair peeked out from under his navy wool beanie. He saw Rebecca watching him and waved.

AJ gave Rebecca a sly grin. 'Well, he's a little young for you, but I see the appeal.'

Rebecca smacked her hand. 'Stop it!' she whispered.

She waved to the younger man. 'Sean!'

He finished giving his order, paid the cashier, then jogged over to their table. 'Hey, small world,' he said. 'Didn't think I'd run into a superspy here.'

Rebecca rolled her eyes, and Sean gave AJ a sheepish grin.

'Oh, shoot. Is that classified, or—'

'If it was, I'd already have you in a black site by now,' Rebecca said, a mischievous gleam in her eye. 'Sean Tyler, this is Special Agent Alej—'

'For God's sake, please don't call me that,' AJ said, laughing. She held out her hand as Sean's grin grew wider. 'My friends call me AJ.'

'AJ, pleased to meet you,' he said, shaking her hand eagerly. 'Wow, are your eyes two different colors?'

She nodded. 'They are, just like my mother's. It's called heterochromia.'

'Wow,' Sean repeated, gazing back and forth between her blue and brown irises. 'They're beautiful.'

'Oh, what a charmer you are,' the older woman said, with only the slightest note of sarcasm in her voice.

Rebecca gestured to a free chair. 'Sean and I have a mutual friend. Sean, care to join us?'

The young man stuck his hands in his pockets and shook his head. 'Thanks, but I can't. I'm working, have to get back to the office.'

'Sean works at Human Rights Watch,' Rebecca explained to AJ.

'Oh, over on Washington Street?' AJ asked.

Sean nodded. 'Yep. Making a coffee run. You know, new guy in the office and all.'

Suddenly, AJ's eyes opened wider, and her mouth formed a tiny O. 'Wait, Sean Tyler? You're the human rights worker we traded for that Chinese hacker, right?'

The young man gave her a sheepish grin. 'Yeah, that's me. Not exactly what I'd like to be known for, but beats the alternative.'

AJ gave Rebecca a knowing look. 'So that means your mutual friend is…'

Rebecca shifted in her seat. 'Yes, Tom worked with Sean's father, Jack.'

'Hey, speaking of, do you know if Tom's in town?' Sean said. 'I left him a couple voicemails, but…'

Rebecca frowned. 'I'm sorry, I can't discuss that. But I'll let him know you're trying to get a hold of him.'

Sean nodded. 'Right, of course. It's just that—'

'Tyler!' a voice at the counter shouted. 'Six large chai lattes, one medium flat white!'

'That's my order,' Sean said, hiking his thumb over his shoulder.

'It was good to see you, Sean,' Rebecca said. 'Call my office, and let's set up some time to grab lunch, okay?'

Sean nodded. 'Yeah, will do. And AJ, you should come too.'

AJ smiled but said nothing. Sean headed for the counter.

'Poor thing,' AJ said, watching him go. 'He looks like a little lost puppy dog.'

Rebecca sighed and rested her chin on her hands. 'Yeah. Kid barely knew his father. Tom is his only connection to Jack, and he isn't exactly—'

A loud chime sounded from her cell phone. Rebecca frowned and picked up the phone, checking the screen. 'Damn. It's Paulis.' She furrowed her brow as she read the text. 'AJ, I'm sorry, I have to go. The DNI is on the warpath.'

AJ waved her hand. 'Go, go. We'll talk more later.'

Rebecca stood and the two women hugged. 'Don't you dare leave town without calling me, okay?'

'Of course,' AJ said, kissing her cheek. 'Now *ve, ve!* The longer you make him wait, the worse Maddison's mood will get.'

As Rebecca exited the café, Sean returned to the table, carrying a pair of white paper bags. 'Oh shoot, I missed her. But, uh, hey, I was thinking maybe I could get your number, and—'

AJ stood and kissed him on the cheek. '*Muy suave.* You get an A for effort. But an F for timing. Here, try one of these.'

She slid the plate of scones closer to him, then leaned in close and whispered into his ear. 'I hear they're better than sex.'

Sean cocked his head and watched as AJ left the coffee shop. He grabbed a half-eaten scone off the plate, popped it in his mouth, and chewed.

'Naw,' he said, chuckling to himself. Then he exited the café and headed out into the cold.

12

SAPPORO, JAPAN

The snowfall in Sapporo dwarfed that of Tokyo. Considered one of the snowiest cities in the world, towering mounds of white powder flanked the sidewalks, blocking pedestrians' views of the city's busy streets. Heated pipes beneath the concrete melted some of the snowfall, keeping the walkways clear. But the frigid night temperatures caused the puddles of water to freeze, resulting in slick patches of ice in some of the less well-trodden areas of the city.

After arriving in New Chitose Airport, Caine purchased a suitcase and some winter clothes from local shops, then changed at his hotel. He was now sitting on a stool in a small ramen shop, clothed in dark denim jeans, a gray cable-knit sweater, and a black Montbel puffa jacket. Lightweight thermals beneath his clothes helped fight off the chill. Even within the warm noodle shop, the air still held a frigid bite.

The shop was in Ramen Sapporo Yokocho, better known as 'Ramen Alley'. World-class ramen shops lined either side of the narrow, lantern-lit passageway, featuring styles from all across Japan. Crowds usually filled the area, and long lines of customers often snaked out into the street. But it was late in the day, and Caine had missed the lunch rush.

Still exhausted, and now starving as well, Caine spooned the rich soup into his mouth. The restaurant served ramen in the popular Hokkaido style, a miso-based broth topped with corn and a pat of butter. It was a heavy meal, but it had been hours since he had last eaten, and he didn't know when he would get another chance.

His belly full, he paid and exited the shop. Outside, he slipped on a gray beanie, black gloves, and a pair of Masunaga tortoiseshell sunglasses. Then he trudged through the snow, heading back to the address Koichi had given him.

The apartment building was fifteen minutes from the shop. It was his second time walking past the six-story brick and concrete building. And just like before, he spotted a white Toyota Crown sedan parked across the street. A pair of men sat in the front seat of the sleek, sporty automobile. One of them sipped a cup of coffee, while the other scrolled on his cell phone. They both wore rumpled suits and dark sunglasses. They looked up as Caine walked along the sidewalk, crossing between them and the building.

As Caine continued to the edge of the building, the sedan's engine rumbled to life. A puff of steaming exhaust smoke burst from the tailpipe as it pulled away from the curb. About two blocks down, it turned right on Nishi-Dori Street and disappeared behind a snowbank.

Caine turned the corner and ducked into an alley. His breath turned to mist in the cold winter air. Peering around the corner, he watched the street for a minute. The white sedan did not return, and he saw no other cars take its place.

Taking a deep breath, Caine weighed his options. While it could have been a coincidence, all his instincts screamed that Kanako's apartment was under surveillance. By whom, he couldn't say.

Koichi claimed he had settled the girl's debt with the local yakuza drug dealers. But in Caine's experience, when drugs and money were involved, things were rarely that simple. It was possible the girl had started using again, or got herself into some other trouble.

He continued down the alley. The narrow passage snaked right, running between the rear of the apartments and a bland gray-brick building. According to the map on his phone, the other building was a youth hostel. Air-conditioning units bristled from the side, jutting out above his head.

Tiny balconies ran up the side of Kanako's building, each just large enough to hold a small table and a single chair. Behind their metal guardrails, sliding glass doors reflected the cloudy sky overhead. Caine paused next to a row of vending machines. Colorful sports drinks and flavored coffee beverages sat in rows behind the machine's neon-lit transparent panel.

He looked up at the apartment building. A call box, which allowed the residents to buzz in guests and delivery men, guarded the front doors. Even if Kanako were there, he doubted she would buzz in a random *gaijin*. There were ways to defeat the simplistic security system, but if anyone else was watching the building, he didn't want them to see him enter.

He eyed the balcony directly above him. Robberies and break-ins were rare in Japan. There was a good chance the building's residents would leave their balcony doors unlocked, especially since they were so high above the street. The lowest balcony was about twenty feet above the ice-slicked pavement. Too far to jump, even with a boost from the vending machines.

He glanced at the AC units protruding from the other building. The alley itself was only a few feet wide. He did some quick mental calculations, then climbed up onto the vending machine. The machine wobbled and shook as he stood on the top.

Facing toward the alley, he eyed the nearest AC unit. It was about four feet away, and a little higher than his perch on the machine. Taking a deep breath, Caine jumped off the vending machine. He heard a metallic crunch as his foot landed on the AC unit. Its metal support brackets buckled beneath his weight, but they held as he vaulted off again, launching himself back towards the opposite side of the alley.

His gloved fingers wrapped around the balcony railing. A thin coating of snow and ice ran along the narrow metal beam. He felt his grip slipping as he dangled above the alley floor.

His right hand slid off. He quickly grabbed one of the vertical metal rails and pulled himself up. His scrambling feet found purchase on the snow-covered balcony, and he climbed over the railing.

Taking a second to catch his breath, he glanced at the AC unit across the alley. It now hung at a precarious angle. The surrounding bricks were cracked and crumbling.

Who needs AC in this weather, anyway? he thought. He glanced through the frost-covered sliding glass doors.

The apartment beyond was dark. He listened for any sounds of movement inside, but heard nothing. Reaching out, he grabbed the door handle and gave it a gentle pull. The door slid open.

After stamping his feet to shake off any loose snow, Caine entered the apartment and closed the balcony door behind him. He walked through the sparsely furnished room, unlocked the front door, and exited into the corridor beyond. Then he took the elevator up to the fifth floor.

Exiting the dingy elevator car, he paced down the corridor, making his way to Kanako's apartment. The carpet beneath his feet was drab and worn, its crimson-red color muted to a dull maroon by years of dirt and grime. The apartment doors glistened with fresh white paint, and a chemical smell lingered in the air. A metal door marked an emergency exit at the far end of the corridor. Although he spotted no security cameras mounted to the ceiling, he kept his head down as a precaution.

Caine stopped in front of unit 508, Kanako's apartment. Kneeling, he examined the lock on the door. A series of scratches and grooves marred the brass metal surface. Caine recognized the marks instantly.

Someone picked the lock. Looks like Koichi was right to be worried.

Reaching into his coat pocket, he pulled out his own lock pick and tension bar, a set he had purchased from a locksmith before leaving Tokyo. He glanced left and right down the corridor, making sure he was alone. Then he inserted the tension bar and picked the tumblers of the lock. Within seconds, the door swung open. He entered the apartment.

Caine tensed. The air inside the apartment reeked of rotting meat and chemicals. Caine knew the scent well.

It was the stench of death.

His footsteps creaked across the floor as he crept along the unit's outer wall. The apartment consisted of a common living/dining area with a tiny, connected kitchen. A counter separated the kitchen from the main room. A small corridor led from the living room to the bedrooms.

Once he was certain the living room was clear, Caine ducked behind the tiny kitchen counter and grabbed a knife from a wood block.

The sink was half full of murky water and piled with dirty dishes. Clumps of old rice and rotting chicken floated in the mire, contributing to the apartment's foul odor. Women's magazines and empty delivery food containers lined the counter.

Caine eased the refrigerator open with his foot. Food, including cans of diet soda, a carton of milk, and a bag of lettuce, filled the plastic shelves. The lettuce leaves were brown and wilted. Caine grabbed the milk carton and checked the expiration date. It had gone bad three days earlier.

Setting the carton down, he exited the kitchen and stalked down the hall. The bathroom door was ajar, and he glanced in as he walked past. The room was empty. Bottles of cosmetics and lotions covered the sink.

The door to the first bedroom was ajar. He nudged it open and leaned into the room, holding the knife ahead of him in a hammer grip with the blade's tip up. Gauzy scraps of lingerie and a few inside-out T-shirts littered the floor. The futon bed was unmade, its sheets and blankets gathered at the foot of the mattress.

A few papers and books lay stacked on the nightstand. Flipping through them, Caine found an envelope stuffed with Japanese yen notes. He slipped through the bills inside, counting about 300,000 yen. A direct deposit stub in the back was addressed to Kanako Natsuki and listed 'Paris Nights LLC' as her employer.

Caine set down the envelope and picked up a folded matchbook cover from the nightstand. The picture on the front showed a pretty Japanese model, dressed as a French maid. The words 'Paris Nights New Club' were printed under her picture. He slipped the matchbook in his pocket as he glanced around the room.

A folding closet door hung half-open on the far side of the room. Caine pushed the door open and examined the tiny cubicle. Half the hangers on the rod were empty. A series of depressions dented the carpet on the floor... Kneeling, he inspected the markings. They resembled the impressions of a suitcase's wheels.

Caine left the room and continued on to the second bedroom. The rancid smell hovering in the air grew worse. Caine opened the door. The room was even more disheveled than the first. Someone had tipped over a cheap wooden dresser, scattering its clothes across the floor. Beams of light lanced through the slitted blinds, reflecting off the shards of a shattered mirror in the corner.

The air was thick with the scent of decay, along with an acrid, chemical smell, like mothballs. Caine spotted a scrap of black cloth peeking out from under the bed. Kneeling, he covered his nose and mouth with his sleeve. The stench grew even stronger. As he peered under the bed, he saw why. Grabbing the cloth, he dragged it out from under the bed.

It was the hem of a silk robe. A pale, slim leg emerged from the shadows. The limb was stiff and cold, more like a beam of wood than flesh and bone.

Caine pulled the corpse out from under the bed. He sucked in his breath as he saw the fiery red hair spilling down the dead body's back.

Kanako!

13

Her corpse was face down. Grimacing, Caine reached under the body and rolled it over. She wore no makeup, and her skin was pale, tinged blue around the nose and mouth. Her loose black robe was open, and only a pair of baby-blue panties covered her naked skin underneath. Bruises and cigarette burns painted a grisly mosaic across her torso.

Caine clenched his fist.

Someone tortured her, he thought. *But why?*

Her eyes were open, their brown irises nearly eclipsed by the twin black circles of her dilated pupils. She peered straight up at the ceiling. Her lips hung open, her face frozen in a blank, empty expression. A pale white visage, with no trace of emotion behind her lifeless features.

Caine pulled the robe closed and tied the belt around her waist, covering her injuries. He placed his fingers on her eyelids and pulled them down, holding them closed for a few seconds. Rigor mortis had set in, and he knew they would open up again on their own. But for at least a few brief moments, he could give her corpse the illusion of peace.

Caine was no stranger to death. He had seen it up close and personal many times in his years in the field. Sometimes, his was the hand that took a life, erasing a person from existence as casually as one might swat a fly. Other times, he had stared death in the face, certain that his own demise was all but inevitable.

But this... To tell Koichi that his estranged daughter, the man's own flesh and blood, was dead, and brutalized in such a manner... Caine stared at the body, struggling to decide how to break the news to her father, searching for something he could say to blunt the pain. But in the end, there was nothing. Kanako was dead. What else was there to say?

A strand of the girl's red hair lay across her lips. He brushed the fiery lock aside, then froze. Something about her hair didn't feel right. He ran his fingers through her crimson tresses again. The strands of hair looked real, but felt synthetic to the touch, like nylon or acrylic fibers.

He tugged at the hair, and it came loose from the girl's head.

It's not a dye job after all, Caine thought. *It's a wig!*

The natural hair underneath was short, dark, and slicked back tight to her skull. He stared at the girl's face more closely, then looked at Kanako's picture on his phone. The corpse's eyes were a few millimeters closer together, her lips a bit thinner. The resemblance was there, but this was not Kanako.

His eyes darted to a fallen picture frame, lying face down on the floor by the nightstand. He carefully picked it up. The frame contained a photo of three women laughing in a park. They wore winter clothes and stood in front of a series of snow sculptures.

Caine recognized Kanako instantly. She was wearing the red wig in the picture, and next to her stood this woman. Whoever she was, a blue knit hat covered her sleek, dark hair. In the picture, she was planting a kiss on Kanako's cheek.

They could be twins, Caine thought, looking closer at the picture. If someone had been targeting Kanako, they could have easily mistaken this woman for her, especially if she was wearing the red wig.

In the photo, a third Japanese woman stood behind them, embracing them both. She was winking at the camera, her lips tilted up in a mischievous smirk.

Caine set the broken frame on the nightstand. He erased the message on his phone. Before he could type a new one, he heard a noise from the apartment's living room.

The front door creaked open. He heard footsteps.

He slipped his phone into his pocket and pressed himself up against the wall next to the doorway. The footsteps came closer. The doorknob jiggled, then the door cracked open.

Caine heard rustling in the hallway. Mentally, he identified two sets of footfalls, two potential attackers. He caught a glimpse of a man in a gray plaid suit with a peaked lapel, entering the room. The man held a pistol in his right hand.

Caine struck. Swinging his arm, he plunged the knife blade into the man's shoulder before he cleared the doorway. A plume of blood jetted from the wound. The man gasped in pain, and the gun fired. A lamp on the opposite side of the room exploded, sending a shower of sparks into the air.

Releasing his hold on the knife, Caine grabbed the top of the man's pistol with his left hand. He slapped his right hand under the barrel and twisted the gun backwards until the muzzle faced his opponent.

As he wrenched the pistol free from the man's grasp, he spotted a second intruder moving in the hallway. The man opened fire, and three gunshots rang out. Caine felt a bullet whiz past his cheek, barely missing him. Dust and plaster flew into the air as the stray shot struck the wall behind him.

The other two shots hit the bleeding man with dull, fleshy thuds. He jerked and writhed in the corridor, blocking the shooter's line of fire. Caine planted a forward kick into the wounded man's gut, sending him careening down the hall.

As the two men stumbled back into the living room, Caine raised the pistol. He recognized the weapon by feel, a SIG Ultra Compact 1911, chambered in 9mm. He worked the trigger, and a pair of crimson holes erupted from the lead man's chest. Blood stained the front of his white dress shirt.

The injured man collapsed to the floor. Sunlight streamed through the open blinds, allowing Caine to get a better look at the intruders. Both men were Japanese, but the one bleeding out on the carpet was taller, lankier. Caine's other opponent was on the shorter side, and heavyset. Instead of a suit, he wore a leather jacket with a sherpa collar over a gray thermal. He had a shaved head, and several scars and bruises marked his scowling face.

Caine circled around the two men and fired again.

Click.

The weapon jammed.

The remaining attacker's bruised lips curled into a savage grin. He raised his pistol.

Caine hurled the useless weapon at the man's face. The shooter slipped his head to the left. The pistol flew past him and over the counter, landing on the kitchen floor with a metallic clatter.

The intruder fired, but Caine's sudden movement threw off his aim. The window behind Caine shattered. A freezing wind rustled the curtains as it whipped through the apartment.

Caine was already moving, charging towards his attacker. The gun went off again, but the man was shooting wild, and the bullet struck the ceiling. Caine grabbed his opponent's shooting arm by the wrist. Plaster dust rained down around the struggling men. As Caine forced the pistol away and down, his opponent threw a left hook.

Caine grunted as the blow rattled his skull. Pivoting, Caine drove his shoulder into his opponent's chest, forcing him back. They slammed into the kitchen counter. Caine yanked the man's sleeve up and stabbed his knuckles into the radial nerve on his forearm.

Yelping in pain, the man's arm spasmed, and the gun fell to the floor. Caine kicked it away across the carpet, then slammed the top of his skull into his opponent's face. The blow connected with a loud crack, and the man's neck snapped back. But before Caine could follow up with another attack, his barrel-chested opponent threw another hook into Caine's abdomen. The blow struck his bandaged wound, and Caine gasped in pain.

Breaking free from Caine's weakened grip, the bald thug slammed a knee into Caine's opposite side. As he doubled over in pain, his opponent grabbed Caine's jacket in his fists and hoisted him up into the air.

Caine kicked at the man with his legs, but before he could land a solid hit, the man swung him into the cabinets hanging above the kitchen counter. The drywall crumbled around him, and the entire cabinet unit dislodged from the wall and collapsed on the kitchen floor.

Shaking his head to clear his blurry vision, Caine threw up a knee, and felt the blow connect with the thug's jaw. The man roared in pain and lowered Caine back to the ground. But instead of releasing him, he spun Caine around, then heaved him over the counter.

Caine rolled over the dust-covered marble slab and crashed onto the splintered cabinets below. The wooden beams smashed beneath him, and he winced as he felt sharp splinters pierce his skin.

Heavy footsteps stomped through the apartment. He heard the man pause… Then he heard the metallic click of a pistol slide racking.

He found the gun! Caine thought.

His hands scrambled over the debris, searching for a weapon. The footsteps lumbered closer. As the man rounded the corner of the kitchen, Caine's fingers wrapped around the butt of the SIG Ultra Compact he had discarded earlier.

Caine rolled over onto his back, raised the weapon, and pulled the trigger, hoping the impact of being thrown across the room had cleared the jam.

Again, the pistol refused the fire.

The thug grinned and raised his own gun. He took a step forward.

Caine kicked the refrigerator open as hard as he could. The metal door slammed into the thug with a loud crack. The man stumbled backwards, more surprised than hurt.

The words of an old instructor from the Farm, the CIA's training center in Virginia, echoed in the back of Caine's mind...

Glock, SIG, Smith & Wesson... A gun is a gun. And guns jam. When yours does, remember these three little words. TAP, RACK, BANG.

Caine slammed the butt of the pistol on the floor, then racked the slide back, clearing the jam and loading a fresh round in the chamber. He raised the pistol and aimed.

Blam! Blam! Blam!

Caine emptied his magazine as he shot through the refrigerator door. Bubbling soda water and sour milk spattered the floor as bullets tore through the containers lining the door's shelf. The thug jerked and spasmed behind the door, then toppled over. He struck the floor with a loud thud, and his pistol fell from his hand.

Gasping for breath, Caine scrambled to his feet and examined his foe. The man coughed, sending a fine red mist into the air.

Grabbing the man's gun, Caine heaved him into a sitting position and rested his back against the kitchen wall. He winced as the exertion tugged at the stitches in his side. Glancing down, he pulled up his sweater and examined the bandages around his abdomen. Blood flecked the white gauze, but his stitches appeared to have held.

The thug coughed again, then peered at Caine through half-lidded eyes.

Caine slapped the man in the face. The thug's dull, vacant expression turned into a snarl of rage.

'Wake up, asshole,' Caine snapped. 'Who are you? What are you doing here?'

The man chuckled, then exploded into a fit of coughing. Caine examined the ragged red holes torn through the thug's jacket.

'You've got a ruptured lung. Probably a torn intestine as well.' He turned and examined the refrigerator. It was still half open, and light streamed through a series of bullet holes puncturing the thin metal door. 'Guess they don't make 'em like they used to.'

'*Jigoku ni ochiro*,' the man wheezed. *Go to hell.*

'Tell me who sent you, and I'll get you to a hospital.'

The man grinned. '*Byakko no me o miru to iu koto wa, shi o chokushi suru to iu koto. Sugu ni wakarudarou...*'

Caine translated the Japanese words in his head. *To look into Byakko's eyes is to stare death in the face. You will see. Soon...*

'Who the hell is "Byakko"?' he snarled.

The man's eyes rolled back into his head and his body slumped over. Caine felt his neck. There was no pulse. Caine examined the man's pistol. It was another SIG Ultra Compact, identical to the first. He jammed both guns into his pockets, then patted down the dead bodies. He removed the cash and IDs from their wallets and found two spare mags for each pistol.

He returned to the bedroom, grabbed the picture from the nightstand, and removed the photo from the frame. He glanced at the girl's body on the floor. Whoever she was, her eyes had once again opened. Dark and lifeless, they peered up from her pale face, like two bullet holes in the snow.

Caine stared back at her for a few moments. Then he folded the picture, slipped it into his coat, and left the apartment.

14

MCCLEAN, VIRGINIA, USA

Rebecca shifted in her seat as she watched the images playing on a large-screen TV. Her gaze flicked away from the monitor and lingered over the eclectic decor in Alex Maddison's office. A red Turkish rug lay in the center of the room, placed above the wall-to-wall industrial navy-blue carpet. Office store chairs sat around an antique cherry wood table. Outdated computer equipment and IKEA desks lined the walls, and cheap plastic blinds, some crinkled and bent, covered the windows, blocking the sunlight from outside.

This place looks more like a telemarketing company than the office of the director of National Intelligence, she thought.

Michael Paulis, the D/CIA, sat next to her. The tall, heavyset African American man grunted as the scene on the TV changed. She turned her attention back to the screen.

The aerial footage on the monitor was crisp and clear. A United States Carrier Strike Group traversed a dark, slate-blue sea. The vessels in the group ranged in size from a massive aircraft carrier to smaller destroyers and frigates, all surrounding the larger ship.

A voiceover spoke as the footage played.

'Every year, right around this time in February, the United States sends ships, troops, and supplies to South Korea, where it takes part in a series of war games and battlefield exercises,' the narrator said, speaking in a smug, nasal voice. 'Some claim this show of force is meant to deter the threat of a North

Korean attack. Others say it's all to prepare for an inevitable conflict with China. But one fact is undeniable...'

The footage dissolved to a medium shot of a man sitting behind a news desk. His curly blond hair was perfectly quaffed, and the circular glow of a ring light reflected in his baby-blue eyes.

A graphic flew in from the side of the screen that read 'The Rowan Report, featuring Carter Rowan'.

The host, Carter Rowan, wore a blue blazer over a crisp white dress shirt. A paisley silk scarf wrapped around his neck, peeking out from the unbuttoned collar of this shirt. He pointed a finger at the camera, addressing his unseen audience.

'You, my dear viewers, are paying for it. Millions of your hard-earned tax dollars are being spent to prop up one of the largest economies in the world.'

Is this moron wearing an ascot? Rebecca wondered as the video continued.

'Meanwhile, here at home, we're still reeling from the previous administration's disastrous economic policies. Open borders, crumbling infrastructure, and a failed trade war with China... Is it so wrong to ask why we put the defense of South Korea, and many other countries as well, ahead of our own citizens' needs?'

As the video continued playing, Paulis removed his glasses and polished them with a small cloth.

'Didn't President Kemper kill the joint infrastructure bill about five minutes after he was sworn in?' he asked in a deep baritone voice.

The director of National Intelligence, Alex Maddison, pointed the remote at the TV and turned the volume up a notch. 'Not the point, Michael. Keep watching.'

'The Democratic People's Republic of Korea, better known as North Korea, hasn't attacked their southern neighbor in at least five decades,' Rowan said, his voice taking on a sarcastic tone. 'And reports of any North Korean missile capable of reaching the United States are dubious at best. But there's something worse in the air than the usual deep state military industrial complex shenanigans.'

Paulis frowned and checked his watch.

A new graphic floated behind Carter Rowan's head, displayed over the image of a young woman in a hospital bed. Angry red sores covered her face and arms. A doctor examining her turned to the unseen cameraman.

'Hey!' the doctor shouted. 'This is a closed area, you're not allowed—'

The footage cut to a chart, displaying case numbers of a new virus. An animated red line climbed higher and higher as it moved toward the right-hand side of the screen.

'It's not just waste, fraud, and abuse we have to worry about,' Rowan continued. 'Multiple cases of an unknown virus have broken out in states like Virginia, New York, and California. And while the symptoms may seem mild at first, this mysterious illness has already claimed the life of at least ten American citizens. In every case, the vectors of contagion have traced back to South Korea. Tourists, visiting government officials, or immigrants, legal and otherwise, spreading this plague through ethnic enclaves in major cities. Leading some doctors and CDC officials to refer to this terrifying new outbreak as... the K-Pox.'

Maddison popped open a Styrofoam container sitting on his desk and removed a large Italian sandwich. The thick hoagie roll dripped with oil and vinegar dressing.

'You ever try Caffe Bottega, in Fort Evans?' he asked, tearing off a chunk of soggy bread and popping it in his mouth. 'Goddamn geniuses, I tell you. I send my assistant every day at lunch. Takes forty-five minutes each way, but it's worth it.'

'Talk about a waste of taxpayers' money,' Rebecca muttered.

Paulis shot her an annoyed glance. He didn't say a word, but she knew the man well enough to get the message.

Don't poke the bear...

Maddison chuckled and bit into his sandwich. The video continued playing. A dramatic closeup of Rowan filled the screen.

'As if all this wasn't bad enough,' the host continued, 'I now have, in my possession, proof that South Korea's Ministry of Health and Welfare knew about this outbreak long before it reached our shores. A laptop recovered from a high-ranking South Korean official reveals deleted government records... Case counts, contagion vectors, mortality rates. They refused to close their borders or declare a public emergency, even though they knew there was a chance of spreading this pestilence to the United States and other countries. Instead of warning us, they covered it up. Why? Money. Millions of dollars in weapons, equipment, and military aid, pouring into their country. Americans were already paying through the nose. Now, we're being asked to pay with our lives.'

'I think I've seen enough,' Paulis said, his deep voice rising above Rowan's monologue.

Maddison nodded, grabbed the remote, and paused the image. Carter Rowan's sneering face froze on the screen.

'What proof is he talking about?' Rebecca asked, watching as Maddison stuffed another bite of sandwich into his mouth. 'We've been working closely with the South Koreans. There's been no sign of any viral outbreak, let alone a cover-up.'

Maddison shrugged as he sucked down soda through a straw. 'I have no idea,' he replied, wiping his mouth. 'But whatever it is, President Kemper's taking this seriously. He's ordered me to shut down Empty Nest, and any other joint intelligence sharing operations you might have going on.'

'Are you telling me a television personality has presented the president with intelligence that neither you, the DNI, nor the CIA, has vetted?' Paulis demanded.

Maddison returned the director's steely gaze as he guzzled another sip of soda through his straw. 'Technically, Rowan's not a television personality. He hosts a streaming podcast. His network fired him a couple years ago after one of his broadcasts led to a billion-dollar defamation suit.'

'Great,' Rebecca said, brushing a strand of copper-red hair from her face. 'So the president is risking our entire Indo-Pacific strategy on the word of a goddamn YouTuber?'

Maddison set his cup down and leaned back in his chair. 'Look, we're not talking about some kid teaching the latest dance craze on TikTok. Rowan's broken big stories before, and his podcast has over fifty million followers. Most of whom support President Kemper's views on America's involvement in foreign military conflicts. And it's not just him. Other influencers are running with this. It's going to be all over the internet.'

'That doesn't make it true,' Rebecca snapped.

'It doesn't matter if it's true,' Maddison replied, glaring back at her. 'What matters is, the voters Kemper needs for reelection believe it.'

'What about the South Koreans?' Paulis asked. 'What's their response to all this?'

Maddison's eyes darted back and forth, sizing up Rebecca and Paulis. 'They denied it all, of course. But Rowan's not lying about this so-called outbreak. I've confirmed those cases with the CDC. Their current theory indicates it's a novel form of bird flu, with a few unusual symptoms, including that damn rash.'

'I read the report,' Paulis said, tapping his finger on a manila folder resting on the table. 'So far, they don't see anything in the virus's genetic sequencing that indicates it's man-made, thank God.'

Maddison nodded. 'Those findings aren't conclusive, of course. They've barely had time to study this. But if it were a bioweapon of some kind, it would be a spectacularly ineffective one. It's spreading fast, but case counts are still relatively low. And it's far less lethal than the common flu. Those ten deaths Rowan mentioned were mostly due to co-morbidity factors. Patients already suffering from pneumonia or immune disorders.'

'Is the CDC really calling it "K-Pox"?' Rebecca asked, her voice dripping with sarcasm.

Maddison shook his head. 'No, of course not. The CDC refers to it as H5N9v-CV, or some other scientific BS. Rowan made up that K-Pox stuff, but it's catching on.'

'Racist prick,' Rebecca muttered.

'Maybe,' Maddison said, speaking with his mouth full. 'But as of now, the South Korean Ministry of Health and Welfare is refusing to allow the World Health Organization to audit their records. They say they want to complete an internal investigation first.'

'Not an unreasonable position,' Paulis replied, peering at the man over the rims of his glasses.

Maddison shrugged. 'President Kemper's always leaned toward isolationist policies, and this is exactly the kind of excuse he's looking for. He hasn't given me the final word yet, but I think he's going to announce the cancellation of Operation Freedom's Spear any minute now.'

Paulis frowned. 'Isn't the Carl Vinson Strike Group already on its way? Those ships are due to arrive in Busan in—'

Maddison shook his head. 'Not anymore. Kemper's ordered them to stop in their tracks while he makes up his mind. Right now, the entire carrier group is sitting on their asses in the middle of the Pacific.'

'And what if Rowan's full of crap?' Paulis asked. 'China, North Korea, Russia... There's no shortage of countries that would love to see the US scale back its presence in the region. Any one of them could be feeding Rowan and these other influencers disinformation.'

Maddison took another sip of soda. 'Of course. But that's just speculation. Can you prove it?'

'We might have—' Rebecca began but stopped as Paulis cleared his throat.

'Not at the moment, no,' Paulis said, shooting Rebecca a sideways glance. 'But given the new intel we have on this Unit 99, we shouldn't rush to—'

Maddison rapped his knuckles on his desk. 'As far as the president is concerned, Unit 99 is South Korea's problem.'

'Alex, you know as well as I do, South Korea plays a critical role in US Indo-Pacific strategy,' Paulis said, raising his voice a notch. 'If these deep-cover operatives have penetrated their government half as much as we suspect, I can assure you, it will become our problem pretty damn quick.'

Maddison sighed. 'Look, all three of us in this room have survived multiple presidential tenures. I don't know about you two, but I plan on surviving this one as well. Intelligence is a product, Paulis, you know that. Right now, Kemper doesn't want what you're selling.'

Maddison swallowed another bite of his sandwich, then looked up at them.

'So get me a better product. Something the president can't ignore. Otherwise, Freedom's Spear is dead in the water. He's going to turn those ships around. And God help us, if Rowan's right? That will be the least of the fallout from this.'

* * *

The heels of Rebecca's Manolo Blahnik slingbacks tapped a furious beat as she stomped down the corridor outside Maddison's office.

'This is insane,' she muttered, barely able to control the volume of her voice. 'I knew Maddison was a self-serving prick, but this is beyond the pale, even for him! He's—'

'He's giving us an opportunity,' Paulis grunted.

'What?' Rebecca pivoted to face him as they reached the elevator. 'What do you mean?'

Paulis glanced around, seeing if anyone else was in earshot. A few employees shuffled past, but none paid them any mind. He pressed the button next to the elevator doors.

'You notice anything odd about that briefing?' he asked.

'You mean aside from the fact that Maddison chews with his mouth open?' she muttered.

The heavyset man chuckled. 'And his interior decorating leaves a lot to be desired. But that's not what I meant. It was just us. No FBI, no NSA, no HHS, even. Maddison is playing his cards close to the vest on this one.'

Rebecca narrowed her eyes. 'Like he said, we're the last remnants of the previous administration.'

Paulis nodded. 'Thanks in no small part to him. I always knew Maddison went to bat for us. But I was never sure why. Until now.'

'If we manage to turn this around, he looks good for keeping us on,' Rebecca whispered, tapping her foot on the floor as the elevator hummed.

'And if it blows up in our faces, well, that's on the last guy.' Paulis gave her a sideways glance. 'Don't let the door hit you on the way out.'

'So what do we do?'

The elevator doors opened with a chime. Paulis stepped in, then blocked the door with his arm. 'What we always do. Our jobs. Is Caine still in Seoul?'

Rebecca shook her head. 'No. But he's in the region.'

Paulis frowned. 'In the region? Do I even want to know?'

Rebecca bit her lip but said nothing.

Paulis sighed. 'Never mind. Just get him back here. If Maddison finds out Caine's anywhere near this, he'll file a burn notice on him in a heartbeat.'

'Understood,' Rebecca replied.

'Good,' Paulis grunted. 'In the meantime, let's work this from our end. Find out how reliable Rowan's source is. Where is he getting this stuff from?'

Rebecca frowned. 'Isn't that stepping on the FBI's toes?'

'Caine's not your only asset, Director Freeling.' Paulis gave her a knowing look. 'I seem to recall you getting friendly with a certain FBI special agent?'

The door slid shut, and the elevator began its descent.

Rebecca thought for a moment, then pulled her cell phone from her purse. The clicking of her heels resumed as she headed for the stairs.

'AJ, it's me,' she said, leaving a message. 'Call me back when you can. We need to talk.'

15

Caine sat on the edge of the king-sized bed in his suite at the Knott hotel. The lights of Sapporo spread out before him, twinkling through the open curtains. The distant streets were faint black lines, choked with blinking lights and traffic. Thick, puffy snowflakes fluttered past the windows, descending to join the vast white mounds below.

Caine worked a towel over the frame of the SIG pistol he had taken from the thugs in Kanako's apartment. After stripping the gun down, he'd found the firearm to be filthy and poorly maintained. Carbon build-up and gunpowder residue covered the barrel.

Japan had some of the strictest gun laws in the world, and gun shops were extremely rare. Caine knew finding proper gun oil and cleaning solvent would be next to impossible in the city. But after a quick stop at Don Quixote, a sprawling ten-story convenience store near the hotel, Caine returned to his room with some synthetic motor oil and a few shammy rags.

Now, as he looked out over the snow-covered city, he worked a damp, soapy rag over the disassembled gun, gently washing away the grime and residue, piece by piece. When he finished, he dried the parts thoroughly and set them down on a dry rag.

Using Q-tips from the bathroom, he applied a thin coating of motor oil to the slide and frame, paying close attention to the contact points where metal rubbed against metal.

Satisfied that he had properly lubricated the gun's components, he reassembled the weapon, racked the slide, and tested the trigger. The gun's action was smooth and precise. As far as maintenance went, it wasn't ideal, but he was confident the weapon wouldn't jam again.

As he wiped down the pistol with a fresh cloth, he stared at the lights outside and debated his next move. He glanced at the burner phone on the bed next to him. He had placed several calls to Koichi but received no answer.

He set the gun down, picked up the phone, and dialed another number. After a series of clicks, followed by an electronic tone, a woman's voice answered.

'Tom,' Rebecca said, her voice still heavy with sleep. Caine checked his watch. It was still early morning in Washington DC.

'Yeah, I'm sorry I couldn't call sooner. Things got complicated.'

'Somehow I knew you'd say that,' she replied. She sounded equal parts annoyed and amused. 'Are you still in Tokyo?'

'Negative.'

There was a pause. 'Do I want to know where you are?'

'I don't know,' Caine replied. 'Do you?'

He stood up and walked closer to the window. The snowfall outside grew more intense. A translucent curtain of white haze shrouded the city lights.

'We said no more secrets,' Rebecca said, a note of uncertainty in her voice.

'I'm not keeping secrets,' Caine said. 'But honestly, it might be better for you not to know. It's your call.'

'Just tell me when you're coming back.'

Caine was silent.

'Tom?'

'Look, I know... I know I'm putting you in a bad spot,' he finally said. 'I just need a little more time.'

'What the hell is going on over there?'

Caine sighed and paced back and forth. 'The less you know, the better. Koichi's daughter is in some kind of trouble. It's serious.'

'Koichi? Koichi Ogawa? Isato Yoshizawa's former right-hand man?'

He pictured her biting her lip as she put the pieces together.

'Yeah,' he replied. 'Old guy. Missing a finger.'

'Are you sure this is about helping him?'

'What do you mean?' he asked, glancing out the window.

'I mean, you'd travel halfway around the world to help a friend. But some-times you seem to forget there are people who need you back home, too.'

'Why? What's going on?'

'Anything and everything related to South Korea is blowing up in our faces,' she said. 'Maddison says the president is seriously reconsidering the terms of our alliance. You know there's a carrier group scheduled to dock in Busan in three days? Part of a joint military exercise with the South Korean Navy?'

'Yeah,' Caine said, narrowing his eyes. His voice took on a suspicious tone. 'Operation Freedom's Spear. New name, same drills we do every year. What's that got to do with—'

'He's ordered them to hold. They're parked in international waters, twid-dling their thumbs while President Kemper decides what he wants to do.'

'Why the hell does he want to pull back from South Korea?' Caine asked.

'While you were gone, there's been a series of... outbreaks.'

'Wait,' Caine said, freezing in place. 'You mean some kind of bioweapon, or—'

'No,' Rebecca said. Caine noted the uncertainty in her voice. 'At least, we don't think so. It seems like a naturally occurring virus. But there have been a few deaths. And so far, all transmission vectors link back to South Korea. The media's been having a field day.'

'The media would have a field day if a K-pop singer lost her dog,' Caine muttered.

'You know Carter Rowan?'

'Rowan? The podcaster?'

Rebecca sighed. 'Yes, that's the one. Rowan claims to have intel that shows the South Korean government knew about this virus and covered it up. That they've been deleting government records, hiding how severe it is, so as not to interrupt the military exercises. He's even got people calling it K-Pox.'

'Rebecca, you're the goddamn CIA! Are you telling me President Kemper is ignoring Paulis, and getting his intel from a jackass on the internet?'

'That "jackass" has an audience of fifty million people. Most of them white males over the age of forty. And guess who they favor in the next election?'

'So Kemper's afraid he'll piss off his biggest voting block?'

'Remember, no one cast a single vote in Kemper's name for president,' Rebecca said. 'He's the first VP in history to assume the office after the incumbent resigned for health reasons. He needs to build a coalition, fast. I just wish he wasn't throwing one of our most valuable alliances under the bus to do it.'

'Look, Rebecca... I'm sorry, that all sounds like a shit show. But what difference is me being there going to make?'

'I don't know,' Rebecca admitted, after a brief pause. 'Paulis thinks President Kemper's looking for any reason he can get to sideline the CIA. Or fire the both of us.'

'And a rogue agent operating in the Asian-Pacific region gives the bastard the ammo he needs,' Caine muttered, clenching his fist as he gazed out the window.

'Maybe,' Rebecca said, her tone softening. 'Or maybe I just... want you back here with me.'

'Give me forty-eight hours,' Caine said. 'Please. I'll wrap this up and catch the first flight back.'

'I'll do my best. And Tom?'

'Yes?'

'Don't keep me in the dark, just because you think it's for my own good.'

Caine nodded. 'I won't.'

'Good. And please, be careful.'

There was a click as she hung up. Caine slid the pistol into his waistband, tugged the curtains closed, and left the hotel room.

Outside, the snow continued falling, blanketing the city in a cold carpet of white.

16

TOKYO, JAPAN

St. Luke's Medical Center

The clicking of the woman's heels echoed through the darkened hospital as she pushed a laundry cart down the corridor. It was late, and the hospital was quiet. The cart's wheels squeaked and rattled. A canvas tarp covered the top, stretched tight over its load of soiled sheets and hospital gowns.

The woman's dark hair was styled in a long bob, falling just below her neck. Her eyes held a sharp, inquisitive gleam. She wore a lavender nurse's smock over white pants, and the uniform's fabric was crisp and freshly starched. She moved at a rapid pace, checking the door numbers as she passed by several rooms. Finally, she stopped outside a room near the middle of the corridor. She compared the number on the door to a sheet of paper on her clipboard.

She ran her hands over her smock, smoothing out any wrinkles, then pulled her hair back from her face. Taking a deep breath, she glanced left and right, checking the corridor.

At the end of the dark, quiet hall, two men in black suits paced back and forth near the nurses' station. They were supposed to be guarding the room she was standing by, but she knew one of the men had a crush on the head nurse. He would look for any excuse to remain close to where she worked.

The other man stuck close to his friend. Probably trying to see if he scored the pretty nurse's phone number. Or to laugh at him if she shot him down.

One of the men noticed her and gave a nod. She smiled back, then opened the door and pushed the cart inside. She closed the door behind her.

'*Baka*,' she muttered to herself. *Morons...*

It was a private room, with only one bed inside. The nurses had drawn the curtains over the windows and turned off the lights. The tiny white cubicle smelled like air freshener and alcohol. It was a sickening scent, one that lingered through most of the hospital.

She flicked on the lights and checked the EHR tablet hanging at the foot of the patient's bed. After activating the screen, she tapped in the code she had obtained from her source at the hospital.

The old man lying in the bed coughed, then sat up, squinting at her in the sudden harsh light.

'I didn't call for a nurse,' Koichi grunted. 'What are you—'

'Your chart says you're stable,' the woman snapped. 'Are you in pain? Any fever or infection?'

Koichi stared at her, then narrowed his eyes. 'Oi... Don't I know you?'

The sound of men talking came from down the hall, muted by the frosted glass door.

'*Damare!*' she whispered. 'Be quiet. I need to listen!'

Setting the tablet down, she pressed her ear against the glass.

Koichi slid his feet over the edge of the bed. 'Look, you can't just barge in here. Who sent you?'

The woman ignored him. She turned and threw the tarp off the cart. It was empty, save for a wheelchair sitting inside, along with a small black leather bag. She removed the bag and set it on the counter. Then she withdrew a needle and a small vial of liquid from the tiny satchel.

'I'm sorry, I really don't have time to explain,' the woman said, as she filled the needle with liquid from the vial. She held it up to the light, checking the dosage of fluid inside. Her dark eyes darted around the room, then settled on the old man. A cold, serious expression filled her face.

'All I can tell you is... someone wants you dead.'

* * *

The ding of the elevator doors seemed deafening in the dark, quiet hospital.

Three men exited the bright light of the elevator car, stepping into the dim corridor that ran past the nurses' station.

One of the nurses frowned as the men crossed in front of her desk. They were all tall, muscular, and dressed in suits. They wore long dark overcoats, and expensive-looking black leather gloves.

The nurse turned to another woman working behind the counter.

'More yakuza,' she whispered. 'What are they doing here?'

The other nurse silenced her with a severe look, then hurried off to file a stack of patient records.

As the three newcomers marched down the corridor, the two men guarding the corridor that led to Koichi's room stepped forward, cutting them off.

'*Sore de juubun desu*,' one of them grunted, pressing a hand into the lead man's chest. 'That's far enough.'

The man in the overcoat glanced over the guard's shoulder, then looked the man in the eye. 'You're supposed to be guarding his room. What the hell are you doing out here? Flirting with the nurses?'

'I could ask you the same question,' the guard said, his lips curling into a snarl. 'Nobody sees the *oyabun*. Tetsuo's orders.'

'Tetsuo sent us,' the man in the overcoat replied. 'We have a problem.'

The man in the black suit frowned, then exchanged a look with his partner. 'What problem? Tetsuo said nothing about—'

The man in the overcoat glanced at the nurse, typing on her computer behind the desk.

'Not here,' he grunted. 'Come...'

He put a hand on the guard's shoulder. Two of the men in overcoats escorted the guards around the corner, out of sight of the nurses' station. The third newcomer stayed put, keeping an eye on the nurse. She gave him an uncomfortable glance, then continued with her work.

'Tetsuo is worried,' the man in the overcoat grunted, as they paced down the corridor. 'He has heard rumors. The Kodo-kai organization, from Hokkaido, is moving against the Yoshizawa clan. Tetsuo believes they are sending men here to kill Ogawa-san.'

The man in the black suit shook his head.

'That's impossible,' he grunted. 'This is Yoshizawa territory. The Kodo-kai wouldn't dare attack us here.'

The taller man shook his head. 'I would not be so sure.'

Before the man in the black suit could react, the man in the overcoat pulled him close. With a quick thrust of his arm, he jabbed a stiletto between the man's ribs. His gloved hand covered the guard's mouth, muffling his scream.

As he collapsed to the ground, the second guard uttered a similar grunt of pain. The man in the overcoat glanced over his shoulder and saw that his partner had dispatched the second guard in a similar fashion.

He nodded to a door down the hall.

He dragged the guard's corpse across the floor, taking care to spill as little blood as possible. Then he opened the door and hauled the dead body inside.

As his partner followed him with the second corpse, he wiped the blade of his knife clean on the bed's sheets.

'Hide the bodies as best you can,' he said. 'I'll be back shortly.'

The other man nodded and opened a closet opposite the bed.

The man in the overcoat exited the room, quietly shutting the door behind him. He checked the corridor, making sure he was alone.

His footsteps clicked across the tile as he made his way to another room. He examined the clipboard hanging next to the door.

Although the paperwork was under a different name, he knew this was the room of Koichi Ogawa.

He listened at the door for a moment but heard nothing. Gripping the slim, sharp knife in one hand, he reached down and opened the door.

* * *

Koichi watched as the frosted glass door swung open. A shadowy figure entered the darkened room. The sliver of distant city lights beaming through the curtains revealed only glimpses of the intruder's features. Slicked-back hair, a broad, flat face. Hard eyes, and a cruel slash of a mouth.

'Who the hell are you?' Koichi grunted.

'The Kodo-kai has a new *oyabun*,' the man said, his voice barely a whisper. 'Byakko-san sends his regards.'

Koichi furrowed his brow. 'Byakko-san? Never heard of him.'

The man held the stiletto knife before him. The long, narrow blade glinted in the shadows.

'Figures,' Koichi muttered. 'I've been shot more times than I can count. So they send an asshole with a knife to kill me.'

'I give you my word, I'll make it quick,' the man said, stepping closer.

'*Un*, I bet you will,' Koichi replied.

Before the man could take another step, the nurse emerged from the shadows behind the assassin. She plunged the needle into the intruder's neck. The man yelped in pain as he spun around and stabbed at the woman with his knife.

The nurse sidestepped his attack. The man slashed with the blade again, but his attacks were slow, clumsy. 'Wh... What...' he stammered. 'What did you—'

His eyes rolled back in his head and the knife fell from his fingers. It hit the floor with a metallic clatter and the intruder collapsed. His head struck the cabinets with a loud crack, then he slumped to the floor. A pool of blood grew beneath his head.

The woman in the nurse's uniform kneeled and checked the man's neck for a pulse.

'*Kuso*,' she whispered. 'He's dead.'

'Son of a bitch,' Koichi grunted, standing from the bed. 'I was hoping I could get this idiot to tell me who sent him. And why they're after my daughter.'

The woman stood and lifted the wheelchair from the laundry hamper. 'No time for that now,' she said. 'Caine-san sent me. Obviously, your enemies know where to find you. Which means we have to move. Get in the chair.'

Koichi squinted at the woman in the dim light. 'Now I remember you! You're that lady cop! The one Caine—'

The woman rolled her eyes, then helped the old man off the bed. '*Damare!* We have to move! My name is Mariko Murase, and I'm not with the *keisatsu-chou* anymore.'

'Oh?' Koichi asked, as he settled into the chair. 'You quit, huh? Can't say I blame you. Too much political BS for my taste.'

'Let's just say my superiors encouraged me to resign,' Mariko replied, grabbing the handles of the chair and pushing him toward the door. 'It was less embarrassing for them that way. I'm a *yonigeya* now.'

'A fly-by-night arranger. You're freelance?'

'That's right,' she replied. 'I help people escape from loan sharks and criminals. You know the type.'

'*Hai*. People like me,' Koichi chuckled.

Mariko shrugged. 'Your words, old man. Now be quiet. The goal is to get you out of here without attracting attention.'

Koichi grumbled under his breath as she cracked the door open. The corridor was empty.

She wheeled him out of the room and away from the nurses' station. Koichi glanced up as they passed under the smoked plastic dome of a security camera.

'You got a plan for those?' he whispered, pointing up.

'Already taken care of,' Mariko replied. 'A hacker friend of mine looped the video. By the time anyone realizes what happened, we'll be long gone.'

A door swung open behind her. A man wearing an expensive-looking overcoat stepped out into the hall.

'*Oi*,' he shouted. 'Where do you think you're going?'

'You were saying?' Koichi grunted, glancing up at her.

Mariko broke into a run, sprinting for the end of the corridor.

'Hey, slow down!' the old man in the wheelchair shouted.

'*Tomare!*' the man in the overcoat bellowed. He drew a pistol from inside his coat and fired. Mariko ducked as a glass door shattered beside her.

'You were saying?' she shouted. The chair's wheels squealed as she raced around the corner. Footsteps pounded down the corridor after her. She heard another man shouting... The thug's partner had joined in the pursuit.

'Where are we going?' Koichi demanded, gripping the chair's handles. 'And why don't you shoot back?'

'I told you, I'm not a cop anymore,' Mariko panted. 'I don't carry a gun!'

Koichi shook his head. 'This is embarrassing. Turning tail and running from these *makeinu*.'

Another gunshot roared behind them. White mist exploded from a nearby fire extinguisher.

Mariko spun the chair around another corner. As they raced past a cart filled with medical supplies, she reached out and grabbed a clear canister of liquid. Then she came to a stop at a pair of metal elevator doors.

A sign above the doors read 'Emergency Elevator: Hospital personnel only'.

She swiped her nurse's ID over the security terminal. The doors slid open. She wheeled Koichi in, then slammed the button for the parking garage.

The doors began to close.

Suddenly, a man's hands thrust between the sliding metal panels. The man in the overcoat tugged at the doors with all his strength, forcing them to slide back open. He reached in with one hand and aimed his pistol at Koichi.

Before he could fire, Mariko lashed out with a kick, knocking the weapon from his fingers. She popped the top off the plastic container and threw the liquid in the man's face.

Shrieking in pain, the man clawed at his eyes and backed away. The doors slid shut, and the elevator began its descent.

Koichi raised his bushy white eyebrows. 'What was in that thing?'

Mariko panted for breath. 'No idea.' She turned the cylinder over and read the label on the side aloud. 'Divalproex Sodium. Warning: May cause severe chemical burns to exposed skin.'

The old man grinned. 'Not bad, Murase-san.'

Mariko tapped her foot and looked up, watching the numbers on the control panel as the elevator descended. 'We're not out of this yet.'

Koichi groaned as he bent over in his chair. '*Hai*, sure. But look at the bright side.'

He grabbed the thug's discarded pistol and sat up straight. 'Next time those assholes shoot at us, we can shoot back.'

17

SAPPORO, JAPAN

Caine jammed his hands into his coat as he traversed the snow-covered streets. His gloved fingers wrapped around the grip of the HK Pistol. After his encounter at Kanako's apartment, he found the weight of the gun in his pocket to be comforting.

Banners flapped in the wind overhead, announcing the beginning of the annual Sapporo Snow Festival, a weeklong celebration of the winter season. Despite the cold weather, the city felt vibrant and alive. The Snow Festival was a major tourist attraction, drawing millions of travelers to the area. Crowds of pedestrians meandered through Odori Park, marveling at the beautiful and intricate snow sculptures arranged along either side of the rectangular strip of land.

The sculptures varied in size. Some were about the size of a person, while others formed towering murals of ice and snow, stretching across the park grounds. Prizes were awarded to the winning designers at the close of the festival. Artists from all over the country had worked for days, chipping away at mounds of snow to carve the elaborate shapes and designs.

Earlier, he had stashed his spare pistol and some clothes in a locker at Odori station. Then he used the Snow Festival crowd and the park's congested walking paths to perform an SDR, a surveillance detection routine.

Confident that he wasn't followed, Caine continued along the park's perimeter. Ahead of him, a pair of massive ice sculptures depicted a female anime character with long, flowing hair and an eye patch. Colorful spotlights reflected off the ice, causing the statues to shimmer like diamonds. The twin figures flanked either side of a stage, blocking off the end of the park.

As he drew closer to the stage, Caine heard Japanese pop music blasting from the towering speaker racks. A crowd swayed in front of the platform, waving neon-green light sticks above their heads. Shadowy musicians played their instruments, hidden just behind the sweeping spotlights.

A glowing anime character danced on the stage, belting out vocals with a high-pitched, electronic chirp. Her long neon-green hair trailed behind her, flicking and dancing like jade flame. An eye patch covered one of her big green eyes. She wore an elaborate costume, a combination of futuristic club-wear mixed with Victorian-era white furs. White thigh-high boots sheathed her long, slim legs.

The animated character appeared to be performing in real life, interacting with the flesh-and-blood musicians on stage. But Caine knew this was an illusion. The singer was a holographic projection, reflecting off a nearly invisible transparent screen. Illustrated banners hanging over the stage read 'Snow Ongaku, Festival Icon!'

Masuka Ongaku, Caine thought. *A virtual pop idol.*

The last time Caine had operated in Japan, Hitomi Kusaka, the abused, wayward daughter of a Japanese industrialist, used the software to communicate with Caine, and to hide her identity from her pursuers. Seeing the character again gave Caine an uneasy sense of déjà vu.

As he walked past the stage, the Masuka hologram performed a pirouette and leaped into the air, floating above the stage as the spotlights beamed over the crowd. The audience cheered and raised their glow sticks as the song reached a crescendo. The twirling anime girl glanced over her shoulder, her crackling green hair flowing around her like an electric tornado. She broke into a wide grin, and Caine could have sworn he saw the character wink at him.

He left the stage behind, turning onto Sapporokimae-Dori street and heading south. Dark thoughts clouded his mind, brooding ruminations on his past.

Hitomi was somewhere out there in the world, and Kenji Yoshizawa was, as well. Both people he had risked his life to save. But Rebecca's words still rang in his ear. What was he really doing here? Was it just about paying a debt to Koichi? Or was he avoiding facing something else?

Someone else...

Sean Tyler, Jack's son. Another person whose life he had saved. Sean had reached out to him several times, and it was clear the young man was trying to form some kind of connection with him. But as Rebecca had observed, Caine kept him at arm's length.

That's because you've seen what happens to people who get close to you, a cold-blooded voice whispered in the back of his mind. *After all, look at what happened to Rebecca.*

Up ahead, colorful neon lights pierced the snowy haze. The famous Nikka Whisky sign loomed over the street, an unofficial mascot of Susukino, Sapporo's red-light district. The illuminated billboard depicted a blue-eyed Elizabethan monarch, smiling down on the city. Known as 'The King of Blenders', the character was a nod to the distillery's heritage of crafting fine-blended and single-malt whisky.

Caine realized he had traveled several blocks through the snow without noticing his surroundings, lost in thought.

Get your head in the game, the killer's voice snapped in the back of his mind, cold as the frost-filled air. You just left an apartment with three corpses inside. You're operational now. Everything else can wait.

Through the windows on either side of the busy intersection, Caine saw dark figures lounging in the clubs above street level. Scantily clad cocktail waitresses wove through the dimly lit bars, balancing trays of drinks. Above the street to his left, the women were dressed as Playboy Bunnies. In the next building, cowgirls danced on the bar counter, gyrating their hips as the crowd cheered. Every window, every sliver of glass, offered an additional glimpse into another shadowy den of fantasy and desire.

Caine crossed the street and approached a bland, nondescript office building. A narrow alcove stood to the right of the entrance. A glowing sign hung above the dark passage. The rectangle of light displayed the faces of attractive Japanese women, all airbrushed and photoshopped to inhuman perfection. Each doe-eyed woman wore the frilly white lace bonnet of a French maid.

Beneath the beautiful smiling faces, the words 'Paris Nights' glowed in English. In the sign's right-hand corner, Japanese characters identified the bar as a '*Seku Kyabukura*'. The Japanese term roughly translated to 'Sexy Cabaret'.

Caine checked the address on the matchbook from Kanako's apartment, then ducked into the alcove. A small elevator stood at the end, bathed in neon pink light. Caine pressed the button, and the doors slid open with a quiet chime.

Stepping inside, he noticed there was only one button on the control panel. He pressed it, and the doors rattled closed. With a quiet hum, the elevator rose up into the building, lurching to a stop on the fourth floor.

The doors slid open. Caine glanced out and found himself in a quiet, empty corridor. The floor was clean white marble, and his footsteps echoed through the building as he stepped out of the elevator. The walls were decorated with posters of beautiful women, all dressed in French maid costumes. Antique bulbs surrounding each poster were the only source of illumination on the floor, casting pools of soft light through the shadowy passageway.

Caine walked down the hall, examining the pictures on either side of him. None of the women resembled Kanako, although they were so heavily edited, it was difficult to be sure. The corridor turned right and led to a large black door. A metal plaque on the wall read 'Parisian Nights'.

Caine opened the door. The thumping bass of electronic music pounded in his eardrums. His eyes squinted in the dim light. A willowy hostess in a shimmering white dress emerged from the inky blackness.

'Irasshaimase,' she said in a soft, lilting voice. *Welcome...*

She bowed, then offered him a heated towel on a metal tray. Caine took the towel and rubbed it over his face and hands, then deposited it back on the platter.

The woman's forced smile flickered a bit as she examined his Caucasian features. She bowed again, then took him by the arm and led him to a marble reception counter. A man in a black suit stood behind the desk, giving him a wary look. He pointed to a sign on the wall, beneath pictures of more girls.

'Nihongo nomi desu. Wakarimasu ka?' he said. *Japanese only, understand?*

Caine slid a wad of cash from his jacket pocket. He peeled off 30,000 yen and slid the notes across the desk to the attendant.

'I think we speak the same language,' Caine replied in Japanese.

The man's eyes opened wide with surprise. He swiped the money off the counter and stuffed it in his pocket, then gave Caine a deep bow.

'Arigatou. Please, choose your companion,' the attendant replied, gesturing to the pictures on the wall.

Caine squinted in the dim light. Again, it was hard to be sure given the girl's makeup and costumes, but he spotted a face that resembled Kanako in the collage of beautiful women. On the wall, her picture was labeled 'Hanna', but Caine recognized her wide-set eyes and full lips.

'*Sore desu,*' he said, pointing at the picture. *That one...*

The attendant's face blanched, and he shuffled his feet behind the desk. '*Sumimasen,* excuse me, sir. Hanna is not available this evening. If you like, I could recommend—'

'Okay,' Caine said, scanning the pictures again. He spotted another familiar face. The third girl in the photograph from Kanako's apartment, the one with the enigmatic smile. 'I'll take her, then.'

The attendant gave him a relieved bow. 'Of course, sir.'

The hostess took his arm once more, leading him deeper into the dark, shadowy interior.

18

The hostess sat him in a small, dark booth near the far corner of the room.

She took his drink order, then left with another bow. Caine glanced around the club. A pool of red light beamed down above his seat. Now that his eyes had adjusted to the dim interior, he could see more crimson beams spread throughout the club. Beneath the faint circles of light, shadowy figures reclined on cushioned seats, chatting with women in colorful, sparkling cocktail dresses.

Unlike the girl bars in Susukino, there were no windows in the room. Between the dark interior and the thumping music, he felt claustrophobic in the cave-like chamber, despite the comfortable seating and high-end decor.

'*Konbanwa*,' a voice called out. *Good evening.*

A woman in a short red dress approached Caine's table.

She kneeled and set down a tray. On the tray were a bottle of Nikka coffee malt whisky, a bucket of ice, and two crystal glasses.

'My name is Gaya. Do you mind if I drink with you?'

Her voice was deeper than most Japanese women, with a hint of a throaty rasp, as if she had just smoked a cigarette. Caine knew her offer to drink with him was more than just a social nicety. Hostesses earned commission based on the number of drinks they sold. And of course, as the customer, Caine would be expected to pay for Gaya's drinks as well as his own.

'Of course,' he said, replying in Japanese. 'But I have to admit, I'm a little surprised. I was expecting a French maid.'

The girl's eyes opened wide, and she covered her lips with her hand in an exaggerated gesture of embarrassment.

'*Nihongo jouzu desu ne!* Your Japanese is so good!'

'I get by. I worked in Tokyo for a while.'

She opened the bottle and filled two glasses. 'We stopped wearing those silly costumes,' she said as she slid next to him and handed him a glass. 'The club has a new owner. He didn't like them. I hope you're not disappointed?'

Caine smiled and clinked his glass against hers. 'Not at all. *Kanpai*.'

They each took a sip of their drink. Gaya peered at him over the rim of her glass. She wore her hair in an elaborate updo, decorated with pearls. A matching pearl choker ran around her neck. She was young, in her early twenties, and her makeup had a fresh, natural look.

'May I ask your name?' she asked in an innocent voice, blinking her long lashes.

'I'm Tom,' Caine replied. '*Hajimemashite*... Pleased to meet you.'

She ran her fingers through Caine's hair as she pressed closer to him on the seat. 'You have such beautiful eyes, Tom. *Midori*, like jade. I wish I could wear contacts, like the other girls here, but they hurt my eyes. When I try them, I look like I'm crying!'

Caine had never understood the allure of hostess clubs. There were few things he'd rather do less than pay a woman to shower him with insincere compliments. But this girl was his only lead to Kanako. If he didn't behave like a normal customer, he might scare her off.

'Your eyes are lovely as they are,' he replied, after taking another sip of his drink. '*Me wa kuchi hodo ni mono o iu*... The eyes speak as eloquently as the mouth.'

Gaya blushed and looked away. 'Your mouth speaks eloquently, indeed, Tom. I wonder how it might feel to kiss you?'

'Tell me, Gaya,' Caine said, resting a hand on her thigh. 'How long have you been working here?'

She pursed her lips and looked up, thinking. '*Etto*... Maybe six months? Less than a year, for sure. I used to work at a different club. But I like it better here.'

Caine finished his drink and set the glass down. 'Oh? Why is that?'

She leaned forward and refilled his glass. 'The men here are more handsome. Like you, Tom.'

Caine forced himself to smile. 'Well, I think you're exquisite, Gaya. I usually ask for Hanna. I was hoping to spend some time with her soon. Do you know when she'll return to work?'

Gaya blinked again, and Caine saw a minute crack in her seductive facade... a trembling lip, a twitch in her cheek. Her eyes betrayed the fear hidden behind her carefully crafted appearance. Then, like ripples fading in a dark pond, her face calmed. The beautiful facade emerged once again. She took another sip of her drink.

'Hanna-chan is away, I'm afraid. I'm not sure if she'll come back. You know how it is. Girls come and go here, as they please.' She rested her head on his shoulder. 'Hanna-chan is very beautiful. I can understand why you would prefer her to me. Did you two meet here, at this club?'

Gaya looked up at him. He peered into her eyes, deep, dark pools of mystery. Was she testing him? Trying to catch him in a lie? If he claimed to be a regular at the club, she might wonder why she had never seen him before.

'No, it's not like that. To be honest, I'm kind of worried about her.'

The girl stared at him, her expression blank and inscrutable. 'Worried? Why? Are you her friend? How do you know her?'

Caine sipped his drink and thought for a moment. He removed his hand from her thigh. 'Look, all I can say is, I'm friends with someone who cares about her. Please, do you know where she is?'

Before the girl could answer, the crimson light above them focused into a narrow beam. It spun around them, blinking to the beat of the music. The club's speakers blasted the electronic tune even louder.

Caine tensed, but Gaya grabbed his arm and gave him a reassuring smile.

'Shhh, it's all right,' she said, her lips brushing against his ear. 'This is *dauntaimu*, downtime. You've never been here before, have you?'

'What gave it away?' Caine grunted as Gaya straddled him and leaned back. She reached behind her dress and slid the zipper down. Crossing her arms in front of her, she let the shimmering fabric fall away from her body as she swayed above him.

Caine gritted his teeth. Seku Kyabukura, he recalled, was more or less the equivalent of a lap dance at a Vegas strip club. Only with kissing and touching allowed.

Maybe this is one secret Rebecca doesn't need to know, he thought.

He felt the warmth of Gaya's body as she leaned against him. She pulled the dress down farther, revealing the soft ivory mounds of her breasts, peeking out from black lace lingerie. Her hands caressed his arms and shoulders. She nuzzled his neck. Her warm lips traveled across his skin, her tongue darted at his ear.

He tried to pull away, but she wrapped her arms around his neck and held him tighter, kissing him on the mouth. Then her lips shifted to his ear.

'We can't talk here,' she said, her words barely audible beneath the music. 'I think Hanna… Kanako… is in some kind of trouble.'

Caine tilted his head and grabbed her hips, pulling her close. 'I think you're right. Where can we meet?'

'I have a break in twenty minutes. Can you meet me in the alley behind the club?'

Caine grabbed her hair and pulled her head close. 'I'll be there.'

She kissed him again, exploring his mouth with her tongue. When she came up for air, she smiled and looked down at him with half-lidded eyes.

'I was right,' she breathed into his ear. 'You are a good kisser. But you are holding back. Are you married?'

'It's complicated,' he replied.

She giggled. 'That's what all the men here say.'

She caressed his chest through his clothes, then writhed above him for another few minutes. She kept her eyes closed and said nothing else.

When the song ended, the lights grew brighter, and the volume of the music lowered.

Gaya pulled her dress back on and tugged on the zipper. She slid off Caine and stood before him, then gave a deep bow. 'My turn is over. We must rotate, unless you'd like to request me for—'

'Gaya, don't keep the other customers waiting,' a woman said, her voice cutting through the electronic music like an icy blade.

The hostess from out front approached Caine, flanked by a pair of tall, muscular men in ill-fitting suits. Their dress shirts were open at the collars, and Caine spotted traces of colorful tattoos peeking out from beneath the crisp white fabric.

'Just a moment,' Caine said, giving the hostess a roguish grin. 'I like this girl. I want to pay for more time with her.'

'I apologize for the inconvenience, sir,' the woman said, giving him a slight bow. Her lips curled into a smile, but her eyes were cold and dark. 'But the club's owner wishes to have a word with you.'

There was no hiding the terror on Gaya's face as the woman turned her icy gaze on her. Her skin turned a shade paler, and a shiver ran down her spine. She bowed deeply, then gave Caine a worried look.

'*Sumimasen*,' she muttered. 'Excuse me, I must go.'

As Gaya hurried off, Caine eyed the two thugs standing at the other woman's side. Even in the dim light, he could spot the telltale bulges of weapons beneath their jackets. 'Who is the owner of this place, anyway? Do I know him?'

'His name is Hideo Torazama,' the woman said, bowing deeper. 'But some call him Byakko-san.'

Caine stood up and looked the nearest thug in the eye. 'Byakko-san? That's an interesting name. Mine is Thomas Caine, and I'd like to meet your boss, as well.'

19

The men led Caine through a door next to the club's bar. As the door closed behind him, the pulsing electronic music faded. Only the dull, distant thumping of the bass reverberated through the air.

He found himself in a long corridor. Muted light fell from the ceiling, and the carpeted floor was a deep navy-blue color. One of the men grabbed his shoulder and spun him around. Caine did not resist as the thug patted him down, removing his pistol and wallet.

The man looked at the gun and grunted, then shoved Caine forward. He glared back at the man, then continued walking down the corridor between the two yakuza men. They approached a pair of black lacquered doors at the end of the hall. The thug behind Caine grabbed his shoulder again. They stopped walking.

An intercom panel was installed on the wall next to the doors. One of the men pressed the talk button and spoke rapid-fire Japanese.

Static crackled through the silver mesh speaker. A deep, gravelly voice answered back.

'*Kare o tsurete ki nasai.*' *Bring him in...*

The man in front opened the two doors wide, then stepped aside. The other thug shoved Caine forward again.

'Move,' he grunted.

Caine stumbled into a large square room. The chamber seemed to be an office of some kind, although it was massive enough to be a ballroom or banquet hall. The entire room, from the wall to the floor, was the same blue color as the hall. Like the club outside, there were no windows. The only light came from glowing recessed panels in the ceiling, mounted behind traditional Japanese wood carvings.

A cherry wood desk sat at the far end of the room. Behind the desk, a tall, handsome man paced back and forth, talking on a cell phone. He glanced up as Caine entered the room. Unlike the two thugs, this man's suit was perfectly tailored. The gray pinstriped wool had a satiny luster and looked expensive. His thick black hair was flecked with gray at the temples and slicked back with gel. A neatly trimmed mustache and goatee framed his handsome, angular features.

Caine narrowed his eyes as he noticed two odd details about the man. Several scars and bruises marked his face, as if he had recently been in a fight. And despite the room's dim lighting, a pair of dark designer sunglasses covered his eyes.

'I'll call you back,' the man snapped in English, ending the call. He put his cell phone on the desk and sat in a large padded leather chair. As he steepled his fingers beneath his chin, Caine glanced at a gold-framed relief hanging behind the desk.

In the center of the frame, a tiger, carved from wood and painted white with black stripes, pounced above a pale blue cloud. Gold lightning bolts streaked through the sky, and pink cherry blossoms rose beneath the fearsome animal.

On a small table next to the desk, a game board carved from solid jade glinted in the overhead light. Rows of alternating light and dark squares divided its playing surface, like a chessboard. A series of wooden pieces, each one shaped like a shield, faced each other across the jade board.

A pair of wooden chairs sat in front of the desk. One of the thugs shoved Caine down into a chair, then handed his pistol and wallet to the man in the expensive suit.

Caine watched the man but said nothing. A heavy silence fell over the room.

The man examined the pistol, hefting it in his hands. He ejected the magazine, tested the slide, then slammed the mag back in. He triggered the slide release.

'Perhaps you were unaware, Mr. Caine,' the man said, as he opened a desk drawer and deposited the weapon inside. 'It is illegal to carry a firearm such as this in Japan.'

Caine glanced up at the two thugs flanking his chair. 'Maybe you should tell your men that.'

The man in the sunglasses nodded, then flipped through Caine's wallet. 'It says here your name is Mark Waters. Names are no small matter, of course. A name gives a thing its essence. Its power. You know, many years ago, before my time, the police and the yakuza used to work together.'

The man opened another drawer and removed a bottle of sake and two small glass tumblers. Condensation dripped down the bottle's crystal neck. The man continued speaking as he poured the clear rice wine into the two glasses.

'Back then, the yakuza protected their territory from muggers, con men, rapists and the like. But in 1972, the police decided their presence could no longer be tolerated. And do you know the first thing they did? They gave them a new name. Instead of yakuza, they called us "*boryokudan*".'

'Violent syndicate,' Caine said.

The man nodded as he slid a glass across the desk toward Caine.

'*Hai*. Just so. Two names for the same thing.'

'You have two names as well, Mr. Torazama,' Caine said, staring at the man behind the desk. 'Or should I call you Byakko-san?'

The man's expression was unreadable behind the dark glasses. He raised his glass of sake in both hands, and drank it down, then sipped what liquid remained in the tiny wooden box.

'My name is Hideo Torazama,' the man said, setting the glass down on the desk. 'My men refer to me as Byakko. It is the name Japan gave to the white tiger, a god-like spirit found in Chinese and Korean myths. Do you know the legend, Mr. Caine?'

'I'm not too big on fairy tales,' Caine replied. He drank his own sake. The wine was dry and crisp. It tasted of apples, with a hint of cherry blossom.

'Hundreds of years ago, a brave samurai, Kashiwade no Omihasui, was sent to Korea as an ambassador. As was the custom, he brought his family with him. His wife and young daughter were said to be the most beautiful women in Japan, and together, they brought great honor to Emperor Kinmei.'

Byakko stood and turned around, gazing at the tiger mural hanging behind his desk.

'But then, on a cold, winter night, much like this one, Kashiwade suddenly awoke from a deep slumber. Or rather, something woke him. A noise, a scream. His young daughter, the light of his life, was missing. And worse, he found strange tracks in the snow outside. Blood splattered across a nearby tree.'

The man turned and peered at Caine over the rim of his glasses, his face hidden in shadow.

'Have you ever lost a family member, Mr. Caine?'

Caine stared back at him, his emerald eyes glinting in the dim light. He said nothing.

The man shook his head. 'Your own flesh and blood, torn away from you. Such failure, such shame. It is worse than any pain a man could inflict upon himself, I assure you. And so, enraged at the loss of his beautiful, beloved child, Kashiwade tracked the beast to its lair, determined to avenge his daughter. But tigers are not native to Japan, Mr. Caine. He had never faced such a creature before. It took all his power, all his strength, to slay the mighty beast. And when he returned to his village, he brought with him the animal's skin, as white as the snow on the ground. The Japanese people, inspired by the warrior's tale, adopted the tiger as a symbol of strength and ferocity. They emblazoned the white tiger on shields and banners when they sent men to die in battle.'

'That's a nice story, but it didn't work out so well for the daughter,' Caine said, dryly. 'So is that why they call you Byakko? Are you a symbol to your men? Or do you think you're some kind of mythical beast?'

The older man chuckled. 'Perhaps, Mr. Caine. But there are other, more obvious reasons as well.'

Byakko stepped into the light and lowered his glasses.

Caine narrowed his eyes and leaned forward in his chair, looking closer at the gangster's features. The man's gaze was hypnotic. His eyes were almost as green as Caine's, a bright hazel color flecked with jade. The color was unusual for the Japanese, but more extraordinary than that were his pupils. They were not round, but rather slit-like, stretching vertically through the iris, like a cat's eye.

'I assure you, they are not contact lenses, or some other trick,' the man said, grinning at the look of surprise on Caine's face. 'In medical terms, I have a chromosome 22 partial tetrasomy. Better known as Cat eye syndrome.'

'I'm sure your men find it very impressive,' Caine replied, leaning back in his chair. 'But you didn't bring me here just to tell me an old folktale. What do you want?'

Byakko stood and leaned over the desk. 'You were asking your hostess about a girl that works here. Hanna-chan?'

Bastard must have the booths bugged, Caine thought.

He shrugged. 'So what if I was?'

'Since you claim to be her friend, you probably know this girl's real name is Kanako Natsuki. She has gone missing. She didn't show up for work.' Byakko spread his hands and gave Caine a disarming smile. 'I'm worried about her as well. What exactly is your interest in this girl?'

'That's between me and Kanako,' Caine replied.

The men on either side of him shifted uneasily. Byakko glared at Caine for a moment, then tapped the side of his head. 'Some of my men believe that eyes such as mine can peer into a man's soul. They can see his fears, know his fate. And they can see when he is lying.'

'I already told you, Byakko-san – I'm not big on fairy tales.'

'I don't need mystic powers to know you are lying. My men saw you enter Kanako's apartment. Now, they are missing as well.'

'Sounds like you've got a real employee retention problem here,' Caine said. He glanced at the thug to his right. 'Or maybe you're just hiring the wrong people.'

Byakko gave the beefy yakuza man a look. The man nodded, then threw a right cross into Caine's face. The blow connected with a loud crack, sending Caine flying out of the chair. He sprawled across the blue carpet, then picked himself up, rubbing his jaw.

Byakko paced over to the jade shogi board. He stuck his hands in his pockets as he examined the pieces on the board's green crystal surface. 'Are you familiar with the game of shogi, Mr. Caine?'

Caine stood and rubbed his jaw. He did not answer.

'Japanese chess,' the man said, his strange, cat-like eyes focused on the board. 'It simulates a battle between two great armies. It is said a true master must think three to five moves ahead of his opponent.' He looked Caine in the eye. 'This particular match has been on my mind, as of late. My opponent is gifted, but inexperienced. Checkmate is near, and he has only a few possible moves that will not result in me capturing a piece.'

'I'm not interested in playing games,' Caine replied.

Byakko grinned. 'We shall see.' He sat back in his chair and poured himself another glass of sake. Then he opened another drawer and removed a silver-plated Colt Python revolver. He inserted a single bullet, then spun the cylinder. With a quick flip, he closed the cylinder and tossed the weapon to one of his henchmen.

'Sit down, Mr. Caine,' he said. 'Or my men will shoot you where you stand.'

Caine glared at the two thugs for a moment, then lowered himself back into the chair.

The imposing gangster took a sip of sake. 'Let us test your skill. If you can make three moves without me capturing a piece from your side, you win.'

'What happens if I lose?' Caine asked.

Byakko's grin grew wider, leering at Caine like a Cheshire cat. 'Simple, Mr. Caine. Every time you lose a piece, my man pulls the trigger.'

Caine heard a loud click as the thug behind him cocked the revolver.

The smile vanished from Byakko's lips, replaced by a predatory stare.

'Three moves, Mr. Caine. We begin... now.'

20

Caine examined the game board, forcing himself to ignore the gun-wielding thug behind him. He was familiar with chess, but he was hardly an expert. And he knew the rules of shogi, while similar, were not identical. He struggled to recall the few times he'd played the game with Isato's young son, Kenji.

Maybe this is some kind of bluff, Caine thought. *Does this lunatic really want to shoot someone in his own club?*

'Normally, shogi is played without a clock,' Byakko said, glancing at his watch. 'But in your case, I'll give you thirty seconds for each move.'

'Fine,' Caine said, glaring at the man across the desk. 'Pawn G9 to F9.'

The move brought the pawn close to an opposing knight, but since those pieces had to move in a L shape, Caine was confident his pawn was in safe territory.

Byakko nodded as he moved Caine's pawn a single space. 'A wise move. In chess, at least. But in shogi, a promoted knight may move a single square diagonally as well.'

He slid his knight tile into Caine's space and removed the pawn from the board. His strange eyes glanced up at the revolver-wielding thug.

Click.

Caine winced as he heard the man pull the gun's trigger. Nothing happened, and Caine breathed a sigh of relief.

Guess he's serious after all, he thought. He felt his heart beat faster. A cold sweat dotted his brow.

'One move down,' Byakko said, again glancing at his watch. 'Two to go. You have thirty seconds.'

'And if I run out of time?' Caine asked.

The gangster shrugged and sipped his sake. 'That would be considered a loss, of course.'

Caine's eyes darted over the board, searching for another move. He narrowed his eyes, noticing that capturing his pawn had left Byakko's knight open to attack.

'Rook H9 to F9,' he said. He couldn't help but notice the uncertainty in his voice.

The gangster slid Caine's piece across the board and deposited the knight in a small pile of tiles lying to the side of the jade slab. Caine noted that a similar pile lay opposite his, on Byakko's side of the board.

'You captured your first piece. Well done. But I'm afraid your victory has a cost...'

The gangster grinned as he slid his bishop through a gap in his line of pawns, capturing Caine's rook.

Caine shuddered, knowing what would come next.

Click.

Again, the revolver's chamber came up empty.

'It may interest you to know that your rook was previously promoted to a Dragon King, Mr. Caine,' Byakko said, glancing over the board. 'Such a piece may move one space in any direction, as well as its normal movement.'

This is insane, Caine thought. *I'm playing blind, just guessing.*

He glanced over his shoulder, checking to see if the armed thug was within striking distance. But both men stood just out of reach. Attacking them would be suicide. But how much longer could his luck hold out playing this diabolical game? With two chambers down, that left a 25 percent chance that the next pull of the trigger would bring oblivion. At this range, he would be dead before he even heard the sound of the gunshot.

'Tick tock, Mr. Caine,' Byakko said, grinning at the look on Caine's face.

The men shuffled behind him. He heard the soft rustle of cloth as the thug raised his arm, aiming the revolver once more.

Caine racked his brain, struggling to remember anything about the game that might help him.

'Time is running out,' Byakko said.

Again, Caine heard the men moving behind him, the soft clicking of the gun's cylinder, trembling in the thug's grasp.

His eyes darted to the tiny pile of discarded tiles, lying next to the board.

Those captured pieces, he thought. *In shogi, they can return to the board. It's called a drop, and it counts as a move!*

He studied the board, searching for a safe square, away from Byakko's pieces.

'Five seconds,' Byakko said, his sinister eyes gleaming in the dim light.

'Drop pawn to E4,' Caine shouted, leaning forward in his chair.

Byakko tilted his head as he stared down at the board. He set his drink on the desk, then plucked a piece from his pile. He placed the pawn on the board and tapped it with his finger three times.

'It appears you are a quick learner, Mr. Caine.'

Caine breathed a sigh of relief as he heard the softer click of the thug lowering the hammer on the revolver. The beefy man slid the weapon across the desk. Byakko grabbed it, then deposited it back in the drawer.

'Take him to the meat locker,' he snarled. 'We shall continue this conversation later.'

Caine watched as Byakko's strange feline eyes blinked. The man drank from his glass of sake, then turned and faced the relief on the wall. The two thugs grabbed Caine by the arms and dragged him out of the room.

21

The men led Caine back down the corridor, toward the club. The thumping electronic bass grew louder as they approached the exit.

Caine glanced at the man who had punched him earlier. 'So what's this playroom Byakko-san was talking about?'

The thug gave him a leering grin. 'You'll find out soon, *gaijin.*'

Caine shrugged. 'If someone's going to work me over, I hope they can hit harder than you. Otherwise, we'll be here all night.'

The man glowered but said nothing as the other thug opened the door. The pulsing beat of the music washed over him as Caine stepped back into the club's dark interior. He blinked, letting his eyes adjust to the light.

To his right, a long bar counter stretched along the wall. Men in suits chatted up hostesses dressed in colorful gowns and sequined cocktail dresses. A wall of glass bottles reflected the red spotlights beaming down from the ceiling.

More lights pierced the club's shadowy depths. He caught glimpses of girls straddling men in the booths beyond the main stage, writhing to the music's frenetic beat.

'Keep moving,' one of the thugs shouted. The man grabbed Caine's arm and dragged him forward. As they walked past the bar, Caine glanced to his left. A bartender dressed in a white shirt and black bow tie spun a bottle of vodka around his hand, then poured the clear alcohol into a metal shaker. An attractive Japanese girl in a green dress pointed at the bartender, laughing as a man in his sixties leaned in to light her cigarette.

Caine turned to the other thug. 'You should work out with your friend here. He's got a firm grip. I'll bet he knows how to throw a punch.'

'I'll make sure Byakko-san lets me soften you up first,' the man growled.

'Yeah?' Caine said, glaring at the thug who had threatened him. 'Careful, you might break a nail.'

'*Damare, furyou yarou!*' he bellowed. *Shut up, punk!*

The other yakuza let go of Caine and grabbed his partner's shoulder, but he was too late... The thug wound back with his right arm and threw another punch.

This time, Caine was ready.

Spinning around to face the two men, he raised his arms and dipped his head low. He slipped right, deflecting the punch with his right shoulder. Then he drove his left fist into the man's side as hard as he could.

Even over the thumping music, he heard the man grunt in pain as the blow knocked the air from his lungs. The girl in the green dress spun around in her seat, her eyes wide with shock.

'*Nani?*' she shrieked. What the...

Before the other man could react, Caine reached across the bar and yanked the bottle of vodka from the bartender's hands. He swung it down, smashing the bottle over the injured yakuza's head. The clear alcohol spilled down his face, soaking his clothes and stinging his eyes.

Stepping back, Caine slashed sideways with the broken bottle, tearing a gash in the other thug's suit sleeve. The doused thug rubbed his eyes and advanced on Caine. The stench of vodka clung to his clothes, filling the surrounding air.

'*Koroshite yaru!* I'll kill you, *gaijin!*'

Caine grabbed the cigarette lighter off the bar counter and flipped the lid open. Ducking under another clumsy punch, he ignited the lighter and touched its flame to the man's lapel. The alcohol fumes ignited. Tendrils of fire raced up his clothes, burning his hair and skin.

The patrons at the bar screamed and backed off, giving Caine and his attackers a wide berth. The girl in the green dress pulled the nearest customer in front of her, then scampered over the bar and ducked behind the counter.

The burning man screamed and swatted at the flames crawling up his face. His partner dipped his hand into his suit jacket.

He's going for his gun, Caine thought, pivoting to face him.

Caine stabbed down with the broken bottle. The jagged glass drew blood from the man's arm, and he yanked it back before he could draw his weapon. Howling in pain, the thug swung a left hook with his other arm.

Caine slipped back and the punch missed. The momentum of his attack spun the yakuza man around, leaving him off balance and exposing his back. Caine grabbed the collar of the man's suit jacket and yanked down. The fabric bunched at the thug's elbows, trapping his arms at his side. Before he could shrug free from the jacket, Caine launched into a pair of body strikes, hammering his fists into the man's kidneys. Reaching through the bent-over thug's arm, he felt the butt of a pistol protruding from a shoulder rig. He drew the weapon, then planted a kick into the man's rear, sending him sprawling to the floor.

The burned man rolled on the ground, dousing the flames on his face. Smoke rose from his charred flesh and hair as he grabbed a walkie from his belt and depressed the talk button.

'Send help! Quick! The *gaijin*, he—'

Caine sent a swift kick into the side of his head. He rolled over and sprawled across the floor, unconscious.

Turning, Caine sprinted for the club's entrance, brandishing the pistol at any employees who got in his way. As he neared the door, he heard gunfire roar behind him. A crimson light overhead exploded, showering him with fragments of glass. The music stopped, and the patrons' screams filled the air.

Squinting in the sudden bright light, Caine dived behind the marble reception desk. More gunfire echoed from the club's interior. Chips of rock flew through the air as a barrage of slugs struck the desk.

Caine glanced at the gun he was holding. It was a small striker-fired pistol with a simple, blunt design. Markings on the barrel identified it as a Mexican-produced version of Heckler & Koch's P7 M13. Chambered in 9mm, the grip contained a built-in cocking lever. The gun could not fire unless the grip was squeezed with the appropriate pressure.

Caine felt the lever depress as he gripped the weapon. He leaned around the side of the reception desk and saw the yakuza men pushing and shoving their way through a crowd of patrons, all running for the exit. As the panicked mob surged past the desk, Caine leaped out and ran with them, keeping his head tucked down.

The river of bodies surged out into the corridor. A small crowd gathered in front of the elevator. A man in a rumpled suit pushed the call button over and over, but the lights above the metal door showed that the elevator car was stuck on the second floor.

A few of the terrified club patrons noticed Caine's Caucasian features and backed away, recognizing him from the fight inside the club. Glancing back down the corridor, Caine saw three men in cheap-looking suits pushing through the crowd. One of them shoved the girl in the green dress out of his way. As she struck the wall and fell to her knees, he pointed in Caine's direction.

'There he is! *Kare o yamero...* Stop him!' the man shouted.

Caine turned right and sprinted toward a glowing red exit sign further down the hall. A gunshot rang out behind him. The sign exploded, sending a shower of sparks into the dim corridor.

He threw open the metal door and entered the stairwell. As the door swung closed behind him, more bullets ricocheted off the metal slab. Caine's pounding footsteps echoed through the narrow stairwell. He raced down to the third floor. As he neared the landing, the door ahead of him swung open. A gun-wielding man emerged, half-hidden by the metal door.

Caine threw himself into the air, slamming his shoulder into the door. The metal panel shut, crushing the man's arm in the doorway. Caine heard the crack of breaking bones, and the man's pistol clattered to the floor. As he yelped in pain, Caine swung the door open and grabbed his arm, yanking him into the stairwell. He kicked the pistol away, and it flew through the railing, crashing to the bottom of the stairs.

Footsteps echoed above him. Caine looped his free arm around the gangster's neck and pivoted to look up the stairs, jamming his pistol into the struggling man's back. Two more yakuza entered the stairwell, pistols drawn. They opened fire, but their bullets thudded into the flesh of Caine's human shield.

The echo of gunfire was deafening in the narrow stairwell. As the man jerked and writhed in front of him, Caine aimed his pistol and fired, sending a double tap up the stairs. The lead yakuza clutched his chest, then tumbled forward, rolling down the stairs and landing at Caine's feet.

The yakuza in his choke hold went limp... He was deadweight now.

Backing up, Caine hurled the corpse to the right. The body tipped over the railing, then fell to the bottom of the stairs. Bullets tore into the floor near Caine's feet, sending puffs of dust into the air.

Dropping into a crouch, Caine aimed up the stairs. His gun roared three times. He heard a grunt of pain from above, and footsteps backed away from him. But before he could move, he heard more footsteps moving up the stairs beneath him, followed by men shouting.

Byakko has men throughout the entire building, Caine thought. *If I don't move quick, I'll be pinned down.*

22

Before he could reposition, automatic weapon fire screamed up the stairwell. A row of bullet holes perforated the wall behind him, and a recessed light above his head shattered.

Throwing himself to the ground, Caine aimed down through the railing. He saw three men in suits charging up the stairs. Two men carried pistols, but the lead thug wielded a small submachine gun. From the size and shape, Caine guessed it was an HK MP5, but it was difficult to be sure in the dim light of the stairwell.

Caine fired three times, but his shots ricocheted off the stairs' railing. The three men ducked and pressed their backs against the wall, struggling to get out of the line of fire. Caine fired again. The man in the rear yelped in pain as he collapsed and tumbled down the stairs.

The lead man opened fire. Caine rolled away from the railing as a volley of bullets screamed through the air. Dust and paint chips fell around him like snow, and the echo of the gunshots thundered off the walls.

As he rolled onto his back, he heard a metallic screech. The door on the landing swung open again. Grabbing the tiny pistol in both hands, Caine squeezed the cocking lever. He steadied his aim as another armed man charged through the open door. The yakuza thug fired, but the bullet struck the concrete a few inches from Caine's skull.

Caine squeezed the P7's trigger twice. A ragged crimson hole erupted in the man's chest, followed by another in his shoulder. Blood stained the front of the injured man's white shirt and spattered the door behind him. As the thug staggered back, Caine leaped to his feet, darting towards the wounded attacker. More automatic weapon fire erupted from below.

The wounded man raised his pistol and fired again, but he was wobbling on his feet, swaying from the shock and pain of his injuries. Caine darted left, and the shot went wild, striking the wall behind him.

Before the bleeding thug could line up another shot, Caine grabbed his arm, swinging the pistol away from him. He slammed the man's wrist onto the railing, and the gun fell from his grasp.

The men on the stairs beneath him shouted again. Their echoing footsteps pounded closer.

Caine drove a knee into the wounded thug's groin. The man pitched forward, grunting in pain. Grabbing the man's head, Caine slammed it into the glass window of the fire-hose cabinet. The plate glass shattered, and more blood streamed down the thug's mangled face. He fell to the ground and ceased moving.

Panting for breath, Caine opened the door and peered into the corridor beyond. Like the upper floors of the building, the lights were dim. Most of the bars and cafés lining the floor were closed. He raced into the shadowy corridor.

The door slammed shut behind him with a loud crash. The sound echoed through the hall like a gunshot. Doors of various colors lined the corridor, along with signs advertising the establishments inside. A few were cafés, including a late-night parfait restaurant. But most seemed to be *sunakku*, bars that served small dishes and snacks along with their drinks.

Caine ran to the nearest door and tried the knob, but it was locked. Glancing down the corridor, he noted most of the signs were dim, and steel shutters covered many of the doors. The businesses on this floor all seemed to be closed.

He heard shouting, footsteps thundering around the corner. More men were closing in on his position.

Glancing to his right, he saw a single lightbulb illuminating a plain black door. Caine sprinted towards it. As he threw it open, the footsteps behind him grew louder, and echoed off the marble floor. Caine entered the dark room behind the door and closed it behind him.

Blinking, he gave his eyes a second to adjust to the dim light. He was standing in a small speakeasy. Soft jazz drifted from speakers hidden in the shadows. A bar ran along his left side, and a few patrons sat at the counter, sipping cocktails from tall, elegant glassware. There were only a few tables in the tiny space, and the walls were solid black.

Behind the bar, a young bartender held a silver cocktail shaker in his hands. He wore a black vest and dress shirt with a gold silk tie. His eyes were closed, his brow furrowed in concentration. The ice within the shaker rasped a frenetic beat as he moved it up and down at a rapid pace.

A woman in a burgundy cocktail dress approached Caine and held out her hands, offering to take his coat.

Caine ignored her and instead grabbed a stool from the bar. He wedged it under the doorknob, blocking the entryway. The woman's eyes opened wide as the men outside pounded on the door.

Caine grabbed the woman's shoulders and looked her in the eyes. 'Do not open that,' he said. 'Call the police... *Wakarimasu ka?* Understand?'

The woman gave him a nervous nod, then turned to the bartender. She shouted to get his attention. As he set down the shaker and grabbed his cell phone, Caine made his way to the end of the tiny lounge. A small circular table lay beneath the only window in the room. The young couple sitting at the table looked up from their drinks as Caine approached. Based on their clothes and the woman's makeup, Caine assumed they were on a date.

'*Sumimasen,*' Caine muttered.

Their surprised stares shifted from him to the door as the pounding outside grew louder. Muffled shouting came from the corridor. Caine stepped onto the table and opened the window. The girl gasped. The man grabbed her arm and pulled her away as a frigid wind whipped through the bar, scattering cocktail napkins into the air.

Caine climbed out the window onto a fire escape. The metal platform shook and creaked beneath his weight. Sliding down the ladder, he landed on an identical platform one floor down. He vaulted over the metal railing, plunging down to the snow-covered alley below. A towering snowbank broke his fall. He rolled down the white embankment to the alley floor.

Standing, he brushed loose snow and ice off his clothes.

Before he could turn around, a hand seized his shoulder. Caine reacted on instinct, grabbing the slim wrist and ducking under the arm. He spun his attacker around, locking their arm behind their back and shoving them up against the alley wall.

'Owww!' the woman screamed. 'You're hurting me!'

Caine realized he was holding Gaya in an armlock. He released her and stepped back. The startled woman spun around and fumbled in her purse. Her arm snapped up, holding a silver can of pepper spray.

'*Baka janai no?*' *Are you crazy?*

Caine raised his hands. 'Sorry, you took me by surprise.'

The woman pouted and cradled her arm. She wore a black wool coat over her dress, and a pink knit hat covered her dark hair. 'I told you I'd meet you back here, didn't I?'

Caine glanced at the alcove behind her. A pair of double doors led into the building. Above them, the lens of a security camera peeked out from the corner.

Caine grabbed her arm and pulled her down the alley. 'We have to get out of here. Do you have a car?'

'*Hai,*' she replied. 'It's parked in a garage a few blocks away. What happened to you?' she asked, noticing his disheveled appearance.

'I met the club's owner, Byakko-san.'

'And?'

Caine grunted as they ran through the snow. 'Let's just say we didn't see eye to eye.'

23

Byakko stood over the shogi board, examining the tiny wooden pieces. In his mind, he played out a variety of scenarios, possible ways the game could end. With each move, he predicted his opponent's counter, then his response, and so on and so on. And he knew his opponent would do the same, just as he had taught them to do.

'Soon, this game will end,' he whispered to himself. 'And I promise, we shall reclaim what was taken from us.'

A soft electronic chime echoed from the intercom on his desk. He glanced over and saw a red light blinking on the instrument's panel. There was a video call on his private line.

He poured himself another glass of sake, then pressed the red button. The sculpted relief of the tiger behind his desk parted and slid into a recessed panel behind the wall, revealing a massive TV screen. The screen pulsed with static, then an image filled the monitor.

An Asian woman's face stared back at him. Her features were severe, her eyes obsidian black. She wore a black sweater and appeared to be standing in the cargo hold of some kind of ship. Rust patches covered the curved metal walls behind her, and rows of computer workstations lit the shadows of the cavernous cargo hold.

'You saw the pictures I sent?' Byakko asked, his voice rumbling like thunder.

The woman blinked. 'I did. This Thomas Caine is the man I encountered in Seoul.'

'And now he is here,' Byakko muttered, stroking his goatee. He sipped his sake and glanced at the shogi pieces scattered across the floor. 'But he will trouble us no longer.'

'If he is here, then the CIA knows of our plans,' the woman said. 'The girl must have talked. I told you, this—'

'No,' Byakko snapped, cutting her off. 'I do not believe so. I think Ogawa-san sent him here, to look for Kanako.'

The woman narrowed her eyes. 'Koichi Ogawa? I thought he was dead.'

Byakko finished his sake, then twisted the glass in his fingers, watching the light reflect off its rim. 'Apparently not. But he soon will be.'

'Perhaps. But there are still too many loose ends. The journalist, in DC, for example. He has served his purpose. Now, he is a liability.'

Byakko nodded. 'Very well. Alert our people. It's time to sacrifice another pawn.'

The cell phone on his desk chirped to life. His men were calling him.

'Just a moment,' Byakko said, grabbing the phone and turning away from the screen.

'Yes?' he answered. The woman on the monitor watched as a voice chattered into his ear.

'What?' he bellowed. 'Find them! Kill them both! The *gaijin* must not leave Sapporo alive. Do not fail me again!'

He threw the phone onto his desk. The woman on the screen glared back at him.

'Another problem?' she asked, arching a single brow.

'Caine has escaped. But my men will take care of him.'

'Is he alone?'

Byakko shook his head. 'No, he is with a girl from the club. One of Kanako's friends.'

The woman's expression hardened. 'Send me everything you have on her. My people can help locate her. The sooner we find her, the sooner we find him.'

Byakko stroked his goatee, deep in thought. 'It is not necessary. You should focus on phase—'

'You know what will happen if we fail in our endeavor?'

Byakko waved his hand as if shooing a fly. '*Hai*, you're right. Go!'

The woman nodded, a determined gleam in her dark, pensive eyes. The screen faded to black, then the tiger sculpture slid back into place.

Byakko bent over the shogi board and clenched his fist. Bellowing a cry of rage, he swept the pieces off the board. The wood tiles scattered across the floor.

He blinked his strange feline eyes and examined the few pieces still left on the jade surface. The game had changed. Defeat loomed in the shadows, closer than ever before. But all was not yet lost.

His lips curled into a manic grin.

For victory, he sensed, was still within his grasp.

24

Caine turned the wheel of the tiny Daihatsu Tanto, darting between a delivery van and a Toyota sedan as he navigated the Sapporo City traffic. The windshield wipers made a quiet, rhythmic swishing as they batted away the thick, fluffy white snowflakes falling from the night sky. The little car's engine revved in protest as Caine downshifted and stomped on the accelerator.

'*Oi*, be careful!' Gaya protested, grabbing the door handle to steady herself as Caine swerved around the sedan ahead of them. 'It's a *kei* car, not a Ferrari!'

'You said you wanted me to drive,' Caine muttered, glancing in the rearview mirror.

The boxy, diminutive vehicle was nimble enough. At less than five feet wide, and with a wheelbase of less than eight feet, the little car maneuvered between larger vehicles with ease. But the three-cylinder engine was lacking in horsepower and torque. If it came down to a chase, Caine doubted he would be able to outrun his enemies. And considering the vehicle's sparkling purple paint job, they would be easy to spot if Byakko's people were looking for them.

Gaya sank into her seat. 'I'm too nervous to drive. What happened in there? I heard gunshots and screaming.'

Caine kept his eyes on the road, darting through a traffic light just before it turned red. 'The new owner, Hideo Torazama. Have you met him?'

The girl shuddered. 'Of course. Most of the clubs and bars are owned by yakuza. I knew he was a gangster. But those eyes, the way he speaks... There is something different about him. He scares me.'

'I don't blame you,' Caine replied. 'Look, we don't have much time. You have to leave the city. It won't be safe for you here, for a while at least. Is there somewhere you can go? Family, a friend?'

She ran her fingers through her hair and sighed. 'No, my family and I... It's complicated. I have an ex-boyfriend in Okinawa. He's a *bakayaro*, but at least he won't kick me out.' She glared at him and pouted. 'I knew you were trouble the minute I saw you. I never should have said a word to you!'

'I just want to help Kanako,' Caine replied, keeping his eyes on the road. 'You said she was in some kind of danger?'

Gaya fished around in her bag, then pulled out a crumpled pack of Misty cigarettes. She removed a slim cigarette from the box, slid it between her lips, and lit it with a cheap neon-green plastic lighter. She shook her head as she blew smoke out the window.

'I don't know what that girl was thinking. She wasn't even supposed to be working that night! I guess she needed the money, or—'

'Slow down. What night?'

Gaya's hand trembled as she brought the cigarette to her lips and took another drag. 'There was a private party at the club. Friends of Tora—I mean, Byakko-san. Kanako was still new at the club. She wasn't allowed to work at that event. He only wanted girls who had worked there for a long time. And a few of his, uh, special girls.'

'Special girls?' Caine shot her a quick glance as the car skidded around a corner. A thin layer of snow fell upon the roads, and the car's little tires struggled to grip the ice.

'*Hai*,' Gaya said, slumping back in her seat. 'Look, I'm not saying I'm one of them. But the rumor is some of the girls that work in the club... They owe him favors. Or he has something on them, you know... pictures, videos. Things they wouldn't want their families to see, if you know what I mean.'

Caine nodded. 'I know exactly what you mean. But Kanako wasn't one of those girls?'

Gaya shook her head. 'No. She was really smart. That's why I can't believe she'd pull a stunt like that.'

'Like what?'

'Kanako's roommate, Rise,' Gaya continued, pronouncing the name like reese-eh. 'She was hooked. *Shabu.*'

'Methamphetamine,' Caine muttered. He knew the word 'shabu' was a slang term used by the yakuza to describe the highly addictive stimulant. It literally translated to 'suck'. First, the drug sucked an addict's wallet dry. Then it sucked the soul from the husk of their withered body.

'Yeah,' Gaya said, peering out the window as the city lights rushed by. 'It was sad to watch. She was so pretty. When she wore that red wig, she drove the customers wild. That was all they could even see. Kanako fooled half of them in the club that night, just by borrowing that stupid wig.'

The wig, Caine thought. *The red hair. Could that be why...?*

'She and Rise looked like sisters,' Gaya said, taking another drag of her cigarette. 'She even had that *kankoku no hentai roujin* fooled.'

Caine narrowed his eyes as he translated the words in his head. *Old Korean pervert...*

'Korean? She was talking to a Korean man?'

Gaya shrugged. 'I guess so. He was one of Byakko-san's special guests. They must have brought him in through the back, to a private room. I didn't see him in the club. I only noticed him because he followed Kanako to the ladies' room. Pervert.'

Caine's mind shifted into overdrive as he swerved around a parked delivery truck. 'What did he look like?'

'I dunno. Old. Boring. Glasses. Probably married, I bet. Most of the customers are.'

'Your phone... Give it to me!'

The girl furrowed her brow and blew more smoke out the window. 'What? Who the hell do you think—'

'Please! It's important!'

Muttering a curse in Japanese, the girl rummaged through her purse, then handed Caine a pink iPhone. Sparkling charms hung from its silicone case. 'Here. Jeez!'

Struggling to navigate the little car with one hand, Caine opened the girl's web browser and did a Google search. When the results popped up on the screen, he opened a picture, then handed the phone back to her.

'Was this the guy she was talking to?' Caine asked, steadying the car as the rear wheels fishtailed on the ice.

Gaya furrowed her brow as she studied the screen. '*Sou desu ne*. I think that's him. When the owner saw them talking, he lost it! Kanako ran off, and then he started yelling at this guy, calling him an idiot, asking what he told her. Who is he?'

'Chan Tae Young. He worked for the Korean Ministry of Trade.'

Gaya took another look at the picture. 'Yeah? What's so special about him?'

Caine glanced at the girl, uncertain of how much he should tell her. 'Well, for one thing, he was murdered in South Korea the other night.'

Gaya's eyes opened wide with shock. '*Nani?*' *What?*

'That's not all,' Caine said, deciding the girl had a right to know the danger she was in. 'Your friend, Rise. She's dead as well.'

'*Shinjirarenai!* I can't believe it! Are you—?'

Caine glanced at her as the little car sped around a corner. 'I'm sorry, Gaya. But I saw the body myself. Trust me, if Byakko was involved with Chan, this is bigger than some yakuza turf war. You and Kanako are both in danger.'

'But what do I... What should I do?'

'I'll take you to the airport, give you some money to get a ticket. Do you have any idea where Kanako might have gone? I have to find her.'

Gaya shook her head. 'No, I didn't see her again after that night! I—'

She paused and looked down at the phone again.

'Anything you remember could help, Gaya,' Caine said. 'Please, think!'

'I... I do remember one thing,' Gaya said in a small, quiet voice. She blinked and looked up at Caine, her eyes on the verge of tears. 'Before Byakko-san saw them, they were talking. I think I heard this guy, Chan, mention something about Tomamu.'

'Tomamu?' Caine asked. 'What's that?'

'It's a small town, north of here,' she replied, clutching the phone with both hands. 'It's in the mountains, very remote. There are ski resorts there. Fancy hotels, that kind of thing.'

'Got it. Were they planning to meet there?'

'I don't know,' she said, her voice trembling with fear. 'I only heard him say the name, I couldn't make out the rest. Look, I just wanted to make sure Kanako was okay. I don't want to get involved in—'

Before she could finish her sentence, an engine roared behind the little car. Caine's eyes shot up to the rearview mirror. The blinding glow of high beams flooded the tiny car's interior.

A large SUV rammed the Daihatsu's rear bumper. Caine struggled to control the wheel as the *kei* car fishtailed across the icy road. Gaya screamed, and the phone flew from her hands, clattering to the floor of the skidding car.

'What was that?' she gasped, glancing over her shoulder.

'Byakko found us!' Caine snarled, weaving around a lane of stopped traffic.

'What? How could he—'

'He could have hacked the traffic camera system,' Caine grunted. 'His people probably have your license plate number. And a purple *kei* car isn't too hard to find.'

The lights grew brighter in the rearview mirror. The SUV was closing in again. Instead of ramming them, the vehicle pulled up alongside them. Caine saw the rear window lower down, and a man in dark clothes leaned out, holding an automatic rifle.

'Gaya, get down,' he shouted, throwing the wheel to the left.

Gaya screamed and ducked in her seat as the man in the SUV opened fire. Muzzle flash lit up the night, and the car's rear window shattered.

The tiny car swerved across the street. Horns blared in Caine's wake as he cut off traffic and shot through a red light. Glancing in the rearview mirror, he saw the SUV follow a split second later. A silver Nissan sedan was already turning through the intersection. The black SUV struck the hood of the oncoming car, sending it spinning out of the way with a metallic shriek.

Caine darted right, struggling to keep the other cars between him and his attacker. Up ahead, a sea of blinking red lights filled his vision... A delivery truck blocked the lane. The traffic slowed to a crawl as vehicles maneuvered around the truck.

As a pair of workers in coveralls wheeled a dolly of Asahi beer crates from the back of the truck, Caine steered into the gap between the traffic and the side of the road. The tiny car was just small enough to thread the narrow ribbon of pavement without going up on the curb.

Twin howls echoed behind him. Glancing in the mirror, he muttered a curse. A trio of bright lights followed him down the narrow strip of pavement, and they were gaining fast.

Motorcycles, he thought. *High-power crotch rockets*. He knew there was no way the tiny car could outmaneuver those.

As the men rolled the dolly of beer towards a neon-lit bar, Caine jerked the wheel right. The little car bounced over the curb and up onto the sidewalk. He slammed his fist down on the horn. The two workers looked up, their shocked faces lit by the twin beams of his oncoming headlights.

Behind him, he heard the motorcycle engines rev higher as they followed him up onto the sidewalk. The lead rider raised his arm and held out a small weapon. A submachine gun of some kind, Caine guessed by the look of it.

'Gaya, stay down!' he shouted.

'*Touzen da!*' she snapped back. 'You think I want to get shot in the—'

The rider opened fire. A quick burst of gunfire tore through the air, and the rear windshield exploded behind them. Gaya shrieked as glass shards rained down onto her seat.

The two workers released the dolly and sprinted out of the way, letting the wheeled cart roll across the sidewalk. The brakes of the little Daihatsu squealed as Caine swerved around it.

The rider behind them opened fire again, oblivious to the dolly that had stopped in his path. Caine heard a series of metallic pings as the bullets tore through the *kei* car's rear door. Then the rider's front tire struck the dolly.

Both the cycle and its rider flipped into the air and crashed through the plastic crates. The glass bottles shattered, filling the air with spray as the bike slammed down and skidded across the concrete. Sparks shot from the motorcycle's crumpled metal frame.

The rider landed several meters away. He struck the ground with a bone-snapping crack, then tumbled several times, rolling across the sidewalk.

He didn't get back up.

Caine's lips curled into a savage grin, but his victory was short-lived. The other bikes sped around the toppled dolly and continued pursuit. And as Caine turned around the corner and skidded back out into the street, the black SUV reappeared behind them.

'Do you know where you're going?' Gaya shrieked, plucking shards of broken glass from her hair.

'Yeah,' Caine grunted. 'Away from the people shooting at us!'

As the two motorcycles raced closer, Caine threw the wheel to the right. Cutting across the median of the road, he sped into oncoming traffic. Brakes screamed and horns blared as he cut in front of a row of cars, then sped through the entrance of a Buddhist temple.

The motorcycles followed, swerving after him. Directly ahead of Caine, a flight of concrete stairs led up through a series of red wooden arches. A rotund, ash-filled urn sat at the top of the stairs. Smoke wafted from sticks of incense poking out from the ash and mingled with the falling snow.

Caine spun the wheel, the car skidding across the snow-covered ground. He darted to the right, shooting behind a long row of stacked sake barrels. White paper lanterns hung above the barrels, swaying in the frigid breeze.

The motorcycles raced along the other side of the barrels. The lead rider opened fire with his submachine gun. Bullets tore through the paper lanterns overhead, but they couldn't pierce the thick wooden barrels.

As Caine neared the end of the row, he swerved right. Shooting out from behind the barrels, the tiny car lurched towards the lead rider. The bike veered away, narrowly avoiding a collision. Caine spun the wheel and crashed through a wooden fence, skidding back out onto the icy pavement. The little car fish-tailed, then sped down a side street.

The SUV roared after them. The walking street was barely large enough for the larger black vehicle, and the motorcycles behind it couldn't get a shot. Caine leaned on his horn as a pair of salarymen in rumpled suits stumbled out of a standing bar down the street. A woman in a long wool coat grabbed them both by the shoulders and yanked them back into the bar. She flipped Caine the bird as he sped by.

The SUV crashed through a sign on the ground advertising drink specials. Caine watched as the armed man in the back leaned out the window again. Cursing, he threw the wheel to the left, zigzagging across the street.

Dozens of bicycles filled a rack on the left side of the walking street. Pedestrians mingled there, securing their bikes, talking, and sipping warm drinks from Styrofoam cups. Caine leaned on the horn. The crowd scattered as he skidded across the snow towards them. At the last second, he veered to the right, swerving around the bikes.

The man in the SUV behind them opened fire. Bullets ricocheted off the car's roof. Then the SUV struck the bikes. Sparks flew from their metal frames as the rampaging vehicle tore them loose from the rack. The SUV's engine roared in protest, as it shoved the mass of mangled bicycles down the street like a plow moving snow. The armed man ducked back inside as the SUV fishtailed behind the pile of twisted metal.

Caine threw the wheel to the left, drifting across the snow into the cross street. As the car straightened out, the squeal of brakes echoed ahead of them. Horns blared, and another pair of black SUVs skidded to a stop, cutting off the street. Men exited the vehicle, armed with MP5 submachine guns.

Caine checked the rearview mirror. Behind them, the mass of bicycles skidded across the snow as the SUV exited the walking street and roared towards them.

Caine glanced left and right, searching for a way off the street. He swerved around a stopped car. A bright yellow sign hung over a dark alley, running perpendicular to the street. A line of people waited on the sidewalk as pedestrians sauntered in and out of the passageway.

The roar of the SUV behind them grew louder. Caine squinted as the vehicle's blinding headlights filled the rearview mirror.

Caine spun the wheel and accelerated toward the yellow sign.

Gunfire crackled through the street as the men ahead of them opened fire. People abandoned their stopped cars, ducking for cover or fleeing from the snow-covered street. The Daihatsu's front windshield exploded into glass shards. The frigid wind blasted their faces, and Gaya's hair whipped around her face. She ducked low in her seat, whimpering in fear.

The tiny vehicle bounced up over the curb and onto the sidewalk. Between Caine's horn and the gunfire in the street, the line of pedestrians scattered, fleeing in all directions.

Gaya peeked up, looking over the dashboard. 'That's Ramen Alley! It's too narrow, we won't—'

The crash of metal cut her off. The SUV behind them collided with another parked car. Caine gripped the steering wheel as the *kei* car plunged into the narrow gap. The high-pitched roar of the engine echoed off the brick walls. Sparks flew from the side of the car as the passenger side-view mirror tore clean off.

The crowd ahead of them screamed and ran, ducking into the tiny ramen shops on either side of the alley. Caine squinted and ducked as the little vehicle struck a low-hanging sign, ripping it off its moorings. The swaying metal plaque crashed into the street behind them.

The little Daihatsu was about four and a half feet wide, barely small enough to thread through the narrow alley. Clearance was tight, and Caine struggled to keep the wheel steady. The sound of grinding metal echoed through the passageway as the car scrapped against the brick walls.

Glancing back, Caine saw the headlights of the two motorcycles enter the alley behind them, still in pursuit. But the SUVs were too wide to follow.

'Look out!' Gaya shouted.

Caine returned his attention to the cramped alley ahead. A crowd of pedestrians fled before him, revealing a long bench jutting out from the driver's side of the wall. Caine threw the wheel to the left. The tiny vehicle scraped against the opposite wall, sending a trail of sparks through the air behind them.

But there still wasn't enough clearance.

The corner of the bench caught the driver's side front fender. The little car shuddered as the fender tore loose, the metal peeling off like the lid of a sardine can.

As the detached fender spun on the ground behind them, the little car shot out of the alley. Caine sped through an intersection, narrowly avoiding oncoming traffic. He merged with the traffic on Sapporo Ekimae-Dori street. Weaving around a row of taxicabs, he darted in front of a delivery van, hoping the large vehicle would hide the little Daihatsu from their pursuers.

Caine checked the rear-view mirror, but the towering van on their six blocked his view. Gaya poked her head up, glancing left and right. Her pale skin dripped with sweat, and her mascara was running. Caine ran his fingers through his hair. It was soaked with perspiration as well. Despite the vehicle's broken windows and the freezing temperature outside, it was sweltering inside the tiny cabin.

The car's engine was under the seats, and Caine knew he was pushing it to its limit. And generating excess heat in the process. He doubted the car could take much more strain.

'Do you see them?' he asked, as they raced past another row of glittering ice sculptures and neon-lit bars.

Gaya shook her head. 'No. I think we lost them!' She gave Caine a panicked look. 'This is insane! What do they want?'

'I don't know,' Caine grunted, swerving around a yellow delivery truck. 'But if they're after Kanako, she's in more trouble than she realizes. Can you think of anything else she said? Anything that might help me find—'

The roar of a motorcycle engine drowned out his words. The lead bike pulled up behind the rear passenger side door. Muzzle flash exploded from the rider's gun, and bullets tore through the rear seat. Tufts of upholstery foam exploded into the cabin.

Caine threw the wheel left, swerving towards the bike. The motorcycle veered away, barely avoiding a collision. As the bike's engine screamed in protest, it jumped up onto the center island and collided with the ice sculptures. The ice shattered, and the bike flipped, catapulting the rider into the air.

As the mangled bike skidded across the snow, the rider crashed into another shimmering statue. The beak of a massive hawk, carved from a solid block of ice, pierced the rider, then snapped off under his weight. The impaled man struck the ground and rolled to a stop, blood staining the ivory snow beneath him.

Caine narrowed his eyes as he examined the road ahead. Police had blocked off the next intersection. A crowd of pedestrians wandered along the other side of the barricade. Traffic was diverting to the left and slowing to a crawl.

A similar barrier blocked the opposite side of the street, and snow sculptures filled the narrow strip of land in between.

Odori Park... The Snow Festival!

Leaning on his horn, Caine maneuvered through the stop-and-go traffic. The car's engine revved louder as he raced toward the barricades. The remaining motorcycle roared through the street, but a black Audi sedan screeched to a halt, cutting it off behind them.

'Brace yourself,' Caine shouted, gripping the wheel tight. Gaya threw up her arm and pressed her hand against the dashboard. The Daihatsu struck the nearest barricade, snapping the wood in two. The crowd scattered out of their way as the little car raced between the rows of snow sculptures.

The screech of brakes filled the air. Another pair of black SUVs skidded to a halt behind the second set of barricades, blocking their path.

To Caine's left, a massive wall of snow rose from the ground, sculpted into the facade of a castle. To his right, the glass walls and marble columns of a bank's pavilion shimmered in the neon lights.

'They found us!' Gaya gasped. 'We're trapped!'

Caine spotted a gap in the buildings, a narrow space between the bank's columns. 'Not yet, we aren't,' he muttered. 'Hold on!'

He threw the wheel to the right, and the car darted between the columns. But a split second later, the front wheels dipped, throwing Caine and Gaya forward in their seats. As his stomach lurched, and broken glass flew from the back window, Caine realized the opening between the pillars was not another alley, or a passage between buildings.

It was a flight of stairs, plunging down into the Sapporo Underground.

The little car's engine screamed, and the rear wheels flew off the landing. A white marble wall filled the shattered windshield ahead of them as the car plunged down the stairs.

hard window, but crashed through-most of between the glass was not whole, alley, or a passage between buildings.

It was a flight of stairs, plunging down into the subground underground.
The little car engine screamed, and the rear wheels flew off Daihatsu. A white marble wall offer the shimmer a window doubled of where as the car plunged down the walls.

26

The tiny car shook and rattled as it careened down the marble stairs. Gaya's hair flew in her face, and her purse tumbled off the seat, spilling its contents on the floor.

Caine could barely see out the shattered windshield as the bouncing motion of the car jostled him in his seat. The stairs spiraled to the left, and he struggled to keep the car from crashing through the guardrail and falling to the level below.

Sparks flew from the crumpled metal hood as the driver's side struck the wall. The rear end fishtailed, and the engine wheezed as the little car rounded the corner and bounced down the remaining steps. With a high-pitched roar, the Daihatsu skidded off the stairs and onto a smooth marble floor.

They were in the Sapporo Underground, a sprawling network of tunnels and underground shopping centers beneath the city streets. The Underground provided access to major subway stations throughout the city, as well as Aurora Town and Pole Town, two popular subterranean shopping arcades.

Smoke billowed from the Daihatsu's tailpipe, and the high-pitched rev of the engine echoed around them, bouncing off the walls and ceiling of the underground passageway.

Women in long winter coats and men carrying briefcases walked along either side of the tunnel. They stared in shock as the mangled car rushed past them. Screams of terror replaced their surprised glances as the remaining motorcycle roared down the stairs and its rider opened fire.

Caine held the wheel in a white-knuckled grip as he sped through the underground tunnel. The passageway was wider than the above-ground alleys, and the two vehicles swerved around pedestrians as they darted between support columns.

The rider fired again, sending bullets ricocheting off the tunnel walls. The car's driver-side mirror exploded into shards of glass and plastic.

Information booths and art displays raced past on either side of the tunnel. Caine glimpsed a colorful mural displaying Masuka Ongaku in her snow festival furs. Her neon-green hair ran along the length of the tunnel wall, and her massive, glowing green eye seemed to follow him as he drove by.

As they flew past an art exhibit of giant robot statues, smoke billowed from the Daihatsu's exhaust. The engine sputtered and wheezed.

Caine glanced left and right, searching for some way out of the tunnels. The car was on its last legs, and he knew the engine wouldn't hold out much longer under the strain. Multiple passages split off from the main tunnel, but they were all too small for the car to fit through.

More gunfire erupted behind them. Caine spun the wheel, veering to the right side of the tunnel as bullets tore chunks of concrete from the floor. Pedestrians leaped onto benches, or pressed against the walls, clearing a path as the little car careened past them.

He heard a metallic clanking sound coming from Gaya's side of the car. At first, he thought they might have broken an axle going down the stairs. But as the vehicle straightened out, he spotted a tiny metal canister rolling out from under her seat.

Gaya's pepper spray...

Before he could react, another volley of bullets tore into the Daihatsu's rear bumper. A salaryman in a rumpled gray suit jerked and writhed, caught in the spray of gunfire. He slumped to the ground as the motorcycle screamed past him.

Caine veered to the left, swerving around a row of colorful paper-mache animals. He peered through the shattered windshield. Plywood sheets and barricades blocked the tunnel up ahead. A narrow walkway led through the construction, but it was barely wide enough for two people to fit side by side.

Caine checked the rearview mirror. The rider swerved behind them and fired another burst from his MP5. Bullets tore through the animal statues, sending a colorful confetti of paper scraps into the air. Caine looked closer at the bike's rider in the mirror. The man wore black motorcycle leathers and a matching helmet. His visor was open, and his dark, beady eyes squinted through the noxious exhaust that belched from the Daihatsu's tailpipe.

'Gaya, give me your pepper spray,' Caine snapped, weaving around another column. 'Hurry!'

The barricaded section of the tunnel raced closer. The whining of the car's engine and the roar of the motorcycle echoed through the confined space.

'*Hai, chotto matte,*' Gaya grunted as she rummaged beneath the seat of the tiny car. 'Can you at least drive straight for a minute?'

'Not if you want to avoid getting shot,' Caine snapped, slaloming between another pair of columns.

Gaya grabbed the little silver canister. Her head popped back up, and she handed the pepper spray tube to Caine. Her eyes opened wide as she peered out the shattered front windshield.

'Here, take—*Oi!* Look out!'

A trio of pedestrians stumbled out of a stairwell and sauntered into the middle of the tunnel. There was a male in his twenties, flanked by a pair of girls who looked about the same age. They were all dressed in club clothes, and they wobbled on their feet, struggling to maintain their balance. They looked intoxicated and showed no sign of noticing the pair of vehicles racing toward them.

Caine banked right while the motorcycle banked left. One of the girls laughed and pointed at the mangled Daihatsu, giggling as it screamed past.

The motorcycle swerved behind them again and opened fire. Gaya screamed as bullets ricocheted off the passenger sidewall.

Caine kept his eyes on the rearview mirror, following the movement of the bike. Both vehicles sped closer to the barricade. A group of people exited from the station on the other side. They pointed at the oncoming vehicles, then hurried back the way they came.

'Gaya, keep your head down,' Caine said, watching as the bike raced around a column behind them. 'Close your eyes and cover your nose if you can!'

The terrified girl didn't answer, but Caine was already turning the wheel with one hand, drifting to the left of the motorcycle. As the bike sped closer on the driver's side, Caine reached one arm out the window. The rider raised his weapon, preparing to fire again.

Caine squeezed the pepper spray's trigger.

A cloud of white mist exploded from the canister, filling the air behind the little car like a smoke screen. Caine squinted as the mist expanded, filling the tunnel. He felt a slight burning in his nostrils and his eyes teared up. Some of the vapor had made its way into the cabin, but most of the cloud stayed behind the speeding vehicle.

The barricade rushed closer. They were less than a hundred meters away. The motorcycle vanished behind them, lost in the noxious pepper-spray cloud.

The bike's engine roared through the tunnel as it burst from the cloud and sped along the driver's side of the vehicle. The rider's eyes were swollen, and his face was flushed. Tears streamed down his cheeks as the pepper spray burned his eyes and nostrils.

Caine dropped the canister and swung open the driver's side door. Then he gripped the wheel with both hands and slammed on the brakes.

Smoke billowed from the tires as the tiny car screeched to a halt. A split second later, the motorcycle collided with the open door, tearing it off the vehicle with a horrendous metal shriek.

The impact spun the Daihatsu around in a circle across the smooth marble floor. The bike flipped into the air, sending the rider careening into the plywood barrier. He hit the wood with a loud crack, then fell to the ground. The skidding bike slammed into his torso, and his gun clattered across the floor.

He slumped against the barricade and his head lolled to the side. Blood dribbled from the corner of his open mouth.

Caine shook his head, struggling to clear his vision from the stinging fumes. The Daihatsu's engine sputtered and coughed, then died. He glanced over at Gaya. She was leaning against the passenger door, facing away from him.

Caine coughed, then unbuckled his seat belt. All pedestrians in the area had fled. An eerie silence filled the air, a stark contrast to the gunfire and roaring engines that had echoed through the tunnel moments earlier.

'We should go,' he said. 'The police will be here any minute.'

He shook Gaya's shoulder. She did not respond.

'Gaya, are you all right?'

He turned her head to face him. Her dark brown eyes peered up at him, glazed over, lifeless. Glancing down, he saw beams of light shining through a row of bullet holes in the metal door. A pool of blood stained the seat and dripped onto the floor below.

Clenching his jaw, Caine felt her neck for a pulse. There was nothing.

She was gone.

He gently lowered her head and brushed her hair from her face. Then he examined the contents of her purse, still spilled on the floor. He found a small pack of sanitary wipes. Grabbing one, he wiped down the steering wheel, door, and any other part of the vehicle he'd touched.

As he stumbled from the wreckage, he heard a wet, rasping cough echo through the tunnel – the injured rider struggling to lift the wrecked bike off his mangled body. The twisted metal frame pinned him to the ground.

Caine limped over to the rider's discarded MP5. He picked up the gun and approached the coughing man.

'Fuck you, *gaijin*!' the rider hissed. Another fit of coughing wracked his body. A fine red mist spattered the marble floor beside him.

Caine stood over the injured man, holding the gun at his side. His emerald eyes glared at the thug, blazing like gemstones in the dim light. The swirling white mist of the pepper spray filled the tunnel behind him.

'To look into the White Tiger's eyes is to stare death in the face,' the thug wheezed, as more blood dribbled down his chin. 'You will—'

Caine planted a foot on the wreckage lying atop the wounded man. He pressed down with all his weight. The thug gasped and ceased his ranting.

'Save your breath,' Caine said. 'I've already heard it. This time, I've got a message of my own for Byakko-san.'

'Wha... What is it?' the man gasped, as Caine let up on the mangled bike's frame.

'Don't worry,' Caine snarled. 'I'm sure he'll get the point.'

Caine raised the gun and fired a burst point blank into the man's face.

As the last shot echoed through the tunnel, Caine heard men shouting in the mist, footsteps heading in his direction. Wiping the gun clean, he tossed the weapon in a garbage bin and jogged to the nearest stairwell.

A few minutes later, he emerged onto the street. He flipped the collar of his jacket up and tilted his face down as the cold wind blasted his skin. More snow fell from the sky.

27

Caine's eyes shot open. He jerked awake, gasping for breath, reaching to his waist for a gun that wasn't there.

The gentle rocking of the train shook his body. His breathing slowed, and his heart stopped racing. He remembered where he was.

Blinking, he sat up and glanced out the window. The morning was cloudy and the sky was gray. Wisps of pink and orange clouds, the last vestiges of sunrise, clung to the distant horizon. Then the train snaked through a mountain valley, and all Caine could see was white.

A thick blanket of snow covered the ground. Gnarled, blackened trees reached out from the frozen ground like claws. Crows clung to their branches, their shadowy wings silhouetted against the blinding white landscape.

After escaping the subway, Caine had retrieved his go bag from the locker, then spent the night in a capsule hotel, a cheap facility that rented tiny, coffin-like chambers to businesspeople and drunken travelers who had missed their trains home.

It was risky staying in Sapporo after the chaos in the underground. But the next train to Tomamu didn't leave until the morning, and he needed a place to lie low. He considered stealing a car and making the drive himself, but the odds of being stopped along the way were too great.

Caine had slept in such places many times before. But that night, sleep had eluded him. Gaya's face haunted his dreams. Pale skin, black, lifeless eyes. Snowflakes dusted her hair, and her lips were a pale icy blue.

In the dream, Caine cradled her head in his arms as her blood dripped from the door frame. The blood froze into crimson icicles that clung to the mangled metal door. A cold white mist engulfed the wrecked car. Shadowy, translucent figures surrounded them, hanging just out of sight in the swirling haze.

Shhh, it's all right. This is dauntaimu, downtime...

He heard her voice whispering in his ear, even though her lips remained still.

The dream had repeated throughout the night. After tossing and turning for a few hours, he finally gave up and turned on the TV. He kept the volume off and just stared at the images on the tiny screen until it was time to leave.

Now, after catching the morning train to Tomamu, the dream had returned. Only this time, the face kept changing. Gaya, Sue Mi, Kanako...

No, not Kanako, he reminded himself. *Rise...*

Two of the women he barely knew. The third he had never met. And yet they were all connected to him. All connected to Byakko, somehow.

Then it was Rebecca's face he saw. He felt an icy touch on his shoulder. Looking up, he saw Sean standing in the haze behind him, his face just as pale and lifeless as the woman in his arms.

It was then that he woke up.

As he stared out the window at the bleak, endless white landscape, he felt his burner phone vibrate against his leg.

Pulling it from his pocket, he checked the screen and saw he had missed a call.

In Japan, it was considered rude to talk on one's cell phone in public, especially on trains and buses. So he left his seat and exited the car. There was no one else in the connecting corridor between cars, so he tapped the screen and returned the call.

After three rings, there was a clicking sound, followed by a series of quiet beeps. Then, a woman's voice answered the phone.

Rebecca...

'Hey,' she said. 'How's your trip going? Did you catch up on those K-dramas I told you about?'

Caine was so glad to hear her voice that, for a moment, he forgot the proper response. He blinked, clearing his mind.

'Yeah, I did,' he finally replied, his voice hoarse and scratchy. 'I preferred *Boys Over Flowers*. I think I've had enough of revenge.'

'Are you all right?' Rebecca asked. 'You sound exhausted.'

'Had an encounter with the local wildlife,' he said, staring out the window as a flock of crows took flight from the branches of a Japanese oak tree.

'I don't even want to know what that means,' she sighed. 'Tom, I need you to get back here. I've tried to be patient, but—'

'Wait,' he said, cutting her off. 'I think what I'm involved with here is connected to what happened in Seoul.'

'What? How do you mean?'

Caine paused, gathering his thoughts. 'I spoke to someone, an... asset. They saw Chan Tae Young here, in Sapporo. A few days ago.'

'That doesn't match his known itinerary,' Rebecca said. 'But he's faked travel records before, to slip away from surveillance.'

'There's more,' Caine said. 'Chan was meeting with a yakuza gangster. A man named Hideo Torazama. He goes by another name in the underworld. Byakko. It means White Tiger.'

He heard her soft breathing through the static. 'North Korea has a history of working with organized crime groups,' she said, her voice quiet and thoughtful. 'This asset of yours... Can you bring them in for questioning?'

'She's dead.' Caine spat the words from his mouth. 'Byakko's men killed her. They nearly got me too.'

He heard Rebecca tapping on keys. 'Oh my God... I'm seeing reports now about a gunfight in the streets. You drove through the Sapporo Underground?'

'It's better if you don't know the details.'

'Tom, if Maddison finds out you're still operational, you're going to get burned. And this time I won't be able to—'

Caine glanced through the window into the next car, making sure no one was listening to their conversation.

'Rebecca, look. The only person who can link Chan and Byakko together is on her own here, in the mountains of Japan. I have a... I don't know, call it a gut feeling. Something big is about to go down, and Kanako Natsuki is part of it.'

Rebecca sighed. 'I have some intel that might corroborate your theory.'

'What's that?' Caine said, his voice taking on a sharper tone.

'The woman you encountered in Seoul, the one in the market? Facial ID software clocked someone matching her appearance, disembarking at New Chitose Airport. Her passport was in the name of Jiwoo Park, but that's probably a cover. She's a blank slate, as far as we can tell.'

'She must be working with Byakko, somehow,' Caine said, thinking back to the chase through Sapporo. 'You said yourself, the North Koreans have worked with the yakuza before.'

'Yeah, but never this directly,' Rebecca replied. 'That's a pretty big leap.'

'Byakko found me within minutes, in a city of nearly two million people. He had to be using drones or he had someone hacking traffic cams. Either way, it felt more like an intelligence operation than the usual gangster tactics.'

'Something this so-called Unit 99 could easily pull off,' Rebecca said. 'Where are you now?'

Caine didn't answer.

'Tom, for Christ's sake, just—'

'See if you can find anything linking Chan to a place called Tomamu. According to my contact, he was talking about it with Kanako before she went missing.'

'So that's where you're going now?'

'Like I said, it's better if you don't know. And send me everything you have on this Jiwoo Park.'

Rebecca took a deep breath. He heard her clicking a pen. 'Fine,' she said. 'But if this lead pans out, you read me in, and this op goes on the books. Our relationship doesn't change the fact that I'm your boss. I don't need you to protect me. I can fight my own battles.'

Caine grinned. 'No arguments here, Director.'

'Good. I'll be in touch.'

She hung up.

Caine pocketed his phone and returned to his seat. He watched the blur of the snow-swept mountains speed by as the train chugged through the countryside. Occasionally, they would streak past a dilapidated wooden shack, or a frozen waterfall, shimmering in beams of sunlight that pierced the gray clouds above. There was a fairy-tale-like beauty to the stark, empty landscape.

Then he thought of Byakko, and his strange, cat-like eyes. In fairy tales, monsters lived in the woods.

As the train carried him deeper into the frozen forest, he felt the skin on his neck tingle. He had left Sapporo behind, but he couldn't shake the feeling that he was heading straight into the tiger's den. He'd told Byakko that he didn't believe in fairy tales. And that was true.

But he had slain plenty of monsters in his life.

28

CHIBA, JAPAN

Koichi squinted across the table at Mariko. The woman returned his stare, her dark brown eyes betraying no sign of weakness or emotion. She didn't even blink.

The old gangster furrowed his brow and sighed. He tossed his cards face down on the table.

'Fold,' he muttered. 'I've played cards with killers who've put more men in the dirt than I can count. But I've never seen a poker face as good as yours.'

Mariko glanced down as she scooped up the cards and reshuffled the deck, the faintest hint of a smile on her lips. 'Try working in a government bureaucracy as a woman for a few years. You quickly learn to hide your true feelings.'

Koichi nodded. '*Hai*, I can imagine. I wouldn't last five minutes in a place like that.'

Mariko shrugged. 'Well, I lasted five years. So I hope you're prepared to pay up.'

As Mariko dealt them each a new hand, the old man glanced around the room. They were staying in a cheap, run-down love hotel in Chiba, just outside Tokyo. After escaping the hospital, Mariko had switched vehicles, parking her White Acura SUV in a private lot, and hiding Koichi in the rear of a battered tatami delivery van.

It was usually about an hour's drive from the Tokyo metro area to Chiba. But Mariko took them on a complex winding route, merging on and off freeways, doubling back onto surface streets, and making frequent stops at Lawson and other convenience stores. Once she was certain they were not being followed, she continued along the normal route, taking the Express Route Number 9 the rest of the way to Chiba city.

Chiba was close to Narita Airport, and although nowhere as popular and crowded as Tokyo, it was still a bustling metropolis. Finding them, or the dilapidated love hotel where they were hiding, would be no small task in a city of over a million people.

As Koichi examined his cards, the windows rattled and a low rumble shook the paper-thin walls. The room's pink velvet curtains were drawn, but through a torn hole in the fabric, Koichi could see the blinking lights of the SkyTrain flash as the monorail screeched past the hotel room.

'So what's the deal with you and Caine-san?' Koichi asked. 'You two an item?'

Mariko laughed. 'You sound like my grandmother. I swear, you yakuza guys are worse than a bunch of *obasan*... You love your gossip.'

The old gangster shrugged. 'Just trying to make conversation. You look different from how I remember you. You seem happier. Not that anyone could tell from that damned blank expression of yours.'

Mariko tossed a plastic poker chip into the center of the table. 'Do you want to talk or do you want to play? I call.'

As Koichi examined his hand, another faint smile played upon Mariko's lips. 'And for your information, I am happy.'

'I knew it,' Koichi said, wagging a finger. 'You're happy he called you, right?'

She shook her head, laughing more. '*Damare*, shut up! It's not like that. Tom and I let off some steam once. We had some fun, nothing more. He's a good friend. Well, as much as a man like that can be friends with anyone. Let's just say we understand each other.'

Koichi discarded two cards, and Mariko dealt him new ones.

'He has someone in his life, and he's happy, I think. I am glad for him.' She gave a little shrug. 'And me, I have this...'

Koichi looked up, examining the shabby little room. 'A love hotel in Chiba? I'd say you got the short end of the stick.'

Mariko rolled her eyes. 'No, *baka*. My job. I help people now. Really help them. No commissioners or department heads breathing down my neck, telling me what I can do, or fretting about what might look bad for the department. You know, 80 percent of my clients are women? Victims of abuse. Someone like me... I'm the only one they can turn to. I help them disappear, start a new life.'

Koichi gave her a thoughtful look. Then he grabbed a beer can from the table. Droplets of condensation rolled down the silver metal sides. He took a sip of beer, licked his lips, and sighed.

'There's an old proverb,' he said, glancing up at Mariko. '*Akusai wa hyaku-nen no fusaku*. A bad wife spells a hundred years of bad harvest.' He ran his fingers through his wispy gray hair and sighed. 'Me? I've always found the opposite to be true. My father was not a good man, certainly not a good husband. And my mother... She reaped a bad harvest, all right.'

'Was he a good father, at least?' Mariko asked in a quiet voice, peering over her cards at the old man sitting across from her.

Koichi shrugged. 'Hard to say. I'm not exactly a son to be proud of.'

'Tom says you're doing all this, risking your life, to protect your daughter?'

Koichi nodded. '*Hai*. Funny, eh? I'm not much of a father either, I suppose. My daughter, Kanako, she doesn't even know I exist. And yet, I'd do almost anything to protect her.'

'Then she's lucky to have you. Whether she knows it or not,' Mariko replied. She laid her cards down. 'Royal flush.'

Koichi tossed his cards down in the pile. '*Sugoi!* Unbelievable! All right, give me the cards. This time, I shuffle!'

Mariko gathered the cards up from the table. Suddenly, she froze as someone knocked on the door.

'Hurry,' she whispered. 'Get in the bedroom.'

'Relax,' Koichi said, dealing himself new cards from the deck. 'It's just the kid. I texted him when we left the hospital.'

'What if he was followed?' Mariko hissed.

Koichi held up the pistol he had taken from the hospital. 'I hope he was. Then I can stop hiding and start shooting.'

Mariko grabbed her own pistol from under the table, a small Glock 27 chambered in .40 S&W. She stalked toward the door, holding the gun in a two-handed grip. She avoided standing in front of the peephole, instead taking a position just to the left of the door frame.

The knock sounded again.

'Who is it?' Mariko shouted. 'What do you want?'

'*Oyabun?* It's me, Junko!' a voice called out.

Mariko opened the door. Junko entered the room carrying a plastic Family Mart shopping bag. Mariko checked the corridor, then shut the door behind him.

Junko grinned at Koichi and held up the bag. '*Oyabun*, I brought you cigarettes, and some—'

Before he could finish his sentence, Mariko grabbed his jacket, swung him around, and threw him up against the wall. She jabbed the barrel of her pistol into his spine.

'Don't move!' she commanded. 'Spread your legs. Hold your arms out to the sides. Drop the bag on the floor.'

'I'd do as the lady says,' Koichi grunted. 'She used to be a cop. Doesn't think too highly of us yakuza.'

'*Daijoubu desu*, okay!' the young man shouted. He dropped the plastic bag and spread his legs. Mariko kicked the bag aside, then frisked him for weapons. She removed an HK pistol from his waistband and a folding knife from his trouser pocket.

'Who the hell is this woman?' Junko grunted, as Mariko continued to frisk him.

'Never mind that,' Koichi demanded, standing from the table. He grabbed the plastic bag off the floor and pulled out a pack of Seven Stars menthol cigarettes. The pack was already open, so he removed a cigarette and stuck it between his lips.

He flicked open a zippo lighter and touched the flame to the cigarette's tip. 'Give me the news, kid,' he muttered. 'Good, bad, all of it.'

'Tetsuo's telling the other men that you're dead!' Junko exclaimed. 'He says Goro's people attacked you at the hospital. He's making a power play, says the group needs new leadership.'

'Let me guess,' Koichi chuckled. 'He nominated himself for the job?'

Mariko finished her search and released the young man's arm. She stepped back, dropping the gun and knife on the table.

'If he knew about the hit at the hospital, then—' she began.

'Then he must have sent those idiots to kill me,' Koichi said, finishing her sentence. 'At least I know who's gunning for me.'

Koichi's cell phone vibrated on the table. He glanced at the screen, then picked it up.

'*Moshi moshi*,' he grunted, glancing up at Mariko and Junko.

'It's me,' Caine answered. 'Are you at the safe house in Chiba?'

Koichi glanced at the others in the room. '*Hai*, I am. I'm here with Murase-san and Junko-kun.'

'Put me on speaker.'

Koichi tapped the screen, then set the phone down on the table.

'Tom, are you all right?' Mariko asked, leaning over the table. 'Things got heated at the hospital. I ditched my phone to be safe.'

'I'm fine,' Caine replied, his voice crackling through the tiny speaker. 'I had a run-in with a yakuza in Sapporo. Calls himself Byakko.'

'Second time I've heard that name tonight,' Koichi replied. 'He's working with Tetsuo. They sent men to the hospital to finish me off. Don't know why he wants me dead. I never heard of the guy.'

'His real name is Hideo Torazama,' Caine replied. 'And trust me, you'd remember if you crossed paths. His eyes are—'

'Like a cat?' Koichi said. He squinted and rubbed his temple as he blew a puff of smoke into the room. 'Torazama... Now there's a name I remember.'

'What do you know about him?' Caine asked.

'Hideo was a punk kid from Otaru. That's up north, a little town on the coast. His father used to be with the Koda Kai. We, uh, rumbled a few times. Back when Isato and I were climbing the ranks of the Yoshizawa clan. But Hideo's family was *zainichi*... immigrants, mixed blood.'

'Japanese soldiers and their Korean wives, stranded when the empire fell,' Caine replied.

'*Hai*, just so,' Koichi said. 'As I recall, Hideo was some kind of kid genius. His father wanted him to become a shogi prodigy. Made him play against the best shogi masters he could find. If Hideo lost a match, he made him sleep in the ice shed overnight. Oh, and he had the kid wear contact lenses to cover those *kimyou* eyes of his.'

'I could see how they might unnerve an opponent.'

Koichi chuckled. 'Yeah, well, it didn't matter. Hell, I've got nothing against Koreans. Probably have some Korean blood in me myself; lots of yakuza do. But in those days, no way was a *zainichi* kid going to be accepted into polite society, if you know what I mean.'

'What happened to him?' Caine said, his voice crackling with static.

Koichi scratched his nose. 'Well, this was back in the eighties. Way I remember it, there was a big push by the Japanese government to force the *zainichi* out. But after the Korean war, South Korea wasn't in any shape to take in refugees. So that left the North. Rumor was, the Japanese government was in cahoots with a group called "Chongryon". They had ties to North Korea. Told the *zainichi* a paradise awaited them in Kim's communist utopia.'

'Must have been a rude awakening,' Caine replied.

'Heh, yeah, right. Instead of a paradise, they got poverty, disease, and forced labor. Hell, things were worse for them there than they were in Japan. Once word got out, Chongryon ran out of volunteers. So their contacts in the Japanese government, ugh, encouraged the remaining *zainichi* to get the hell out. Unofficially, of course.'

'That's terrible,' Mariko said, leaning over the table. 'Was Hideo's father taken?'

Koichi nodded. 'A rival in the Koda Kai sold him out. Framed him for a murder and led the cops right to his door. They dragged his ass to a refugee ship and sent him on his way. Grabbed his wife too. Probably got a kickback for every body they rounded up. But somehow, in all the commotion, little Hideo got left behind.'

Mariko gasped. 'That's awful. He was just a child?'

Koichi glanced up at the ceiling, thinking. 'Mmm, guess he would have been around twelve years old. Another Koda Kai boss felt sorry for him, took the kid in. That's where he got the Torazama name from. So overnight, Hideo went from a shogi prodigy to a yakuza punk. A few years after that, someone killed the guy who was taking care of him. Hideo tracked the bastard down, slit his throat in front of a whole *izakaya* full of customers. Didn't take long for the cops to round him up and throw him in jail.'

Koichi shook his head, then took a long sip of beer. 'As far as I knew, he died in Fuchū Prison. Someone knifed him in the shower, right around the time I first met you, Caine-san.'

'Believe me, Torazama-san is very much alive,' Caine replied. 'I think he's working with the North Koreans. His men treat him like he's some kind of prophet, or god.'

Koichi nodded. 'Fucking *baka* morons. I suppose we yakuza love our superstitions. But what does all this have to do with Kanako?'

'Torazama owns a club in Sapporo. Kanako was working there and I think she saw something she wasn't supposed to.'

'Did he... Did he hurt her? Is she—'

'No,' Caine said, cutting him off. 'As far as I know, she's alive. A friend of hers thought she might be in a town called Tomamu.'

Koichi coughed. 'Tomamu? What the hell is she doing at a ski resort?'

'That's what I'm trying to find out,' Caine replied. 'It looks like this all might be connected to an investigation my own people are working on.'

Junko peered out the curtains as he took a drag from his cigarette. His eyes opened wide with surprise. A pair of black SUVs were blocking the street outside, their taillights flashing.

'Uh, *Oyabun*?' Junko muttered, backing away from the window. 'I think you need to see this.'

Mariko peered through the curtains. 'They found us!' She glared at Junko. 'Were you followed?'

He shook his head. 'No, I swear!'

'His car,' Caine said, his voice crackling from the phone on the table. 'Byakko was able to track me in Sapporo. I think his people hacked the traffic cams. Junko's Lexus is flashy, easy to spot.'

Mariko grabbed the phone. 'Tom, we have to move. I'll contact you once we're safe.'

'Go,' he said. 'And be careful.'

'*Jaa ne*... See you soon.'

She hung up the phone and slung a duffel bag over her shoulder. 'There's a fire escape at the end of the hall. Ogawa-san, can you—'

Koichi nodded. 'I'm an old man, but I'm not an invalid. I'll make it.' He glanced over at Junko. 'Better give the kid his piece back.'

Mariko glared at Junko for a moment, then handed him the HK pistol. 'You make a mistake like that again, I'll shoot you myself. *Wakarimasu ka*?'

The young man's nostrils flared and his lips curled into a snarl. But a second later, the angry look melted away. He looked down and shuffled his feet. 'I understand. It won't happen again.'

Mariko patted his shoulder. 'Good. Let's go.'

She listened at the door for a second, then opened it and stalked out into the corridor, gun raised.

The three of them hurried to the fire exit at the end of the hall.

29

TOMAMU, JAPAN

Tomamu Station was little more than a small main building and an enclosed walkway leading over the tracks. A thick layer of snow blanketed the building's roof, and powdery flakes filled the air with a milky haze.

A single road ran past the station, a strip of pavement flanked on either side by walls of snow piled several feet high. To the south, a steep hill rose in the distance, more snow and blackened trees, as far as the eye could see. There was no town or city to speak of within walking distance. The only vehicles parked outside the station's waiting area were shuttle buses, leading to various hotels and ski resorts.

Now what?

The snow and wind blasted his face as he exited the train. Tomamu was farther north than Sapporo, and it was noticeably colder once he stepped onto the platform. A chill ran through his body, despite his warm clothes. He hefted his bag over his shoulder and trudged through the thick snow, making his way up a rickety flight of stairs and through the walkway that led over the tracks.

Once he emerged on the other side of the platform, he followed the crowd through a sliding glass door into a small, heated waiting room. Most of the crowd exited to the parking lot, where they loaded into the waiting shuttle buses. Steam wafted from the vehicles' engines as the passengers filed on, one by one.

Caine grabbed a stack of flyers from a rusting metal rack and sat on a steel bench. He pretended to flip through them as the remaining passengers shuffled past him. The last tour bus disappeared into the snow, and Caine was alone in the station. Outside, the wind picked up, howling louder. It whipped particles of snow and ice off the ground into a swirling haze.

One flyer advertised an Ice Village at the nearby Hoshino Ski resort. The village was built every year to celebrate the winter season. Workers built it from ice blocks and geodesic domes. Its grounds included an ice-skating rink, a ramen shop, a boutique hotel, and even a cocktail bar.

As Caine examined the flyer, his phone buzzed in his pocket. He pulled it out, hoping it was Mariko, confirming they were safe. But instead, it was a text from Rebecca:

> No hotel reservations under Kanako Natsuki or Chan Tae Young within a twenty-mile radius of Tomamu.

Caine sighed and stretched his legs. Finding Kanako without an address would be next to impossible, even in a remote town like this.

A second message popped up on the screen.

> Found one reservation at a campsite called 'Glamping Stay' under the name Yi Jun Kim.

Caine stared at the screen, thinking.

Yi Jun Kim was a common South Korean name, and an alias used by one of Chan's assistants. They had booked hotels under that name when traveling with Chan, both for rendezvous with his mistresses, and clandestine meetings with his North Korean handlers.

Standing, Caine examined the rack of flyers until he found one advertising 'Glamping Stay'. It was roughly a twenty-minute drive from the station, and they provided a free shuttle bus to guests.

Looking up, he checked the schedule on the wall. The next train would arrive at the station in two hours. And with it, a fresh round of shuttles and buses.

Caine sighed and sat back down. He leaned back and closed his eyes. For now, there was nothing to do but wait. Outside, the wind continued to howl. Snow clung to the windows, blotting out the frozen landscape that lay beyond the glass.

* * *

A few hours later, Caine was sitting on a fur-covered lounger inside a white geodesic dome. The spacious interior of the dome was heated and looked more like a luxurious hotel suite than a camping tent.

The structure sat in a snow-covered field, surrounded by a dozen identical white domes. The field was freshly plowed, and a wall of piled snow surrounded the campground on all sides, blocking the view of the nearby road.

A panoramic window filled one side of the dome, giving Caine a view of the sun as it sank behind the distant mountains. The sky was dark now, with a few fiery traces of orange and pink lining the snow-swept horizon. Pitch-black darkness soon engulfed the last glimmers of daylight.

Caine grabbed a pair of tongs and dropped a paper-thin sliver of beef into a pot of boiling broth. Each dome came with a portable stove, and the staff stocked the refrigerator with local meats and vegetables. Everything one would need for a satisfying hotpot meal.

Caine removed the meat and deposited it on top of a bowl of rice. He ate with chopsticks, savoring the perfectly marbled wagyu beef. Then he washed it down with a sip of ice-cold Yebisu beer.

Earlier, at check-in, Caine paid for several nights up-front in cash. The owner gave him a wary look when he wrote the name 'Patrick Bailey' in the registry. At first, he assigned Caine a dome in the southwest corner of the campsite. Caine pointed to the map, insisting on a different dome. One that offered a view of Yi Jun's tent, as well as the spectacular sunset.

The owner shrugged, then handed him a new set of keys.

In the time he had spent inside the luxurious tent, Caine had seen no one come or go from Yi Jun's dome. Once, he walked the grounds, pretending to marvel at the heavy snowfall. The structure's interior lights were on, but Yi Jun had drawn the curtains, covering the windows. He couldn't see if anyone was inside, but there were no fresh tracks leading from the tent.

Caine dipped another slice of beef into the boiling broth. As he ate, he monitored Yi Jun's tent, watching for any sign of movement. His restless thoughts turned to Sean.

Caine had risked his life to rescue the young man from China, where corrupt actors within the NSA had plotted his assassination in order to derail a prisoner exchange. Years ago, he had promised Jack that he would look out for the young man. But despite that, on the few times he had spent time with Sean since returning from China, he felt profoundly uneasy in his presence.

After years on the run, Caine had to admit he had still not fully adjusted back to his life in the States. Friends, loved ones, stability... These things all seemed like strange luxuries when, only a few years earlier, his survival depended on anonymity. No attachments, nothing to hold him down, nothing to stop him from running at a moment's notice.

Rebecca... The killer's voice, the cold, logical whisper he could never fully silence, echoed through his mind. *Remember what happened to Rebecca...*

He stared at the icicles outside the dome's window. Droplets of water slid down the long, shimmering ice daggers.

After his betrayal, he had left Rebecca behind, cut her off for her own protection. And the second he re-entered her life, danger and violence had followed in his wake. She had endured multiple attacks on her life, one of which had left her in a wheelchair, unable to walk. Unable to run...

And Sean... Did a similar fate await him as well? Caine couldn't help but wonder if the best thing he could do for Jack's son was to keep him at arm's length. To stay away, and hope the specter of violence lurking in the shadows of his past remained there.

The door to the tent outside his window swung open. Caine snapped to attention, banishing the dark thoughts to the back of his mind. He turned off the burner, plopped another piece of beef into his mouth, and finished his beer.

A shadowy figure dressed in warm, heavy clothes exited the dome and trudged through the snow.

Caine threw on his ski parka and gloves. Then he exited his own tent and followed in the other man's footsteps. The wind howled and bit at Caine's skin. Snow filled the dark sky, lit up by the campground lights.

The two men marched through the swirling haze, heading for the distant lights of another shuttle bus.

30

SPRING VALLEY, WASHINGTON DC, USA

Special Agent Zavala glanced out the window as she drove her Volvo sedan down the tree-lined road. Along either side of the smooth, winding street, houses crouched behind ivy-covered brick walls and wrought-iron fences. Although their architecture varied from sleek modern structures of metal and glass to sprawling colonial brick mansions, the homes shared several elements in common.

They were all set back from the road, partially hidden by both natural and man-made barriers. They were all larger than the average American home, with most being three stories high and several thousand square feet. And they were all expensive. The median home price in the upscale neighborhood was 3.7 million dollars.

But Zavala knew the area had a darker side to its history as well. Secrets lay buried beneath the rolling hills and tree-lined parks, things that the neighborhood's residents probably didn't know, or didn't care to discuss.

During WWI, long before Spring Valley earned its status as a desirable suburb, the land had served as a chemical weapons testing ground for the US Army. From time to time, construction in the area unearthed shells laced with mustard gas, arsenic, and other deadly agents.

In the thirties, the land was developed for residential use. And the neighborhood prohibited home ownership by African American and Jewish residents. Richard Nixon, and other famous residents, signed pacts vowing never to sell their homes to those of Black or Semitic descent.

It didn't matter how nice the streets were, she thought. *People were people. And you had to take the good with the bad.*

As she turned onto Glenbrook Road, another house came into view. The brown wood and stucco building looked like a cross between a traditional American ranch house and an Asian pagoda, and icicles hung from its steep, sloped roof. A Korean flag fluttered in the breeze, hanging from a pole that rose above the snow-covered lawn.

A crowd of people gathered outside the residence's wrought-iron fence. The mob ignored the steely-eyed glares of the security guards patrolling the home's perimeter. They marched along the sidewalk carrying picket signs, their breath misting in the cold winter air as they chanted and shouted at the people within the fence.

'Go home and take your K-Pox with you!'

'You're the disease. God is the cure!'

'K-pop sucks. K-Pox blows!'

A pair of DC metro police cars were parked down the street. Uniformed officers waved traffic past the demonstration.

Zavala shook her head as she left the protestors behind in her rearview mirror. It had not occurred to her that Carter Rowan lived so close to the South Korean ambassador's residence. It would almost be funny. If not for the fact that protestors like the ones surrounding the house might think Rowan's conspiratorial rantings, and the president's refusal to condemn them, were a tacit approval to take matters into their own hands.

'The more things change, the more they stay the same,' she muttered to herself.

She turned down a narrow street leading to the gated community of West-over Place. As she approached the security gate, more protestors filled the streets, marching back and forth. Unlike the group outside the ambassador's house, these people were a mix of ethnicities... White, Black, Asian, Latino. They carried signs that read, 'Hate is the real disease!' Another proclaimed in big bubble letters, 'Rowan is a liar!'

Zavala slowed down and honked the horn. A few members of the crowd gave her dirty looks and shouted insults at her, but they cleared a path as she approached the security booth. The sound of broken glass echoed through the air. Zavala turned and saw several protestors flinging empty bottles at the metal fence.

The private security guard manning the booth leaned out the window. 'Hey,' he shouted. 'This is private property! Get your asses off the street or I'm calling the cops!'

He turned and gave Zavala a suspicious look. 'What do you want?'

She opened her window and showed the man her FBI badge. 'Special Agent Alejandra Zavala. I need to see a resident of yours. Carter Rowan.'

'Yeah?' the guard replied, his eyes still focused on the protestors marching along the sidewalk. 'You got a warrant?'

'I don't need a warrant to ask to see him,' she replied. '*Mira*, look... Are you going to give me a hard time about this?'

He passed her badge back through the window. More bottles shattered against the fence. The guard muttered a curse, then slammed his palm down on the gate controls. The gate swung open.

'Fine. But if Rowan complains, you'll have to leave.'

'You don't think he'll be happy to see me?' Zavala replied, flashing the guard a smile.

'That guy isn't happy to see anyone,' the guard grunted. He punched a number into his cell phone as Zavala drove through the gate.

Probably calling the police, she thought. *Which means I better make this quick.*

Within the gated community, brick townhouses and condos lined the streets. Narrow walkways and paths wove between the densely packed buildings. Most of the townhouses were three stories tall and built in the Georgian style. They reminded Zavala of the famous row houses in San Francisco, only much less colorful. She parked her SUV at the curb and walked to Rowan's condo.

A short flight of concrete steps led up to the townhouse's black lacquered door. She rang the bell. Buzzing and hammering echoed from the house next door, which shared a wall with Rowan's residence. The intercom crackled to life, but she could barely hear it over the construction noise.

'Who is it?' a high-pitched, nasal voice asked through the speaker.

'Mr. Rowan, I'm from the FBI. I was hoping I could ask you a few questions. I promise I won't take up much of your time.'

The speaker was silent for a few seconds. The whine of a power drill came from the neighboring house.

'What's this about?' Rowan asked, his voice crackling with static.

'We're concerned about your safety, Mr. Rowan. There's a mob outside, and I wanted to see if there had been any threats or suspicious behavior you noticed recently.'

'Oh. One second.'

She heard the rattle of a chain and the click of an electronic smart lock.

'Come in, the door's open.'

Zavala glanced around, but aside from the construction next door, the neighborhood seemed quiet. There were no other pedestrians on the walkway. She opened the door and entered the townhouse.

The foyer was clean and modern, with white walls and polished wood floors. To her right, the entrance braced off into a large, open living area. A gray sofa faced a wide-screen TV mounted above a white fireplace. Leather Herman Miller chairs flanked an oval coffee table.

Ahead of her, a short flight of stairs led to an elevated dining area. The kitchen filled the rear of the house. It was dim inside, despite the floor-to-ceiling windows in the kitchen and living room. Beyond the glass panels, the overcast winter sky cast little light, and the snow covering the backyard seemed to take on a deathly gray pallor.

Rowan himself stood at the top of the stairs, a few feet above Zavala. He wore faded tan khakis and a pink Oxford shirt beneath a blue cashmere sweater. Felt slippers covered his feet, and Zavala spotted the glint of a gold watch on his wrist... She recognized it as a Rolex Datejust, a popular watch with wealthy politicians and celebrities alike.

'Please come in. Sorry about the racket.' Rowan sipped from a glass of clear liquid, garnished with a slice of lime. 'Between those lunatics outside and my neighbor's construction, it's been a real mess around here. Pathetic.'

The construction noises next door continued, muted through the house's walls. Power drills buzzed, and hammers pounded a staccato beat.

'Thank you for seeing me,' Zavala said, holding out her badge as she advanced up the stairs. 'Sounds like quite a commotion. Though I imagine a man in your position would be used to such things.'

Rowan gave her ID a cursory glance, then chuckled. 'Truth be told, I'd be worried if they didn't show up. In my business, if you aren't pissing people off, you must be doing something wrong. Here, follow me.'

Rowan led her to the kitchen table. Letters, postcards, and scraps of paper covered the wooden surface.

'This week's haul,' Rowan said. 'Hate mail. Bunch of radical lunatics who think I'm a racist just because I dare to tell the truth.'

Zavala pulled out a pen from her jacket and slid one of the letters aside. 'The truth?' she said, scanning the letter's contents. 'What do you mean?'

Carter laughed, a surprisingly high-pitched giggle. 'Well, you know. Isn't it obvious?'

Zavala squinted as she continued reading the letter. 'I'm sure you have a better pulse on it than I do.'

Rowan shrugged. 'Right now, it's this Korea thing. But every day, people whine and complain about America's problems. Not enough jobs, not enough money, not enough entitlements. But every day we import five thousand new problems, instead of fixing the ones we've already got.'

'I assume you're talking about illegal immigration?' Zavala asked.

'That's a big part of it,' Rowan said, taking another sip of his drink. 'It terrifies me. I mean, at some point, when do we wake up and realize this isn't our country anymore?' He shot her a quick glance, as if noticing her for the first time. Another high-pitched giggle escaped his lips. 'No offense, Ms. Zavala. I'm not implying—'

'This note here isn't a threat,' Zavala said, interrupting him. She tapped the paper with the end of her pen. 'It's a letter from an Asian American mom. She said after your last broadcast, her daughter was assaulted at school. She's not even Korean, she's Vietnamese.'

'Oh, I didn't read that one,' Rowan replied. 'But there are plenty more that are clearly threats. I told all this to the agents that came out yesterday. I said they could take the letters with them, but they—'

'If these threats are related to your story about Korea, have you considered they could be linked to your source?'

'Well, it's a little more complicated than that,' Carter said.

Zavala crossed her arms and narrowed her eyes, observing him as she spoke. 'I'm afraid I don't know much about TV. What do you mean?'

Rowan gave another brief laugh. 'Well, first of all, I don't do TV. Not anymore. I'm what you call an "online influencer". I don't work for a network. I work for myself. Or, in this case, an online media collective.'

'Online media collective,' Zavala repeated, blinking behind her glasses. 'What is that, exactly?'

'Welcome to the twenty-first century,' he replied with a giggle. 'It's kind of like the digital equivalent of a network. A group that works with multiple creators to produce and distribute content.'

Zavala nodded. 'Got it. So the group you worked with on this story was...'

'I believe they were called Credo-com. Based in Tennessee. And yes, they came to me with some ideas for the story. Fantastic deal, I got exclusive rights for my channel. All I had to do was allow them to repurpose some clips for their own use.'

'But you checked their sources, right?'

'I mean,' Carter began. He paused for a moment. 'Well, the case count is all over the news. It's public record, I didn't make it up.'

Zavala peered at him over the rims of her glasses. 'But the files linking these cases to South Korea, and the evidence that their Ministry of Health and Welfare was under-reporting cases... That all came from these Credo-com people?'

'Yes.' Carter nodded. 'Exactly.'

'And you verified their information before you ran the story?'

Carter tilted his head and squinted at her. 'Well, I mean... It wasn't just me. Everyone was running this story, it was all over the internet... Look, I believe everything I said. The American taxpayer has a right to know they're funding the defense of a country who—'

He stopped mid-sentence and stared at her. 'Oh... Now I see. You're not here about some threat at all, are you?'

'Mr. Rowan, I—'

The man gathered up the letters and swept them off the table. He shoved past her and paced down the stairs into the living room.

'Your field director doesn't know you're here, does he? Well, you can bet that's going to change. Now get your goddamn ass out of my house!'

Zavala followed Rowan into the living room. He opened a chestnut armoire and stuffed the letters inside, then pulled a cell phone from his pocket. He tapped the screen and held the phone to his ear.

'This is harassment, and I swear I...' His voice trailed off. He removed the phone from his ear and checked the screen. 'No reception,' he muttered. 'Are you doing this? Jamming my phone?' He paced closer to the TV, holding up his phone as he tried to find a signal.

'No, of course not,' Zavala replied. 'Look, Mr. Rowan, I think—'

Zavala suddenly noticed the construction noise next door had stopped. She frowned and checked her phone. She too had zero bars, despite having perfect reception in the area a few minutes ago.

She turned her head, noticing movement in the front yard. A team of men filed out of the house next door. They all wore blue jumpsuits, white caps, and black Prohear headsets.

Zavala had seen similar headgear before. Such protection was normally worn by shooters, to protect their ears from the deafening roar of gunshots.

She drew her pistol, a compact Glock G19 MOS. 'Mr. Rowan, get away from—'

Kablam!

The sound of the first blast was deafening. A series of explosions rippled through the adjoining wall, one after another. Fragments of glass and plaster tore through the air like shrapnel.

Zavala dived behind the wall separating the living area from the foyer. A wooden beam punched through the drywall, missing her head by inches. A metal pipe scraped against her arm, tearing the sleeve of her jacket. Plaster dust filled the air, swirling around her in a smoky haze.

Choking and gasping for breath, Zavala staggered to her feet. She peered around the corner, struggling to see through the swirling dust. Rowan was buried under a pile of debris. She ran over to him. Something sparkled in the dusty haze... The gold watch on his wrist.

Kneeling, she felt for a pulse. There was none.

The frigid air from outside cleared the dust. She peered through the shattered windows. The men in white jumpsuits were filing out of the courtyard. Raising her pistol, she opened fire.

Her gun roared twice, and the man in the rear dropped to the ground. Zavala charged the broken window, leaping through the opening and rolling into a crouch on the snow outside.

Two of the other men took cover behind a stone arch leading out of the courtyard. They returned fire. Bullets kicked up puffs of snow near Zavala's feet.

'FBI!' Zavala shouted. 'Drop your weapons, now!'

Another hail of gunfire cracked through the air. Zavala rolled again, taking cover behind the corpse sprawled across the snow. She heard bullets whine overhead, felt the impact as they thudded into the dead man's flesh.

Then they stopped.

Zavala peered over the body. The two remaining men broke cover and continued down the walkway. She leaped to her feet and raced after them. Her panting breath left puffs of mist in her wake.

She took cover behind another stone column as the two men sprinted toward the parking lot. The security guard exited his booth and charged toward them.

'Hey,' he shouted. 'What the hell is going on here?'

One man turned and raised his weapon. It was a pistol of some kind, though Zavala couldn't tell the make from her hiding spot.

Holding her pistol in a two-handed grip, she swung out from behind the pillar and fired again. The echo of her twin shots thundered through the cold winter air. The man holding the gun fell to the ground.

The security guard froze, panicked by the sudden gunfire. An engine rumbled to life, and tires squealed at the far end of the lot.

Zavala saw a white van loop around the parked cars, barreling toward the exit.

The security guard stood directly in the vehicle's path, staring at the body on the pavement.

'Move!' Zavala shouted. Breaking cover, she charged toward the lot. The man took a step backward but remained stunned by the sudden explosion of violence. The mob outside shouted louder. More bottles shattered against the fence.

Zavala ran faster, pumping her arms and driving her legs into the snow. She vaulted the interior fence and landed on her feet. The white van raced closer, barreling toward the security gate.

Zavala reached the guard and grabbed his arm, dragging him back to the security booth. Together, they dived through the open door and hit the floor. The van struck the gate, snapping the wooden barrier clean off. The passenger side of the vehicle scraped against the booth, shattering the tiny cubicle's glass windows and tearing the open door off its hinges.

She locked eyes with the terrified guard lying prone beneath her. 'Are you okay?'

He nodded. 'Yeah. I mean, I think so.'

Zavala was already moving, rolling off him and charging out of the booth. She stood in the driveway, aiming at the van as it tore down the street.

She fired, and the vehicle's rear window exploded into glittering shards. But it wasn't enough. The van's brakes screeched as it barreled around a turn and disappeared from her sight.

Muttering a curse, Zavala spun around and stalked over to the body sprawled across the pavement. The man was still alive, and a low groan escaped his lips. He coughed, spraying crimson droplets of blood across the pale slush beneath him.

Zavala kicked his pistol out of reach, then kneeled next to the man. She grabbed her cell phone and dialed her field office. 'This is Special Agent Zavala. I'm at Westover Place. There's been an explosion, Carter Rowan's dead. Notify SIOC I've been involved in a deadly force incident. Shots fired, multiple suspects down. Need perimeter security, EMS, and Evidence Response Team on site. And a bomb tech, as well.'

'Stand by,' the operator at the field office replied. 'I'll connect you to—'

The man lying on the ice coughed up more blood. Zavala hung up, knowing the FBI would send units to her location anyway.

She examined the man lying on the ice. He was Asian – Korean, Zavala guessed. But based on his team's equipment and precision, there was no way these people were protestors. This was a military black op. An assassination. And Zavala was certain when the Evidence Response Team combed the rubble in the adjoining house, they would find the corpses of Rowan's neighbors in the debris. With bullets from these men's weapons in their skulls.

'Who are you?' she said, keeping her weapon trained on the dying man. 'Who do you work for?'

The man glared up at her and smiled. 'Defend unto death, our strong and prosperous nation,' he gasped. 'And our... glorious leader...'

His lips opened as he leered at her. Zavala narrowed her eyes. A tiny red capsule was lodged between his teeth. He bit down, breaking the capsule.

'No!' she shouted, jamming her fingers into his mouth. But she was too late. A thick white foam gushed between his teeth. His eyes fluttered, then rolled back into his skull. She felt his body spasm in her arms, then go limp.

He was dead.

Sirens wailed in the distance. No doubt neighbors had heard the gunfire and called the police. She used her sleeve to wipe the saliva and foam off her fingers. Then she unzipped the jumpsuit and patted the body down. Aside from the pistol, the man was unarmed. She found a wallet in the rear pocket of his jeans.

The canvas billfold held a few US dollars, some scraps of paper with Korean writing, and a small plastic identification card. It was not a driver's license, or any other ID she had ever seen. She set it down on the ground and took a picture of both sides with her cell phone.

'Guy must have come in from Baltimore,' the security guard said, ambling over to the body. 'Hey, thanks for... well, for what you did back there.'

Zavala gave him a curious look. 'No problem. Baltimore, *en realidad*? What makes you say that?'

The guard pointed at the plastic card. 'It's the closest port city. My brother-in-law works the docks there. That's a TWIC. Transportation Worker Identification Credential. Guys working the cargo ships need them to come ashore, access port facilities and stuff.'

Zavala slipped the card back in the wallet and stuffed it in the man's pockets. She stood and took a deep breath, shivering in the cold air.

'*Gracias*. Thank you. Look, the police and FBI are gonna be crawling all over this place in a few minutes. I need to make a private call before they get here. Mind if I use your booth?'

The man nodded but gave her a surprised look. 'No problem, but I mean, aren't they your buddies?'

Zavala gave the man a sad smile. 'Yeah, sure. We're all one big, happy family.'

She strode into the security booth and pressed herself against the wall. She dialed a number on her cell phone.

'AJ?' Rebecca answered.

'*¡Escucha!* Listen,' Zavala whispered back. 'You were right, Rowan was definitely in something dirty.'

'Did you arrest him?'

'It's a little late for that,' Zavala said, glancing out the shattered window. The sirens wailed closer. Red and blue lights flashed at the end of the driveway. 'He's dead. It was an execution, a professional job.'

Rebecca sucked in her breath on the other end of the call. 'Oh my God, are you okay?'

'Yeah, but I'm about to get dragged into the red tape. I was here under false pretenses, and if the director gets wind I was helping out the CIA—'

'Look, this is my fault, I asked you to—'

'Forget that. I'm texting you an ID I found on one of the assassins. I think he entered the country as a cargo ship worker, through Baltimore.'

'I'll get someone on it right away,' Rebecca replied.

'Have them look into something called Credo-com, as well. Some kind of online media conglomerate. They were Rowan's source.'

'AJ, thank you,' Rebecca said. 'I owe you for this, big time.'

'I just hope it helps you find a lead,' Zavala said. 'Because my hands are about to be tied.'

She hung up, texted Rebecca the photos, then slid the phone back in her pocket. She stepped out of the booth as a phalanx of metro police cars and SUVs with FBI markings swarmed into the parking lot.

31

TOMAMU, JAPAN

Caine rode in the rear of the bus, only occasionally glancing at the man he was following. The vehicle's high-beam lights cut through the snowstorm, illuminating the narrow, winding road that carried them up the mountain. They had been driving for about ten minutes, and in that time, Caine had seen no other buildings along the way. Just the deep, dark forest, trees, and snowbanks illuminated by the moving pools of light.

Caine had caught a glimpse of the man calling himself Yi Jun when he first boarded the bus. He had a round, cherubic face, and despite his thinning black hair, there was something child-like about his features. His eyes peered out from behind thick round glasses, nervously darting around the bus.

Although most of the passengers were Japanese, Caine was not the only Caucasian face aboard the vehicle. A couple dressed in white Patagonia parkas sat a few seats ahead of him. They whispered to each other in German and pointed out the windows at shimmering snow-covered trees.

The woman turned to read a signpost as the bus rumbled around a sharp corner. She noticed Caine watching her and gave him a nervous smile. Caine nodded, then stared out the window. A frozen river sparkled in the moonlight as the bus continued its ascent.

Lights pierced the darkness ahead. Caine saw a pair of glass and metal towers rising above the hills, silhouetted against the luminous snow. The chairs of a ski lift hung suspended in the air, swaying as the wind blew.

The bus pulled up to the hotel. Caine read the illuminated sign near the entrance.

Hoshino Resorts...

The vehicle's brakes made a hydraulic hiss as the bus came to a stop. Yi Jun leaped to his feet and peered over the shoulders of the passengers near the front of the vehicle, waiting as they disembarked. He seemed eager to get off the cramped bus. Caine kept his eyes on the German couple, paying as little attention to the nervous Korean man as he could without losing sight of him.

If he let the man get too far ahead of him, he could lose him in the crowd. But he knew if he stuck too close, seemed too interested, he would likely be spotted. Yi Jun didn't seem like a professional, but he was clearly jumpy and on edge.

Caine stepped off the bus and followed the crowd into the hotel lobby. Inside, the heated air was warm and dry, and smelled of cleaning products and incense. Dozens of tourists, both Japanese and foreigners, milled about, clomping across the damp carpet in their snow boots and ski gear.

Directly ahead of him, modern chairs surrounded a carved wooden dais. Silvery-gray birch trees rose from the wooden platform, their dappled trunks reaching up to the ceiling. Flickering candles lined the dais. A few guests sat in the chairs, sipping hot beverages from Styrofoam cups.

Caine followed the crowd down a corridor branching off from the main lobby. At the end of the carpeted passageway, a Japanese woman dressed in sparkling jewel-studded white furs stood behind a ticket desk. Posters on the walls displayed pictures of dazzling ice structures, a fairy-tale village surrounding a frozen lake. Caine recognized the pictures from the brochure at the train station.

So this is the Ice Village, he thought. *Could Kanako be here? Had Yi Jun been sent to meet her for some reason? What part could she possibly play in all this?*

Caine watched Yi Jun purchase a ticket and slink through a pair of doors behind the desk. The air grew chilly as the line moved closer and closer to the end of the corridor. The people ahead of him zipped up their coats and donned hats and gloves. A woman in a pink ski jacket hugged her body, rubbing her sides for warmth.

A few minutes later, he got his ticket and exited through the doors. Outside, snow continued to fall, lit up gold by warm yellow lights hanging from the nearby trees. An illuminated path led down the hillside, flanked on either side by dark forest groves.

Caine spotted Yi Jun about thirty meters ahead of him. He could pick him out from the crowd by his furtive, nervous movements. The other tourists stopped to admire the beautiful light displays and scintillating ice sculptures arranged along the path. But Yi Jun hurried along, oblivious to the stunning snowscape surrounding him.

Caine increased his pace, closing the gap between them as he weighed his options. He could continue following Yi Jun and see where the man led him. Or he could intercept, try to get some intel from him before whatever meeting that was about to take place went down.

As he continued down the path, he saw bright lights through the trees, heard the delighted shouts of tourists in the distance. The faint chimes of music rang out across the snow. The Ice Village was just around the bend. He was running out of time to decide.

Caine gritted his teeth and made up his mind. The short, flustered-looking man kept to the edge of the trail. Caine was only a few meters behind him now and closing fast.

He waited until they were on a darkened section of the path between the glowing lights dotting the dark forest. Then he accelerated, sprinting past the little Korean.

As he ran, Caine pivoted, jabbing his fist into Yi Jun's solar plexus. As the man grunted in pain, Caine jutted his leg in front of his target.

Still staggering from the blow to his lungs, Yi Jun tripped over Caine's leg and fell face-first onto the snow-covered path. The night was cold, barely above freezing, and the snow along the trail was packed hard by foot traffic. Yi Jun's skull struck the icy ground with a loud crack.

'*Sumimasen*, excuse me!' Caine exclaimed. 'I didn't see you in the dark. Guess I got a little too excited to see this Ice Village. Are you all right?'

Yi Jun picked himself up and kneeled on the snow-covered path. He blinked, then squinted up at Caine. He touched his face with his hands, then frantically brushed them over the ice.

'My glasses,' he said in English. 'I need my—'

Caine kneeled next to the man. His gloved hands wrapped around the twisted metal frames of the man's glasses, hiding them from view. 'Let me help you,' he said. 'They must be here somewhere.'

He slipped the broken frames into his pocket as he pretended to search. As he brushed his hands across the ice, a few tourists passed by, giving the two men strange looks. Then they continued on their way. Caine glanced over his shoulder. Between the darkness and the falling snow, he was confident if he moved quickly, they would not be seen.

He walked over to the edge of the path. 'Ah, here they are! Sorry, looks like a lens broke.'

Yi Jun hurried over. 'Where are they? I must get—'

Caine exploded into motion, clamping a gloved hand over the man's mouth and dragging him off the trail into the trees. Yi Jun kicked and screamed, but Caine's thick leather gloves muffled his cries. Within seconds, the trail was far behind them. The terrified man's feet dragged a long trail through the snow. Icicles hung from the gnarled tree branches above them, glinting in the moonlight.

They were alone.

Caine slammed a knee into the struggling man's gut. Yi Jun ceased his muffled cries, wheezing as the wind exploded from his lungs. Caine drew his pistol from inside his jacket and aimed it at the terrified man's head.

'Make another sound, and you die.' Caine glared at the man over the barrel of the gun.

Yi Jun stared back at him, frozen like a deer in headlights.

'If you shoot, people hear. They come,' he said in a quiet voice.

'Maybe. But that won't do you any good, will it?' Caine replied, adjusting his aim. 'I don't want to hurt you, but I will if I have to. Last chance. Nod if you understand.'

Very slowly, Yi Jun nodded his head.

'Good. Now, what are you doing here?'

'I was sent here to... to meet someone,' the man said. His teeth chattered in the cold.

'Who sent you?'

'Chan Tae Young. He is the minister of—'

'I know who he is,' Caine snapped. 'Chan is dead.'

The man's eyes opened wide in surprise. 'What? When did he—'

'Never mind that,' Caine said. 'Who are you meeting?'

'I don't know her name,' he replied, his teeth chattering louder. He hugged his body for warmth as snow swirled around them. 'I just have a picture on my phone.'

'Show me. Give me your phone, very slowly,' Caine ordered.

The man nodded and reached a hand inside his jacket.

'Easy, now,' Caine said, gesturing with the gun.

With slow, halting movements, Yi Jun slid a cell phone from the jacket's pocket and tapped the screen. He showed the phone to Caine.

Kanako's picture filled the screen.

Caine glared at the shivering man. 'Why her? What's so important about this woman?'

'I swear, I don't know,' the man said, raising his hands. 'I am to give her this phone. And a room key. That is all I know!'

'Room key?' Caine snapped. 'Where is it?'

'Here.' Yi Jun reached into his jacket again. Caine stepped back and kept the gun leveled at the man's head. He nodded again and slowly withdrew a plastic card stamped with the Hoshino Resorts logo.

'Please, that's all I know. Chan Tae blackmail me... Caught me charging expenses to the Ministry. Bar tabs. Vacations. Gifts for girlfriends. He make me do things for him, hide secrets. But he tell me, I do this last thing for him, and he erase evidence. I never meet this woman before, I don't know her!'

Caine thought for a moment. This man, Yi Jun, was clearly terrified. Either he was telling the truth, or he was one of the most skilled liars Caine had ever met. Either way, it seemed more likely that he was a civilian asset cultivated by Chan, rather than an enemy operative. But that still didn't answer the question foremost in Caine's mind.

What the hell did Chan want with Kanako? This went far beyond an affair, or a romantic infatuation with a hostess.

Whatever it was, Caine knew there was only one way to find out.

'All right. We're going to walk back to the path. Then you're going to turn around and leave this hotel. Don't come back. Do you understand?'

'Yes, *Ihaehabnida*. I understand!'

'Good. Now, stand up. Turn around.'

Yi Jun rose on shaking legs, and turned to face the dark, distant path. 'Thank you, thank—'

Caine looped his right arm around the man's throat and squeezed tight. His right hand pressed against the back of Yi Jun's head, forcing the man's neck deeper into the hold.

Yi Jun kicked and thrashed, but after a few seconds, his movements slowed, and his muffled cries turned to whispers. Caine kept the hold tight, cutting off the supply of oxygen to his brain.

His body went limp, and Caine dragged him deeper into the forest. He propped him up against a tree and stripped the laces from the man's boots. Then he tied his wrists behind the trunk. He stuffed one of Yi Jun's gloves in his mouth as a makeshift gag.

Before he left, he zipped up the unconscious man's parka and pulled the fleece-lined hood over his head. Caine hoped that would be enough to stave off the cold and prevent frostbite. But he couldn't risk the man alerting the authorities. Or worse, Unit 99, the mysterious faction of North Korea's intelligence apparatus that Chan Tae Young, this man's boss, had been working for.

Because one thing was certain: Kanako, Chan, and Byakko were connected. And whatever the secret was that bound them together, someone thought it was worth killing to protect.

32

CHIBA, JAPAN

Mariko swept her pistol left and right, scanning both sides of the alley. A slick of melting ice covered the pavement, and powdery white snowbanks shimmered in the street lights at either end of the dark passageway.

'Clear,' she whispered. 'Let's move!'

Junko emerged from the hotel and took a position to the right of the door. Koichi followed, moving at a slow but steady pace.

The door creaked shut behind them. Their footsteps echoed off the brick walls as they made their way to the eastern end of the alley.

'Where did you park?' Junko asked, glancing over his shoulder.

'In the garage, but it's too risky,' Mariko replied. She peered at the street ahead of them. 'If Tetsuo's men block the entrance, we'll be trapped. We'll have to take public—'

'*Asoko ni imasu yo!*' a voice shouted from the opposite side of the alley. *There they are...*

More footsteps echoed through the dark passage, running after them.

'Move,' Mariko shouted as she spun around. 'Get him out of here!'

She planted her feet and raised her gun. A trio of shadowy figures raced towards her, their feet splashing in the puddles of melted water. She opened fire.

Her gun roared twice as she sent a double tap toward the nearest man. The first shot ricocheted off the alley wall, but the second struck the man's shoulder. He grunted in pain, then ducked behind a dumpster for cover. The two other men moved to opposite sides of the alley. One took cover behind a series of water pipes running along the wall; the other ducked into a shallow brick alcove.

Junko grabbed Koichi's arm, but the old man yanked it away.

'I don't need help walking, *baka*!' he shouted.

Mariko fired again, then turned and sprinted after them. 'Keep moving!' she shouted. 'Go right!'

Gunfire exploded behind them, and sparks flew from the pavement near their feet. Junko returned fire as they herded Koichi from the alley and turned the corner, moving along the side of the building.

Junko tried to flag down a cab, but Mariko shook her head, glancing over her shoulder as they hurried down the snow-covered sidewalk.

'There's no time to wait for a cab. They're right behind us. There's a station at the end of the street. Keep moving!'

They jogged past the rear entrance of a bar. A few men huddled around the metal door, smoking cigarettes and chatting to each other in low, mumbling voices. They nodded at Mariko as she walked past, but she ignored them.

A few minutes later, the men chasing them rounded the corner. One of them bumped into a bar patron, causing him to drop his cigarette in the slush beneath his feet.

'*Oi!*' the man shouted at the yakuza thug. *Hey!*

The yakuza leered at the man and brandished his pistol. The bar patrons instantly backed off, raising their hands and shuffling back into the bar.

The armed men spotted Mariko and the others, nearing the end of the street.

One of them opened fire. Cars veered away from them as muzzle flash lit up the night. Brakes squealed as cars came to a halt, allowing Mariko and Junko to help Koichi cross the pedestrian walkway.

The yakuza men rushed after them. Mariko paused to fire another shot, but the bullet twanged off the traffic sign next to the intersection.

She turned and followed Junko and Koichi across the street.

Ahead of them, a flight of stairs led up and over the street. A sign reading *Chiba Urban Monorail* hung above the concrete structure. Next to the stairs, a poster of a red cartoon animal decorated the wall, celebrating Chiba's Winter Festival.

Bullets whined past Mariko's head. The shots tore through the poster, revealing metal and concrete underneath.

Junko helped Koichi up the stairs, ignoring the older man's grumbling. 'Is there an elevator?' he shouted.

'No time, keep going!' Mariko replied.

A low rumble filled the air. Mariko glanced up. Blinking lights snaked around the distant buildings, following the long track suspended above the city. The Urban Monorail, better-known as the SkyTrain, was heading for the station.

'We have to go faster,' Mariko snapped. 'Here, let me help.'

She threw Koichi's left arm around her shoulder, and together she and Junko lifted him up the stairs.

'*Hazukashii!* This is embarrassing,' Koichi muttered.

'Would you prefer a bullet in the back?' Mariko countered.

The old gangster grimaced. 'At this point, I think I just might!'

As they reached the top of the stairs, a row of station gates blocked their progress. Each gate consisted of a small plastic barrier next to a terminal. Swiping an IC card, or a phone with the correct app installed, would open the gate and charge the proper fare once the passenger exited at another station.

Mariko released Koichi and spun around. She dropped into a crouch and aimed down the stairs. A group of pedestrians gathered on the street below, backing away from the station as the yakuza men stormed up the stairs.

Junko reached into his pocket, grabbed his cell phone, and swiped it over the station terminal. The plastic barrier swung open, and he dragged Koichi through the gate.

Mariko aimed at the lead man and fired. The man clutched his chest and fell backwards, tumbling down the stairs. The other two men shifted to the side, letting the body roll past them. One of them aimed his pistol and fired. The bullet ricocheted off the metal railing, barely missing Mariko. She leaped to her feet and ran after Junko and Koichi, hopping over the gate.

Hydraulic brakes squealed as the SkyTrain car pulled into the station. The doors slid open, and a few passengers departed, hurrying to the exit stairwell on the opposite side of the elevated platform. A few of them shot worried glances at Mariko, Junko, and Koichi as they jogged toward the suspended train car.

A chime echoed through the station. The train was preparing to depart.

Junko sprinted ahead and grabbed the door, preventing it from closing. A loud buzzer sounded. There were only a few people left in the car, and they shot annoyed glances at the young man.

'*Karera o yamero!* Stop them!'

Mariko heard the voices shouting to her left. She frowned as she ran from the train car. Three more men shoved their way past the travelers on the exit staircase, moving against the crowd.

Koichi froze near the car doors. His lips curled into a snarl. The man in the lead of the new group was Tetsuo. The old gangster raised his pistol and fired.

The people on the train screamed, ducking for cover as the gun roared. The shot struck a light mounted on the ceiling. Sparks cascaded over Tetsuo's head. He ducked behind a blinking vending machine for cover.

Before Koichi could fire again, Mariko shoved him into the train car.

Gunshots exploded behind her. The other two men had ascended the stairs and entered the platform. The window to her right shattered as bullets struck the glass.

'Everyone, stay down!' she shouted. She tackled Koichi and threw him to the floor of the train car as Junko returned fire. He stepped away from the car, continuing to fire, forcing the men to retreat.

'Junko, get in the car!' Mariko shouted. She heard the doors clatter shut. Raising her head, she glanced out the shattered window. Tetsuo stepped out from behind the vending machine and raised his pistol. Mariko swung her gun up, bracing the weapon on the sill of the shattered window.

The train car lurched into motion just as she fired. Her bullet struck the vending machine. Sparks flew from the front panel as the glass shattered. Colorful bags of snacks spilled onto the station floor.

Tetsuo's pistol roared twice. Another train window shattered. Junko ran for the opening, struggling to catch up to the car as it slid along the track.

'Jump!' Mariko shouted. 'You can make it!'

But before the young man could take another step, Tetsuo's pistol thundered again. Junko's eyes opened wide, and his mouth gaped in a grimace of pain. He stumbled, then fell, collapsing on the station floor. Tetsuo fired again, and Junko's body thrashed on the ground.

The last thing Mariko saw was Junko's pleading eyes staring up at her, his hand reaching out toward the departing train car. Blood dripped from his fingers.

Then the SkyTrain swung out of the station, carrying them high above the street. Icy wind rushed through the broken windows, blowing Mariko's hair in her face.

Koichi staggered to his feet, squinting at the distant lights of the station as the SkyTrain snaked through the night.

'That's twice now that kid has saved my life,' he said. He shook his head and slumped down in a seat. 'What a waste. Should be me bleeding out back there. Not him.'

Mariko looked Koichi in the eye. She opened her mouth to speak, but something about the man's expression stopped her cold. No words came. There was nothing she could say. She had never seen someone, anyone, look so old and so tired.

She rested her hand on Koichi's shoulder. He nodded, then turned and looked away, staring out the window at the cars and people in the distant streets below.

* * *

Tetsuo watched the SkyTrain snake along its track and vanish behind some nearby buildings. He adjusted his jacket, then strutted onto the platform, a savage grin on his face.

Junko, he thought. *A kusogaki kobun? That was who Koichi turned to in his time of need? A kid and a woman?*

A few shocked passengers huddled on the edges of the platform. Tetsuo glared at them and waved his gun.

'What the hell are you looking at?' he shouted. '*Koko kara deteike!* Get out of here!'

The few remaining passengers bowed, then hurried down the stairs, departing the station as quickly as they could. A woman dropped her purse on the ground, and Tetsuo kicked it after her.

'Take your shit with you!'

He shook his head and holstered his weapon. Then he pulled a cigarette from a crumpled pack in his jacket. He slipped it between his lips and patted his pockets.

Junko groaned. Blood seeped from his wounds and stained the concrete platform beneath him.

Tetsuo leered down at him, the unlit cigarette dangling from his lips. 'Get him up,' he muttered.

Two of his men grabbed the young gangster's arms and hauled him to his feet. Junko gritted his teeth, struggling not to scream. His lips twitched, and his face went pale.

'Let's see what we have here,' Tetsuo muttered. He patted down Junko's jacket and grinned as he felt a slight bulge in the chest pocket. Slipping his fingers into the pocket, he removed a metal zippo lighter. He flicked it open, lighting his cigarette, then blew a puff of smoke in Junko's face.

'You blew it, kid,' he said. 'Koichi and his kind... They're the old guard. It's time for a fresh start. But I'll make you a deal. Tell me where the *gaijin* is, this Caine-san, and maybe you can be part of this organization's future. Instead of a bloody stain on its past.'

Junko's head lolled on his shoulders. Then he looked up. His eyes focused, and his lips curled into a manic grin. He spat a glob of bloody saliva into Tetsuo's face.

'Fuck you... Traitor!'

Tetsuo grimaced and wiped the mess away with his sleeve. His nostrils flared, and his eyes simmered with rage. He raised the pistol, preparing to strike Junko's head.

Sirens wailed in the distance.

One of the other men grabbed Junko's pistol from the ground, then leaned closer to Tetsuo. 'We should go. The police will be here soon.'

Tetsuo glared at the man, then gave him a faint nod. 'Fine. Bring the kid along. He'll tell us what we want to know, eventually. After all, we've got a long night ahead of us.'

He turned and descended the stairs. His men dragged the wounded Junko behind him.

33

TOMAMU, JAPAN

The Ice Village glittered against the dark night sky. Each building in the village was constructed from blocks of ice, and their walls shimmered like diamonds in the sun. White domes capped most of the structures, similar in size and design to the tent Caine had briefly stayed in earlier.

Ice skaters circled a frozen pond next to the village. Their skates cut long white trails in the ice, as colored lights swept across the pond's glassy surface. More lights lit up the frozen water from below, making the spinning and twirling figures appear to be skating across a glowing sea of colorful glass.

As Caine approached the village's entrance, he heard shrieks and laughter from behind him. Turning, he saw an older man in a ski jacket sliding down a chute lined with ice, holding a giggling young girl in his lap. More tourists whizzed through the air, zip-lining from the top of the hill down to the village grounds.

Caine walked under a shimmering arch with the words *Hoshino Ice Village* carved across its sparkling surface. Sticking to the attraction's outskirts, he meandered past the ice buildings, pretending to marvel at their construction, along with the rest of the tourists.

He sauntered through a convenience store, whose ice shelves held a variety of snacks and desserts, as well as drinks that heated themselves when their bottles were opened. After that, he followed a group of people through a shimmering tunnel that led into an igloo-like structure.

A bed, carved entirely from ice, sat upon a raised platform in the center of the dome. Luxurious fur blankets and pillows adorned the ice bed, and a sign on the wall advertised the room's availability for nightly rental, weather permitting.

As he exited the dome, he again moved to the outskirts of the village. Tourists meandered along the winding paths between the ice buildings, their breath misting in the frosty night air. Snow continued to fall from above, but the wind was gentler in the clearing, and the buildings served as a buffer against the chill.

Certain he was not being followed, Caine checked a nearby map of the village, then headed to a dome marked 'Ice Bar'. The entrance was lower than the other buildings, and he had to duck to enter the structure.

On the other side, he found himself standing in a glowing white lounge. Blocks of ice served as stools, arranged before a curved, frozen counter. Shelves carved from the walls held an astonishing array of colorful bottles, high-end liquor, and spirits from around the world.

Ice tables ran around the edge of the dome, and couples sat enjoying their cocktails, murmuring to each other beneath the low, relaxing tones of electronic music. Behind the counter, a pair of bartenders dressed in white fur coats and hats prepared more drinks. They served them to customers at the counter in frost-covered glasses.

The light inside the bar was dim, and candles flickered on the frozen counter. A woman sat apart from the other guests, her face half-hidden in shadow. She wore a black parka with a fur-lined hood, and gray wool leggings. High black socks covered the leggings for extra warmth, and sleek, expensive-looking leather boots sheathed her feet.

Caine approached the bar and sat on a block of ice next to her. A fur-clad bartender hurried over.

'Yamazaki, single malt, *o kudasai*,' Caine said.

The bartender grabbed the amber bottle from the shelf behind him. 'How do you take it?'

Caine glanced around the icy interior. 'On the rocks, of course.'

Caine heard the woman give a low chuckle. The bartender poured his drink and slid it across the counter. Caine was surprised to find that even the highball glass itself was carved from ice.

He took a sip, then turned to the woman. 'I have a strange feeling you're waiting for someone.'

The woman turned and gave him a cautious smile. Her hair was no longer red, but Caine recognized her instantly.

It was Kanako.

'You Japanese is very good,' she said. 'But I'm afraid—'

'Chan Tae Young is dead,' Caine replied, cutting her off. He watched her face to see how she reacted to the name. 'And Yi Jun isn't coming.'

Her smile faded. She tilted her head and narrowed her eyes. 'I'm sorry, I don't know who that is.'

'No?' Caine sipped his whisky. 'Then why did Gaya see you two talking at the Paris Nights club in Sapporo?'

Kanako stood up. 'I have to be going. Enjoy your stay.'

Caine grabbed her wrist. She looked down at him in shock. Her lips parted, but no sound came out.

'Gaya is dead too,' Caine whispered. 'I'm here to help. Your life is in danger.'

The girl's nostrils flared, and Caine saw a brief look of shock cross her eyes. Then it vanished, and her expression turned cold.

'I'm sorry to hear about Gaya, but that's not my concern. Who are you?'

Caine nodded at her drink. 'Please, sit. I'm here to help. I'm a friend of your father.'

The girl shook her head, as if she could not believe what she was hearing. 'My father? My father is dead.'

'No, he survived the attack. He faked his death to throw off Torazama's men.'

'Attack?' The girl sat down and stared at Caine, her brow furrowed, her lips curled into a frown. 'My father died of cancer years ago. Before my mother—'

'I don't know what your mother told you, but your father's name is Koichi Ogawa. He's alive, but your boss, Hideo Torazama, tried to have him killed. And now he's looking for you.'

'Torazama?' Kanako sipped her drink. 'He's just a yakuza thug. Byakko-san, the great White Tiger... Why are men so foolish?'

'He's more than just another gangster, Kanako. He and Chan are mixed up with some very dangerous people. They're working for a hostile foreign government.'

She took another sip of her drink but said nothing. When she turned to face him, her dark eyes were unreadable.

Caine slid the hotel room key from his pocket and placed it on the frost-covered bar. 'Chan sent you here to give you this, didn't he? What's in this hotel room?'

Kanako's hand shot out to grab the key. Caine slammed his hand down on top of hers, preventing her from taking it. 'Kanako, this isn't a game! Your life is in danger!'

'You think I don't know that?' she said, her voice rising in pitch. She glared at him with dark, desperate eyes. 'Rise was an addict. I hoped... I hoped she would get out, get clean. That's why I worked her shift at Torazama's party.'

'Is that where you met Chan?'

She shook her head. 'He had been to the club before. He was infatuated with Rise and me. When I met him at that party, he said... he said he had something that could help us. A secret we could use to blackmail Torazama. I was supposed to meet him here. He gave me a code, to a hotel safe.'

Caine glanced around the dimly lit bar. The bartenders were busy helping other customers. The couples at the tables murmured among themselves. No one paid any attention to Caine and Kanako.

Caine returned his gaze to the beautiful woman sitting next to him. She lowered her hood and brushed a lock of jet-black hair behind her ear. 'Please, I need this,' she pleaded in a quiet voice. 'You don't understand... This could get me out of the clubs. A new life, no more drugs, no more hostess bars.'

'Kanako, if you need money, your father would—'

She uttered a bitter laugh and took another sip of her drink. 'You keep talking about this father of mine. If he really is alive, why have I never met him? Why didn't he ever try to find me?'

Caine sighed. Getting involved in a domestic quarrel between Koichi and his daughter was the last thing he wanted. And the longer they stayed here, the more danger the girl would be in.

'Kanako, look. It's complicated. What your mother told you... I'm sure she had her reasons. But right now, we don't have time to—'

'What's the rush?' She leaned closer to him, smiling. 'Don't you like me?'

She reached out and touched his cheek. Her hand traveled down his arm, caressing his bicep.

'Kanako, stop,' he said.

Her hand moved to his leg as her lips parted. 'Help me out,' she purred, leaning closer. 'I'll make it worth your while, I promise.'

Caine let go of the key card and grabbed her arm, removing it from his leg. 'Stop it. That's not why I'm here.'

The woman snatched the card off the counter and stood up. 'Idiot,' she sneered. 'Look, I don't know who you are, but you can either let go of my arm or I scream.'

He glared at her, then released her arm. She spun around and stalked out of the bar. Caine muttered a curse as he tossed a few yen notes on the counter. He followed her outside.

As he ducked under the shimmering arch, he saw Kanako stomping through the snow a few meters ahead of him. He started to follow but froze. He felt the familiar tingle on the back of his neck, the instinctive sense of danger, honed by years of experience in the field.

He was being watched. They both were, he was certain of it.

Scanning the crowd, he spotted a Japanese man wearing a blue parka and a red beanie hat. Something about his body language seemed off. Although he stuck to the outskirts of the village, he walked with a purposeful stride, moving against the crowd, as if he was trying to keep pace with Kanako.

Caine jogged through the snow, catching up with the determined young woman.

'Kanako, wait!' he said, cutting her off before she reached the dark, winding path that led up to the hotel.

She stomped her feet in the snow and rolled her eyes. 'Can't you take a hint? Whoever you are, I don't need your help.'

Caine glanced over her shoulder. The man in the blue jacket was gone, and no one else caught his attention. Had he been mistaken? Was it just another tourist?

But the feeling of being watched was still there, creeping across his skin like an annoying insect he couldn't brush away.

'Kanako, please, listen to me. I know you don't believe me, but you're in danger here.'

The woman narrowed her eyes and pursed her lips. 'When I came on to you, you said that wasn't why you were here. Well, why *are* you here? What do you want?'

'Torazama tried to have your father killed,' Caine said, looking her in the eye. 'And your father was worried you were next. He sent me to find you.'

'I told you, my father is—'

'No, he's not. He's alive. And I promised him I'd keep you safe.'

The woman tapped her foot and glanced back, eying the crowded village. Then she looked Caine in the eye.

'Look, I am not leaving until I get what I came for.' She held up the hotel key. 'You want to protect me? Fine. You can come with me.'

Caine nodded. 'Great. Let's go.'

'What did you say your name was?'

'You can call me Tom.'

The girl shook her head. 'All right, Tom. But I'm telling you, you would have been better off just letting me leave that bar.'

'Story of my life,' Caine replied. 'After you.'

She started up the path. Caine glanced behind him but saw no one else who aroused his suspicion. He caught up to the girl and stayed by her side as they walked through the glowing lights hanging from the trees.

34

Kanako stood a few feet away from Caine in the elevator, shooting nervous glances at him as they ascended the resort tower. Caine ignored her and tried to send a text to Mariko, but there was no cell reception in the tiny metal box.

'So this yakuza guy, Koichi Ogawa,' she said, glancing at her nails. 'You're telling me he's my father? And my mother lied about him?'

Caine slid the cell phone back in his coat pocket. 'Yeah. The kind of life he leads... They both decided it would be better for you in the long run.'

She peered up at him, her eyes wide and curious. 'But he sent you to find me. So you must know him pretty well, right?'

'Honestly?' Caine looked down at her and shrugged. 'I hardly know him at all.'

'Then why did you come?'

Caine sighed. 'I owed him.'

She gave him an incredulous stare. 'You owed him? That simple?'

He nodded. 'For me, yeah. It was.'

She shook her head. 'Unbelievable. So, do you think they were right?'

'What do you mean?'

'Was I better off without him in my life?'

Caine stomped his feet to shake the melting snow off his boots. He glanced up at the glowing numbers on the elevator car's display.

'That's not for me to say, Kanako. I... I don't have a family, and I honestly don't know if he made the right decision.'

'You're old enough to be my father,' she said, shooting him a withering glance. 'What would you have done?'

Caine looked her in the eye but said nothing. The elevator came to a stop, and the doors slid open with an electronic chime.

'*Nijuuyonkai*,' a woman's recorded voice chirped. *Twenty-fourth floor...*

Kanako started to exit the car, but Caine blocked her with his arm. He leaned out the doors, glancing in both directions. There was no one else in the carpeted lobby.

Each floor of the resort's tower contained four luxurious suites. Each was accessible by a short corridor that branched off from a central lobby area.

Caine stepped out and grabbed the edge of the elevator door to keep it from closing. Kanako exited and gave him a nervous look. 'You really think someone is following me?'

'Yes,' Caine replied. 'The sooner we leave here, the better. Let's go.'

He led her down a corridor and paused in front of a door marked with a silver number plaque.

2403.

He placed a finger over his lips and made a shushing sound. Kanako nodded and moved behind him. Caine drew his pistol from inside his jacket. With his other hand, he swiped the key card over the lock.

There was a soft click, and a tiny light near the door handle blinked green. Caine opened the door and peered into the darkened room. He crept along the outer wall, holding his pistol in a two-handed grip.

The luxurious suite was narrow and angular, an L-shaped block of rooms wrapping around the corner of the resort tower. The entryway led to the living area, a spacious room with white walls and birchwood furniture. The pale green curtains were open, revealing the rolling hills and dark forest surrounding the hotel. The snow-covered ground reflected the moonlight, a luminous carpet of white beneath the night sky.

Caine cleared each room in the suite, moving through them one by one. In addition to the living area, there were two bedrooms, a glass-enclosed bathroom with breathtaking mountain views, and a smaller guest bathroom. All appeared freshly cleaned, with no signs of any recent guests.

Once he was certain the suite was empty, Caine gestured for Kanako to enter. She stepped inside and closed the door behind her. Caine flipped a light switch on the wall. A pair of lamps in the living room bathed the suite in a soft, warm glow.

'Let's get what you came for, and get out of here,' Caine said, peering out the window. Floodlights illuminated the hotel grounds outside, reflecting off the glittering white snow.

In the distance, a line of skiers snaked through a series of pylons, waiting for a chairlift to carry them up the mountain. Farther down the hill, he saw garages housing snowmobiles and ATV quad cycles. A few snowmobiles were parked in a row, facing a winding trail that cut through the snow-covered mountain. One by one, pairs of tourists clad in cold weather gear straddled the vehicles and sped off, vanishing into the pale white hills.

'Do you have a car?' he asked, watching as another snowmobile raced off into the distance.

'*Hai*, I drove here from Sapporo,' she replied, as she entered the main bedroom. He heard the closet door slide open. 'Why don't you make yourself a drink? It might help you relax.'

Caine ignored her and tried texting Mariko again.

> Found Kanako. Leaving for Sapporo shortly.

As he tapped the keyboard, he heard a series of beeps, followed by the metallic thunk of a safe door opening.

He pressed send, then slipped the phone back in his pocket. He was about to call out to Kanako and tell her to hurry, but instead, he froze in place.

He heard footsteps in the corridor, just outside the door.

'Kanako, be quiet,' he hissed, moving closer to the door. 'Someone's coming!'

He pressed up against the wall, hiding in the shadows. The footsteps stopped. Peering around the corner, he saw a shadow move across the thin sliver of light beneath the suite's door. There was a quiet beep, and the door-knob turned. The door creaked as it swung open. Footsteps echoed through the foyer as the intruder entered the suite.

Caine waited, listening as the footfalls came closer and closer to his position. A shadowy figure entered the room.

As Caine surged toward the intruder, he noted the man's blue parka and red beanie.

The guy from the Ice Village, Caine thought. *He followed us...*

The man spun around, hearing Caine's footsteps. But he was too late. Caine swung the butt of his pistol, clubbing the side of the intruder's head. The man staggered back, raising an arm to ward off any further blows. Caine grabbed the man's jacket, bunching up two fistfuls of the blue fabric in his hands.

He yanked the man towards him and threw up a knee, driving it into his opponent's solar plexus. The man grunted in pain and doubled over. He made a retching sound, but Caine pressed the attack, swinging him around, then hurling him through the air.

The man tumbled over the back of the couch and crashed down onto a glass coffee table. The table shattered beneath him, covering the floor with glittering shards and scattered magazines.

Caine circled around the sofa, aiming his gun at the prone man.

'Get up,' he snarled. 'Hands behind your head.'

The man groaned in pain, then staggered to his feet.

'Turn around, face the window,' Caine ordered. As the man obeyed, Caine glanced over his shoulder. He caught a glimpse of Kanako creeping from the darkened bedroom.

'*Nani?*' she gasped. 'What the—'

'Go outside,' Caine said to her. He refocused his attention on the man in the blue parka. 'I'll take care of—'

Click.

Caine recognized the sound at once. It was as intimate as the sigh of a familiar lover.

It was the sound of a safety being released on a pistol.

'Drop your weapon, Tom,' Kanako said in a firm, commanding voice.

'Kanako, what are—?'

'I don't want to hurt you, but I won't ask again,' she snapped.

Caine lowered his gun. Slowly, he kneeled and set it down on the carpeted floor.

The man in the blue parka turned around. Blood dripped from a gash across his face, and a purple bruise marked his forehead.

'Kick it over here,' the man said, glowering at Caine.

Caine kicked the pistol away. He turned to face Kanako. Her purse was slung over her shoulder, and she held a small Glock 19 pistol in a two-handed grip, aimed directly at him. Her dark eyes regarded him with a defiant stare as she peered down the barrel.

Caine knew that model of pistol well. It didn't usually come equipped with a thumb safety, but some police and military organizations had the optional accessory installed at the factory.

'Are you working with Torazama?' he asked, his emerald eyes returning her dark, smoldering stare.

'Don't be ridiculous,' she said.

'*Baka gaijin*,' the man behind him grunted.

Caine heard the plastic rasp of zip ties looping together. The man grabbed his arms and pulled his hands behind his back. The thin plastic straps bit into his wrists as they were zipped tight.

'We're Naikaku Jōhō Chōsashitsu,' the man said, dragging Caine toward the door.

'Naicho?' Caine said, using the organization's abbreviated name. He gave Kanako a surprised look. 'You work for the Cabinet Intelligence and Research Office?'

She gave him a sly grin as she stowed her weapon back in her purse. 'You seem surprised. Maybe you thought I was a damsel in distress?'

The man dragged Caine into the corridor, and Kanako followed, keeping pace as they entered the elevator.

'I guess you were right,' Caine muttered as the doors pinged shut.

'About what?' She kept her eyes on the elevator doors.

He glared at her as the elevator carried them down the tower.

'I should have left you back in that bar.'

35

Caine flexed his wrists in the back seat of the SUV. The plastic straps bit into his skin, but he felt their grip loosen. He'd been subtly working on them, bending and stretching the thin plastic as much as he could without drawing attention.

Once they exited the hotel, Kanako and the bruised man, a Naicho officer named Sota, led him to a gray Honda SUV waiting near the hotel's valet area. Another man with a young but stern face sat behind the wheel, and the engine was already running. He had given Caine a silent, somber look when Sota shoved him in the back seat. Judging by his lack of surprise, Caine assumed he had been waiting for them. Kanako must have texted him while she was out of sight, alerted him to Caine's presence.

Now, dark trees and luminous snow-covered hills raced past the window as the SUV cruised down the winding road leading away from the hotel. It had not stopped snowing since Caine had arrived in Tomamu, and the wind had grown stronger, making the road treacherous despite the vehicle's snow tires. The vehicle shuddered as another gust blasted the passenger side.

'*Maji ka yo?* You won't believe who this guy is,' Sota said from the front passenger seat. He swiped at a heavy-duty tablet, and Caine saw images from his CIA file fill the glowing screen.

Kanako slipped a crumpled white envelope from her purse and removed what looked like a thumb drive from inside. A similar tablet sat on her lap, and she plugged the drive in, frowning as data filled the screen.

'Who is he?' she muttered, her eyes focused on the screen.

'Thomas Caine, CIA Special Activities Division. Remember the drone attack at Skytree Tower?'

She turned and gave Caine a suspicious look, narrowing her eyes. 'That was you? You're really CIA?'

'Technically, I was freelance then,' Caine replied. 'What did you find in the safe?'

'Says here he's supposed to be in South Korea,' Sota said, still reading from the tablet's screen. 'There's a flag on his file. Standing order for all intelligence agencies to apprehend and return him to the US embassy.'

He turned around in his seat and gave a smug grin. 'Looks like you pissed off your own people, as well as ours. They burned you!'

'Wouldn't be the first time,' Caine replied.

'What the hell are you doing here?' Kanako asked.

'You first,' Caine replied. 'Why were you working in Torazama's club?'

She stared at him for a moment, then nodded. 'North Korea has a long history of working with the yakuza, and other organized crime syndicates. Usually just fraud and money laundering. Petty crimes to fill their supreme leader's coffers. But recently, intel suggested the Kodo Kai organization was escalating their involvement.'

'After Hideo Torazama took control,' Caine replied. 'And the drug charges, your trouble with the gangs?'

She shrugged. 'Just part of my cover. I was trying to get into Torazama's inner circle. I made contact with Chan at the club. He was terrified, said he was looking for a way out. But he couldn't go to his own government. He said there were dozens of sleeper agents, North Korean operatives, who had lain dormant for a decade or more. He offered to turn over his list of contacts, in exchange for protection in Japan, for him and his family.'

'That's what was in the safe?' Caine asked, nodding at the tablet in her hands.

She glanced at the screen and frowned again. 'That's what I was expecting to find. But this... I don't know what this is.'

Caine craned his neck, struggling to see the screen more clearly. He glimpsed snippets of computer code, a series of archived logs and dates, most of it in Korean. But Kanako turned the tablet away from him before he could see more.

'Your turn,' she said. 'What are you really doing here?'

'I told you the truth,' he replied. 'Koichi Ogawa is your father. Someone in his organization sold him out to Torazama, so he reached out to me and asked for help. He didn't know who else he could trust. You have to understand, Koichi thinks you're a hostess in over her head. You're his daughter, and he thought you were in danger.'

She shook her head. 'That's... a lot. I don't have time to deal with family drama right now. But even if all that is true, how would he even know about me? Why did he think I was in trouble?'

Caine sighed. 'He's had men keeping an eye on you for years. When you disappeared, Torazama had them killed. He must have thought they were involved somehow. He couldn't take the risk that they might report back to Koichi.'

She brushed her hair behind her ear. 'What was he afraid they would report?'

'I'm not sure,' Caine said. 'But right now, US–South Korean relations are rapidly deteriorating. There's some kind of outbreak, a virus... People have died, and a journalist in DC claims he has evidence the South Korean government knew about it. That they covered up reports of cases, and allowed it to spread to—'

Kanako squinted at the tablet again. '*Sore wa kyoki da*, that's insane.'

'Yeah,' Caine replied. 'Apparently, the lunatics are running the asylum right now, because the president believes this idiot. He's about to call off a series of joint military exercises, unless I can find proof this asshole is lying. And I think Chan and Byakko are involved, somehow.'

Kanako continued studying the data on her tablet. 'Most of these records are encrypted. But the fragments I can read are from South Korea's Ministry of Health and Welfare.'

Caine struggled to break free from the plastic cuffs binding his wrists.

'Kanako, please. If Torazama is working with North Korea, he could be trying to drive a wedge between the US and our Pacific allies. That's why he killed Koichi's men, that's why he's been trying to find you. He knows you're with the Naicho, and he wants to stop the info on this drive from getting out!' He held up his hands. 'Cut me loose. We can work together to stop—'

'Are you crazy?' Sota exclaimed from the front seat. 'You assaulted a Naicho officer, and your own government disowned you. We're taking you back to your embassy. You're officially their problem now.'

Kanako looked up at her partner. 'Sota-san, wait. This can't be a coincidence. What if he's—'

'I don't care if he's Santa Claus, we're not cutting this guy loose. The last time he operated on Japanese soil, he shot up a concert at the Tokyo Dome, caused a massive traffic pileup in the Yamate Tunnel, and detonated a—'

'I also stopped a drone from taking out half of Sumida ward,' Caine snapped. 'We're wasting time working against each other.'

The SUV shook as another gust of wind blasted the side. The vehicle's high beams illuminated the falling snow, a cloudy white haze obscuring the road ahead.

'Turn the car around,' Kanako said. She set the tablet down on the seat and rummaged through her purse.

'*Chotto matte. Nani?*' the young driver said, glancing up at them in the rearview mirror. *Wait, what...?*

'*Iie!*' Sota snapped. 'No! Keep going!'

'I said turn around!' Kanako held up a Böker ceramic folding knife with a black handle. She flicked the blade open and looked Caine in the eye. 'If I cut these off you, you promise you won't run? We share intel, pool our resources?'

Caine nodded. 'Trust me, I want Byakko as much as you do. I'm not going anywhere.'

'Natsuki-san, don't do this!' Sota shouted. 'When the director finds out, he'll—'

A shrill beeping echoed through the cabin, cutting Sota off. It took Caine a second to recognize the sound.

It was the vehicle's collision sensor.

High-beam lights flooded through the passenger windows. The roar of an engine drowned out the howling wind. Caine squinted in the harsh glow and threw up his hands, bracing himself against the door.

Crash!

Another vehicle tore across the snow, ramming the side of the Honda SUV head on. The impact sent the Honda tumbling off the road. The SUV crashed through the trees on the driver's side as it tumbled down a steep, snow-covered hill.

In the glare of the high beams, Caine saw the black sky and pale ground invert, flipping over and over. He heard the crack of wood as trees and branches snapped beneath the rolling vehicle's weight. Kanako's tablet flew into the air, striking the side of his head. The rear windshield shattered, cold wind whipped through his hair.

Then, with a final crash, the truck landed upside down in a snow-covered clearing. Caine's head struck the metal frame with a loud crack. Darkness engulfed him. Kanako was shouting, but her voice was a muted echo, as distant and intangible as the groaning wind.

36

LANGLEY, VIRGINIA, USA

CIA new headquarters building

Rebecca tucked a loose strand of fiery red hair behind her ear as she leaned over Sandra Basu's shoulder. The young Indian American woman wore a teal dress with a vintage floral print and batwing sleeves. Her hair was pulled back in a neat, tight bun, and data from the screen reflected in the lens of her glasses. Her bright clothes stood out in the sea of grays and blacks worn by other employees on her floor.

At twenty-four years old, Sandra was one of the younger analysts working at the East and Southeast Asia Group, part of the CIA's Directorate of Analysis.

She's got a promising career ahead of her, Rebecca thought. *Assuming I don't get us both fired in the next twenty minutes.*

Data streamed across her screen, faster than Rebecca's eyes could follow.

'Anything yet?' she asked, glancing over Sandra's shoulder. The other analysts on the floor were all engrossed in their work, typing away in their cubicles.

'Just cross-referencing with Baltimore Port Authority,' Sandra replied. The data cleared from her screen, and a digitized image filled the monitor.

Rebecca leaned closer. It was a duplicate of the file AJ had texted her.

'It's the same ID,' she said, examining the picture on her phone. 'So this guy really is a deckhand from a cargo ship?'

Sandra highlighted several portions of the image. 'Not quite identical. The credential number is the same, as is the name, Okubo Yoshi. But the ID your contact sent has been altered.'

Sandra tapped a key, and the picture from Rebecca's phone slid onto the screen, side by side with the other document. A series of glowing dots highlighted differences in the two men's faces.

'Someone replaced the original file to allow the assassin to access the port in Baltimore,' Sandra said, leaning back in her chair. She glanced up at Rebecca. 'I'm sorry, but isn't this really the FBI's territory?'

Rebecca patted the woman on the shoulder. 'It absolutely is. And if anyone asks, make sure you mention that you told me that.'

Sandra adjusted her glasses and swallowed. 'Uh, is someone likely to ask me about that?'

Rebecca ignored the question. 'Can you tell me anything else about this guy? Employment history, last port of call, anything?'

Sandra cracked her knuckles, then tapped the keyboard again. 'It looks like someone tried to erase the work history associated with the file. But I was able to retrieve the man's last post. He was assigned to a cargo feeder vessel, registered in Japan. Its name is the Eiko Maru.'

'Japan?' Rebecca repeated, raising a single brow.

So Caine was right, she thought. *Japan and South Korea, Chan Tae Young and Hideo Torazama.*

'Yes, the Eiko Maru is owned by Sagawa Express, a Japanese freight company. There were rumors of yakuza influence on the board of directors. Japan's Cabinet Intelligence and Research Office investigated, but their findings were inconclusive.'

'Cross-reference their report with a name,' Rebecca said. 'Hideo Torazama.'

Sandra typed on her keyboard. More data flashed across the screen. 'Hideo Torazama is believed to own Sagawa Express, through a series of holding companies purchased by the Koda Kai.'

A red circle blinked in the center of the screen. Lines and arrows emerged from the center like a digital web, linking the glowing dot to various other corporate entities.

'Oh, look here!' Sandra stopped typing and pointed at the screen.

'What's that?' Rebecca asked, struggling to read the tiny Japanese characters.

'Cyber-Sekai Capital,' Sandra said, reading off the screen. 'It's a Japanese venture capital firm. They popped up in my other search. They're the primary funder of Credo-com.'

'Rowan's source,' Rebecca said, a triumphant smile on her face. 'Excellent work, Sandra. For now, let's keep this between—'

Rebecca's phone chirped. Glancing at the screen, she saw it was a Japanese number calling, but not one she recognized.

Tom must have a new burner phone, she thought.

She answered the call. 'Tom, good timing. You won't believe what—'

'This isn't Tom,' a woman's voice answered. 'My name is Mariko Murase. I'm a friend of Tom's.'

'Tom gave you this number?' Rebecca asked, unable to hide the note of suspicion in her voice.

'*Hai*. He told me to call you if... If I needed to find him.'

'I remember your name from Tom's reports, Murase-san,' Rebecca said, again glancing around the room. 'But I'm afraid I'll need a bit more info than that if you want me to trust you.'

'*Wakarimasu*. I understand,' Mariko replied. 'He also told me to tell you... If you liked *The World of the Married*, you'll love *Cheat on me if You Can*.'

He shared our code, Rebecca thought. She was surprised, but under the circumstances, she needed all the help she could get.

'I'm not much of a K-Drama fan,' Mariko said. 'I assume that's some kind of code. I believe Tom is in danger. His enemies know that he is in Tomamu. I'm hoping I can get to him before they do. So, can I ask you to trust me now, Director Freeling?'

Rebecca nodded. 'If Tom trusts you, that's good enough for me. I'll send you his last known address.'

'Thank you. I'll do my best to—'

'I have some other intel for you as well, Murase-san.'

'Please, call me Mariko.'

'Director?' Sandra bit her lip as she stared at the screen. A red warning symbol flashed in the right-hand corner.

Rebecca covered the phone's mic. 'What the hell is that?'

'That's a burn notice,' Sandra replied, clicking on the blinking square. 'Filed by the office of the DNI.'

'A burn notice on who?' Rebecca asked.

Sandra tapped another key. Rebecca clenched her jaw as Thomas Caine's image filled the screen.

'Mariko?' Rebecca said, speaking into her phone again.

'*Hai?*'

'Do you still work for the Security Bureau?'

'No. I am now *furiiransu*... Freelance.'

'Good. Because Caine just got burned. And we're running out of time.'

37

TOMAMU, JAPAN

'Tom! Wake up! *Oi*, wake up!'

Caine blinked. His vision was blurry, and at first he thought he was looking at the star-filled sky, tiny pinpoints of white light glittering against the velvet black night.

Kanako slapped his face. 'Tom, wake up! We have to move!'

His vision cleared. Shaking his head, he realized it was not stars that filled his vision, but falling snow, lit up by the overturned SUV's headlights. He was hanging upside down in his seat. He felt a dull throbbing, a pounding along the side of his skull. Crimson droplets of blood pooled on the mangled metal and ice beneath his head.

He craned his neck. Kanako was crouched below him, upside down in his inverted vision. Her dark eyes glinted in the shadows, reflecting the headlights' glow. She breathed a sigh of relief as she saw him regain consciousness.

The crack of gunfire echoed through the trees. A bullet ricocheted off the SUV's crumpled metal frame, only a few inches from his skull. He tried to unbuckle his seat belt, but his hands were still tied together.

'Your knife,' he grunted, his voice hoarse and weak. 'Cut me loose! Hurry!'

She frantically searched the wreckage, patting the crumpled metal roof with her hands. 'I can't find it,' she said. 'I lost it in the crash, along with my tablet!'

More gunfire erupted from farther up the hill. Bright orange muzzle flash lit up the dark shadows between the trees.

Glancing to his left, he saw a jagged metal fragment jutting from the mangled passenger door. He sawed the plastic cuffs back and forth against the makeshift blade. The thin plastic cut easily, and within a few seconds, he was free.

After flexing his wrists to get the blood flowing, he reached down and slammed his fist on the seat-belt fastener. It released with a click, and he tumbled out of his seat. He grunted in pain as his bruised skull struck the metal roof.

'Sota-san,' he whispered. 'Are you all right?'

A low groan came from the passenger seat. Sota's head craned back, turning to face Caine. His beanie had fallen off, and a fringe of dark, thinning hair hung from his upside-down skull. His face was a mess of blood and bruises.

'My gun,' Caine said. 'Give me my—'

'Kid... *Oi*, kid, you okay?' Sota gasped. He ignored Caine and turned to face the driver.

The young Naicho officer's skin looked pale in the headlights' glow. Shards of broken glass pierced his face, and his head hung at an odd angle. His arms dangled in the air, like a carcass hanging from a hook.

He did not respond.

'Sota-san!' Caine hissed. 'We have to get—'

Another barrage of gunfire struck the car. Sota jerked in his seat as bullets tore through the shattered window. Caine ducked, and Kanako crawled out of the car, taking cover behind the metal hulk.

Caine glanced at the wheel at the ceiling, near Sota's dangling head. A pair of pistols lay on the floor, Sota's Glock, and his own HK.

'Kanako, cover me!' he shouted.

'Go,' she replied.

She popped up from behind the hood and fired into the dark grove up the hill, aiming where the last bursts of muzzle flash had lit up the trees. As she squeezed off two more rounds, Caine crawled into the front of the vehicle and scooped up the guns.

He felt Sota's neck... There was no pulse. He didn't bother to check the driver. The man's lips had already turned blue. He was obviously dead.

Caine crawled into the rear of the vehicle, then emerged from a shattered window next to Kanako. Bullets sparked off the car's metal frame. The muzzle flash was closer now, moving through the dark, distant trees.

Caine braced his arms on the front end of the wreckage and returned fire, sending a double tap into the shadowy trees. He heard a yelp of pain echo through the shadows.

Farther up the hill, the headlights of the vehicle that had rammed them pierced the falling snow. He heard the squeal of brakes, and another set of lights joined them.

He glanced over his shoulder. They were in a clearing several hundred feet wide, nestled between the two clumps of forest. The glowing towers of the resort rose up behind the trees. Beyond that, jagged snow-capped mountains pierced the dark sky.

'We can't stay here,' he said, his eyes scanning the forest, looking for any signs of movement, or more muzzle flash. 'If we don't have enough ammo to hold them off, and if they send men around, we'll be boxed in.'

'Just cover me,' she said, dropping to her hands and knees. 'I need that tablet.'

'Kanako,' he growled, 'we don't have—'

'Just give me a minute!'

Caine ducked behind the engine block as more gunfire tore into the wreckage. The muzzle flash was closer now, near the edge of the grove on the mountain. Caine saw a shadowy figure lean out from behind a tree.

His gun roared twice. The man staggered from the grove, then collapsed in the snow.

'Kanako, we have to move. Now!'

The woman gritted her teeth as she stretched her arm under the overturned driver's seat. 'I see it... It's stuck between the door and the seat!'

She wrenched the plastic slate loose, then scurried out of the vehicle. The tablet's screen was dark and cracked, but the flash drive was still attached. She pulled the tiny memory stick loose and slipped it into her pocket.

'Got it,' she said. 'We move single file, one at a time. The other provides covering fire.'

'Right,' Caine said, peering over the smoking hood. 'You first. Go!'

Kanako sprinted across the snow. As she ran, Caine stepped out and opened fire. The echo of his gun roared over the howling wind. He couldn't see any movement in the trees through the swirling snow. He could only hope his wild shots convinced the enemy to take cover.

As he fired, he narrowed his eyes. Two more sets of headlights appeared on the mountain road above them. Pools of light lit up the snow-covered hill, giving it a silvery gleam.

Kanako paused halfway to the opposite grove of trees. She kneeled in the snow and took aim. 'Go!'

Caine turned and sprinted toward her. More gunfire ricocheted off the SUV's frame. Kanako returned fire, targeting the orange blossoms of light in the forest.

Caine reached her position and spun around. As he aimed, he saw a line of men emerge from the trees. There were at least eight of them, all carrying submachine guns of some kind. They opened fire, sending puffs of snow exploding into the air.

'There's too many!' Caine shouted. 'Keep moving!'

He fired a few wild shots at the approaching men. Then he grabbed Kanako's arm and the two of them sprinted for the dark forest. Caine's breath misted the air as his feet dug into the thick white powder. They crossed the treeline into the forest. Bullets whistled through the air. A staccato drumbeat echoed through the night as slugs tore into the surrounding trees.

Caine ducked behind the thick trunk of a nearby oak. The snow and ice covering its branches shimmered in the moonlight, making it look as though the tree was carved from crystal. He winced as another bullet struck the trunk with a loud crack. The impact sent snow cascading down from the higher branches.

Caine leaned out and scanned the clearing. He spotted the group of men still advancing across the field. They were past the wreckage now, and halfway to the grove.

He aimed and squeezed the trigger. The roar of his gun reverberated through the trees. One of the men sprawled backwards, falling into the powder. The howling wind carried his anguished cry across the frozen ground.

The other men returned fire. Bullets screamed through the trees. Frozen branches shattered, raining down on Caine like diamond shards.

He broke cover and sprinted after Kanako. The freezing air stung his face, and his lungs felt like they were on fire. Kanako gasped for breath, winded from sprinting through the deep snow.

'Keep going!' Caine shouted. 'They're getting closer!'

As they raced through the grove, Caine squinted... The light up ahead, beaming through the trees. The hotel towers rose up in the distance. They were nearing the resort grounds.

The staccato beat of gunfire continued behind them. They exploded from the trees, and struggled up another snow-covered slope, heading for the resort. As they crested the hill, the roar of an engine rose above the wind. A single headlight pierced the snow, racing toward them. A second light followed in its wake.

Caine stopped and aimed his gun at the approaching vehicle, squinting as the headlamp blazed closer.

A pair of snowmobiles emerged from the white haze. They sputtered to a stop a few feet away. A man in his thirties rode the first vehicle. Caine could barely see his face behind his fur-lined trapper hat and goggles. A younger couple rode the vehicle behind him, and their colorful winter gear looked like expensive designer brands.

'*Nantekotta?*' the man shouted. 'What the hell? You're blocking the—'

He stopped mid-sentence. His eyes opened wide and his jaw dropped as he noticed the gun in Caine's hand.

Kanako held up an ID and stepped closer. 'Government business,' she said. 'We need to borrow one of your vehicles. Are you a guide for the hotel?'

The man nodded, dumbstruck.

'Take the other vehicle and get out of here. It's not safe,' she said in a sharp, authoritative voice.

Caine doubted the man could see Kanako's ID in the swirling snow. But he obeyed her command and dismounted the snowmobile. Caine climbed onto the idling vehicle. He glanced up at the older man.

'I'm sorry, but I'll need your goggles as well.'

The man pulled them off his head and handed them to Caine.

Kanako climbed on behind him and wrapped her arms around his waist. Caine slid the goggles over his eyes. As the guide explained what was happening to the couple, muzzle flash lit up the trees once more. Bullets streaked across the trail, burying themselves in the deep snow.

The young woman screamed, and the guide clambered on the back of their vehicle.

'*Ike!*' he shouted. 'Go, now!'

Caine gunned the throttle of his own snowmobile and sped down the trail. Behind them, he could hear the other vehicle veer away and head up the slope, back towards the hotel.

The echoes of gunfire faded into the distance.

'I think we lost them!' Kanako shouted.

Before Caine could answer, a loud thumping noise drowned out the howling wind. A circle of light blazed down across the snow. Caine looked up. A dark shape hovered in the air above them.

A helicopter swooped over the field. As it flew above them, more headlights crested a hill in the distance. A pair of vehicles bounced over the hill and came crashing down in the snow. Caine squinted at them as they roared closer. They were SUVs, like the ones they had left behind on the road. But their tires were locked into wheel drive track systems, metal brackets that allowed the spinning wheels to drive snowmobile-like treads.

'I don't think we lost them,' Caine shouted.

'*Joudan janai yo...* No kidding!'

As Caine piloted the snowmobile off the trail and swerved around a nearby hill, the helicopter opened fire.

38

Icy wind blasted Caine's face as he gunned the snowmobile's throttle. Turning the handlebars, he skidded around the hill. The vehicle's treads kicked up a plume of snow behind them. The roar of the engine was deafening. But louder still was the crackle of automatic weapon fire blazing from the helicopter above. Bullets thumped against the wood of the nearby trees.

The trail dipped low, and the snowmobile dropped behind the hill, blocking the line of fire. But the twin SUVs followed, spitting clouds of snow behind them as their treads tore through the powder. The metal brackets mounted to each wheel raised the vehicles' frames off the ground by about two feet. They loomed over the low-slung snowmobile, like lions running down a sleek gazelle.

A rider leaned out from the rear of the closest vehicle and opened fire with an MP5, spraying bullets across the snow. Kanako yelped as a slug ricocheted off the snowmobile's rear, missing her leg by inches.

Caine veered right. The vehicle's front skid bounced in the air as he left the trail and charged into a low clearing. As the two SUVs followed, the helicopter circled around the hill and dropped low, hovering directly in front of them. Peering through his goggles, Caine recognized the aircraft as a Kawasaki BK117. Its fuselage was decorated in the red and white colors of Japan's HEMS, the Helicopter Emergency Medical Services network. The main cabin was large and bulbous, and seemed out of proportion with the chopper's narrow, delicate tail. But Caine knew the design had stood the test of time, and since the eighties it had developed a reputation for reliability in tough working conditions, including inclement weather.

The rear door slid open, and a figure in black winter gear leaned out, aiming an automatic rifle in their direction.

Caine turned the wheel again, speeding towards an outcropping of trees. Bullets thudded into the surrounding tree trunks, then the helicopter swooped above them. One of the SUVs careened through the snow, roaring up on his left side. The vehicle was close enough for Caine to see the rider. A dark-haired woman in white winter gear sat behind the wheel. She turned and glared at him through the window.

It was Jiwoo Park, the woman he had battled in the Seoul marketplace.

Caine returned her stare. She arched an eyebrow and her lips curled into a faint smile. She threw the wheel to the right, sending the truck skidding across the snow towards the snowmobile.

Caine braked hard, dropping behind the SUV as it swerved in front of them. The driver's side of the SUV scraped across the trees, lighting up the shadows as sparks cascaded from its crumpled metal sidewall.

Caine gunned the throttle, racing by the passenger side of the vehicle as the woman straightened out from the crash. A man leaned out the rear window and took aim, but Kanako raised her pistol and fired. The front passenger window shattered. Her next shot struck the man with the gun, and he fell limp, his body hanging out the open rear window.

'Nice shooting!' Caine shouted back.

'It would be easier if you stopped skidding back and forth!'

Caine gunned the throttle. 'For them, too!'

The second SUV surged ahead, bouncing over a snowdrift. It came crashing down a few meters behind Caine, and the passenger opened fire. Muzzle flash blazed through the swirling haze, and bullets whined above Caine's head.

Kanako twisted behind him, struggling to get a shot at their attacker. Caine ducked low in his seat and steered left, drifting towards a narrow gulch that cut through the countryside.

'Hang on!' he shouted.

The snowmobile's engine wailed as the vehicle leapt into the air, then slammed down into the gulch. The snow was packed harder in the narrow crevasse, and the front skis wobbled back and forth as Caine struggled to control the speeding vehicle.

More bullets streaked above them. The SUV skidded up to the edge of the crevasse, sending loose snow and rocks tumbling down onto their heads. The passenger leaned farther out the window, balancing his leg on the sill as he struggled to aim his rifle at the speeding snowmobile below.

Kanako aimed her pistol. 'Slow down,' she said in a calm, level voice. 'Just a bit.'

Caine gently squeezed the brakes. The snowmobile dropped back, and the SUV raced ahead of them. The passenger opened fire, his bullets thudding into the snow on the opposite side of the crevasse, just ahead of them.

Kanako fired twice.

Their attacker uttered a strangled cry of pain as her bullets tore into his thigh. He dropped his rifle and fell out the window. He rolled down the side of the crevasse, striking the ground just ahead of Caine. The snowmobile's head-lamp lit up his face as his eyes opened wide in shock. He threw up his hands, a futile attempt to ward off the vehicle charging toward him.

Caine gunned the throttle. Kanako wrapped her arms around his waist and squeezed tight.

Crunch!

The snowmobile bounced over the wounded man. A sickening, grinding sound echoed through the crevasse as the vehicle's treads tore into his flesh. Then the vehicle slammed back down, and the mangled corpse tumbled behind them, leaving a crimson trail across the pure white snow.

Gunfire tore into the snow and rocks. The second SUV, driven by Jiwoo, raced along the opposite side of the narrow crevasse. Caine glanced left and right, searching for a way out of the gorge. They were stuck in a kill box, with enemies on either side.

'*Mite!*' Kanako shouted. 'Look!'

Ahead, the powdery snow gave way to jagged gray rocks. The walls of the crevasse narrowed, funneling them toward the dangerous terrain.

'I see it!' Caine shouted.

He spotted a shallow section of the crevasse wall, a steep slope just before the rocks. He twisted the handlebars and the vehicle drifted left, riding up the side of the crevasse. The vehicle's skids flew into the air as they leaped out of the crevasse and slammed back down into the clearing. The front shock absorbers groaned as they absorbed the impact, and the rear treads fishtailed through the snow.

Jiwoo's SUV swerved behind him. The other truck leaped over a narrow section of the gorge. Both vehicles resumed their pursuit across the snow. The helicopter swooped overhead, strafing the field with gunfire.

Kanako clenched Caine tighter and ducked as more bullets screamed past them. The snowmobile's skis slashed across the frozen ground, sending a barrage of sleet and ice into Caine's face.

Wiping a gloved hand over his goggles, Caine examined the terrain ahead of them. Towering snowbanks wound through the countryside, flanking a narrow mountain road. A snowplow lumbered through the narrow trench. The heavy yellow vehicle resembled a bulldozer with a massive blue wedge mounted at the front. The metal blade shoved the accumulated snow out of the way, sending white plumes cascading to either side of the road.

Caine darted around a grove of pine trees, staying as close to the trunks as he could for cover. He pointed the vehicle's skids at the tallest snowbank he could find, a few meters ahead of the approaching plow. He twisted the throttle, increasing speed. The vehicle exploded from the trees, making a beeline straight for the road.

Jiwoo and the other SUV veered in opposite directions, circling the trees, then meeting on the other side of the grove. The rear passenger leaned out the window and opened fire. Muzzle flash lit up the night.

'Hold on!' Caine shouted.

Kanako gripped him tighter. The snowmobile raced up the bank and sailed into the air. Caine caught a quick glimpse of the snowplow's metal blade. It was only a few meters away, and filled the entire road, with no clearance on either side.

Then the snowmobile landed on the other side of the road, spraying ice and powder from its rear treads.

Caine glanced over his shoulder. One SUV leaped across the road after him. It barely made the jump, and the vehicle's front bumper slammed into the ground on the other side. The metal and plastic bar tore loose and hung from the SUV at an angle as the vehicle bounced across the snow.

The second SUV's engine roared as it sailed into the air. Its front end dipped low and struck the edge of the snowbank. The vehicle fell into the road, tipping over onto its passenger side. A second later, the snowplow struck.

Sparks flew from the wreckage as the plow shoved the mangled SUV down the road.

The other SUV roared closer, and Caine saw the driver through the front windshield... Jiwoo glared back at him. Suddenly, a shocked expression filled her face, and she veered left.

Caine's head spun around. A large grove of trees loomed ahead of him, and the ground dipped at a sharp angle. More jagged rocks thrust up from the snow.

Caine steered around the rocks and plunged into the shadowy grove. As the snow-covered branches slapped his face, the roar of the helicopter swooped overhead. A barrage of gunfire tore through the trees, sending branches and snow flying through the air.

Caine struggled to steer with one hand as he raised the other to ward off the foliage. They were nearly through the grove, and he saw the steep, moonlit slope just a few meters ahead, through the trees.

Suddenly, a massive branch struck his arm. He heard Kanako scream behind him, felt the snowmobile's weight shift as she flew off the back. Before he could react, the snowmobile exploded from the trees and skidded down the steep slope.

Caine struggled to turn around, but he was going too fast. He squeezed the brakes, bleeding off speed so he could turn without flipping over. As he spun the handlebars, another engine roared over the wind. Jiwoo's SUV swerved around the grove, slamming into the rear corner of his snowmobile. His front skis lifted off the ground, and the snowmobile's rear end swung around.

Caine winced as he felt a crushing pain in his right leg. The snowmobile was stuck horizontally in front of the SUV, its front skids tangled between the mangled bumper and the brackets holding the treads. His leg was pinned between the two entangled vehicles. He kicked and thrashed, struggling to free himself, but it was no use.

Glancing up, he saw Jiwoo's face leering in the driver's seat. Reaching into his jacket, he drew Sota's pistol and opened fire, sending three shots into the windshield. The woman ducked as a spiderweb of cracks exploded through the glass.

Caine turned and looked ahead of them. Through the spray of ice and snow, he saw a deep, rocky gorge cutting through the mountain. They were racing towards the edge, picking up speed as the angle of the slope increased.

Turning, Caine adjusted his arm. He fired three more shots into the engine block. Smoke rose from the SUV's crumpled hood, but the vehicle continued surging down the slope.

Jiwoo's head popped up behind the windshield. Her cold, arrogant features contorted into a grimace of fear. She threw open the door and leaped from the SUV. As her body rolled across the snow, Caine looked over his shoulder again. The gorge was less than a hundred meters away, and the truck was picking up speed.

Caine wrenched his leg, but it was no use. He was caught in a vise between the twisted metal frames of the two vehicles. Glancing down, he saw the yellow metal bracket that attached the treads to the spinning front tires. Lowering his aim, Caine aimed at the bracket and opened fire, emptying his magazine into the metal clamps.

He heard the shriek of tearing metal as his bullets struck the clamp. One of the metal brackets snapped, and the clamp lost its grip. The tread flew loose and the bracket dislodged from the vehicle. As the front right tire dipped, the hanging bumper caught in the snow and tore loose. The snowmobile swiveled away from the truck.

Caine yanked his leg free and dove off the vehicle. A shock wave ran through his body as he struck the snow at a bone-rattling speed. He continued tumbling down the steep slope, his flailing arms and legs unable to slow his descent. He heard the motor of the SUV rev higher as it launched off the rocks and flew into the air, carrying the damaged snowmobile with it.

A split second after that, Caine felt his stomach lurch as he rolled over the edge and plummeted through the frigid air. A winding ribbon of pale blue ice rushed toward him, shimmering in the moonlight. The two vehicles struck first, shattering the frozen river and sinking into the churning, dark water.

Caine hit the water a few meters away and sank like a rock. The frigid water felt like white-hot needles of pain, stabbing at his skin. His breath exploded from his lungs. The darkness swallowed him, and before he could even get his bearings, the current sent him tumbling away beneath the ice.

* * *

Jiwoo staggered to her feet, gasping for breath. She winced as she felt a burning sensation in her torso. Glancing down, she saw her winter coat was torn, and blood stained her clothes. A mottled bruise colored her skin near the wound. The result of a rock or branch she had struck in her tumble across the ice.

Ignoring the pain in her side, she sidestepped down the slope, moving closer to the gorge. Peering over the edge, she saw the lights of the SUV beaming up through the water as it sank. Chunks of ice spiraled through the water around the site of impact, and churning white rapids carried bits of the wreckage beneath the frozen river's surface.

She scanned the trees along the riverbanks. Her breath misted the air, and the wind blew her hair behind her as her eyes darted left and right. There was no sign of the American, Caine. She doubted he could have survived the fall. And even if he did, the currents would have carried him under the ice.

The thumping of rotor blades roared overhead. The helicopter hovered just above the ground, farther up the slope. She turned and limped through the snow, ducking her head to ward off the bitter wind and frozen hail.

As she approached the hovering aircraft, a pair of her men emerged from the trees, dragging a struggling woman through the snow. Jiwoo stood beneath the rotors, rigid as a statue. The prop wash sent her hair streaming behind her. As the men approached, their captive glared up at her.

It was the girl, Kanako.

'You're too late,' Kanako said, shouting over the noise of the helicopter. 'My government knows I'm here. They know everything.'

'We shall see,' Jiwoo replied. 'I suspect they will soon have other concerns.'

She nodded to the rear of the chopper. The cabin door slid open, and the two men dragged her inside.

Jiwoo looked over her shoulder, casting one last glance over the snow-covered cliff. Then she turned and climbed up into the helicopter. She slid the door closed, and within seconds, they were airborne.

The helicopter pierced the clouds as snow continued to blanket the ground below.

39

Caine's body tumbled through the dark water as the current carried him downriver. His lungs burned, and his body felt numb. Moonlight reflected off the ice above, giving the frozen surface a ghostly luminescence. Beneath the pale, translucent sheet, the water was pitch black, a liquid shadow embracing him in its frozen grasp.

As the raging water swept him along, his spinning body struck a rock. Pain radiated through his shoulder. He opened his eyes, but the freezing water and limited light reduced his vision to a blur. Gnarled shapes reached out from the darkness, like grasping claws. Fallen branches, rocks, and other debris lined the riverbed, but it was impossible to see anything clearly.

Fighting against the current, Caine oriented himself to face the silvery ice overhead. He kicked his feet, swimming up and away from the submerged debris. His hands touched the cold, rough surface. Bubbles streamed from his sealed lips as he pounded at the ice, but he could not break through. The swirling water carried him farther downriver. His hands slid along the ice, unable to find purchase.

The water swept him away, and again he tumbled through the darkness. A few seconds later, the motion ceased... The river grew deeper, and the current slowed. Caine shook his head, struggling to think clearly. He knew that in free-diving situations, panic and fear were the greatest enemies. The faster his heart beat, the sooner he would use up what little oxygen he had. He forced himself to relax and gently drift in the water.

Kicking his legs, he drove himself back up to the icy surface. He pounded his fist against the frozen barrier. The ice wasn't thick, but the water slowed his movements. He couldn't generate enough force to break through.

He knew from his training he could hold his breath for about three minutes underwater. How much time had elapsed since the river had carried him away? He had no way of knowing. He felt dizzy, light-headed. As he peered up through the ice, a red haze filled his vision.

He blinked. Darkness closed in around him. The soft, glowing light of the ice seemed to recede into the distance, like a tiny pinpoint of light. He couldn't touch it, even though he knew it was less than a meter above him.

The darkness closed around him, drowning out what little light remained. His arms and legs went limp. The water cradled him in its frozen embrace.

'*Shhh, it's all right.*' He heard Gaya's voice, a faint echo reverberating through the shadows at the edge of his consciousness. '*This is dauntaimu.*'

No, Caine thought. *Not yet.*

Forcing his limbs to move, he spun himself away from the ice and dove deeper, plunging to the bottom of the river. The surging water had deposited him into a deep pool, and it took him a few seconds to find the bottom. The pressure of the deeper water increased the oxygen saturation in his blood. He felt the fog in his head lift, and his thoughts grew clearer.

It was an old diving trick, but he knew it wouldn't buy him much time. His lungs burned, and his extremities were numb from the cold. Swimming over the bottom of the pool, his hands searched for a loose rock or branch, anything that might help him shatter the ice above. His probing fingers touched a sharp metal surface. He couldn't see the object in the gloom, but he grabbed hold and tugged it free from the rocks.

Bubbles streamed from his lips as he kicked his feet and ascended back to the ice. His heart pounded in his chest, and he felt the crimson haze clouding his vision once more. As he neared the moonlit ice, he glanced down at the object in his hands.

It was a narrow, pointed slab of composite material, some kind of plastic. A bent metal strut protruded from the object's rear. The twisted, worn metal looked as if it had snapped off whatever it was once attached to.

Snowmobile ski, Caine thought. *It must have broken free in the wreckage. The current carried it along with me.*

He slammed the pointed end of the ski into the ice, fighting against the water. The tip struck the surface with a dull thud that echoed around him. He jabbed it up again, angling the pointed end of the ski to slice through the water more efficiently.

Bubbles exploded from his mouth. A crimson haze surrounded his vision once more. The ice grew darker. His oxygen-starved brain was shutting down. He was running out of time.

He thrust the ski into the ice again. A tiny white crack ran across the surface. He heard a sound, like shattering glass, echo through the water. His limbs seemed to otherwise move in slow motion, but he forced himself to strike with the ski again. The crack grew larger, a shimmering spiderweb moving across the frozen shroud.

His vision went dark. He couldn't see, couldn't feel. He was moving on instinct, not even aware of what his body was doing. The neurons fired, racing from his brain to his arms. And again, he stabbed at the ice with the ski.

The ice shattered, and his head popped up through the hole, gasping for breath. He coughed as the freezing air struck his lungs, but he continued panting, sucking in oxygen in great gulps.

He felt a surge of strength as adrenaline flooded his body. He pulled himself up from the ice, and lay on his belly, prone against the frozen river's surface. Inch by inch, he dragged himself across the surface, carefully distributing his weight so as not to break the ice and fall through again.

His soaking-wet body shivered in the wind. His arms and legs felt like frozen jelly, but he forced himself to keep moving. Finally, he reached the riverbank. Standing on shaky legs, he stumbled as he tried to walk. He leaned on a nearby tree for balance and continued gasping for breath.

As he got his bearings, he heard a distant thumping, echoing above the wind. Glancing up, he saw the lights of a helicopter ascending into the clouds.

Jiwoo and her men are leaving, he thought. *Which means they got what they came for.*

Kanako.

It was possible the young woman had escaped. She was clearly tough and resourceful. But on foot, in the woods, with only a pistol... He doubted she would have made it far before the men pursuing them had taken her.

His teeth chattered as he watched the helicopter vanish into the swirling snow. Rubbing his body for warmth, he turned and stalked into the forest. He had to assume Byakko, the White Tiger, had captured Kanako, along with whatever intel she had retrieved from Chan Tae Young. Which meant whatever the gangster was planning, the clock was ticking.

And time was running out.

40

OTARU, JAPAN

International waters, 45 minutes later

Kanako stumbled as the ship rolled beneath her feet. Black clouds gathered on the horizon, and white-capped waves flecked the dark seawater. She gasped as she lost her balance and fell to the deck.

Looking up, she saw a crane moving above her. A metal cargo container dangled from the steel cables running from the jib arm. The red metal box was forty feet long and eight feet wide. It spun in a lazy arc as the wind and waves rocked the massive cargo ship.

The helicopter that had carried them from Otaru sat on a helipad in the center of the deck. More cargo containers filled the bow in stacks of three. On the starboard side of the ship, two armed guards led a row of men, women, and children across the lurching deck. One by one, they filed into an open container.

In the distance, a smaller cargo ship bounced over the waves, moving away from the larger vessel. Two more smaller ships remained nearby, moored to the larger ship's hull. As the deck shifted again, Kanako heard the shriek of metal, followed by a low groan. The ships were rubbing together, colliding in the rough sea.

Jiwoo glared down at Kanako. One of her men dragged the Japanese woman to her feet. She nodded at the people in the distance.

'Who are they?' she asked.

Jiwoo turned and watched as the people continued filling the container. Her expression was blank, unreadable. 'They are not your concern.'

She marched ahead, and the men shoved Kanako after her.

'This weather is getting worse, and my government knows where I am,' Kanako said, her voice brimming with confidence. 'You won't be able to offload all this cargo before they—'

'I am not interested in your lies,' Jiwoo said, cutting her off. 'We will talk soon enough. I shall employ great pain to purify your words. We will get to the truth, you and I.'

'The truth?' Kanako replied with a bitter laugh. 'The truth is, you work for a gangster who takes advantage of women and children and traffics them around the world. Where are these people from? The Philippines? China? North Korea? You're selling your own people for—'

Jiwoo spun around. Her arm lashed out, striking Kanako across the face with a deafening crack. The blow knocked the woman back, and she fell to her knees.

'My people?' Jiwoo hissed. 'What do you know of my people? The Japanese are the puppets of the West. First you, then your American masters, tore my country in two. Starved our children, slaughtered our men, raped our women. Even so, we prevail. The American tyrants strangle us with economic sanctions, spreading famine and disease across our land. And all the while, you wait patiently by the table as they feed you their scraps. Choking on the ashes of your former empire.'

Kanako glanced back at the bedraggled people. A wave crashed over the side of the vessel, dousing the huddled mob in cold water. The guards shouted and screamed, herding them on.

'We can't change the past,' she said. 'But what of these children? What future will they have?'

Jiwoo's features hardened into a cold, emotionless mask. 'Those children have already endured more hardship than someone like you could imagine. Their sacrifice, along with our great leader's wisdom, shall return our nation to prosperity.'

Jiwoo marched ahead. 'Pick her up,' she called back to her men. 'If she resists again, throw her overboard.'

* * *

Jiwoo and her men led Kanako into the superstructure at the rear of the ship, a white tower rising from the stern. Upon entering the tower, Kanako was surprised to see that a large plastic tent took up most of the space inside. Within the clear plastic flaps, more women and children huddled on the floor.

A security guard wearing an oxygen mask tapped the screen of a tablet. He called out names in Korean. A few women in the group raised their hands and shuffled forward. As the guards asked them a series of questions, another woman sat down in a folding chair. A man wearing a white coat handed her a small white nasal inhaler from a plastic container. Dozens of similar devices lay nestled in the container's foam-lined compartments.

The woman inserted the inhaler into her nostril, then took a deep inhale, breathing the contents into her lungs.

As the armed guards led the woman outside, Jiwoo stepped into a small elevator running along the superstructure's rear wall. Kanako struggled, but one of the guards dragged her in. The other remained behind, as there was no room for him in the tiny car.

Kanako glanced at her captors, sizing them up. Jiwoo returned her stare, her eyes unblinking, unreadable. The armed man pressed the barrel of his submachine gun into Kanako's torso.

The message was simple. Trying to fight her way out of the tiny car, with her arms bound behind her back, would be suicide. Kanako ignored them and stared at the elevator doors as the car descended into the ship's hull.

They only traveled a short distance before the doors opened again. The guard shoved her out into a dark metal corridor. Again, the deck swayed beneath her feet, and the hull groaned around her. Water dripped from the rusted ceiling as waves battered the ship.

They guided her down the corridor to a shiny metal security door near the stern. Jiwoo swiped a card over a security terminal, and the door slid open. White mist drifted out, and the air felt cooler beyond the door.

She put up a token resistance as they dragged her into the dark room, but there was little she could do with her arms restrained. Glancing around the cavernous chamber, she saw it was a meat locker or refrigerated room of some kind. Frost clung to the walls, and frozen beef carcasses hung from hooks on the ceiling.

As her eyes adjusted to the dim light, she gasped. A body lay on the floor. The young Japanese man's face was beaten and bruised, and he was naked from the waist up. Yakuza tattoos covered his torso, and a pale rime of frost clung to his skin.

As far as Kanako could tell, he wasn't breathing.

Hideo Torazama, the man known as Byakko, stood at the far end of the room, wiping blood from his hands with a rag. Although he stood with his back to her, she recognized the tattoo of the white tiger which adorned his back. The design rippled as the muscular man flexed his arms and shoulders.

'Natsuki-san,' he growled, addressing her without turning around. 'Welcome aboard. I apologize for the cold. I find sparring in such extreme temperatures toughens the body. Just as practicing shogi hones the mind.'

'You're wasting your time out here,' Kanako snapped. 'My government is already—'

'The Japanese government is just as clueless as the Americans,' Byakko said. He spun around to face her, his cat-like eyes gleaming in the dim light. 'They both allow hate and fear to fester, even as ignorance tears them apart from within.'

Jiwoo held up the memory stick she had taken from Kanako. 'The traitor, Chan, left this in a hotel room.'

Byakko plucked the tiny sliver from her fingers. He squinted at it, holding it up to the light. 'Ah, poor Chan. He was quite taken with you, Kanako. The fool had whores in every city, but he threw away his life for you. A Naicho agent working undercover in my club. You could say he died for you. Romantic, I suppose.'

'Even Chan knew you were psychotic,' Kanako said. 'You're responsible for the viral outbreak in the United States and South Korea, aren't you?'

Byakko grinned and gave her a modest bow. 'Of course. The H5N9v-CV virus, better known as K-Pox. Catchy, don't you think? Rowan was a fool, but he had a flair for the dramatic. Still, it was not my hands that crafted this pathogen. Chan Tae Young delivered the virus to his handlers in Unit 99 years ago.'

'The refugees above decks,' Kanako replied, her eyes meeting the man's sinister stare. 'You're infecting them with this sickness, then trafficking them around the world. To what end? How many have died for your insane delusion?'

Byakko chuckled. 'Surprisingly few. This virus was an abandoned project, a joint effort between US and South Korean bio companies. Some sort of test organism, designed for developing vaccines. Unit 99 thought it was useless. Not lethal, they said. Too weak to be effective. But I showed them that in the proper hands, a tiny needle can be deadlier than the sharpest sword. So long as it injects just the right dose of poison into an enemy's veins.'

Kanako squinted at him in the dim light. 'Not lethal? Then why? What can you hope to gain?'

'Oh, there have been deaths, of course,' Byakko replied. 'The sick, the elderly. Those with weakened immune systems. But death, on a mass scale, was not my goal. At least, not yet. This so-called K-Pox was never meant to kill. But it did have one redeeming feature. Its gene sequence was designed to appear natural, rather than man-made. Making it the prefect infiltrator. A saboteur, rather than an assassin.'

The tall, muscular man returned the thumb drive to Jiwoo, then dropped the rag he was holding on the floor. One of his men handed him a fur-lined coat, which he threw over his bare torso.

'Natsuki-san, have you ever heard the term "R-Naught"?'

The woman glared back at him but said nothing. Byakko grinned.

'It's a term used in virology and the study of communicable diseases. It represents the number of people a single infected individual can be expected to spread the pathogen to before they die. That's the tricky thing about viral weapons. The more lethal they are, the less effective they become.'

'In other words,' Kanako said, staring into the man's unnerving feline eyes, 'they kill the host before they can spread.'

'Very good,' Byakko replied. 'But as I said, mass death was not my goal. Sickness. Disease. Vermin... For centuries, xenophobes and racists around the world have played on these fears. Blamed immigrants and marginalized populations for plagues and outbreaks. For example, did you know the so-called Spanish flu actually began in British Army camps throughout mainland Europe?'

Kanako's eyes opened wide as she grasped the meaning of the man's words. 'You wanted the virus to spread. To build resentment in America, drive them away from their South Korean allies.'

The man's cat-like eyes shimmered in the dim light. 'Yes, their Mutual Defense treaty, an alliance that has stood for decades. Crumbling in a matter of weeks, thanks to my genius. When the self-appointed "leader of the free world" bows to the whims of extremists and demagogs, weaponizing hatred and fear requires nothing more than a few keystrokes. And as my virus spreads, a virus of another kind burns across the internet.'

Byakko gestured to his men. One of the guards slashed Kanako's coat with a knife. Another man grabbed a small control box hanging from a cable. He pressed a button, and a chain lowered from the ceiling. The metal links clanked and swayed as a large hook descended from above. The first man tore the remains of her coat from her body. She shivered in the freezing chamber, her breath misting the air.

His men looped the zip ties binding Kanako's hands around the hook. One of them grabbed the control box, and the chain rose back up, dragging Kanako into the air. She kicked and squirmed, but could not free herself from her bonds as she dangled above the frost-covered floor.

'But you're sending those people into Japan as well,' she said, gasping as her arms and shoulders burned in agony. 'Why? What does Japan have to do with—'

Byakko's unnerving eyes leered up at her as she dangled from the chain. 'The United States tore my country in two,' he snarled. 'But it was Japan that ripped my family, my flesh and blood, away from me. Soon, both countries will pay the price for their complicity.'

He grinned and clasped his hands behind his back. Jiwoo stood beside him, looking up with her familiar empty stare. She rested her hand on the taller man's shoulder.

'As far as my employers are concerned, I have completed my task,' Byakko said. He slipped a pair of sunglasses from his coat and covered his strange eyes. 'The United States carrier group has halted en route to Seoul. The first brick in the wall has fallen. More will follow. And soon, their alliance will shatter.'

'No one will believe South Korea covered up a pandemic,' Kanako spat. 'Your story falls apart with just the slightest scrutiny!'

'Oh? Even as we speak, the president is conferring with his advisors. I'm confident he will soon announce that Operation Freedom's Spear has been aborted. And as the death toll rises, military aid to South Korea will end as well.'

'Death toll? But you said—'

'In life, as in shogi, patience is the key to victory,' Byakko growled. 'The first strains of the virus were non-lethal, slow-acting. Perfect for building fear, stoking the fires of resentment. Now comes checkmate, the killing stroke. The people you saw above? In forty-eight hours, they shall become contagious. And they will deliver a somewhat upgraded form of the virus. Its lethality will limit its spread, but I am confident the death toll will number in the tens of thousands. Both in the United States, as well as South Korea and Japan. The president's lapdogs in the Pacific.'

As Byakko and Jiwoo turned to leave the chamber, Kanako spat on the floor. 'And what about you, Torazama-san? How much did your North Korean masters pay you to murder innocent women and children?'

The man spun around. His sneer turned into a feral snarl. He ripped off his glasses, letting the full weight of his unnerving stare bore into Kanako's frightened eyes.

'Money? This was never about money. This is my chance to reclaim my legacy. And to enact my revenge. There is no price I would not pay, nothing I would not sacrifice for such an opportunity.'

He paused, watching as Kanako's body shivered in the cold. She swayed back and forth on the hook, the chains clanking in the dark recesses of the ceiling.

'You have a fiery temper, Natsuki-san. But the cold... It saps one's strength. Makes it hard to think clearly. As a boy, my father would punish me when I lost a shogi match. He would force me to sleep in our shed, out in the snow and ice. Then, I would replay the game. And if I lost again...'

His words faded, and he grew silent. He gazed at the frost covering the chamber's metal walls. He was breathing hard, panting almost. Tiny clouds of mist drifted from his mouth.

His eyes traveled back to the hanging woman. 'Let us see how you fare after a few hours in the cold. By then, Natsuki-san, I will have already won. Soon, this ship will be on its way to the bottom of the sea. Taking you along with it.'

He turned and exited the room, followed by his entourage. Jiwoo remained, staring up at Kanako with her cold, dark eyes.

'You will not live to drown,' the woman said, the faintest trace of a smile playing across her lips. 'You will beg to tell me all you know. And when we are finished, I shall mark you, as I have marked so many others. I will watch you gasp your last breath.'

She stared at Kanako for a few more seconds, her eyes wide and unblinking. Then she spun around and followed the others out of the room.

The door slid shut, leaving Kanako alone in the freezing darkness.

41

TOMAMU, JAPAN

Caine stumbled into his domed tent, grabbed a fur blanket off the bed, and wrapped it around his shoulders. His lips were blue and his hair and clothes were still damp. He poured himself a tumbler of whisky from the bar, then threw the drink down, his teeth chattering against the glass. The alcohol warmed his throat and eased the chills running through his body.

He knew the effect was just a rapid dilation of blood vessels that gave the illusion of warmth. But he didn't care.

He poured himself another drink.

After taking a sip, he gathered his clothes and stuffed them into his bag. He debated traipsing back out into the snow to take a warm shower at the main building. But it was too risky. Earlier, after exiting the dark, frozen woods, he had stumbled upon a small back country road. A kind local driving a white Toyota Yaris Cross had stopped to pick him up.

The weathered old woman had squinted her eyes and pursed her lips when she saw Caine's soaking-wet clothes and half-frozen hair. Shaking her head, she muttered, '*Kankoukyaku*... Tourists. Lucky you don't all freeze to death!'

She had dropped him off at the campsite, then motored off into the swirling snow. But Caine knew it was only a matter of time before police reports searching for a soaking-wet American circulated on all the local radio and TV stations. Sooner or later, she, or another witness from the resort, would lead the authorities to his door.

He had to move quickly.

Hs stripped off his wet rags, then threw on clean, dry clothes. Clean thermals, a pair of jeans, and a wool sweater. He would have to keep the wet coat until he could purchase another one.

As he stashed his remaining dry clothes in his bag, it suddenly occurred to him that he had no idea where to go next. He'd been so focused on survival for the last several hours, he had not had time to plan his next steps. If the White Tiger really was working with the North Koreans, Caine doubted they would bring Kanako back to Sapporo. Whatever they were planning, they had already drawn too much attention to themselves. They would want somewhere more remote, a place they could interrogate her without attracting attention.

But where?

Before he could dwell on the problem any further, a noise outside snapped him to full alert. He could not say exactly what it was he had heard. A breaking twig, shuffling footsteps. Whatever it was, it had registered with his subconscious, alerting him that someone was outside the tent.

He froze in place. Footsteps crunched across the snow outside... Someone was circling around his dome. The curtains were drawn over the panoramic window, but the lights were on. Caine darted to the side, making sure his silhouette would not give away his position through the sheer fabric panels.

The footsteps continued. Caine counted at least three different people. He grabbed a steak knife from the sink, then stood next to the door. There was no place to hide in the domed tent, other than under the bed. And with multiple people searching the dwelling, he doubted he could remain hidden there for long.

He heard a clicking sound come from the door, the rasp of a metal tool. Someone was picking the lock.

He took a deep breath and raised the knife. The door creaked open.

Footsteps entered the dome.

He tensed, preparing to strike...

'Tom? Are you here?' a woman's voice called out.

Mariko!

Caine emerged from the shadows, grinning. Mariko stood inside the dome, flanked by a pair of beefy-looking Japanese men. She gasped when she saw him.

'*Nantekotta...* What the hell? Are you okay?'

Caine nodded and took a step towards her. He stumbled, suddenly exhausted. He had been running on adrenaline for hours. He needed food, sleep, and warmth.

Mariko embraced him, then led him to the bed. 'Here, sit down. *Hidoi...* You look terrible!'

'Thanks,' Caine muttered. 'Nice to see you, too. Speaking of which, what the hell are you doing here? You're supposed to be with—'

Mariko rolled her eyes. 'Koichi? Please, that old gangster will outlive us all. It was a close call, but now that he knows who the traitor in his organization is, he's managed to surround himself with allies. He sent me here to help you.'

Mariko noticed the half-empty glass of Scotch on the table. She drank it, then refilled the glass and handed it to Caine. He nodded his thanks.

'Sounded like you ran into trouble,' he said, after taking another sip.

She crossed her arms, hugging her body. 'Mmm. Tetsuo, Koichi's second, made a play for him. For all their talk of loyalty, I never met a yakuza who wouldn't turn on his own mother to get a bigger cut.' She turned and smiled at the men standing in the doorway behind her. 'No offense.'

One of the men shrugged. He sat down at the table and poured himself a drink. The other paced back and forth in the tent.

Caine nodded. 'Makes sense. So Tetsuo sold him out to the White Tiger. You're lucky you made it out of there alive.'

Mariko hugged herself tighter. 'Not all of us were so lucky. Junko...' Her voice trailed off.

'The kid with the fancy car?' Caine asked.

She nodded.

'Is he dead?'

She shook her head. 'No. He is hurt, but alive. Or at least he was. Tetsuo captured him when we fled the safe house.'

Caine took a long swallow of whisky. 'So that's how Jiwoo and her men found me.'

Mariko looked down at the floor. 'Junko-kun fought bravely. He would never give you up if he could—'

Caine shook his head. 'No one can hold out forever, Mariko. It doesn't matter now, anyway. Byakko's people have Kanako. And I have no idea where they've taken her.'

Mariko smiled. 'Then it's a good thing I found you as well.'

Caine narrowed his eyes. 'What do you mean?'

'I spoke to your... friend. Rebecca.' Mariko's smile grew wider, warmer. 'She's been trying to reach you. She seems like a very intelligent woman. You're lucky she's on your side.'

'Damn straight.' Caine stood. This time, he appeared steadier on his feet. 'Did she have new intel?'

'North Korean operatives assassinated a journalist in DC. Someone named Carter Rowan.'

Caine furrowed his brow. 'Calling Rowan a journalist might be a little generous, but go on.'

'A friend of Rebeca's, an FBI special agent, was on site. They found something on one of the killers. Evidence pointing to a ship named the Eiko Maru. It's parked in international waters off the coast of Otaru.'

'Koichi said Hideo Torazama, the White Tiger himself, is from Otaru. That can't be a coincidence.'

Mariko looked him up and down. A slight frown crossed her lips. 'Ogawa-san has rented a private helicopter. It will take us wherever we need to go, but—'

'But what?' Caine asked, his emerald eyes glaring at her in the dim light.

'Tom, you're exhausted. You're in no condition to—'

'Where's the heliport?' Caine demanded.

'Tokachi-Obihiro Airport,' one of the men grunted. 'Two-hour drive in this weather.'

'Then I can sleep on the way,' Caine said, grabbing his bag. 'Let's not waste time.'

'Tom...' Mariko sounded uncertain.

Caine looked her in the eye. 'The longer we stay here, the more likely it is the police will find us. If we're detained, we may never get to the bottom of whatever this White Tiger has planned. And Kanako... She's not just Koichi's daughter. She's like us.'

Mariko squinted and tilted her head. '*Wakarimasen*... I don't understand.'

'Koichi had it all wrong. The drugs, the hostess bars, that was all a cover. Kanako isn't some troubled young girl. She works for the Japanese government. She's a Naicho officer, investigating ties between the yakuza and North Korean Intelligence. And right now, she's on her own. She needs backup.'

Mariko sighed. 'We are *ronin* once more, it seems.' She turned to one of the men. 'You, carry his things.'

The muscular thug stood and grabbed Caine's duffel bag from his hands.

Mariko turned back to Caine, a serious look on her face. 'You say she needs backup? We will have to suffice. But we're stopping along the way for some hot tea.'

She scrunched her nose as Caine threw on his damp outerwear.

'And we must find you a new coat. You'll freeze to death in that thing. And you smell like a wet dog.'

Caine grinned as he followed her out the door. 'I've been called worse.'

42

OTARU, JAPAN

International waters, 12 hours later

Black clouds gathered in the sky, leaving little room for what small amount of sunlight there was to shine through. The sea churned and roiled beneath the wooden fishing vessel, tossing the ship into the troughs between waves like a child's toy in a bath. The radio in the boat's cabin bleated a series of storm warnings, spaced between bursts of static. Although not yet at typhoon levels, the storm was moving closer to the coast, and the white-capped waves already exceeded three meters in height.

Caine clutched the railing running along the bow as the ship lurched up, buoyed by another surging wave. Rain pelted his face and beaded up on the black waxed canvas slicker he wore over his clothes. Mariko stood next to him, gripping the railing with both hands. She gasped as the ship plunged back down, slamming into the sea and sending a light spray into the air.

'The storm is moving closer,' she shouted. 'If it gets any worse, we won't be able to stay out here for long.'

Caine squinted as he peered at the clouds on the horizon. The wind whipped the rain and spray into his face like icy needles, but he didn't flinch as the boat surged ahead.

'We'll make it through,' he finally said.

'How do you know?'

He shrugged. 'I've spent my share of time in stormy waters.'

Mariko stared back at him as raindrops pelted her face. She shook her head. ' *kureijii da...* This is crazy!'

Caine nodded. 'Probably. Glad I'm not doing it alone.'

Mariko's features softened, and she looked away. Suddenly, the ship lurched again. Waves crashed over the bow, and her foot slipped on the wet deck. Caine grabbed her waist, steadying her as the boat crashed back down.

'We'd better get back inside,' he shouted.

'I hate boats,' she shouted as he helped guide her along the narrow passage between the side of the hull and the cabin. Another wave crashed over the side, dousing them both in freezing water.

'I can't imagine why,' he shouted back.

He opened the cabin's side door, fighting against the wind. The two of them entered the ship's bridge, and Caine shut the door behind them. The tiny room smelled of smoke, sweat, and brine. The vessel's captain, a short, stocky woman named Tomoko, clenched a lit cigarette between her lips as she fought to keep the wheel steady. Caine didn't know her exact age, but her sunbaked, cherubic face had a patina like well-worn leather. Tufts of long gray hair flared around her ears beneath her orange wool cap.

The two yakuza men who had accompanied Mariko steadied themselves against the rear wall of the cabin as the boat pitched and rolled in the violent sea.

'Can't you keep this damn boat steady?' one of the men grumbled. The other blanched as the bow plunged down the face of a wave.

'Look at you two,' Tomoko grunted, still puffing on her cigarette. 'Bunch of *yowamushi...* cowards.'

The pale man vomited in a trash can. His partner shook his head and glared at the woman.

'Women on land, men at sea,' he muttered.

'She got us this far,' Caine said, shooting the man a stern glare. 'I wouldn't want to pilot a boat in this weather.'

Tomoko glanced back at him over her shoulder. 'Yeah. You want to take the wheel, tough guy?'

A massive wave crashed over the bow, splattering the cabin's window with sheets of water. The yakuza thug grunted and shook his head.

The woman nodded. 'That's what I thought.'

Mariko laughed as she struggled to keep her balance. 'They're not so bad once you get to know them,' she said. 'And I have to admit, I don't think I've ever seen a female fishing captain before.'

Tomoko spun the wheel, steering the ship down a trough between waves. 'All the men I know in this business are pushing seventy. Industry needed fresh blood, so they offered me a shot. Sure, you don't see many women working trawlers like this one, but that doesn't mean we don't exist.'

She turned back to the two yakuza men, as the sickly one retched again. 'So watch your tongue. And if ya spill yer guts on my deck, I'll kick your ass overboard, *wakarimasu ka?*'

Before the man could answer, a beep sounded from the marine radar display bolted next to the wheel. A tiny green light blinked within the haze of the storm on the square display.

'There she is,' Tomoko grunted. 'The Eiko Maru. She's a big one, over 100,000 tons.'

'Is that too large to dock in Otaru's ports?' Mariko asked.

Tomoko shook her head. '*Iie*, no. Otaru's port can handle bigger ships than that. Officially, she's filed a notice of repair, something about rust damage on her hull. They're using smaller feeder ships to transfer her cargo. Sounds like bullshit to me, if she can weather a storm like this.'

'Koichi said Torazama's group is involved in human trafficking,' Caine said, peering out the window. Rain and sea spray pelted the glass. 'Sending smaller ships into multiple ports spreads out the risk, makes their movements harder to track.'

'Like a shell game,' Mariko replied. 'The authorities never know which ship is hiding the contraband, if any.'

A dark shape emerged from the mist, bobbing on the waves ahead of them. As Tomoko's boat surged over another wave, the ship in the distance became clearer. Its hull was massive, three football fields' worth of iron and steel. The vessel was nearly empty of cargo, and only a few colorful stacks of metal containers filled the fore and aft sections. The rest of the sprawling deck was open space, with the ship's bridge tower rising from the stern.

A skeleton of bright blue metal beams surrounded the ship, allowing the massive gantry cranes mounted overhead to slide fore and aft. One of the crane jib arms hung out over the roiling ocean. A red metal container swung from the crane's steel cable like a pendulum, lowering to the deck of a smaller cargo vessel lashed to the main boat.

'They're unloading cargo in this weather?' Tomoko exclaimed. 'They must be crazy!'

'Or they're on a tight schedule,' Caine said, keeping his eye on the ship as they moved closer. He turned to Mariko. 'I have to get ready. You know what to do?'

She nodded. '*Hai*. We will be ready.'

Caine moved to the back of the cabin, balancing as the deck swayed upon the waves. He opened a series of plastic crates, revealing an assortment of diving gear and weapons. Unzipping a rubber waterproof bag, he pulled out a black neoprene dry suit and hung it on the hook. Then he removed his rain slicker and tugged off his sweater.

'Sorry, it's faster to change here, instead of lugging all their gear below decks,' he said, as he unbuttoned his pants.

Mariko blushed. 'Of course.'

She turned around to give him some privacy. Tilting her head, she gave Tomoko a surprised look. The older woman leered at Caine's lean, muscular torso. Tomoko noticed her stare and shrugged.

'What? Every job has its perks, eh?' she said with a raspy cackle.

* * *

The cargo vessel's hull creaked and groaned as it shifted atop the roiling sea. The mighty ship displaced a massive amount of water. A system of ballast tanks and bilge keel fins fought to keep the ship stable in the churning waves. But even with these advanced systems in place, the deck still rolled beneath the crew's feet.

Byakko stood with his hands behind his back, allowing his knees to flex as the ship moved around him. He maintained perfect balance, glaring at the shogi game on the large screen as his men stumbled around him.

An alarm sounded, dragging his attention away from the game. Glancing at one of the smaller monitors, he watched as a massive wave crashed into the ship's bow. Seawater flooded the deck, and the hull creaked again as the ship tilted to port.

'Sir, we're taking on water,' one of the crewmen shouted.

Although Byakko knew the ship's bridge received the crewman's transmission as well, he did not wait for the captain to reply. Instead, he stepped behind the man's chair and examined his instruments.

'Lower starboard ballast to 80 percent,' he growled.

The crewmen looked up, surprised to see the yakuza gangster hovering so close to his chair. 'Uh, aye, sir.'

He tapped some commands into his keyboard. The sound of hydraulic pumps echoed through the control room, and the ship slowly righted itself.

'How much longer until we offload our cargo?' Byakko asked.

The crewman checked his screen. 'Four more containers to go, sir. This storm is really slowing us down. The last container almost fell into the—'

'I'm not interested in excuses,' Byakko growled. 'Get it done. We're behind schedule as it is!'

'Yes, sir!'

The crewman hunched over his terminal, nervously tapping keys as more waves battered the hull.

A shrill alarm beeped from another crewman's terminal. Byakko glanced over at the sound. The man's radar display showed a blinking red dot moving closer to their position.

'What is that?' he demanded, striding across the shifting deck.

The crewman checked the data on his screen. 'Unknown, sir. It's a vessel of some kind. Too small to have Automatic Identification System installed.'

'Warn them off!' Byakko ordered.

The crewman nodded and tapped his keyboard. 'Opening a channel.'

He adjusted the microphone attached to his headset. 'Attention unidentified vessel. You are in violation of International Regulations for Preventing Collisions at Sea. Repeat, you are in violation of IRPCS. Move off to a safe distance immediately.'

The radio squawked with static. Finally, a gruff woman's voice answered back, crackling through the speakers. 'Check your instruments. We're within the safety zone and licensed to operate in these waters by Japan's Ministry of Agriculture, Forestry and Fisheries.'

'Tell them if they don't move off, we will consider them pirates and shoot them on sight!' Byakko demanded.

The crewman gave Byakko a nervous look. The gangster's impenetrable stare gazed down upon him, his cat-like eyes reflecting the glare of the computer screen.

Gulping, the crewman nodded and tapped the transmit key. 'Negative, repeat negative. You are in international waters. If you do not move off to a safe distance, we will consider you hostile and will defend ourselves accordingly.'

'*Ochitsuke*, relax,' the voice responded. 'We've cut our nets and we're moving off. But I'm filing a protest with MAFF, you *kusottare—*'

The crewman cut the transmission. The red dot blinked on the radar screen. The boat moved away from them, circling the area at a slow, steady speed.

'They're falling back,' he said, relief in his voice.

'Keep an eye on them,' Torazama replied, still staring at the radar screen. 'If they move any closer, alert me immediately.'

'*Hai*, yes, sir,' the crewman replied, bowing his head.

Torazama peered at the screen for a few more seconds. Then he turned and paced back toward his larger screens. His footsteps echoed through the cargo hold.

'Load the next container!' he bellowed.

A guard nodded and exited the control room. On the monitors, guards marched another row of bedraggled men and women onto the ship's deck. One by one, they filed into a cargo container near the bow. The gantry crane swung back around and swayed above them, its hook twirling in the wind.

Twenty feet below the surface, the sea was dark and calm. Between the roiling waters above him and the dense clouds choking the sky, little sunlight made its way down into the depths. Caine swam at a steady pace, kicking his fins to propel him through the dark, churning ocean. Although he could only see a few feet ahead of him in the cloudy green water, the sea felt empty, devoid of life. Like a graveyard.

Most fish and other sea creatures were sensitive to barometric pressure and knew to take shelter during storms like the one raging above. A distant, muted thumping echoed through the depths, the churning of massive waves rippling through the water. A faint tapping rang out as Caine swam on. Raindrops, pelting the water's surface.

He checked the dive computer strapped to his wrist. According to the compass, he was still on course. He kicked his legs harder, continuing on his way through the cold jade depths.

The dry suit he wore was thick and stiff. It was far less flexible than a wetsuit, making his swimming motions feel slow and awkward. But it kept the freezing water from penetrating his body, save for the areas of his face not covered by the suit's hood and goggles. Although he didn't have far to swim, spending any amount of time in the cold water without such gear would have sapped his strength and likely caused hypothermia. The suit made him more buoyant, but a weight belt, along with his gear, kept him level in the water.

Several waterproof bags trailed from his harness, and he carried a modified speargun in his hands.

After swimming for a few more minutes, he spun around in the water, peering up through the bubbling haze. A black shape filled his view, floating on the surface. Although he could see very little of it through the churning ocean, he could tell it was massive, large enough to blot out the daylight over a significant portion of the water's surface.

Dropping his weights, Caine kicked his fins beneath him and ascended toward the surface. As he swam closer, the shape grew clearer, more details emerged. He was about thirty feet away from the keel of the massive cargo ship. Time and tide had scraped away patches of red paint from the hull, revealing streaks of dull gray metal underneath. Barnacles and crustaceans clung to the exposed patches of the hull, forming jagged clusters of organic matter against the smooth, curved metal. Weld lines, arranged in neat perpendicular rows, ran up the hull to the surface, marking where the steel plates joined together.

As Caine swam alongside the crimson keel, he noted several dark circular vents arranged along the hull at regular intervals.

Intake valves, he thought. They pumped seawater into the ship's ballast tanks, helping to keep the vessel steady in the churning sea.

The waves above grew more intense. Caine struggled to maintain his position, fighting against the violent currents. A deep, metallic groan echoed through the water, followed by a series of clicks and screeches. Glancing up, he saw a second, smaller shape, near the larger ship. The surging waves had slammed the two ships together, and their hulls scraped against each other.

Caine adjusted his approach. Surfacing between the vessels would be suicide. If they collided again with him in between, they would crush his body to a bloody pulp. He swam to the starboard side of the larger vessel. As he approached the stern, he saw the dark, ominous shape of the ship's screw. The propeller's massive scythe-like blades hung motionless in the green ocean haze. Algae clung to the thirty-foot screw, and a few strands of seaweed swayed in the water behind it, caught by the massive blades.

As he neared the surface, the violent motion of the waves swept him up, thrusting him out of the water as if plucked from the sea by a giant's hand. The hull of the cargo vessel rose before him, a towering wall of steel painted navy blue above the waterline. Then he felt his stomach lurch as the wave dropped him again, plunging him down fifteen feet.

Boarding a ship from the sea in these conditions was crazy. Standard procedure called for an aerial descent from a helicopter. Or, at the very least, ascending from an inflatable Zodiac raft. As it was, he had to tread water, fighting to keep his position in the violent sea. If he swam too close, a rogue wave could pick him up and slam him into the side of the ship.

As he waited for the next wave to pass, Caine reached down to one of the waterproof bags hanging from his harness. He opened the bag and pulled out a nylon cord attached to a carabiner clip. He snapped the clip onto a metal loop at the tip of the harpoon loaded in his speargun.

Another wave undulated beneath him. The roiling water tossed him closer to the vessel. Caine held his breath, certain he would collide with the metal hull. But instead, he bobbed in the ocean, roughly ten feet away from his target.

Raising the speargun from the water, he pulled up his goggles and aimed the weapon at the white railing running along the deck. He felt the water surge beneath him, lifting him up once more. He waited until he crested the wave, then squeezed the harpoon gun's trigger.

With a quiet hiss, the spear flew from the barrel, soaring up and over the ship's railing. The nylon rope unspooled from the bag, trailing through the air behind the slim black shaft. The spear struck the deck with a quiet clanking sound. Caine slung the speargun over his shoulder and pulled on the nylon line. The spear released a series of metal prongs from its tip. They caught on the railing, acting as a grappling hook.

Tugging on the line, Caine activated a tiny pulley system. A long, lightweight caving ladder released from the waterproof pouch, running up the side of the ship's hull. Caine grabbed the ladder as another wave swept him up.

Spitting out his regulator, he unbuckled his air tanks and let them fall. They struck the ocean with a splash and sank beneath him. He kicked off his flippers one by one, then began his ascent. The lightweight ladder flapped and twirled in the wind. Caine wrapped his arms around the guide ropes, clutching them to his chest. He used his feet to propel himself up, stepping on one carbon fiber rung at a time.

As he neared the top, the motion of the ladder grew more violent. The twin ropes twisted around as a massive wave ran under the ship's hull. Caine felt himself spinning in the wind, his back turning to face the ship. The ladder bucked again, slamming him against the metal hull. His foot slipped off the wet plastic rung.

As the hull plunged back down into the water, freezing spray pelted Caine's face. He steadied himself, clutched the ladder to his chest, and continued his climb. Finally, he made it to the top. Clambering over the railing, he lowered himself to the deck and dropped into a crouch. Glancing left and right to confirm he was unseen, he reeled in the rope ladder and stashed it back in the watertight pouch. Then he set down the other watertight bag on the deck. He released the clamp, unfolded the top of the pouch, then unzipped it.

He pulled off the dry suit's rubber hood and replaced it with a black wool beanie for warmth. Next, he opened a smaller case inside the bag. He grinned as he examined its contents.

Koichi had provided him with an HK SFP9 Maritime pistol. Despite Caine's preference for Berettas and SIGs, the SFP9 was ideal for his current situation. Originally designed for German KSM combat swimmers, the pistol was now standard issue for the Japanese Self Defense Force.

Which explains how Koichi was able to get a hold of one so quickly, Caine thought.

The finish on the Maritime model was resistant to saltwater, and a drainage system allowed the gun to fire quickly after surfacing. Per Caine's request, the 9mm pistol's barrel was modified to accept a suppressor, which also lay in the case. He removed the thick black tube and screwed it onto the end of the barrel. Although some referred to such devices as 'silencers', Caine knew the pistol would be far from silent. Anyone nearby would hear the shots. But at least the suppressor would prevent the sound of gunfire from echoing all throughout the ship.

He loaded a magazine into the pistol, then slid it into his shoulder rig. He grabbed two spare mags and dropped them into pouches on his belt. Then he gathered up the empty waterproof bags and crept along the deck, making his way to the superstructure at the rear of the ship. Metal stairs ran up to the Accom deck and Navigation platform. Above those, the glass-enclosed bridge perched at the top of the superstructure tower.

The ship rocked beneath his feet. Waves crashed over the railing, dousing the deck with water. As he approached a white metal hatch leading into the tower, he spied a storage locker mounted to the wall. Opening the locker, he stashed his gear inside. As he closed the lid, he heard the creak of metal, followed by a loud thunk.

Someone was opening the hatch, he thought.

Pressing himself against the wall, he drew a Cold Steel SRK knife from a sheath strapped to his left arm.

A pair of men stepped out of the superstructure and onto the soaking deck. They wore gray waxed canvas ponchos over their uniforms. Black balaclava masks covered their faces. Each man carried a Mineba PM-9 submachine gun. The weapons resembled Uzis, with a second handgrip mounted beneath the barrel. They hung from bandolier straps, swaying under the men's arms.

As the first man approached the metal stairs, the one in the rear turned to close the hatch. His eyes bulged in surprise as Caine lunged from the wall.

Before he could make a sound, Caine plunged the knife into his right shoulder. The blackened blade scraped against bone as it severed muscle and tendon. Caine looped his free hand behind the guard's head, holding him in place as he slammed the top of his skull into the bridge of the man's nose.

The blow struck with a loud crack, and the guard grunted in pain. The other man spun around and raised his weapon.

Caine drew his pistol and fired under the arm of the reeling guard. The gunshots sounded like loud coughs thanks to the suppressor. The double tap struck the other man center mass. He stumbled backwards, dropping his weapon.

Caine grabbed the shoulder strap of the impaled guard's PM-9, then hurled the man to the side. As he wrenched the gun from the man's body, he charged forward, planting a forward kick into the other guard's solar plexus. The force of the blow sent him flying over the railing. He uttered a brief, strangled scream, barely audible over the wind and waves. Caine heard a quiet, distant splash as he struck the sea below.

Spinning around, Caine stormed over to the impaled guard. The man rose on shaky feet and grabbed the knife's hilt. Yanking the blade from his shoulder, he raised the weapon overhead, preparing to stab Caine. Blood trickled from the wound, staining the rivulets of water running along the deck.

Caine aimed his pistol low and fired a single shot into the man's foot. The guard dropped the knife and howled. His cry of pain quickly turned to a muffled grunt as Caine drove his left forearm into the man's throat. Shoving the guard back, Caine slammed the man against the bulkhead and rested the barrel of his pistol under his chin.

'You can either follow your friend, or you can make yourself useful,' Caine snarled.

'Whaaa... What do you want?' the guard stuttered.

'How many people are aboard this ship?' Caine asked, glaring into the man's eyes.

'We are at half crew. Captain, pilot, and officers on bridge. Rest, below decks.'

'And the girl, the one Jiwoo captured. Is she alive?'

'Yes! She is below decks,' the man said, shivering as the wind blew sea spray over the railing. 'In the stern, refrigerated section. I can take you, I have key!'

The man's eyes darted down to his poncho.

'Slowly,' Caine said, taking a step back. He kept his pistol aimed at the man's head.

The guard brushed aside his poncho. He unzipped a pocket on his jump-suit, then removed a small white key card.

'See? I help you! Take you to—'

Caine fired. The gun coughed and the guard's head snapped back, spraying the wall behind them with blood. As he slumped to the ground, Caine grabbed the plastic card and shoved it into a pouch on his harness. Then he stripped the poncho and balaclava from the corpse.

Beneath the poncho, the man carried a battered New Nambu 57 A pistol in a shoulder holster. Caine took the weapon, then heaved the dead body overboard. As he threw the man's poncho over his clothes, the rain and waves washed away the crimson trails of blood from the deck.

44

The ship's heating systems warmed the superstructure's interior, although a damp chill still clung to the air. Caine kept his head down as he made his way across the deck plates, toward a small elevator at the rear of the tower. He noted a small security camera in the room's corner, near the door. But he doubted whoever was watching it could tell his skin tone while he wore the black ski mask.

Folding tables and chairs leaned against the wall, lashed together with bungee cords to prevent them from sliding about in the turbulent storm. A few crumpled papers and shredded plastic sheets littered the floor. Caine picked up a piece of paper and unfolded it. The form was in Japanese, but whoever had filled it out had written their answers in Korean.

The elevator doors opened with a chime, and Caine stepped into the narrow little car. There was only one level beneath the superstructure, so he pressed the down button, keeping his face turned away from the camera as the doors slid shut. The ship continued to roll across the violent sea as the elevator descended into the bowels of the ship.

The storm outside was growing worse. Caine knew winter typhoons were rare, but not unheard of in Japan. If the wind increased any further, Mariko and the others would have to head back, or risk capsizing in the massive waves.

Bracing his arms against the sides of the elevator, Caine struggled to keep his balance as the car tilted to the side and the interior lights flickered. A few seconds later, the ship righted itself, and the car came to a stop.

The doors slid open. Caine exited and turned right, following a narrow corridor toward the stern of the ship. He kept his pistol in his hand, hidden beneath the poncho as he made his way down the narrow passage. Pipes and cables ran along the wall, and small lights dotted the ceiling above, surrounded by protective metal cages.

To his left, metal doors led to the ship's galley and mess hall, along with crew's quarters and a door marked 'Electrical'. This last door piqued Caine's interest. He knew from experience that a ship's generators and electrical systems were usually accessed from the engine room. He was tempted to try his key card on the door, but instead he pressed on.

The corridor turned left. In the center of the rear wall, another door led to the stern, guarded by a blinking security terminal. The lights flickered, and the hull groaned as another wave battered the ship. Caine flexed his knees to absorb the rolling motion. As the ship leveled out, he tapped his key card on the terminal. A light flashed green, and the door slid open.

Caine swept his pistol left to right as he stormed into the room. Chains clanked in the shadows, and the hull continued to creak and shift around him. Squinting, he saw what looked like a skinned corpse hanging in the darkness. Caine rushed toward it, fearing the worst.

'Kanako,' he hissed. 'Are you—'

The ship listed again. The fleshy mass swung closer to him. As it swayed into the light, he saw it wasn't a human body at all. It was a frozen beef carcass, hanging from a hook in the ceiling. A tremor ran through the deck as the ship crashed down again, and waves battered the outer hull.

A low groan sounded from the darkness.

Caine spun around, holding his pistol in a two-handed grip. He stalked toward the sound. Another shadowy figure hung from the ceiling, swaying as the ship rocked back and forth. Chains clanked above, as another low groan escaped the woman's lips.

Kanako!

He rushed toward her, his head darting left and right, ensuring no one else was in the room.

Her skin was pale. Ice crystals sparkled like diamonds in her inky black hair. Her eyes were closed, and a tiny puff of breath slipped between her parted lips. A small control box hung from a cable nearby. Caine grabbed it and pressed the button. He heard the clicking of a winch as the chain lowered the woman to the ground.

Stripping off his poncho, he wrapped it around the barely conscious woman and hugged her to his chest, letting his body heat warm her skin. She shivered, and her eyes fluttered open. She looked up at him, squinting.

He pulled the ski mask up, revealing his face.

'Tom... Is that you?'

'It's me,' he replied, rubbing her arms. 'Are you all right?'

'We have to... Have to stop—'

'We will. Can you walk?'

She nodded, and he helped her to her feet. She leaned against him, swaying as blood flooded back into her numb limbs. 'There are people aboard... refugees. Women and children. You were right, he's infecting them with something, causing an—'

'I know,' Caine replied. 'He's manufacturing a pandemic and using online influencers to spread disinformation. Causing tension between the US and South Korea.'

She shook her head. 'The way he talked... Somehow... Somehow this is personal for him.'

Caine handed her the guard's New Nambu pistol. 'Let's get you out of here. This room is freezing.'

Kanako took the gun, then rolled her shoulders and neck. She stood up straighter. 'There's one more thing. Byakko and the woman, the North Korean...'

'Jiwoo Park. What about them?' Caine asked, making his way to the door.

'I think they're together.'

'Working together?'

She shook her head. 'No. More than that. I mean, like, *together*. You know?'

Caine tilted his head as he processed this new info. Kanako flanked the door, and pressed herself against the wall, holding the pistol in a two-handed grip.

'I don't know if it's important,' she said. 'Just thought you should know. Are you ready?'

Caine took up a position on the opposite side of the doorway. He nodded, then swiped his key card across the security terminal.

The door slid open, and the two of them stalked into the corridor. Kanako swept her gun to the left. Caine covered the right side of the passageway. Peering around the corner, he spotted a pair of guards approaching from the ship's bow. The men spoke among themselves in low whispers as they adjusted the grips on their weapons.

Caine darted back and gestured to Kanako. She followed him as he rushed around the opposite corner. They proceeded down the corridor, staying close to the wall.

Up ahead, voices came from the open mess hall door. Caine heard foot-steps echoing over the metal deck plates. He slid the key card over the security terminal next to the electronics room. They both ducked inside. The door slid shut just as two more men entered the corridor.

'Do you think they saw us?' Kanako whispered. She pressed her back against the wall near the door.

Caine shook his head. 'I don't know.'

He glanced around the room. Unlike the corridors outside, the lights in the small metal cubicle were red, bathing them both in a crimson glow. Racks of electronics covered the walls, and bundles of insulated cables snaked beneath the shelves. Computer components and circuit boards filled slots in the rack, numbered with reflective stickers.

A black binder hung from a chain, dangling from the shelf. On the oppo-site wall, a bank of small monitors displayed video feeds from cameras mounted around the ship. Caine searched the shelves, checking the IO ports of the motherboards installed in the racks.

'The files you retrieved from Chan,' he said, peering behind a row of shelves. 'My guess is they prove Byakko's people hacked the Ministry of Health, altered records to make it look like the South Korean government covered up these outbreaks. They've already killed one of the influencers they used to spread the story.'

'That was just the first stage,' Kanako said, peering closely at the moni-tors. 'Byakko told me the latest version of the virus is lethal. He intends to spread the infection both here, in Japan, and in the United States. South Korea, as well. Those people he's infected... They're all going to die, unless—'

'We have to get that intel to our governments, along with registry informa-tion on all the ships that took cargo from this vessel. There must be a vaccine, or antivirus. Otherwise, Byakko-san and his men would be infected as well. Is the USB drive here?'

Kanako shook her head. 'No. Jiwoo took it with her.'

Caine stopped searching the racks and eyed the wall of security monitors. He pointed to a screen that showed a view of a dark windowless control room. Byakko stood on a raised platform that overlooked the lower deck. He seemed focused on a series of larger screens hanging over the room. Jiwoo stood by his side, her hands resting on a railing.

'It must be with them, in that control room. That's not the bridge. It has to be down here, below deck somewhere.'

Kanako tucked a lock of damp hair behind her ear as she squinted at the screen. 'Camera B17,' she said, reading the metadata in the lower corner of the screen. She grabbed a binder from the desk and flipped through a series of laminated pages. 'Here!' She pointed to a ship's schematic. 'That's in the middle of the ship, one deck up.'

'I interrogated a guard before I found you. He said this ship was running with half the normal crew complement.'

'For a vessel this size, that means maybe fifteen people?'

'Thirteen,' Caine replied, looking her in the eye. 'Two of them are on their way to the bottom. And that number includes the bridge crew. We can take the other guards by surprise.'

'Wait,' Kanako said, grabbing his arm. 'There are still at least a dozen refugees on board.'

Caine nodded. 'Fine. After we take care of Byakko and Jiwoo, we free the refugees, put them in lifeboats.'

'It's not that simple. This is a North Korean spy ship. Byakko told me that by the time our governments realized what was happening, this ship would be at the bottom of the ocean.'

Caine examined the monitors. 'He's rigged the ship to explode.'

Kanako placed herself at the door as footsteps clanged across the deck plates outside. Whoever it was, they continued walking past the door.

'Yes,' she whispered. 'If we run in there, guns blazing, he could kill everyone on board.'

'Including himself,' Caine said, weighing the options in his mind.

Kanako bit her lip. 'Like I said... I think this is personal for him. I believe he's willing to die to see this through.'

Caine thought for a moment. 'Do you know where the refugees are?'

'I think so.' She examined the row of monitors, then pointed at a view that showed the bow deck of the ship. Only three cargo containers remained, stacked in a small pyramid. A helicopter was moored to the deck between the containers and the superstructure at the stern.

'There,' she said, pointing at the containers on the screen. 'I saw guards loading them into those containers when they brought me on board.'

'Then we need a distraction,' Caine said. 'Something to give you enough time to get them on the lifeboats while I go after the USB stick.'

Kanako raised her eyebrows and sighed. 'Got any ideas?'

Caine thought for a moment. He grabbed the binder and flipped through the ship's schematics.

'As a matter of fact, I do.'

Reaching down to his belt, he slid a small walkie from a waterproof pouch and turned it on. 'Mariko, do you copy?'

Static crackled from the tiny speaker.

A few seconds later, Mariko's voice answered. 'I copy. Go ahead.'

'What's your position?'

'We're off the Eiko Maru's port bow, and keeping our distance,' Mariko replied.

'Copy that. I'm going to need you to get closer.'

'How much closer?'

Caine glanced at Kanako and gave her a confident smile. 'A *lot* closer.'

45

Byakko paced back and forth across the control room's upper platform, unaffected by the rolling of the ship in the turbulent sea.

'Status report,' he bellowed, his deep, guttural voice echoing off the curved metal walls.

'Feeder Ships One and Two have diverted to ports in Hakodate,' one of the men below replied, consulting the data on his screen. 'The storm has not affected those waters as severely. We have rerouted our people there for pickup and debriefing.'

'Excellent. And what of the shipments bound for Baltimore and Seoul?'

'Cargo has been delivered, sir. There was only a 10 percent mortality rate in transit, due to starvation.'

'I told you we would need to provide sufficient food for the journey,' Jiwoo said, glaring at Byakko. 'Will this affect our—?'

'This affects nothing,' he snapped. 'We only need one live subject to spread the infection. We shall have far more than that.'

The woman nodded. 'What about the memory stick we retrieved from the Naicho officer?'

Byakko focused his feline stare on another crew member. The man hunched over a computer terminal, squinting at data on the screen. 'You, there. Have you confirmed the veracity of the data?'

The crewman tapped his keyboard. '*Hai*, yes, sir. The data appears to be valid. Currently checking file access artifacts to confirm no copies were made. It will take approximately six minutes to complete.'

'Excellent.' Byakko ran a hand through his thick salt-and-pepper hair. 'Hopefully, we have contained the damage caused by that lecherous coward, Chan. Once you finish the scan, wipe the drive's memory and dispose of—'

Before he could complete his orders, the lights in the control room flickered, then dimmed. The room went dark, save for bursts of static filling the screens around the chamber.

'Power outage, sir!' one of the crewmen shouted. Crimson emergency lights blazed to life.

Another massive wave pummeled the ship, sending groaning vibrations through the hull. As the vessel righted itself, a low electronic hum filled the room, and the lights returned to normal. Boot screens replaced the static on the monitor screens.

'What happened?' Byakko demanded. 'Are we back online?'

'Yes, sir. Systems rebooting. We should have full power in a few seconds.'

Jiwoo narrowed her eyes as live feeds from all the security cameras around the ship filled the monitor screens, one by one.

'Wait,' she said, pointing at one of the crewmen's stations. 'You, there! Transfer camera D4 to the large monitor.'

The crewman nodded and tapped his keyboard. The image glowed to life on the central screen, replacing the shogi game Byakko had been playing.

On the monitor, a woman sprinted across the deck. She raced toward the cargo containers stacked near the bow.

'The woman, Kanako,' Jiwoo said. 'She has escaped.'

Her lips curled into a frown as she stared at the images on the screen. 'Letting her live was a mistake. I should have slit her throat back on that mountain, let her bleed out in the snow.'

'Then do so now,' Byakko snarled, pointing at the screen. 'And throw her body overboard when you're done.'

The woman offered him the faintest trace of a smile. 'With pleasure.' She turned to two armed guards standing over the workers below. 'Come with me.'

She strode down the stairs to the lower deck, and the men followed. They exited a door on the port side of the control room.

Byakko peered at the screens, watching as the ship's bow surged over another wave. 'That fishing trawler we picked up before,' he said. 'What is its current position?'

A crewman below stared at his screen, then shot a nervous glance at the yakuza boss standing above him. 'Radar and sonar systems still rebooting, sir. We'll be sensor blind for a few more minutes.'

Byakko glared down at the man but said nothing. He returned his attention to the large center screen. The massive, glowing shogi board resumed above him. The gangster focused on the board, noting the pieces and their positions, playing out multiple scenarios in his head.

Victory seemed near. And yet, he knew matches could be won or lost based on moves players made in the final rounds. A sudden capture, an unexpected piece returned to the board.

A nagging sensation buzzed in the back of his mind, a maddening sense that he had overlooked something. But still... the game continued.

'Pawn E9 to D9,' he said, staring at the screen. The tiny glowing shield moved ahead one space.

He had placed the piece in danger, daring the enemy player to capture the pawn. And when they did so, he would strike, placing the opposing king in checkmate. Victory or defeat hinged on the next few moments. For him, for Jiwoo.

And for his opponent as well.

* * *

An icy wind, heavy with spray and mist, swept across the massive cargo ship's deck. Kanako's hair whipped behind her. She felt the warm buzz of adrenaline surging through her limbs as she made her way across the heaving deck. Gripping the metal railing to her left, she took another step forward, flexing her knees to absorb the motion of the ship.

The sea stretched as far as the eye could see, slate gray and dotted with white-capped swells. Water surged over the bow, flooding the deck as the ship rose and fell between the waves. The weather was getting worse by the minute, and angry dark clouds engulfed the sky overhead.

She made her way past the helicopter moored in the center of the cargo deck and approached the three red metal containers stacked near the bow. Releasing her grip on the railing, she staggered across the deck, struggling to keep her balance as the ship rocked beneath her feet. Behind her, an orange lifeboat hung from a pair of white bracket arms. The tiny boat creaked as it swayed back and forth.

Another wave battered the ship, and the deck tilted towards the starboard side. Kanako's feet skidded across the wet deck, and she slammed the side of the metal container. As the ship righted itself, she heard the creak of metal straining against gravity.

Glancing up, she saw a series of ratchet straps... Nylon webbing, tightened with metal turnbuckles, and hooked to the deck. Metal scraped above her head. Looking up, she saw the top cargo container shift and slide as the ship surged over another wave.

A twist lock mechanism adorned each corner of the containers. They were designed to lock together, making it more difficult for the massive metal containers to move in bad weather. But the locks on these three containers were loose. Whoever had stacked them had neglected to tighten the connecting bolts.

They must have been in a rush, she thought. *The crew had rushed to offload as much cargo as they could and tie down the rest.*

Cargo... People.

Bracing herself against the door, she grabbed the container handle and jerked it down. The door swung open with a loud creak. Peering into the opening, at first she saw only darkness. But as her eyes adjusted to the dim light, she saw faces hiding near the back of the metal box. Terrified eyes stared back at her from the darkness. Women, children, and a few elderly men.

The fetid air inside the box reeked of excrement and sweat. Vomit covered the floor and left corner wall. A frail, older woman slumped against the opposite corner. At first, Kanako thought she was dead. Then, a low groan escaped her lips, as the cold sea air rushed into the metal box, blasting away the rancid odor.

Kanako didn't know what nationality these people were. Their facial features were a mix of Chinese, Korean, Filipino, and more.

'Does anyone speak English?' she asked.

A young girl, no more than eight years old, raised her hand.

Kanako kneeled and smiled, bracing herself as the ship crashed down another wave.

'I'm a friend. I'm here to help,' she said. 'We have to get off this ship. It's too dangerous here. Do you understand?'

The girl turned and spoke Korean to one of the older women. That woman nodded and spoke to another. Within a few seconds, multiple languages echoed off the metal walls as various groups of refugees spread the word.

Kanako glanced over her shoulder. The orange lifeboat on the port side swayed on its hooks. An orange plastic shell covered the tiny boat's hull, and white metal stairs led to the entry hatch on the roof.

'The deck is very slippery, so we'll go in groups of three, okay?' Kanako said, pointing toward the lifeboat. 'Turn the hatch clockwise, and climb in, like this. See?'

She made a twisting motion with her hands. The older woman nodded and adjusted her clothes.

The boat shifted again, and Kanako nearly lost her balance as the deck tilted back, and the ship climbed up the surface of a steep wave. As the bow crashed down, she stepped aside and pointed at the boat again.

'Okay, move! Go!'

Three of the refugees limped from the container and scurried past her, huddled against the cold. She watched as they climbed up the stairs and opened the hatch. As they climbed inside, she gestured to another group of three.

'You're next. Come on, let's go!'

She stepped aside as the next group of women and children ran for the boat. A young girl screamed as waves crashed over the railing, but one of the other women grabbed her and carried her up the stairs.

As they entered the lifeboat, Kanako heard footsteps echoing across the metal deck, people running toward their position. Turning, she saw another blast of water crash against the side of the boat, filling the air with spray. Through the mist and haze, she spotted three shadowy figures stalking along the side of the deck.

Two of them carried submachine guns of some kind.

'Everyone, get down!' Kanako shouted. She kicked the metal door closed, then ducked alongside the container. Gunfire exploded around her, ricocheting off the metal box. The nylon straps groaned. Sparks flew from a turnbuckle as a stray shot hit the metal latch. The buckle gave way, and the strap snapped loose. Kanako heard the scream of metal grinding against metal.

Looking up, she saw the container perched at the top of the stack shift as the boat rolled across the waves.

Breaking cover, she sprinted forward, dropping to a crouch and skidding behind the skeletal blue framework that held the cargo crane aloft. Behind her, the container skidded off the stack and fell, striking the deck with a deafening clang.

Bullets ricocheted off the metal beams surrounding her. Raising her pistol, she sighted over the barrel and opened fire. Her shots struck the deck a few feet ahead of her target. Aiming as the ship lurched and rolled was nearly impossible, but she hoped she could at least drive these attackers back, give the remaining refugees in the container time to escape to the boat.

As the ship rolled starboard, she let go of the metal beam and slid along the tilting deck. Her feet struck an empty cargo pallet, stopping her a few meters from the anchored helicopter. She rose up from her cover and fired again. Her shot struck the guardrail, missing the nearest man by a few inches.

As he returned fire, Kanako saw the Korean woman, Jiwoo, moving ahead of the two men. She advanced on Kanako's position, while the two other men concentrated their fire on the cargo container.

The agent worked the trigger, firing on Jiwoo until the slide racked back and the trigger went dead. But it was nearly impossible to hit her target as the boat heaved upon the churning sea.

Dropping her now useless weapon, she ducked behind the pallet. Gunfire shredded the canvas tarp above her. Kanako kept her head down, wincing as bullets screamed overhead. Glancing back, she saw the refugees in the cargo container huddling behind the door. More gunfire sparked off the walls of the metal box.

The boat rose over another wave, and the loose cargo container slid forward a few meters. Kanako held her breath, watching as the massive container scraped closer to her. But it stopped short as the bow crashed down, and spray exploded over the deck.

The armed men froze as well. Jiwoo turned, ceasing her assault as the sound of grinding metal echoed through the air.

Before they could press their attack, more gunfire whined across the deck. Kanako narrowed her eyes and turned to the port side... The shots had not come from the men or Jiwoo.

Who was firing?

As another wave blasted the deck, a fishing trawler emerged from the haze, cresting over a nearby wave. Several men and a lone woman stood on the bow. Muzzle flash leapt from their weapons as they opened fire. The boat surged closer, moving to within a few meters. The guards retreated, spraying cover fire at the trawler.

Jiwoo raised her submachine gun and aimed at the new boat.

Kanako charged across the deck, tackling the woman to the ground. Jiwoo glared up at her, surprised by her sudden burst of motion. She gripped the barrel of the submachine gun, preventing the woman from aiming the weapon in her direction.

The trawler drifted closer. The woman on board aimed her pistol and fired three shots, striking the nearest guard. He dropped his weapon and screamed in pain as he toppled over the railing. Kanako heard the distant splash as he struck the water.

As Jiwoo struggled beneath her, Kanako turned to the remaining refugees. 'Go now! Run!'

They filed out of the container and climbed into the lifeboat, ducking as bullets whizzed overhead.

Another wave pounded the ship. The deck tilted starboard. Kanako and Jiwoo rolled across the ship, colliding into another metal beam. The gun tumbled from Jiwoo's grasp and clattered across the deck. Both women struggled to grab hold of something, anything. The angry gray sea loomed before them, like a hungry beast eager to swallow them whole.

46

'We're taking fire,' the guard shouted, his voice crackling over the comm system. 'Vessel off the port side, it—'

A burst of static drowned out his words, and the lights flickered once more. The deck rolled beneath their feet. Byakko clutched the platform's railing to steady himself.

'What is he talking about?' he demanded. 'Who is shooting at them?'

'Radar systems are still offline, but sir... Look!' One of the crewmen tapped his keyboard, sending a camera feed to the main screen. Byakko's cat-like eyes squinted as he glared at the images before him.

A fishing trawler closed in on the cargo vessel, approaching from the star-board bow. As it drew nearer, he could make out people perched on the bow, strapped to the guardrails with safety lines. They peppered the cargo vessel with gunfire, driving the guards back, away from the female agent, Kanako.

One of the guards screamed and clutched his chest, before plunging over the side, into the violent ocean. The other backed off, taking cover behind the bulkhead.

'That trawler,' he snarled. 'Why did we not see it approach when—?'

'Radar system is still offline, sir,' the operator called back, checking his screen. 'It's not responding.'

Byakko glared down at him as the hull groaned around them. 'Then get off your ass and get to the electronics room. Reboot manually if you must!'

'Yes, sir!'

The crewman left his station and ascended the metal stairs to the command deck. The ship's lights flickered again as he approached the door but quickly returned to normal. He tapped the security terminal, and the door slid open.

As Byakko's eyes returned to the screens, gunfire erupted behind them. The crewman jerked and writhed. Bullets tore bloody holes in his chest and torso. His body collapsed to the deck, a soft death rattle wheezing from his throat.

Byakko spun around, but before he could react, another man entered through the open doorway. At first, it appeared to be one of the guards patrolling the lower corridors. But as he stepped closer, Byakko predatory stare fell upon Caine's emerald-green eyes. The guard's hands were zip-tied in front of him. Caine stood behind the bound man, holding a pistol to his head. With his free hand, Caine swept his PM-9 submachine around the room.

He aimed the weapon at Byakko.

'It's over,' Caine snarled.

The yakuza gangster raised his hands and grinned. 'An interesting move, Mr. Caine. One that, I must confess, I failed to predict.'

'More like checkmate,' Caine replied. 'Anyone moves, you die.'

The gangster's eyes blazed with a manic gleam. 'I am prepared to sacrifice anything to achieve victory. Can you say the same?'

'If your man down there doesn't drop his weapon, we're about to find out,' Caine replied, his eyes darting to the lone remaining guard on the lower level.

Byakko nodded. 'Do as he says.'

The guard set his weapon down on the deck, then stepped back.

'I guess the North Koreans aren't paying you enough to die for their cause after all,' Caine said, locking eyes with the gangster's unnerving stare. 'Step away from the railing and keep your hands where I can see them.'

'You think this is about money?' The man sneered as he took a step back. 'You know nothing. I would die a thousand deaths if it meant—'

'And Jiwoo?' Caine asked, cutting him off. 'I know she's on board as well. Are you willing to take her with you?'

The man's lips curled into a snarl, but he said nothing.

That got under his skin, Caine thought. *Maybe Kanako was right...*

'The memory stick you took from Kanako,' Caine said, shoving the guard forward a few steps. 'Where is it?'

The man with the cat-like eyes nodded to the technician's station below. 'Right there,' he said. 'You were so close and yet victory still eludes you. Even if you could recover the data, the damage has been done. There is nothing so easy to manipulate as ignorance and fear.'

'We'll see. You worked with Chan Tae Young to hack South Korea's Ministry of Health records. Make it appear they covered up the virus you've been spreading. But Chan preserved the original database. Once the intel on that drive goes public, your whole story falls apart. People will know the truth.'

Byakko chuckled. 'The truth? Mr. Caine, approximately 7 percent of the world still believes the earth is flat. Truth, lies... Meaningless concepts in a world where disinformation can go viral in a matter of seconds. To quote your famous author Mark Twain, a lie can travel halfway around the world while the truth is still putting on its slippers.'

'I think he said "boots",' Caine replied. Keeping his weapon trained on the yakuza gangster, he glanced at the technician. 'You. Bring me that memory stick. Now.'

The technician shot a nervous look at Byakko. Then his eyes darted to Caine. 'The data,' he said. 'I erased it. The drive is empty.' His voice trembled with fear.

'As I said,' Byakko replied with a smirk. 'You're too late. The fuse has been lit.'

Suddenly, an alarm wailed through the control room. Orange lights flashed overhead. The ship lurched again, even more violently. The guard staggered forward, but Caine grabbed his shirt, holding him in place.

'What happened?' Caine asked. He jabbed the pistol's barrel into the captive guard's back.

Byakko squinted at Caine. 'I have no idea.' He turned to the technician manning the radar console. 'You, report!'

A radar image filled all the screens in the room, showing a glowing mass sweeping across the ocean, heading right for both ships.

'Sir, radar is back online! The storm's getting worse. There's a rogue wave approaching from the west. It... It's massive!'

'How massive?' Caine snapped.

'At least twenty meters tall!' The terrified man looked over his shoulder at Caine and Byakko. 'That's big enough to capsize the ship!'

Keeping the PM-9 trained on Byakko, Caine slammed the pistol butt into the back of the guard's skull. As he crumpled to the deck, Caine holstered the weapon and grabbed his walkie with his free hand.

'Kanako, you and the refugees need to get below decks,' he shouted into the radio. 'Kanako, do you copy?'

The crackling of static was the only response.

47

The sea yawned before Kanako and Jiwoo as the deck tilted to port. From the corner of her eye, the Naicho agent saw the orange lifeboat sway on its twin cables, swinging like a pendulum over the churning ocean waves. She heard the screams of the refugees echoing inside the plastic shell.

As the ship righted itself, Jiwoo's discarded weapon clattered across the deck, sliding closer. The two women stood frozen, each waiting to see what the other would do. The North Korean woman's cold, emotionless eyes locked with Kanako's own, unblinking, revealing nothing. Kanako stepped left, then right, trying to confuse the woman. She raised her hands and took a step back, presenting a smaller target.

The ship tilted in the opposite direction, heaving starboard. The gun slid closer. Jiwoo's eyes flicked down for a fraction of a second, watching as the weapon bounced across the deck. In a sudden burst of motion, she dove for the gun, but Kanako was already moving.

As Jiwoo slid across the deck, the Naicho agent kicked the gun aside, knocking it several meters away. She stomped down, aiming for Jiwoo's neck. The North Korean assassin rolled sideways, avoiding the blow.

Spinning around on the water-slicked deck, Jiwoo swept Kanako's legs out from under her. Kanako's breath exploded from her lungs as her back slammed into the deck. Jiwoo pounced atop her, grabbing her hair and slamming her head down. She felt Jiwoo's cold, bony fingers lock around her throat.

Despite her petite size, the woman's arms rippled with lean, sinewy muscles. Her grip was like iron. Kanako's vision blurred.

Kanako drove a knee up into her attacker's solar plexus. Jiwoo grunted in pain but maintained her grip. Still struggling, Kanako thrust her palm up into her opponent's nose, then struck with another knee. She felt the suffocating grip loosen around her throat. Gasping for breath, she wedged her foot against Jiwoo's abdomen and kicked up, flipping the woman over her.

As both women staggered to their feet, the ship pitched starboard again. They stumbled across the deck, slamming into the blue skeletal beams of the crane. Before Kanako could even catch her breath, Jiwoo slammed her forearm into the Japanese woman's throat. With her free hand, she drew a knife from a sheath at her belt.

Kanako grabbed her opponent's knife hand by the wrist, blocking her strike. She struggled to knock the woman's arm away from her throat, but she was growing weaker, losing her strength. The assassin peered down at her with a cold, emotionless stare. There was no rage, no hate, no fear in Jiwoo's expression. Just a detached clinical gaze, watching, waiting, to see when the spark of life faded from Kanako's own eyes.

The Japanese woman swung her free arm in a hook, striking the other woman in the jaw. Jiwoo's head snapped back, but her stranglehold was unaffected. She shook her head, fighting off the pain. Then her eyes locked with Kanako's once more.

Metal creaked and groaned above them. Looking up, Kanako saw the cargo crane's hook overhead, swaying back and forth as the ship rolled across the waves. Glancing to her right, she saw a gray box mounted to another metal beam a couple of feet away from them.

Another wave tilted the deck beneath them, allowing Jiwoo to bear down with all her weight. Her lips curled into a faint grin as she saw Kanako's eyes flutter. Her legs thrashed, but she wasn't able to land a kick.

As the ship dipped in the opposite direction, Kanako dropped her right arm and reached out. Her fingers grazed the edge of the gray box. She flipped open the cover. Inside, a red switch protruded from a gray panel. Yellow Japanese warning labels covered the inside lid.

Jiwoo heard the metal click of the panel opening. She turned her head, and saw the button, watched as Kanako's fingers curled into a fist. Snarling, the North Korean woman pushed harder with her knife hand, struggling to drive the weapon into Kanako's abdomen. The sharp blade hovered a few inches away from her exposed skin, moving closer by the second.

Gritting her teeth, Kanako slammed her fist down on the button. The sound of clanking metal echoed above them, followed by a loud hiss. The crane's metal cable plunged toward them. Muttering a curse, Jiwoo broke away, stepping back as Kanako dived to her right. The heavy hook fell between them, stopping just a few inches short of the deck.

Gasping for breath, Kanako massaged her aching throat as she staggered to her feet. Her eyes opened wide as she saw the massive hook swing toward her. She sidestepped, dodging the metal cable as it struck the railing with a loud clang.

Jiwoo charged toward her and launched a kick, but this time, Kanako was ready. She threw up her knee, ducked her head, and kept her elbows in tight, blocking the strike. Rotating her leg to throw her opponent off balance, she launched a series of jabs, followed by a left hook. Jiwoo staggered back, then slipped on the wet deck. She fell backwards, groaning in pain. Kanako prepared to strike. But as Jiwoo picked herself up from the deck, the ship tilted again. A dark shadow engulfed the two women. Jiwoo's eyed opened wide.

Kanako spun around. A wall of water surged toward them, blocking out the sun. It towered over the two women as it roared closer. Behind them, Kanako heard more gunfire ricochet across the deck. Then she heard shouting. The men on the fishing trawler retreated below decks as the boat motored away from the cargo vessel.

The deck heaved beneath Kanako's feet, rising faster than before. She heard the creak of the metal cable swaying behind her. From the corner of her eye, she saw Jiwoo stagger to her feet and race toward her. But the deck continued rising, and the woman gasped with exertion, as if running up a steep hill.

Grabbing the swaying cable, Kanako hurled it toward the charging woman. The cable swung out, slamming Jiwoo in the gut with the heavy steel hook. The impact knocked her backwards, and she tumbled down the sloping deck, rolling toward the opposite guardrail.

The roar of the approaching wave grew louder, drowning out all other sound. Kanako debated rushing for the lifeboat. But as the wave's shadow engulfed the deck, she realized there was no time. She had only seconds to act.

Grabbing the swaying cable, she looped the hook around the guardrail, then grabbed hold of the steel fibers. Wrapping her arms and legs around the cable, she looked up to see the wave cresting above the ship. The deck yawned beneath her, almost vertical now. Jiwoo screamed as she tumbled over the railing and plunged into the cold, angry sea.

Then the wave hit. Thousands of gallons of seawater pummeled the ship's hull. Kanako ducked her head and held on for dear life. Her own screams were lost in the furious, guttural howl of the sea.

48

Alarms blared through the control room as the hull groaned. Caine felt his feet skid across the platform's metal grill. As the hull tilted at a steeper angle, Byakko leapt over the guardrail and struck the floor. He rolled sideways, unable to stop himself as the ship leaned farther and farther sideways.

Caine lost his balance and slid towards the stairs, tumbling through the air as the deck swung vertically. The swaying lights above flickered, then went dark. Red emergency lights spun to life, flooding the room with an infernal glow.

At the last second, he grabbed hold of a guardrail. He dangled in the air, watching as Byakko crawled along the wall, moving toward a control panel near the port-side door.

Caine raised the PM-9 with his free hand. Before he could fire, he saw motion from the corner of his eye. The remaining guard on the floor was perched atop a control console. He had recovered his weapon. Muzzle flash blazed through the dark chamber as he opened fire.

Bullets sparked off the guardrail, missing Caine's head by inches. Caine swung his weapon over and fired wild. The console next to the guard exploded, flooding the room with a blinding glare. The armed man jerked and writhed, then dropped his weapon. He lost his balance, toppled off the console, and rolled toward the opposite wall.

The hull groaned louder. Sparks cascaded through the room as computer monitors tore loose from their consoles and collided with the opposite wall. For a moment, Caine was certain the ship would capsize. But then the metal support beams creaked, and an inaudible sigh echoed through the bulkheads. The ship slammed back down, righting itself on the storm-wracked sea. The colossal wave moved on.

Caine felt like he was in free fall. He lost his grip on the railing and toppled over the side. As he struck the floor, he rolled behind a bank of monitors.

Gunfire exploded from the far corner of the room. Peering over the console, Caine saw Byakko crouched beside a workstation. The man flipped up a small, clear panel on the console, revealing a yellow button underneath.

Caine aimed the PM-9 and fired. Bullets sparked off the console, but the rocking motion of the ship threw off his aim. The gangster slapped his palm down on the button, then vaulted over the computer table.

A new alarm wailed through the control room. Caine felt a tremor run through the ship. He braced himself against the nearest console as the deck lurched beneath his feet. The motion was more sudden and violent than before, and was over in an instant.

More creaks and groans echoed through the hull. Cold seawater bubbled through the grates beneath his feet.

He triggered the charges, Caine thought. *The ship is sinking!*

As the water rose to his ankles, gunshots tore through the chamber. The monitor above him shattered, sending bright sparks cascading into the water below.

'As I said, Mr. Caine, I'm willing to die for my cause!' Byakko shouted. 'But I'd much rather have you go down with the ship!'

Caine ducked behind another console. Byakko fired again. Then Caine heard a loud click as the man's pistol emptied. Leaning around the console, Caine returned fire. Orange fire erupted from his PM-9 as he sprayed the room with gunfire.

Byakko broke cover and sprinted for the door. Bullets splashed through the water at his heels. As he ducked through the exit, an armored panel slid down from the ceiling, sealing the exit. Caine charged after him. As his footsteps splashed through the frigid water, he felt the hull dipping toward the stern.

By the time he reached the door, the panel was nearly closed. He pressed his hands against it, struggling to keep it from shutting, but it was no use. The armored plate hit the floor with a loud thunk. Glancing back, Caine saw identical panels covering the other exits.

A shiver ran through his body as the water lapped at his shins. The monitors hanging from the ceiling swayed as the ship tipped backwards at a steeper angle. The ship was going under. And he was trapped inside.

He heard a strangled gasp behind him. Spinning around, he saw the radar operator, the lone survivor in the room, pounding on the doorway opposite him. The man shouted in Korean as his fist battered the metal panel.

'*Jebal! Mun-eul yeol-eojuseyo...* Please! Open the door!'

Caine splashed through the water, stalking towards him. He grabbed the man and spun him around. Startled, the crewman shivered and hugged himself as he looked up at Caine.

'Don't kill me,' he pleaded. 'I'm just a technician, I don't—'

'Your boss isn't coming back,' Caine snapped. 'We're both going to drown in here unless we work together. Is there an override for these doors?'

'I... I don't know. Maybe—'

Caine grabbed the man by the collar of his jumpsuit and dragged him through the water. 'Then find it! We're running out of time!'

'Okay, okay!' the man said, running his hands through his dark hair. 'I'll try!'

As he tapped the keys on the nearest computer console, Caine snatched the walkie off his belt.

'Kanako, do you read me? Are you okay?'

Static crackled from the walkie.

'Kanako!' he shouted again. 'Do you copy?'

'Yes, I copy!'

Caine sighed with relief.

'The refugees and I made it to the lifeboat. We're heading for the trawler now. Where are you?'

Caine watched as the technician called up a new screen on the computer. Six white boxes blinked on the monitor, flashing in the dim glow of the emergency lights.

'It's a long story,' he replied. 'Just get to the trawler. I'll contact you shortly.'

He cut the transmission, watching as the technician typed a series of numbers into the boxes. The screen flashed red. The words *ACCESS DENIED* blinked on the monitor.

'It's not taking my clearance code,' the Korean man said, pounding his fist on the table. 'I can't—'

'Try again!'

The man clenched his jaw and continued typing. Caine moved to the console with the orange memory stick. He checked the screen and confirmed that the technician had told him the truth. The data was erased.

Slinging the submachine gun over his shoulder, he called up the system logs, searching the computer's hard drive. But there was no sign of the missing files. The memory stick was wiped clean.

'Is there a backup for this system?' Caine shouted.

The technician gave him a confused look. 'What? There's no time for that now, we have to—'

Caine aimed the PM-9 at the man. His emerald eyes blazed in the crimson light as he peered over the barrel of the weapon. 'Backup. I won't ask again.'

'In the bridge, there's a backup server for all the systems down here,' the man said, his eyes wide with terror. 'I doubt they had time to wipe it before they abandoned ship!'

The harried technician wiped dripping hair from his face, then finished typing another string of letters and numbers.

Again, the screen flashed red. *ACCESS DENIED.*

Caine felt the water's chill lapping at his knees.

The man shook his head and backed away from the console. 'No use,' he sobbed. 'My codes don't work. We... We shall die here!'

Caine shoved him aside and stared at the screen. The white boxes reappeared. There were six of them, all in a row. He narrowed his eyes, remembering Byakko's test back at the club...

'The shogi game,' he said, peering at the boxes. 'The one that was on the large screen before. Where is it?'

'I... I don't know, I—'

'Bring it back! Now!'

The technician typed a series of commands on another keyboard. The shogi board filled the central monitor. An identical image flickered on the other screens in the room, disrupted and out of sync, due to the damaged monitors and fluctuating power.

Caine looked up, noting the positions of the pieces on the boards. 'No, that's not right. Are there other games saved in the memory?'

'What difference does it make?'

'Just show me!' Caine demanded.

The technician tapped a key, cycling through various games. As the screen refreshed, the positions of the pieces changed. Finally, Caine recognized the configuration.

'There,' he said, pointing at the screen. 'Stop there!'

The technician gave him a confused look. 'What does this have to do with anything? It's just a stupid game.'

'Not to Byakko,' Caine said, examining the board.

Three moves, without losing any pieces...

He considered the pawn, the same piece he had moved before. Knowing now how the opposing knight moved, he glanced at a neighboring pawn. An opposing pawn blocked its movement. But if he captured that piece with a Silver General...

Glancing at the piece's position on the board, he typed in G7, followed by F8. The two boxes stopped flashing and glowed solid white. He scanned the board again. The technician sloshed through the water and pounded on the nearest door.

'Help,' he screamed. 'Help!'

Caine ignored him. Moving to the next piece, he selected a Rook. The shield-like tile had a yellow outline, signifying it had been promoted. That meant besides moving in a straight line, as it did in chess, it could also move one space diagonally.

'H9 to G8,' he muttered to himself as he typed. The boxes accepted the input and turned solid white as well.

Two more to go...

He searched the board, looking for another legal move. The trick he had played before, dropping a piece back on the board, would not work this time. There was no way he could see to convert such a move to alphanumeric characters.

The water was up to his waist now. He shivered, and his fingers trembled as the cold gnawed away at him. The hull creaked and groaned. He felt his feet sliding backwards.

The boat's stern had dipped below the waterline. He was running out of time.

There, he thought... *In the enemy's corner – a lone pawn!*

He had missed it before, as the shield designs were all so similar to his untrained eye. But it was only one space away from the promotion box on the opposite side of the board.

'B8 to A8,' he said, typing in the last characters. The red lights stopped spinning, and the doors slid open. Water sloshed out into the corridor, and the technician stumbled forward, tripping in the flooded passage.

Caine pushed through the deepening water, following him outside. The corridor running along the port side tilted back at a steep angle. Seawater cascaded down the stairwells, flooding into the passage like tiny waterfalls.

Caine grabbed the technician and spun him around. He clutched the man's jumpsuit in his fists as the water sloshed against his chest.

'The bridge! How do I get there?'

The man looked over Caine's shoulder, his eyes wide with panic. 'Elevator, end of hall. It runs up the superstructure tower. But... you can't—'

Caine released him and turned around. The rear of the corridor was completely underwater. Furniture from the mess hall and crew's quarters drifted in the water, carried by the rushing current. Caine waded toward the flooded portion of the passageway, shoving a floating mattress out of the way.

'Hey, where are you going?' the technician shouted. 'You can't make it. The corridor is flooded!'

'That's my problem,' Caine snarled as the water rose to his neck.

'But what about me?' the technician wailed.

'That's your problem,' Caine shouted back.

He took a series of rapid, shallow breaths. As he sucked in oxygen, he closed his eyes and relaxed his limbs. He pictured the elevator in his mind, remembering the layout of the ship. He forced himself to focus solely on his objective, driving all thoughts of fear and drowning from his mind.

He continued taking rapid breaths, increasing the rate at which his lungs expelled carbon dioxide from his blood. When he felt light-headed, he stopped and opened his eyes.

Then he dived beneath the dark, churning water.

[faded ghost text from previous page bleeding through]

49

Caine kicked his legs and swam ahead, pulling himself deeper into the flooded bowels of the ship. The overhead light barely breached the depths of the flooded corridor. Beneath the churning water, visibility was reduced to less than three feet.

As he progressed down the corridor, a dark mass appeared ahead of him, just before the left turn leading to the elevator. Squinting through the swirling haze, Caine swam closer. A metal bed frame and a few loose chairs clung together, forming a barricade in the narrow space.

Forcing himself to remain calm, Caine grabbed one of the chairs and pulled the legs from the wire mesh of the bed frame. It came loose, and he hurled it behind him, letting it sink to the floor a few feet away. Bubbles drifted from his mouth as he repeated the action with the other chair. He tugged at the leg, but he could not free it from the metal frame.

He pulled harder, and more bubbles streamed from his lips. A dull, burning pain rose in his chest.

Narrowing his eyes, he released the chair and swam closer to the blockage. He blinked... The chair leg had a wheel at the end, and the wire from the bed frame was entangled in the caster. Reaching through the mesh of the bed frame, he grabbed the leg and popped the wheel off.

He pulled again, and the leg came free. The bed frame shifted in the water, sinking to the bottom of the corridor.

Caine expelled some of the trapped air from his lungs as he kicked forward, swimming down the rest of the corridor. As he remembered, the passageway turned left. The elevator doors sat in the center of the connecting passage. They were closed, and the security panel mounted next to them glowed, filling the depths with a faint, blinking light.

As more bubbles escaped his lips, Caine braced his feet against the edge of the elevator door. He jammed his fingers into the crack between the two panels and pulled. At first, the doors refused to budge. Caine grunted and pulled again. His shoulders and arms burned, and the pain in his chest grew.

Finally, the doors parted a few inches. Massive air bubbles erupted from the tiny car inside the shaft. Caine pulled harder, and the gap between the doors grew larger. Caine forced himself not to breathe a sigh of relief – he knew he couldn't afford to lose the oxygen. If the car had been stuck above deck, there would be no way to pass through into the elevator shaft.

Releasing the door, he swam through the opening and into the car. Little light from outside penetrated the tiny chamber, and Caine had to feel along the wall with his hands as he swam up to the roof. A few seconds later, his head struck the panels at the top of the elevator car. He blinked, allowing his eyes to adjust to the dim light. The burning in his chest grew more intense. He knew he only had a few minutes of air left in his aching lungs.

He could just barely make out the square outline of the maintenance hatch set in the elevator car's roof. Swimming up to it, he grabbed the tiny lever and twisted it clockwise, releasing the lock. Then he shoved up on the metal square. The hatch rose a few inches, then stopped.

A metallic scrape echoed through the water. Caine gritted his teeth and pushed harder. It was difficult to exert force on the hatch while floating in the water, so he braced his free arm against the opening and rammed his shoulder into the metal panel.

It refused to give way.

Bubbles streamed from his lips. He felt his heart race as the fire in his chest grew even more intense. He was running out of time. And with each passing minute, the ship slipped deeper into the hungry depths.

Reaching through the tiny opening, he flailed his hands around, struggling to find whatever was causing the obstruction. His probing fingers brushed against metal legs, then a slab of plastic.

A folding table, he thought. *From the lower deck. It must have fallen into the shaft somehow, as water rushed into the stern.*

A dim red haze filled his peripheral vision. His heart thumped in his chest, so loud he could hear it beat through the water like a panicked drum. He tried to shove the table aside, but he could barely get a grip on the leg, and it was wedged tight against the elevator shaft's walls.

As more bubbles trickled from his lips, he spun around in the water, hanging upside down in the shaft. Grabbing the edges of the square opening, he kicked up with both legs, slamming his feet into the hatch.

It didn't budge.

He kicked again, harder. He heard metal scrape above. The hatch opened a few inches. The burning in his chest turned white-hot. Every instinct screamed at him to breathe, but he tamped the fear and panic down. As the last bubbles rose from his grimacing mouth, he kicked again.

The metal scraping grew louder, and he felt the obstruction shift. The hatch exploded open.

Barely able to see, Caine swam through the opening. He kicked his feet and paddled his arms, crawling up through the cold blackness. Higher and higher he rose, until finally, a tiny circle of dim light filled what remained of his vision. And as he swam through the freezing water, that too faded...

A second later, his head broke the surface. He gasped, sucking air into his tortured lungs. His vision returned, and the pain in his chest faded. The hull creaked and groaned around him. His eyes slowly adjusted to the dim light. Looking around, he saw he was in the flooded elevator shaft, bobbing about halfway up the superstructure tower. A ladder led up the side to a pair of doors, and a tiny crack of light beamed in above, the only illumination in the dark metal shaft.

Shaking his head to clear the last remnants of fog from his mind, Caine swam over to the ladder and pulled himself from the icy water. The tower now hung at an angle, forcing him to hug the ladder to his body as he ascended. The angle grew steeper by the second, as the ship's stern dipped farther and farther beneath the sea.

As he neared the top of the ladder, he heard a noise above. It sounded like smashing metal and breaking glass. Caine climbed faster, moving as silently as he could. The elevator doors were open just a crack, and Caine peered through into a bright, window-filled chamber. He glimpsed modern electronics... Radar, navigation systems, next to a ship's wheel.

He had reached the bridge.

A dark figure rushed past the door. Caine heard more crashing. Whoever it was, they were destroying the electronics on the bridge.

Reaching up, he gently tugged at the door panels. The mechanism was stiff and difficult to move, but the smashing and crashing of the man on the bridge covered the sound as he forced them open. Caine drew his pistol and held the gun up, watching as rivulets of water spilled from the drainage notches cut into the barrel and slide. He knew the gun was designed to fire reliably after immersion in saltwater.

Looks like we'll put that to the test, he thought. Shimmying through the tiny opening between the door panels, Caine eased into a crouch. To his right, a crewman in a blue jumpsuit was swinging a fire axe into a towering electronics rack. Sparks cascaded through the air as the blade slashed through the delicate components.

Grunting with exertion, the man swung the axe again, oblivious to Caine's presence on the bridge. A tremor ran through the bulkheads, and Caine felt the deck tipping beneath his feet. The axe-wielding man spun around.

Caine raised the pistol. 'Drop the axe and step away from—'

The man bellowed an angry roar and swung the axe over his head. He charged toward Caine, his eyes simmering with hate and rage.

Caine fired. The cough of the suppressor echoed through the tiny chamber. A crimson hole erupted in the man's forehead, and blood spattered the wall behind him. The axe fell from his hand and clattered to the deck. His body followed, collapsing face down.

Caine looked down the shaft behind the elevator doors. The water level was rising and had almost reached the bridge. Holstering his pistol, Caine grabbed the USB stick from the pouch on his belt and moved over to the forward console. The deck shifted beneath his feet once more. Glancing out the windows, he saw the ship's bow rise into the air. White spray cascaded down the sides of the hull, and the cargo containers shifted across the deck. One of the helicopter's mooring clamps broke loose, and the aircraft's tail swung back toward the stern.

The walkie at his waist crackled to life. 'Tom, do you copy? Tom?'

It was Mariko's voice. Caine snatched the radio from his belt and hit the transmit key. 'I copy, go ahead.'

'Tom, get off the ship! It's sinking fast. There isn't much time!'

'Tell me something I don't know,' Caine muttered back. 'Did Kanako make it?'

'Yes, we've transferred her and the refugees on board. We've taken on some water, but we're still seaworthy. But another wave like that...'

Her voice trailed off.

Caine frantically searched the console, looking for the computer server.

'Got it. Byakko infected the refugees with some kind of virus. I don't think they're contagious yet, but probably best to keep them below decks. Just to be safe, over.'

'*Hai*, we will. Where are you?'

'I'm on the bridge.' Caine spun around. He clenched his fist as he stared at the sparking cabinet at the rear of the control room. 'I'll get off soon. I have to do something first. Don't wait for me! Get the hell out of here, now!'

'*Nani?* What are you talking about?'

Caine stalked over to the damaged rack. Grabbing a bent metal panel, he ripped the cover off, revealing rows of servers mounted beneath. Their lights were dim, and the axe had slashed the cables running between them. A few stray sparks leapt from the torn bundles of wire.

'So much for that idea,' he grunted, watching as another burst of sparks fell from the dangling wires.

'What was that?' Mariko asked, her voice crackling from the walkie. 'Did not copy, over.'

'Never mind. Look, I might not make it, and if another wave like that hits the area, your ship could capsize. You've got the refugees, and you've got Kanako. You have to—'

A burst of static came from the speaker. 'Yes, I'm here!' Kanako's voice snapped. 'And I already told you, I'm not some wayward daughter who needs saving. I'm a Naicho agent, and I—'

'I know!' Caine snapped. 'Which means there's a chance both our governments will listen to you! They have to know the truth before it's too late. Now go!'

As the hull creaked and groaned, Caine turned off the walkie and slipped it back into his belt. He kneeled in front of the rack, following the wires to a metal case. Several hard drives sat in the boxy enclosure. Grabbing the multi-tool from a pouch at his waist, he undid the screws holding the drives in place. He slid the drive assembly from the rack and examined it.

The storage unit was about the size of a large toaster. Caine set the unit down on a nearby console. Then he grabbed the largest waterproof pouch from his harness and dumped out its contents, letting the supplies cascade across the deck and roll back towards the gaping elevator shaft. He slid the drives inside. They fit, just barely.

Slinging the pouch around his shoulder, Caine exited the bridge and stepped out onto the navigation platform. The open deck faced the rear of the ship. Two lifeboat brackets hung from the platform. Caine's heart sank as he confirmed that both were empty. Either Byakko and his surviving crew had taken them, or the massive wave had torn them loose.

Water covered the rear deck and rose up the stairs on either side of the bridge. The vessel's stern was completely submerged.

Caine ducked back into the bridge and peered out the forward windows. The sea stretched out before him. A lone lifeboat swung from its brackets near the starboard bow. The superstructure tower now leaned back at a thirty-degree angle.

Caine grabbed the dead crewman's axe from the deck. Hefting the weapon overhead, he swung the blade into the nearest window. The tempered glass shattered, and an icy wind blasted through the bridge, sending loose papers and navigation charts swirling in the air.

Using the axe's shaft, he cleared the jagged shards from the window frame. Then he climbed up onto the console, squinting in the harsh wind. He stepped out onto the other side of the window and balanced on the edge of the sill.

Then he let go. Caine slid down the sloped surface, gaining speed as he raced toward the upended deck.

50

The freezing wind whipped through Caine's hair as he slid down the angled superstructure tower. The deck rushed up to meet him. He bent his legs, flexing his knees to absorb the shock of impact. As he slammed into the base of the tower, water sloshed over the bulkheads on either side of him. He shivered as he staggered to his feet, and water droplets stung his face.

Ahead of him, the bow continued to rise. The distant lifeboat creaked and swayed as the ship heaved in the violent sea.

Before Caine could even catch his breath, he heard a deafening metallic shriek, something scraping across the deck. Looking up, he saw a lone cargo container hurtling towards him at a terrifying speed. At the last second, it struck the tail of the helicopter. The impact sheared the slim metal structure clear off, sending it bouncing towards him down the sloped deck.

Caine dove sideways as the tail section collided with the wall. The rear rotor blades tore deep gouges into the metal, missing his skull by inches.

As he stood up, an angry roar bellowed above him. A shirtless man dove off another cargo container and tackled him to the ground. Caine drove his knee up and threw the man over his shoulder.

Staggering to his feet, Caine drew his pistol. But a swift kick knocked the weapon from his hands. The gun slid across the deck, then plunged into a pool of water on the deck behind him.

Byakko stood before him. The man's feline eyes glinted in the morning light.

'It's over,' Caine said, crouching to maintain his balance as the deck rolled beneath his feet. 'Our governments already know—'

'Your government knows nothing, Mr. Caine.' The man nodded at the satchel slung around Caine's neck. 'That data will never leave this ship. And neither will you!'

Byakko launched a low kick. Caine threw up a knee, blocking the strike. But the rolling motion of the deck flung him off balance. He fell to his left, hitting the shallow water flooding across the deck with a splash.

The gangster brought his leg down, aiming for Caine's skull. Caine rolled sideways, narrowly avoiding Byakko's heel as it splashed into the water.

Caine leapt to his feet and charged, tackling Byakko to the ground. He slammed his forearm into the man's throat, driving his head under the shallow water. With his free hand, he launched a series of rapid punches into the man's solar plexus.

Bubbles erupted from the older man's sneering lips. He glared up at Caine, his cat-like eyes almost iridescent in the dark, swirling water. His lips curled into a smile.

Heaving his legs out of the water, he wrapped them around Caine's neck and locked his feet together. Releasing his choke hold, Caine struggled to free himself from the vise-like grip.

Reaching down to his waist, Caine slid his knife from its sheath. He drove the blade into Byakko's thigh.

The man roared in pain and released his hold, rolling away from Caine through the pool of water. He plucked the knife from his leg, then licked the blood from the blade.

'First blood is yours, Mr. Caine,' he snarled.

Caine stepped back as a tremor ran through the deck. The ship's welds were buckling, struggling to support the weight of the rising bow. If they snapped, the vessel would break in two.

Another shiver ran through his body. His movements felt sluggish, as if he were fighting through molasses. The water and the cold sapped his strength. Byakko's breath misted the air as he charged forward. Naked from the waist up, the freezing temperature did not seem to affect him at all.

The gangster launched a roundhouse kick. Caine hooked the man's foot in his arm, stopping the blow in midair. But Byakko quickly shifted his weight, launching the opposite leg into the air. The blow struck Caine's chin, and stars exploded across his vision.

Stunned, he released the gangster's leg and stumbled backwards. Byakko landed on his feet and pressed the attack, pummeling Caine with a series of rapid punches and low kicks.

'When I was a boy, I thought my father harsh and cruel,' the man snarled, launching another punch. Caine barely blocked the strike. He slipped backwards, ducking under the mangled helicopter tail, to avoid a follow-up kick.

'Now, I see he was wise,' the gangster continued, following Caine through the wreckage. 'He prepared me for hardship. Taught me to be strong, in both body and mind.'

'It doesn't take strength to kill innocent people,' Caine snarled.

'They are but a means to an end,' the gangster snarled. 'You remember the story I told you back in Sapporo?'

'Kashiwade,' Caine wheezed, stalling to catch his breath. 'And the white tiger.'

The man with the cat-like eyes nodded. '*Hai*. Unlike that coward, I will protect my family. The United States tore my homeland in two. Japan tore away my flesh and blood. Now, I will do whatever it takes to defend that which is mine!'

Water sloshed over the decks, filling the narrow gulf between the tower and the angled deck. Caine shivered again as the freezing sea rose to his knees. He had no idea what the man was raving about, but as they fought, the angle of the deck grew steeper and steeper. Soon, it would be impossible for him to make the climb to the lifeboat at the bow.

As the bow rose, Caine heard more metal scraping. From the corner of his eye, he saw another cargo container shift, sliding a meter down the deck.

'What about Jiwoo?' Caine asked, looking the man in the eye as he backed away through the water. 'She's on her way to the bottom now. You couldn't protect her.'

Byakko bared his teeth, then lunged at him, splashing through the pool of seawater. He launched another kick, but Caine hop-stepped backwards, darting out of reach. The gangster launched into a second attack, throwing up his other leg. Caine reversed his stance, and the kick fell short, barely grazing his thigh.

Caine jabbed his knuckles into his opponent's throat. Byakko gasped for breath, and his hands clutched his bruised esophagus. Caine pressed the attack, driving a knee into the man's abdomen. As Byakko bent over in pain, Caine looped an arm around the gangster's neck, crouched low, and reached for his opponent's knee.

It was just a feint but it worked. The gangster instantly stepped back, leaving him off balance. Caine shifted his weight, yanking the man's leg out from under him. Byakko hit the deck, splashing into the deepening water.

Caine heard metal scraping again, a few meters away. The loose container slid another meter closer. The bow creaked. Metal deck plates to his right buckled, then snapped, revealing gaps between the welding seams.

Distracted by the damage to the ship, Caine failed to notice Byakko spin around in the water. The gangster lashed out, sweeping Caine's legs. As he fell to the deck, the other man rolled away and rose to his hands and knees. Caine leaped to his feet and shook the freezing water from his hair. He took a step toward the gangster but froze.

As the man stood from the water, Caine saw he held something in his right hand... Caine's discarded pistol.

'As I said, Mr. Caine. You will never leave this ship,' Byakko growled. 'Though I must admit, I don't really like guns.'

'Right now, that makes two of us,' Caine growled.

Byakko chuckled. 'I prefer to face my enemies head on. Man to man, as it were. Both in the arena, and across the shogi board. But I'm afraid our time has run short.'

The bow rose higher, sending waterfalls cascading down to the ocean. The sound of metal buckling, support beams snapping, echoed above the raging ocean waves.

'You know, about that story – Kashiwade and the white tiger?' Caine said, panting for breath. 'I think you're forgetting one important detail.'

Byakko's grin grew wider. 'And what would that be, Mr. Caine?'

Another wave surged beneath the vessel, rocking the deck beneath them.

Caine charged forward, his feet splashing through the water. The gangster fired, but the sudden motion of the ship threw off his aim. A plume of blood stained the water as the bullet grazed Caine's bicep.

Before the gangster could fire again, Caine was upon him. With his left arm, he swiped the gun sideways, knocking it off course. Byakko squeezed the trigger, but the shot ricocheted off the tower wall.

Caine grabbed the man's shooting arm with his left hand and drove his knee up, smashing it into the gangster's solar plexus. He looped his free hand around the man's neck and slammed his skull forward, striking the bridge of Byakko's nose with his forehead. Blood streamed from the gangster's crushed nostrils, sending trails of bright crimson running down his bare torso.

The metal scraping grew louder. Caine's eyes darted to his left. He saw the loose container skid down the sloped deck, plowing through the water like a battering ram. It was barreling straight for them.

Caine spun the stunned man around, then fell backwards. He kicked out with his legs, levering the gangster up and over him. Byakko hit the water with a loud splash as Caine rolled in the opposite direction.

Caine staggered to his feet. The gangster rose from the water. The sound of the sliding container grew louder. Byakko spun around. His feline eyes opened wide with terror, and his mouth gaped in a silent scream. He stumbled sideways, but the water slowed him down.

He was too late.

The container slammed into the yakuza gangster, pinning him against the sloped tower wall with a sickening crunch.

Caine grasped his wounded arm and limped through the water. Byakko's head and shoulders were visible, but the rest of his body was trapped behind the massive metal box, crushed to a bloody pulp. The pistol lay in the shallow water at Caine's feet.

He kicked the weapon aside.

A gurgle of pain emerged from the gangster's throat. Blood dribbled from his lips and pooled in the water beneath his mangled body. His shattered collarbone jutted from a gash in his shoulder, a compound fracture that looked as painful as it no doubt felt.

Caine gasped for breath, exhausted from the fight.

'The story,' he said. 'The thing you forgot?'

Byakko groaned and shifted his head, peering up at Caine with a befuddled look. Caine kneeled and looked him in the eye.

'The white tiger died in the end.'

A brief chuckle escaped Byakko's lips. Then the man's strange, cat-like eyes fluttered closed. More water sloshed over the bulkheads. Soon, the icy sea covered his lifeless body.

As Caine stood, he heard more metal plates snap behind him. The bow sagged toward the ocean's surface. But it quickly rose again, as the ship sank even faster.

The ship's falling apart, Caine thought. There was no time to climb for the lifeboat, not with the vessel's hull fracturing beneath him.

He turned and raced for the port-side deck. He tightened the strap of the waterproof bag, making sure the pouch was secure. Then he dove off the edge.

A shock wave of white-hot agony assaulted his nerves as he struck the freezing water below. Ignoring the pain, he forced himself to swim. The wound in his arm throbbed but he knew he could not stop. Soon, the ship would sink beneath the surface. And it would take him down with it if he didn't put some distance between himself and the wreckage.

Inch by inch, he crawled through the raging sea, spitting bitter saltwater from his mouth. Behind him, the Eiko Maru slipped beneath the waves, carrying Byakko with it. Caine felt the sea give way. He, too, plunged beneath the surface, as if the water beneath him had suddenly turned as insubstantial as a cloud. He was sinking, falling deep into the dark, frigid depths.

Somewhere in the back of his mind, he knew he was not really falling. Nor was the wreck pulling him under or sucking him into the ocean's black abyss. Such things were myths. Instead, the sinking ship released large amounts of air into the water. This caused turbulence, which reduced buoyancy on the surface.

Caine forced himself to paddle and kick. He just needed to get far enough away from the wreckage. Then his buoyancy would normalize, and he could float on the surface, catch his breath...

But he was tired. The cold, the pain, the fighting... He felt himself plunging deeper and deeper. The water grew colder. He opened his eyes, but saw only cold, black darkness. And within the shadowy depths, Byakko's eyes glared up at him, glowing like phosphorescent green fire as they sank into the cold oblivion.

Shaking his head, Caine clawed his way to the surface. He was imagining things; his oxygen-starved brain was hallucinating. But no matter how hard he swam, he couldn't escape the ocean's grasp. He seemed frozen, stuck in place, just beneath the surface. His movements slowed. Then stopped. His eyes closed.

A voice echoed in the dim recesses of his mind.

Shhh, it's all right. This is dauntaimu...

And down he went.

* * *

Caine's eyes shot open, and he gasped for breath. His fingers scraped against rough wood. He sat up, glancing left and right.

'Shhh, it's all right. You're safe.' Mariko's smiling face hovered before him, and her hand caressed his shoulder.

He was back on the trawler, sitting on the rear deck. The boat was motoring away from the wreck of the Eiko Maru, making good time on the rough sea.

'What... What happened?' he stammered, his teeth chattering in the cold.

Kanako kneeled next to the other woman and draped a wool blanket over him. 'You nearly drowned, that's what happened. We circled the area, and Tomoko happened to spot you floating on the surface. She's got pretty sharp eyes for an old lady.'

'*Oi*, I heard that!' the woman's scratchy voice shouted from the cabin.

Caine turned to Mariko. 'But I told you to—'

The woman laughed. '*Damare*, shut up! Since when do I listen to you, anyway?'

Caine nodded. 'Thank you. Both of you.'

'*Douitashimashite*,' Mariko replied, grinning. 'You're welcome. And you're not our only passenger.' She stepped aside.

Jiwoo Park sat on the opposite side of the deck. Her clothes and hair were soaking wet. Someone had bound her arms behind her, and her legs were tied together as well. An angry purple bruise marked the left side of her skull. Her cold, dark eyes peered back at Caine with no expression, no hint of sadness or regret.

Caine lumbered to his feet. 'Those people below deck,' he croaked. 'The refugees... How much time do they have?'

The woman looked up at him but said nothing.

Mariko grabbed his shoulder, forcing him to sit back down. 'Tom, it's okay. She already told us. We have enough time to get back to port and isolate them.'

She held up the waterproof satchel he had brought with him. 'She told us there should be info on a cure contained in these drives. Along with shipping manifests that show where the other ships were heading.'

Caine glared at the woman, then took a deep breath. 'How did you get her to talk?' he asked. 'Threaten to throw her overboard?'

Kanako shook her head. 'No. I just told her I'd leave her below deck with the other refugees.'

Caine nodded. 'Smart.'

'If you ask me, it's what she deserves.' Kanako gave him an uneasy smile. 'I should try to contact my people. I'll tell them to alert the CIA as well, share this intel.' She turned and headed into the cabin.

'You should come inside,' Mariko said. 'It's warmer there.'

Caine shook his head. 'Thanks, but after nearly drowning twice, I think I want all the fresh air I can get.'

Mariko smiled. She grabbed another blanket and draped it over him, then sat next to him on the deck.

Caine leaned his head back and breathed the cool, salt-tinged air. Neither spoke as they left the storm behind them, and the sea gradually calmed.

51

LANGLEY, VIRGINIA

CIA new headquarters building, two weeks later

Rebecca shifted in her seat as she watched the screen on the conference room wall. The large glowing monitor was the only source of light in the Sensitive Compartmentalized Information Facility. Metal louvers covered the windows, and electronic shielding in the walls blocked all signal transmissions in and out, save for the hardwired connection to the video monitor.

On the screen, the North Korean operative, the woman known as Jiwoo Park, sat on a metal chair in front of a metal table in a sterile white room. She wore an orange jumpsuit, and her long black hair hung in her face. Dark circles marked the skin beneath her eyes. She looked exhausted, worn down. But as she glanced up at the camera, her face still held the same cold, emotionless expression Rebecca had noted on the security camera footage from the Korean market.

Metadata in the corner of the screen identified the video feed's origin as ADX Florence, a maximum-security federal prison in the Rocky Mountains. How long Jiwoo would remain there was an open question. There were those in the intelligence community who favored transferring her out of the country. Sending her to a black site halfway across the world, where more extreme interrogation measures could be employed, without fear of legal repercussions.

'So this organization you belong to,' a woman's voice off-camera said. 'What was it called again?'

'Unit 99,' Jiwoo replied, looking down at her feet with a vacant stare.

The unseen woman slid a photo across the table. 'Yes. And this man, Hideo Torazama, also known as Byakko, the White Tiger. He was part of it?'

Jiwoo did not look at the photo. 'Hideo's father was repatriated to North Korea, many years ago. When my superiors learned about his son's connections to the yakuza, they realized he could be useful.'

'So Unit 99 recruited him, then?'

Jiwoo nodded. 'Yes. They protected him in prison. Once he was released, they assigned me to make contact. I was young, and Hideo... He desired me.'

Classic honey trap, Rebecca thought. Looking at Jiwoo now, it was hard to see the woman as a seductress. She was attractive enough, but there was something so cold, so harsh about her features. Still, she knew people could wear many masks.

'But this virus... Torazama was willing to die to see your plan through. Why?'

The woman smirked. 'You believe it was for money, yes? But Hideo and I, we were fighting for something much more important than that.'

'What, then? Did he do it for you?'

For the first time, Rebecca saw Jiwoo's icy mask falter. The corner of her lips drooped, her cheek twitched. There was a sadness in her eyes.

'I... When I recruited him, we became intimate. I was careless. After we... I was with child.'

There was silence for a moment.

'And what happened to this child?' The voice asked.

'I returned home. My handlers insisted.' Jiwoo looked up. A single tear fell from her eye and dripped down her pale cheek. 'I gave birth there. The child became a ward of the state, the property of our great and prosperous nation. The only contact we were allowed was Hideo's shogi games. He taught the child to play through the computer. Without that, Hideo would have refused to cooperate.'

'And now?'

Jiwoo stared at the unseen woman. 'I do not know. Hideo devised this plan in exchange for the release of... of our son. Now, that plan has failed. I have failed. They will put our son to work. He will likely die in a labor camp, or perhaps they will send him to fight overseas. A soldier in another land's war. My country will use him as it sees fit, just as it uses me. Because it has no choice. People like you think you can starve us into servility. Beat us into submission, like dogs.'

The interrogator was silent.

Jiwoo tilted her head and stared into the camera.

'Our plan may have failed, but others may yet prevail. There are more of us, more than you know. We are silent. We are patient. And when the time is right, we will strike. Our great and prosperous nation shall shine once more, like a phoenix rising from the ashes of your defeat.'

'Defeat? Why do you think—'

'You think you've won?' Jiwoo shook her head, then smiled. A shiver ran through Rebecca as she watched the woman's face. Her pupils were two black pinpricks, seething pits of rage in the frozen mask of her face. 'All it took to bring you to the brink were a few deaths and some silly videos posted online. Hate and fear fester within your nation's bloated corpse. They are our weapons, left behind on the battlefield. For those who come after me to wield against you.'

For a moment, there was silence.

'What was his name?' the interrogator finally asked.

Jiwoo turned and narrowed her eyes. 'Whose name?'

'Your son. What was his name?'

All traces of emotion drained from the woman's face. Her eyes hardened, and she looked down, allowing her hair to fall across her face once more.

'Ms. Park? Please, don't you think we—'

The woman exploded from her chair, lunging toward whoever sat across from her. The camera tilted at a wild angle, then the screen filled with static.

'It is true?' A deep baritone voice echoed behind Rebecca.

She gasped and spun around. Michael Paulis stood in the doorway, silhouetted by the lights in the SCIF room. He took a step closer, and the static from the screen lit his face.

'I didn't hear you come in,' she said, clutching her hand to her chest. 'You startled me.'

Paulis grinned. 'Nice to know I still have the touch.' He gestured at the screen with his cane. 'Her story, this supposed child... Is it true?'

Rebecca brushed a strand of hair behind her ear and examined the files on the table. 'Impossible to say. Our sources inside the RGB are limited. But North Korea's regime has been known to hold family members hostage or punish them for the supposed crimes of their relatives. Still, even if her story was true, there's no way to confirm the child is still alive.'

Paulis grunted as he stared at the static on the screen. 'She believes he is. You can see it in her eyes. Torn between devotion to country and a mother's love for her child. Tough choice to make.'

'Any country that would force her to make a choice like that doesn't deserve her devotion,' Rebecca said.

Paulis jammed his hands in his pockets. 'That's true. Guess we're lucky in that regard, though none of us are strangers to sacrifice.'

'Director, I'm still working on my report. Did you need an update, or—'

He shook his head. 'No, nothing like that. I wanted to let you know... I have a funny feeling I'm not long for this job, Director Freeling. Thought you should hear it from me first.'

Rebecca stood and flicked on the lights. 'What? When did this happen? Did Maddison—'

'No, nothing like that. Nobody told me anything. But when you've worked in the shadows as long as I have, you can see the knife coming. Even when it's stabbing you in the back.'

He nodded at the stack of files on the table. 'Thanks to Mr. Caine, along with our Korean and Japanese allies, the truth prevailed. The infected refugees were quarantined, and we were able to develop an antivirus quickly enough to save lives.'

'And President Kemper adjusted his stance on Operation Freedom's Spear,' Rebecca added.

Paulis chuckled. 'That's one way to put it. Yes, we won the day. But the underlying problem remains.'

'Which is?'

'In a word? Me.' Paulis shrugged. 'Kemper's looking for a loyalist, someone who'll toe the party line, no matter what. And that's not me. Frankly, I'm surprised I lasted this long.'

Rebecca gathered up the files from the table. 'How can he think that? We stopped a hostile power from exerting influence over his foreign policy.'

Paulis slipped his glasses from his face and polished the lenses with a small cloth. 'I've been at this game for a long, long time, Director. Seen it all, done it all. And I'll tell you, in my experience, some politicians mean well. Some don't. But I never met a single man or woman in DC who didn't crave power. Or who wasn't driven by the fear of losing it.'

'But we can't let them—'

Paulis silenced her with a stern look. 'I didn't come here to argue, or strategize, or enlist allies,' he said, slipping his glasses back on his face. 'What happens, happens. I've made my peace with it. And I'm satisfied knowing I did the best job I could.'

'Then why did you come here?' Rebecca asked, clutching the stack of files to her chest.

'Because when this all goes down, I thought you might get the idea in your head to quit. Maybe out of loyalty, maybe to protest. Hell, maybe you're as tired of all the BS as I am. Can't say I blame you.'

'But?'

'But... I'm here to ask you not to do that. The agency needs people like you, Freeling. If they want you gone, you make them come right out and say it. Don't make it easy for them. And until then, keep fighting the good fight. Is that understood?'

Rebecca nodded. 'I... I think so, sir.'

'Good. Oh, one more thing. I suspect you'll see Mr. Caine before I do. I want you to thank him for me. We didn't exactly get off on the right foot, he and I. But he's proven himself to me. Next time he gets himself in trouble – and he *will* get himself in trouble, I can promise you that – tell him to look me up. I owe him one.'

Rebecca took a deep breath. 'Sir, are you sure?'

'I am.' He turned and exited the room. 'Keep fighting the good fight, Freeling,' he called back to her. 'That's all any of us can do.'

She watched him lumber down the hallway, vanishing as he left the pool of light and returned to the shadows.

52

TOKYO, JAPAN

Roppongi District

Caine stood alone in the cavernous concrete chamber, his wounded arm secured in a sling. He had been in this room before, but now, after only a couple of years, everything seemed different. The street-facing garage doors were rolled up, and sunlight beamed into the empty warehouse. But a gloom still hung over the place, clinging to the room's shadowy corners. The air held a cold, lonely chill. Dust covered what little furniture remained, and scraps of paper, crumpled cups, and other refuse lay scattered across the floor.

The last time Caine had stood in this room, plastic kiddie pools filled with fat, colorful koi covered the floor. He remembered the sound of bubbling water, and the soft crooning of the old caretaker, singing to the fish at feeding time.

Now, empty and abandoned, the place felt like a pale reflection of its former self. A ghost, lingering in the city, abandoned and left to die.

Or maybe I've got it backwards, Caine thought. *Maybe I'm the ghost, haunting this place with my memories of the past.*

A door at the far end of the room swung open, and a group of young Japanese men emerged. They all wore dark suits, and walked with their chests puffed out, hands jammed in their pockets, cigarettes dangling from their lips.

All but one.

Junko stood in the center of the group. Scars and bruises covered his face, and his left cheek had swollen to the size of a baseball. He walked with a limp, all hint of bravado and swagger lost beneath a shroud of pain and shame.

Tetsuo had worked him over good, Caine thought. *Ripped out a couple of teeth, judging by the swelling of his face...*

The battered young gangster glanced up and locked eyes with Caine. He stopped in his tracks. It was then that Caine noticed he clutched a bloody cloth over one hand, applying pressure to a fresh wound. And although the rag covered his fingers, Caine knew removing it would reveal that his left pinkie was severed at the first joint.

'Waters... I mean, Caine-san,' Junko said, his voice slurred by the injuries to his mouth. '*Gomennasai...* I am sorry. I failed you, just as I failed my *oyabun*. Tetsuo, he... He forced me to...'

Caine nodded. 'Forget it, kid. No one can hold out forever. Believe me, I know.'

Junko nodded. 'Perhaps. But I should have done better. Fought harder. But I swear this: I will die before I betray my *oyabun* again.'

Caine held out his good hand. 'Let's hope it never comes to that.'

Junko stared back at him, a pained, haunted look filling his eyes. He did not shake Caine's hand. Instead, he bowed, bending at the waist, his gaze peering down at the floor.

Caine shuffled his feet, unsure of how to respond. Finally, he gave a slight bow in return.

'Take care of yourself, kid. Get that finger looked at.'

Junko stood straight and nodded. Then, after a few surly glances from his entourage, the men shuffled out of the room and into the street.

'Idiots,' a voice croaked from the shadows.

Koichi shuffled out into the room, leaning on a cane. His face seemed even more sunken and withered than the last time Caine had seen him. His shoulders hunched and his arm trembled as he put his weight on the walking stick.

'Still, good men,' he continued. 'Loyal, dependable. Not half a brain shared between them, of course. But then I could say that for most families.'

The tough old bastard had survived more gunshots, beatings, and other wounds than Caine could imagine. Yet now, almost overnight, he had somehow turned old and frail.

Koichi grinned as he saw the expression on Caine's face.

'Ahhh, screw you,' he muttered. 'Let's see how you look the next time you get shot.'

Caine chuckled and raised his hand. 'Hey, I didn't say a word. I'm just surprised you took that kid's finger. Didn't think you had it in you.'

Koichi shook his head.

'I offered him a choice. Said he could leave the yakuza, start a new life, start fresh. Or he could make amends in the traditional way. He said this was his family. And he was willing to sacrifice to remain a part of it.'

The old man gave a tired shrug. 'Not the sharpest tool in the shed, but his heart's in the right place. And there are worse things than losing a finger or two. For some, it's easier to live with pain than failure.'

'What about Tetsuo?' Caine asked.

'Ah, that.' Koichi scratched his nose and glanced around the room. 'Well, let's just say it took more than a finger to make amends for what he did. We discussed the situation and came to a mutual agreement.'

'An agreement?' Caine said, looking the old man in the eye.

'Yeah. He agreed to die. And I agreed to make it quick.'

A black SUV pulled up outside the warehouse. Koichi hobbled to the garage door, and Mariko exited the driver's seat. The passenger door opened, and Kanako stepped out of the vehicle. She wore a long gray skirt and a white wool coat. A black hat and flowing knit scarf completed the winter ensemble.

Koichi beamed at her as the two women approached the warehouse.

'What happened to this place?' Mariko asked, looking as surprised as Caine had been.

The old man shrugged. 'Isato's kid may have been a little shit, but he was right about one thing. This place never made any money. I tried to hold on to it, but in the end—'

A fit of coughing wracked his body. He brought his fist to his mouth as the spasm grew more violent.

'Ogawa-san, are you all right?' Kanako asked. 'Perhaps you left the hospital too soon?'

The old man shook his head. 'No, no. *Daijoubu desu*. I'm okay. Who has time for hospitals? Caine-san tells me you have a rather interesting job, eh?'

'I... I suppose.' She gave the man a nervous smile. '*Gomennasai*, I'm sorry. I'm not sure how to—'

Koichi raised his hand. 'Please, don't apologize. It's my fault, not yours. I... I wanted to honor your mother's wishes. But maybe I waited too long, I should have—'

His voice trailed off as the wind picked up. Kanako gave Caine and Mariko a nervous look, then stepped closer to the old man.

'There's still time, Ogawa-san. Perhaps we could talk, for a bit?'

Koichi smiled. 'That would be delightful, Natsuki-san.'

Kanako blushed. 'There's no need to be so formal. You can call me Kanako.'

Koichi nodded, still beaming. 'Kanako,' he said. 'A beautiful name. There is a teahouse just down the street. We could walk there.'

The girl nodded. '*Hai, sore o shitai desu...* I would like that.'

Koichi turned to Caine. 'Caine-san, I owe you my thanks. I—'

'No,' Caine replied. 'I owed you a debt.'

'If so, you are in my debt no longer,' Koichi replied, shaking Caine's hand. He turned to Mariko. 'But I am in yours, Murase-san. Embarrassing, you being an ex-cop and all. But could be useful for you, eh?'

Mariko smiled. 'I'll keep that in mind.'

She stood next to Caine, watching as Kanako and the old man walked down the street, flanked on either side by banks of shoveled snow.

'I owe you a debt as well, Mariko,' Caine said.

'That's right, you do,' the woman replied, giving him a warm smile. 'The last time I saw you, I was in a... a dark place. Things are better now. I'm happy. I hope you are as well.'

'Working on it,' Caine replied.

Mariko nodded. 'This life we lead, the things we do... It can be hard on relationships. Ogawa-san nearly lost his daughter. Even now, they can never make up for the years they lost.'

She threw her arms around Caine and gave him a hug. 'Don't make the same mistake,' she whispered in his ear. 'You have people back home who care about you. Don't shut them out. That is how you can repay me.'

Caine returned her embrace. He watched as she climbed into the SUV and drove away. Then he pulled his phone from his pocket with his good hand and dialed a number.

The phone rang three times before someone picked up.

'Hello?' Sean answered. He sounded confused, and Caine remembered he was using a burner phone, a number Sean wouldn't recognize.

'Hey, Sean, it's me,' Caine said. 'Sorry, I know it's late there, but—'

'No, man, I'm up, it's all good! Where are you?'

Caine walked down the snow-covered sidewalk. 'It doesn't matter. I'm coming home tonight. Listen, Rebecca helped me find a place, and I was thinking of having some people over.'

The words sounded alien, strange. He felt his heart beat faster in his chest. Despite the cold outside, droplets of sweat broke out on his forehead.

Sean chuckled. 'You? Having people over?'

'Yeah. Look, I know... I know I haven't exactly been...'

'I'm in, man. Let's do it!'

Caine smiled. 'Good. Rebecca wants to introduce you to an analyst from work. And I thought maybe we could talk about Jack. Your dad and I went through a lot together. Did he ever tell you about—'

Sean laughed. 'Let me stop you there. Jack never told me much of anything.'

Caine chuckled. 'Well, there was this one time in Iraq. We were in a bar, in Erbil, and Jack picked a fight with...'

Caine continued talking as he walked down the snow-covered street. Above him, a crow cried out, its black wings silhouetted against the pale gray sky. As it soared overhead, the clouds lifted, and the sun shined through, warming the cold, ice-slicked pavement below.

* * *

MORE FROM ANDREW WARREN

The next book in the Thomas Caine from Andrew Warren is available to order now here:

https://mybook.to/ThomasCaine7

ACKNOWLEDGMENTS

I'd like to thank the following for their very generous help with this book:

As usual, thanks must go to Sam Carver for sharing his expertise regarding weapons and the military. I also greatly appreciated his insights into North Korea and their intelligence apparatus.

Thank you to Matt Fulton, whose *Secrets and Spies* podcast is always loaded and ready to go on my phone. The details he shared about the DNI's office helped bring that scene to life.

Thank you to former defense contractor J. T. Patton for taking to time to chat about how something like the H5N9v-CV virus might actually come to pass.

And special thanks to LCDR Robert Adamcik, USN (ret.) for sharing his knowledge of naval and maritime matters. Without his help, I would have been lost at sea (pun intended).

Matt, J. T., and Robert are all fellow authors as well. If you're a thriller fan, I hope you'll check out their books.

I'd also like to thank friend and fashionista Chanya Roye, whose style advice keeps Rebecca clothed in suitable super-spy attire.

To paraphrase the great Stephen King, what I got right is thanks to them. What I got wrong is thanks to me.

Again, I'd like to thank my editor Vic Britton and the entire Boldwood Books team for all their hard work.

And as always, a very special thank you to my wife, Mimi. She always has Caine's six. Luckily, she has mine as well.

Finally, thanks to you, the reader, for taking the time to read this book. Without you, none of this is possible! I hope you will join me on Thomas Caine's next adventure.

ABOUT THE AUTHOR

Andrew Warren is the international bestselling author of the Thomas Caine thriller series. Andrew was born in New Jersey and has over a decade of experience in the television and motion picture industry, where he has worked as a writer, story producer, and post production supervisor. He currently lives in Southern California with his wife and trusty dachshund sidekick.

Download your exclusive bonus content from Andrew Warren here:

Visit Andrew's website: www.andrewwarrenbooks.com

Follow Andrew on social media here:

facebook.com/andrewwarrenbooks
instagram.com/andrewwarrenbooks
bookbub.com/authors/andrew-warren
bsky.app/profile/aawarren.bsky.social

ALSO BY ANDREW WARREN

Thomas Caine Thrillers

Tokyo Black

Red Phoenix

Fire and Forget

Code Green

Hell and Ice

White Tiger

THE *Hit* LIST

Every crime has a story...

THE HIT LIST IS A NEWSLETTER DEDICATED TO PULSE-POUNDING, HIGH-OCTANE ACTION THRILLERS!

SIGN UP TO MAKE SURE YOU'RE ON OUR HIT LIST FOR EXCLUSIVE DEALS, AUTHOR CONTENT, AND COMPETITIONS.

SIGN UP TO OUR NEWSLETTER

BIT.LY/THEHITLISTNEWS

Boldwood

Boldwood Books is an award-winning fiction publishing company seeking out the best stories from around the world.

Find out more at www.boldwoodbooks.com

Join our reader community for brilliant books, competitions and offers!

Follow us
@BoldwoodBooks
@TheBoldBookClub

Sign up to our weekly deals newsletter

https://bit.ly/BoldwoodBNewsletter

www.ingramcontent.com/pod-product-compliance
Lightning Source LLC
Chambersburg PA
CBHW011759010726
47497CB00012B/3201

9781806560509